To Anne w
good wish

THE NORTH BEYOND

Part 1 : NUMIRANTORO

P.M. Scrayfield

P. M. Scrayfield.

Pen Press

First published in Great Britain

All paper used in the printing of this book has been made from wood grown in managed, sustainable forests.

ISBN13. 978 1 78003-489-8

Printed and bound in the UK
Pen Press is an imprint of
Indepenpress Publishing Limited
25 Eastern Place
Brighton
BN2 1GJ

A catalogue record of this book is available from
the British Library

Cover design by Jacqueline Abromeit

CONTENTS

... the story continues with:

THE NORTH BEYOND
Part 2 : Maesrhon

THE NORTH BEYOND
Part 3 : Haldur

THE NORTH BEYOND
Part 4 : Artorynas

Chapter 1

Night watch

Silence, darkness, emptiness. Silence so deep, so unrelieved by any whisper of air or murmur of life, as to daunt the heart and beat upon the ears of any who strayed into it. Darkness that enveloped all, that lay over the folds of the land like a mantle, heavily as a snowfall lies. Emptiness that was of the silence and the dark, yet greater than both: the earth ached under the burden of its weight. Dark under that silence, the world turned in the empty night. Though the moon rose slowly at the full, its lifeless face served only to stare blankly at the vast barrenness now pitilessly exposed. Down from a scree-scattered hillside the land dropped in an immense sweep, spreading out endlessly under the night until it rose again in the far distance to a higher, bleaker slope. Not so much as an ant crawled in all that wide gape of darkness, devoid as it was of colour, life and warmth.

Suddenly, high across the empty valley, a tiny heart of flame blossomed. Within an instant it had flared and vanished, but so potent was its strangeness that it was seared onto the night as brightness will linger behind closed eyelids. A subtle change crept over the silent, empty darkness. The night seemed alert, filled with listening, as if it stayed its course with bated breath. How could fire flower here, deep in the wilderness? The wilderness where scarcely a bush relieved the withered glens, where no bracken or heather brightened the lifeless slopes; where harsh grasses blew wiry and grey in the searching breeze, and the few meagre streams flowed coldly in their rocky beds.

The wilderness, Na Caarst, that lay around all settled lands, haunted by nameless creatures from the Waste beyond, the wilderness that was feared and shunned by men. But it seemed that one man at least dared to go there: for where fire is, man is; and there was indeed a man on the bare hillside, keeping back the empty night with a tiny seed of warmth and light at the heart of the silent darkness.

Maybe it appeared careless of life, to risk fire here where blindworms might be drawn to it; yet this man had not abandoned caution. His fieldcraft showed in every detail of his bearing: the way he sat with his back to the fire, his eyes wide with night-sight, ever watchful; his weapons, though few, were ready to his hand in the knife at his hip, the sling at his belt, the stave in the crook of his arm; his food was simply meal and water set over the fire, causing no betraying scent, enough merely to stay his stomach with warmth and sustenance before rest.

Indeed a fellow-wanderer would have seen all the marks of a man well-used to journeying far alone, a man who was prepared to put many weary miles between himself and the nearest settled land. Such a wanderer, had he been there to see, would have noted the careful siting of the camp, the fire screened by boulders which also helped to retain its warmth; nor would he have missed the way some rocks had been moved so as to add height and protection to a hollow scrape which could form a refuge if desperate need threatened, and beside which a neat pack was carefully propped.

The lone stranger's garments and equipment, though plain and without any kind of decoration, and clearly the worse for much wear and rough living, were well-made and of good quality, carefully chosen to sustain life should direst need arise. There had been rivers to ford and forests to struggle through, mountains to cross and many trackless miles to tread; and this was a wayfarer who had done everything he could to make sure no disaster that might befall him would snatch away all his means of survival in the wild.

What man could this be, who sat watchful in the night in the midst of Aestron na Caarst? Clearly, a traveller who had come far, a wanderer well able to fare alone without help from other men; but who was this way-worn stranger, where had he come from, what was his errand? He was tall, with lean, muscled limbs that weary miles of journeying had honed to a wolflike endurance. His movements were supple and his stride long; his pace spare and steady, set to continue relentlessly, day on day. He favoured neither hand when working at the tasks of his camping-place, but his right wrist was thicker than the left, and when he stripped it could plainly be seen that his right arm was the more heavily muscled. A sword-arm, and one strengthened by use? Yet though he was carrying weapons and had the look of a man who knew well how to use them, he bore no sword. But alone in the wild a man gains little from a sword, which encumbers him and cannot be used in the hunt: better, if need arises, to strike from afar with the bow and finish the kill with the spear or knife, whether the adversary be beast or man; if man, better still to avoid the encounter.

The man who tended his fire on the cold hillside was dark-haired, except for a white lock above his temple on one side, maybe the mark of an old head-wound. The white strand showed up almost like a feather where the hair blew back from his face in loose, springing locks which might have given his face a slightly womanish cast had it not been for the bleak set of his features. Although not yet into his fourth ten years, he seemed older. A deep line was etched into his brows between his eyes, and stern lines too ran from his nose to the corners of his mouth, which was wide and straight, with a rather delicate upper lip marked by a small scar, and a strong chin below. His forehead was high and his cheeks somewhat hollow. But the eyes, now dark as they swept the wider darkness, were an unexpected tawny colour, framed by dark lashes and brows; like amber, with small sun-sparks in them when touched by fire or torchlight.

The wanderer shifted slightly, moving to bring a new expanse of hillside into view under the wasted moonlight. He leaned forward to stir the mealpot over the fire. It was thicker now; soon it would be ready to eat. Taking out a horn cup, he filled it with warmed water and began to sip it slowly. An old wayfarer's trick, this: the warmth of the cup heated his hands, keeping the numbing cold at bay, while the hot liquid dispelled the chill in his body and dulled his appetite. With his stomach partly stayed, he put the cup back beside the embers and began on the food. This too he ate deliberately slowly, still turned away from the fire, surveying a fresh piece of his surroundings between each mouthful.

Briefly the eyes of the watcher on the hillside dropped from their constant survey of the night as suddenly his stomach twisted within him. What would he not give to exchange his scanty bowl of meal for the generous fare he remembered from his foster-years! His mouth watered and tears stung his eyes, but he turned to scan a new sector of night, forcing himself to repress the memory. Even as a child he had been able to master himself like this: little wonder people had thought him cold. But then, he had always been the misfit, the odd-man-out among the children, the changeling in his father's house; and now he was a hunted man, a man with a price on his head, a price put there by his own father. And even the years spent among his mother's people, though they might have shaped him, had not made him. His mother's people. Yet Numirantoro had lived only long enough to see him once and leave his true name in Arval's keeping.

The traveller moved abruptly, his memory turning back to the night he left Caradward. He saw again in his mind's eye the victory feast – a shameful feast for an ignoble victory. Before him flashed the faces of the nobles, the councillors, the warriors, the servants, the slaves. Yes, by then there had been slaves also. But every face had been frozen in shock as he defied Vorynaas before them all and spoke the words that sealed his doom. He had felt a power in him that night, a power that flooded through his mind and body so that his feet seemed scarcely to press the earth: his path had seemed shining and clear before him. Now, though, his mind turned for the thousandth time to the questions that haunted him. He had been gone so long, heading north and north again like the geese in spring, and still he seemed no nearer to finding what he sought. Was the whole quest a wild goose chase? Time, he knew, was running out; and he had been gone so long: almost five years, which left so little of the seven that were all he had.

Finishing his food, the wanderer washed it down with the last of the water and then stood up to take a final long look all round his camping-place. Methodically he cleaned and put away his utensils, banked the fire to keep it alive until dawn and then prepared for rest, lying in his shallow, scraped-out refuge with his pack and belongings to hand. Time crawled by, but failed to bring him the sweet oblivion of sleep. He might close his eyes, but could not close his mind to the vast darkness at whose heart he lay. Aestron na Caarst was so hostile, so threatening: its silence dinned in his ears, its emptiness oppressed him until he ached at his own homelessness. The small scar at his lip stretched as his mouth set bitterly. Homeless? He had never had a home; he had always been alone within himself, his eyes turned northwards.

Restlessly he moved and turned in his earthy burrow. How unnerving it had been, as day drew to an end, to look across the huge valley where he now lay and to realise he saw the very landscape that had haunted his dreams for years. No wonder he lay wakeful, alone in the midst of the dread that had shadowed his childhood. But now he remembered how Arval had comforted his fear and the memory eased a little of his tension. He had sworn to return, and he would keep that promise: whatever might befall, Arval should not stand alone at the last. At this, his heart darkened again. Arval was called Earth-wise, but how deep was his wisdom? Deep enough to reveal and explain the strange fate that had befallen Numirantoro, yes; but did he really know nothing of what Carapethan had revealed to her son? Surely if he had, he would have told of it; but if not, how could it have happened that such knowledge had been lost or forgotten?

Before sleep finally came, his thoughts took a few final turns, musing now on the strangeness of men: the Earthborn who, living all their lives in the surety only of death, still toil on, year upon year. They dig and delve, they strive and sweat; with effort beyond measure they change the very face of the earth itself, spending their strength that some memory of themselves be left behind, be it words, or heirlooms, or sons. Yet, though men may come and go, and may do good or evil; though they yearn for light, and lust for power, and seek for wisdom, do they ever learn from the mistakes they make? No, the knowledge he now possessed showed that they do not. How strange, that it should now be for him to seek the secret that might prevent disaster overtaking the world once more, that might save men from themselves. But then, it is not who I am, but what I am, that has formed me for this quest, he thought; and as for where the tale springs from the seed, the dark secret that Carapethan revealed to me is where it all began.

I EARTHBORN

Chapter 2

Fair-day in Framstock

It was May-tide in Gwent y'm Aryframan and everyone was caught up in last-minute preparations for the following day's fair. Everyone, that is, except a young man who sprawled on a seat in the garden of his home on the outskirts of Framstock, fast asleep in the morning sun. Children shrieked with excitement, women called to each other as they worked to hang garlands from house to house, men laughed as they exchanged greetings in the street outside. Even the animals seemed to be noisier than usual: geese and fowls chattered and clucked, cattle lowed, a distant donkey brayed determinedly. Everywhere there rose the sound of hammering, sawing, creaking wheels; and still the young man slept on, one hand hanging down where his arm had slipped from the bench and a half-finished piece of osier-work loosely held in the other. Beside him, a dog lay basking in the warmth, occasionally glancing up at him hopefully.

Suddenly there was an outburst of noise close by; from the squeals and yells it seemed that someone had lost a pig and the beast was giving its pursuers a fair run for their money. The dog jumped up, ears alert and tongue lolling. The commotion died down and the dog turned to his young master once more. Surely now he would be ready to take notice of him? But no, still he slept on. The dog could not settle again. He nosed warily at a bee in the lavender, sat down, scratched, yawned. Then he decided on action, licking at the dangling hand. When this produced no response, he whined softly and yelped once or twice. The sleeper stirred and mumbled, but failed to wake. The dog stood up, gripped on the sleeve, tugged, waited. He tugged again. Then, setting his feet and splaying his toes, he began to pull. The arm moved, the young man mumbled again. The dog threw his weight into his efforts, pulling again until, with a mighty heave, he managed to haul the sleeper off the bench completely. Tumbling with a yell of fright, the young man fell in a heap as the half-done basketry rolled away and the dog cavorted triumphantly.

'What the... oh, you silly fellow!'

He fondled the animal's ears, fending off a storm of enthusiastic licking while tenderly feeling one or two sore spots where the ground had hit him rather hard. Then as the sleep began to clear from his head, he registered the sounds of helpless laughter behind him. Turning, he saw his sister leaning on the doorpost, shaking with mirth.

'Well there's sympathy for you, I must say.'

He did his best to sound grumpy, gingerly getting to his feet, but it was no good; he knew it must have looked funny to Salfronardo and her giggles were making him want to laugh too. He sat on the bench again.

'Why did you let him do that?'

'I couldn't resist waiting to see what would happen when you finally fell off,' said Salfronardo, moving out from the door of the house and coming to sit beside her brother on the bench. 'Anyway, what's the matter with you? Why were you asleep? Why aren't you getting ready for tomorrow?'

Ardeth groaned. 'Oh, don't ask me so many questions! I was asleep because I was *tired*, of course. I came out here to make my hat for tomorrow' – he exhibited the unfinished osier-work – 'and the sun made me sleepy, and I must have just dropped off.'

'Fell off, would be more like it,' said Salfronardo, digging her brother in the ribs and causing him to wince. She laughed again. 'You must be getting old, if you're already tired even when it's still morning!'

'Well, I *am* two years older than you,' said Ardeth. 'But if you must know, I didn't get any sleep last night. I mean, I didn't go to bed. I stayed up on purpose, because,' and his voice dropped a little, almost as though he was speaking to himself, 'because I didn't want to miss a single moment of my first night back in Framstock.'

Salfronardo turned on the bench to look at her brother in astonishment, and after a slight pause he turned too, meeting her gaze. His cheeks had coloured slightly, but he looked at her steadily. Then without saying anything, she nodded, and turned back again. She took the wicker-work from him and continued with the weaving, while he stroked the dog's head as it sat leaning against his leg. The sun climbed in the sky and the scent of spring flowers filled the garden. Ardeth took his jacket off and Salfronardo kicked off her shoes. Companionably they sat there, brother and sister, in the familiar home-place where they had lived all their lives before the five years just spent in Caradward.

Salfronardo, though the younger, was slightly taller than her brother and lighter in build. She was well named, for her hair gleamed with fiery sparks when the light glanced upon it, and the same glints danced in her hazel-brown eyes. She was quick in all she did: fleet of foot; eager for new things and places; swift in understanding; as ready with friendship as anger, but sooner to forget wrath than laughter. Ardeth was very like her, but steadier and broader. He was a son of his country through and through, sturdy and steadfast, with thick brown hair and lighter eyes of the same colour. Fresh air and sun had already begun to bleach his hair a little, as happened every summer, and to tan his arms. Both Salfronardo and Ardeth bore the signs that all children in Gwent y'm Aryframan were marked with when they became men and women: he had the tattoo of the springing corn in a flowing design around his right arm just above the elbow, and she had her left ear pierced to hold a small dangling drop of amber, sparking as it caught the sun and matching her eyes. Five years ago they had undergone the rites, just before they had set off with the other youngsters of their age to be fostered in Caradward; and now, at eighteen and twenty, they were home again, exchanging places with the Caradwardans who had lived in Gwent y'm Aryframan.

After a while, Ardeth took his basket-work back from Salfronardo. 'You're not doing it right,' he said. 'I don't want it all neat and finished-off looking. I want it like this' – pulling out a few withies and turning the weaving in a wrong direction or two – 'so it looks sort of, well, more ham-fisted and homespun.'

'But why?' asked Salfronardo. 'I thought you wanted it for the fair.'

'I do,' said Ardeth, 'but when it's time for the storytelling, I'm going to ask for *The Farmer and the Maiden*, and then I'm going to put this on and be the farmer. Just you wait! They'll be asking me to repeat the performance right through to the Midwinter Feast.'

Salfronardo giggled. 'Ooh, *Aryfram ac Herediro*! So who did you have in mind to be the maiden? Couldn't by any chance be Fosseiro, could it?'

'You'll just have to wait and see, won't you,' said Ardeth, ignoring his sister's teasing with infuriating calm and working steadily on at giving his rustic hat a wide, battered edge from which a straw or two dangled.

They sat for a while longer, so quiet now that small birds hopped about the garden and swung singing in the branches. Then Salfronardo returned to their earlier exchange.

'Didn't you like it in Caradward, then? If you were homesick, why didn't you say? Of course I'm glad to be home, but I loved it, especially in Caradriggan. If mother and father will let me, I'm going to go back sometimes, if I can. Lots of friends there have invited me to stay with them. I might go back in the autumn, when this year's foster-kin set out, if I did that I could travel with the ones from our year who've decided to settle there. Then I could be home again long before the bad weather sets in. I thought you enjoyed seeing the metalworkers in Staran y'n Forgarad. You never said anything when you came to Caradriggan for Midwinter Feasts.'

Ardeth smiled slightly to himself. Salfronardo had fired her usual barrage of questions and comments at him, but he noticed that she had spoken much more quietly than usual, her eyes on the ground rather than on him, her subdued manner belying the animation of her words.

'No, no, Caradward was fine,' he said. 'I won't be going back there to live, obviously, so that's why I wanted to see as much of the country as I could rather than stay in the same place all the time. Caradriggan is an amazing city, there's nowhere like it in Gwent y'm Aryframan. It wouldn't suit me to live there, but I'm glad I've seen it and I'll never forget it. And I did enjoy working with old Ironsides in Staran y'n Forgarad; I learnt a tremendous lot.' He smiled to himself again as he spoke the old Outlander's nickname, thinking of the contrast between the heat and noise of his workshop and the peace of the garden where he sat now. 'And that wasn't all I learnt. Spending time in the mountains near the mines, and away south where they work on the plant trials, I picked up all sorts of tips that I can use here at home. No, it's not that I didn't like it in Caradward. It's just that, well, after five years away I realised when it was time to come back that I don't want to be anywhere else but here. *Ever*,' he added with sudden vehemence. 'Not just in Framstock, in Gwent y'm Aryframan, I mean.'

Ardeth picked at his fingers with an air of slight embarrassment at having said so much. Then he stood up and stretched.

'Come on,' he said, 'let's have a walk round and see if there's anything we can help with.'

Salfronardo jumped up too, and gave her brother a little push. 'Helping to try out one of mother's pies, for instance, or helping father to decide which barrel to send to the feast!'

'Yes, that kind of thing,' grinned Ardeth, and they left the garden together, the dog bounding beside them.

A wider world

Time out of mind, each year youngsters from all over Gwent y'm Aryframan had left their homes and gone to be fostered for five years in Caradward, the country that lay to the south east; and in the opposite direction had come young Caradwardans to spend five years under the broad skies of Gwent y'm Aryframan. There were many ties of kin and friendship between the two countries, ties that the custom of fostering served to strengthen, to the benefit of both lands. Gwent y'm Aryframan was the older country; its people had come down from the north in a legendary past. They had found a land of broad, fertile plains well watered by several river systems; to the north and west were high mountains and in the far south the country was bounded by a wide tract of marshland. There were mountains to the east also, much less lofty than those to the north and less extensive than the Somllichan Asan to the west. The Red Mountains of the east came to an abrupt end long before the confines of the forest were reached, but the people of Gwent y'm Aryframan, having plenty of space to roam and settle in their new land, had never spread eastwards through this gap.

So it was that when, some five hundred years after Framstock was built and its flocks and herds established, new people began arriving in numbers from a more north-easterly direction and settled down to found Caradward, the borderland between the old country and the new ran along the line of the Somllichan Ghent and northward to the edge of the forest. The Caradwardans were restless for knowledge, ever seeking new ways to perform old tasks. It had not been long before they discovered ores in the Red Mountains, and their second city of Staran y'n Forgarad was the centre of their metalworking industry. It was situated towards the south of the country, convenient for the mines and home to many folk known to the Caradwardans as Outlanders. Small numbers of these were already settled in the far south when the Caradwardans arrived. They tended to be rather sallow with very dark hair and black eyes widely spaced; they spoke an unknown language among themselves but readily mingled with the newcomers, seeming to regard them with complete indifference. They proved to be skilled and knowledgeable in metalwork and smithying and were now established in numbers in Staran y'n Forgarad, often taking on young Caradwardans in apprenticeships.

The Caradwardans indeed were mainly town-dwellers, although their land contained level plains where crops were grown and developed. Their chief city was Caradriggan, a marvel of wide streets and narrow closes, elegant courts and high towers, houses in wood and stone, and masonry richly carved. Its main wonder was its wall, which was stout and strong and encircled the whole city; for Caradriggan was in the north of the land and looked out towards the forest which Caradwardans shunned. Maesaldron they called it, for beyond it the wilderness that all men feared was almost one with the Waste, Na Naastald which men were reluctant even to name. But in Gwent y'm Aryframan cattle and sheep were moved between pastures, and along the drove roads there had grown up a network of hamlets and wayside inns. Many families lived on farms, mixing crop growing with stock rearing; and most villagers kept hens and pigs. For centuries trade had passed between the two countries, and people; for many a young man had set off to seek his fortune in Caradriggan, and many a maiden had married into the wide acres of Gwent y'm Aryframan. Salfronardo had not been the first to form ties during her foster-years that would shape her future life.

Homecoming

Two years passed after Salfronardo and Ardeth returned to their home in Framstock, years in which much changed for both of them. Ardeth had his own home now, Salfgard in the north, sheltered by the Somllichan Torward and refreshed by the headwaters of the Lissad na'Rhos which flowed south past Framstock. He was wed to Fosseiro;

and now that harvest-time was over the two of them were on their way down the valley back to his childhood home, for Salfronardo was to be married to Arythalt and all her friends and kin were bidden to the feast. Himself, he wished that she had chosen differently. He liked Arythalt well enough but it was easy to see that once Salfronardo had tied the knot with him she would seldom walk in Framstock again. Arythalt was ambitious and had good connections and it was quite plain that he aimed to make his mark among his own people in Caradriggan; and, thought Ardeth, the great men of Caradward are rarely seen in Gwent y'm Aryframan these days.

As their wagon creaked down the valley road, Ardeth and Fosseiro sat together swaying with its motion, Fosseiro waving merrily at passers-by and Ardeth looking about him with a farmer's eye at the countryside they travelled through. The journey brought back to him the return from Caradward two years earlier. He had told the truth to his sister when they talked in the garden that May-tide: his foster-years had passed happily enough. His decision to see as much of the country as he could, to try his hand at all Caradward had to offer, had been a good one. It had opened his eyes to the world, given him new skills, turned him from boy to man. In his last year there he had been so busy that he had barely thought of home. Even now he recalled with a glow of warmth his pleasure at how his bargain with old Ironsides had turned out.

The Outlander was a legend in Caradward, his name a byword far beyond the city of Staran y'n Forgarad. A man of few words, and those uttered in his thick Outland accent, he presented a surly front to the world and clearly gave less than a rusty nail for what folk thought of him. But he was a metal-master like no other and men were only half-joking when they said he must have been brought into the world by forging rather than birth. Yet he had taken well to Ardeth and the two of them had spent much time together. They made a strange pair, Ardeth with his open face and ready smile and old Ironsides darkly glowering; but both had kept to their promise and so it was that after his last Midwinter Feast in Caradriggan, Ardeth had returned to Staran y'n Forgarad. There his months of hard apprenticeship with Ironsides, and his gifts to the old fellow of the grain and stores which he had earned by his labours with those who worked the fields, had been rewarded as agreed. When he bade farewell to the heat of the forge and the roar of the bellows, he took with him not only calluses on his fingers and muscles in his arms from the hot metal and the hammering, but two priceless gifts to bring back to Framstock: for his mother, a beautiful arm-ring worked in both red and yellow gold; and for his father, the secret of how to make the specially-hardened steel invented by the Outlanders of the south and perfected by them in the workshops of Staran y'n Forgarad. The Caradwardans guarded the knowledge jealously, though they were willing to trade its finished products with Gwent y'm Aryframan. Their prices however were high, and Ardeth had hugged himself with delight all the way back to Caradriggan at the thought of the stronger ploughshares and better tools that his father would now be able to make for himself.

He had been reunited with Salfronardo and the rest of the youngsters from Gwent y'm Aryframan for only a day or two when the wagons arrived in town to bring them home from their years of fostering. They had all climbed aboard with their bundles and baggage, and so amid a confusion of barking dogs, shouting children, much laughter and a few tears, they had set off on the westward journey. Kinsmen and foster-families were there to see them off, with the new friends they had made during their stay. Arythalt had been there, Ardeth recalled, but maybe there was no special bond then between him and Salfronardo: Arythalt was a little older and perhaps rather aware of his dignity; and if he looked often at Salfronardo he was not alone, for she was one of the most beautiful young women in all that gathering of people. Three wagons had been sent from Framstock, one for baggage and stores for the journey, and two for sleeping in at night. They were broad and large, with bright coloured awnings, and drawn by teams of four oxen each, slow and steady. Off they rumbled, the harness squeaking and jingling, trundling along the dusty roads now dry and hard in the warm weather of springtime.

It had taken them just over two weeks to reach Framstock, and for almost half that time they had been still within Caradward, going steadily west and a little north towards the gap between the Red Mountains and the forest. Ardeth had wondered, as he had done many times during his foster-years, why the Caradwardans shunned the forest. He could see it in the distance as they journeyed, bright with the many different hues of green in the spring sunshine. Each evening they halted to water and feed the oxen, and gradually the Red Mountains loomed nearer on their left. There was no formal boundary between the two countries, but one day the road began a gentle climb and by evening when they made their camp the Red Mountains were behind them and far, far away ahead the sun went down behind the much higher peaks of the Somllichan Asan. At last they were within Gwent y'm Aryframan and bearing in a more northerly direction for Framstock.

To his own surprise, Ardeth had suddenly wanted the journey, slow as it was, to last even longer. Each day as he rode in the wagon, or walked beside it, he filled his eyes and ears with the sights and sounds of his own country and breathed deeply of its scents. His heart had been suddenly caught up with love so strong it seemed to catch in his throat. There were no words to tell how he felt, as he gazed at the hawthorns white with blossom, the flowering apples and cherries in the wayside hedges, or heard the sound of the streams flowing beside their camping places and the birdsong that filled the air in the upland meadows; no words to measure his delight at the warm sun waking the earth to summer once more, or the scent of bluebells drifting as they plodded on through a shady coppice; no words to explain this sudden longing to possess and be possessed by the land of his birth. He wanted to touch it all, to see it all, to fly over it as the wind flew, to know every rock, every blade of grass, every secret valley. One evening as twilight fell, the thought came to him that this must be how the Starborn felt about the world, if the old stories about them were true. Yes, he thought, surely I feel, however remotely, the love of the As-Geg'rastigan for the earth. As the wagons rolled slowly on, further into Gwent y'm Aryframan, the intensity of his emotion increased almost painfully, so that on the last night of the journey he could barely bring himself to lie down and rest. His companions were eager to travel on late into the day, now that they were so near to home, and he sat out on the shafts of the wagon, moving to the rhythm of the wheels and the heavy fall of the ox-hooves, drinking in the scents of evening as the dew fell and damped the wayside dust; and later he crept from his bed to sit under the huge darkness of the warm night, his face turned up in wonder to the stars that blazed above.

And finally they had seen Framstock in the distance, the drivers encouraged the tired oxen to their best effort at speed, the girls picked flowers from the passing meadows to deck their hair, and as a surge of townsfolk came running out to greet them, they arrived to an even louder tumult than that in which they left Caradriggan. Fathers lifted daughters down from the wagons; returning sons, now large and grown-up, swung shrieking younger siblings through the air; dogs ran round in circles barking frantically; mothers cried, babies howled; baggage was heaved onto handcarts or hefted over shoulders, dust rose in clouds and eventually, with everyone talking at once, the crowd broke up into groups of family and friend and moved off towards home and lodging – for with the May-tide fair taking place the day after next, all the returned fosterlings would be staying in Framstock for the merrymaking and only travelling on to their own homes once it was over.

Salfronardo and Ardeth returned to their childhood home, where their mother wept tears of happiness at their presence, and of wonder at her gift of gold; and their father listened in his quiet way, but with ever-wider eyes and brighter face, to the tale that Ardeth had to tell of what he had learnt from Ironsides the metal-master.

But when the tale was told, when they could eat no more of their mother's lavish home-coming feast, when Salfronardo had talked herself to a standstill on the wonders of Caradriggan, when the lamps had burned low and it was time for sleep, still Ardeth could not rest. He leaned on the sill of the small room that had been his from boyhood, and felt his heart beat and his blood course with joy to be back. In the end he slipped out of the garden door and, quieting the dog, climbed the wall by the damson tree, wandering silently through the old streets of Framstock and out into the fields while the night lasted. At dawn he returned, and ate his morning bread with the rest of the family. But afterwards, though his home-hunger was still not nearly sated, two nights without rest overtook him and so it was that he slept in the garden: a lover's dreamless sleep of sweet, quiet, deep fulfilment.

Wedding guests

As Ardeth's mind turned inwards to his memories, and the hot sun of late summer beat down on him, his hands relaxed on the reins. He and Fosseiro were travelling in a light covered cart drawn by two mules and the animals, feeling their master's lack of attention, slowed from a steady walk to a leisurely amble. It would be the next day before they drew near enough to Framstock to sense the end of their journey and in the heat of afternoon they knew there were still hours to go before the evening halt. Soon their progress was so slow that barely a breath of passing air refreshed the travellers as they sat in the sunshine, and Fosseiro urged Ardeth to quicken the pace. To her surprise, he seemed not to hear her, staring unseeingly before him with a withdrawn expression on his face.

'Ardeth!'

He started, taking in on the instant their erratic progress and correcting matters with an expert's touch on the mules. Then he turned to his wife. 'What were you saying just then?'

Fosseiro shook her head at him indulgently. 'I said, "What on earth are you doing?" You were miles away. What were you thinking about?'

Ardeth smiled his wide grin down into his wife's young face, which looked back at him, open and fresh as a flower. They had been made for each other, these two; from childhood neither had considered any other partner. 'Oh, nothing much, you know,' said Ardeth. 'My mind was just running on from one thing to another.'

'Keeping secrets from me already, are you? I might just run off to Caradriggan with Salfronardo and Arythalt – I'm sure he's got lots of eligible friends,' teased Fosseiro.

'Huh, I bet he has. *Very* well connected, that young man,' said Ardeth, tweaking one of the braids into which Fosseiro had plaited her hair for the journey. 'No, I was just thinking about the journey back from Caradward when my foster-years were over, and about my time there, and about coming home again.'

'Mm. Especially about coming home again, if I know you,' said Fosseiro. 'Remember *The Farmer and the Maiden* at the May-tide fair?'

'Well of course I do!' laughed Ardeth, but inwardly he knew that Fosseiro had turned the conversation in her quiet way. She knew how he felt about Gwent y'm Aryframan, and was trying to lighten his mood, knowing too that he was uneasy about his sister marrying a man from Caradward.

He turned to Fosseiro again, reining in the mules one-handed so that he could put the other arm round his wife, drawing her briefly to him and kissing her on the forehead where a stray wisp or two of fair hair had escaped the braids. So they jogged on down the track, talking now of their plans for their own life at home in Salfgard, now of the forthcoming wedding feast, now of small news of friends and kin; the day wore away, and night followed; and next day brought them down to Framstock.

Marriage gifts

The wedding of Salfronardo of Gwent y'm Aryframan with Arythalt of Caradward lived long in the memories of all who were bidden to it. They were a striking pair. Arythalt, some five years older than Salfronardo, caused many a Framstock maiden's head to turn, for he was tall and dark, with pale skin, jet-black hair and light blue eyes; his brows were wide-arched, his nose narrow and straight but his lips rather full and well-shaped. He had brought a small entourage of groomsmen with him from Caradriggan, including, to Ardeth's surprise, a man by the name of Sigitsar who was an Outlander. But all his companions were clearly men of standing and influence in their homeland, dressed unostentatiously but expensively. They lodged together at the best inn Framstock offered, while Salfronardo and her friends, together with Ardeth and Fosseiro, fitted themselves somehow into the old home-place.

As was traditional, the ceremony that bound the young couple together was simple and brief and it was followed by the gift-giving, the feasting and the storytelling. Arythalt stood forward from his place, and as his glance swept the company a silence of anticipation fell; everyone craned to see what gift he would bestow on Salfronardo. She stood to face him, almost as tall as he, her eyes locked on his face.

'I greet you, men and women of Gwent y'm Aryframan, my friends and now my kin,' began Arythalt. 'Today the honour is all mine, for I receive as my wife Salfronardo, the brightest jewel this land has to bestow. I will call upon my new brother Ardeth to step forth and begin the exchange of bride-gifts, but as is the custom I claim the first place for myself.'

A buzz of speculation went around the hall, for none of the groomsmen came forward and Arythalt seemed empty-handed. He spoke again.

'Salfronardo is well-named flower of fire. Who can say whether the flowers and the fire are in her eyes or her hair? Or do they bloom together in her heart?'

Many of the folk present murmured appreciatively: a silver tongue was well-regarded among them, and none could disagree with Arythalt's praise of his bride. Some of the women wiped fond tears; Salfronardo glowed brighter and the amber drop in her ear waked and sparked. Arythalt put his hand to his sleeve, removing something small from the pocket within the pleating.

'There is nothing I could give that would add to her beauty or her worth, for both are beyond price. Therefore I give her this small token only, which has nonetheless cost me dear, as so it should: and by it I bring only more flame to the fire, more sunlight to the flower, more golden glory to the flower of fire that is Salfronardo.'

He embraced his bride before them all and when he stepped back, they saw that in her right ear there now trembled a second drop of amber, so that the tawny highlights of her eyes and hair were framed by a small matching heart of fire at either side of her face.

Together, Salfronardo and Arythalt turned to the company of their well-wishers, she smiling and sparkling with life and laughter, he seeming a little withdrawn, solemn and exalted of face. A babble of confused noise welled around them, compounded of congratulations, astonishment, admiration and a little unease: for the amber ear-drops of Gwent y'm Aryframan were heirlooms from time out of mind, from an age before the people had made that land their home, from a time when they knew far northern coasts now long forgotten; and no woman had ever worn two such drops as Salfronardo did now. But, they reasoned, she will live in Caradward with Arythalt, and amid the marvels of Caradriggan her loveliness now twice adorned will do her homeland honour; if he has the means to purchase such a jewel, he must be a great man indeed and he has chosen a bride from among us, not his own, so let us drink to their fortune and enjoy the day! And so they stood in their turn and cheered the bride and groom, upping the noise even further when Ardeth emerged from the throng, for he was a popular young fellow in Framstock.

Raising a hand for quiet, Ardeth stood before the bridal couple. He looked into his sister's eyes for a moment or two of silence before he spoke.

'Salfronardo, may you never know sorrow. My gift is a thing I have made myself, so when you wear it, think of me and remember Gwent y'm Aryframan.'

He held out to her a gold necklet, slender and plain without twist or chasing, rounded into gleaming finials as if the precious metal had frozen as it melted. Salfronardo put the circlet on and the gold caught the light, reflecting the amber at her ears. Sigitsar the Outlander leaned forward and stared hard from Ardeth to his craftwork, muttering in his own language. A sound, almost a sigh, broke from the onlookers, as they gazed at Salfronardo. Her eyes met Ardeth's again, and now a roar of approval broke forth, affection for Ardeth and admiration for Salfronardo quite overcoming any feeling that his words had been perhaps a little plain and unfestive for such an occasion. Ardeth turned to the new husband.

'Arythalt, I welcome you as my brother, and I embrace you as my friend.' He clasped right hands with the Caradwardan, and then gripped him shoulder to shoulder. 'I hope Fosseiro and I may greet you and Salfronardo often in Salfgard. We pledge you as our wedding gift one-tenth of all our stock and stores from this day forth for one full year.'

This time the response was immediate, with much whistling and stamping in acknowledgement of such generosity.

Ardeth moved away to join Fosseiro where she sat to one side, and the long line of gift-bearers edged forward to add their good wishes to Salfronardo and Arythalt. Finally all was done, and the bride's father rose in his place to bid everyone enjoy the feast and drink health and long life to the newlyweds; but first he called the company to order for a recitation of the pledge, as was traditional in Gwent y'm Aryframan.

Then the chief storyteller of Framstock walked into the centre of the hall and gave the company *Temennis y'm As-Geg'rastigan ach Ur*, the *Pledge of the Starborn with Earth*, and they heard him out in silence with bright eyes, though many a cheek was already flushed with ale and wine. Afterwards there was laughter and mirth, and favourite tales were called for; one of the groomsmen even gave them a story from Caradward, *Lords of the Wanderers*, and finally, in response to much egging-on, Ardeth and Fosseiro repeated their famous performance of *Aryfram ac Herediro*. At last as the evening grew old, Fosseiro slipped away from the feast and was asleep in Ardeth's small room long before he came to join her.

Foreboding

She woke to find the first light stealing in, and Ardeth leaning at the window, apparently gazing into the shadowed garden.

'Ardeth.'

He turned and came to sit on the edge of the bed. 'So, there's no going back to untie the knot now.'

'Why would anyone want to? What's wrong? There's more in this than Salfronardo marrying into Caradward: you must have known all along that was likely to happen, half the foster-kin do it as often as not.'

Ardeth sighed and rubbed his eyes; they felt gritty from lack of sleep. 'Oh, I don't know. That's partly it, I suppose. Do *you* expect the two of them to come visiting at Salfgard?' Fosseiro made no reply, for none was needed: both of them knew well enough the answer to that question.

'But... That amber drop. No woman born of Caradward owns such a thing. When I laboured at the mines of the Somllichan Ghent and the smithies of Staran y'n Forgarad I saw no amber, and there was none in the workshop of old Ironsides. I asked him about it, and he said even the Outlanders have none. They claim it has a kind of life in it, that it's not found in the earth but only at the sea's edge in the far north. That would be why only we in Gwent y'm Aryframan have it, if it's true that we came from the north too in ages past. We must have brought it with us, that's why it's all so old, why every piece is cherished and handed down the generations in a family. Every single amber drop is an heirloom, and yet someone was willing to sell one to Arythalt – there's no other way he could have got one to give to Salfronardo. I don't doubt he told the truth when he said the price was high, but it should have been beyond price. I don't like it that a Caradwardan could buy himself a piece of our heritage, and I don't like it that anyone in Gwent y'm Aryframan was prepared to sell.'

Fosseiro was silent as the birds began to stir outside. She was at a loss for the right thing to say. 'Who could really know where amber comes from, though?' she tried in the end. 'The sea – I know it's in lots of the old stories, but where is it, how far away? No-one knows now. And another thing, even if Arythalt did buy the drop in Gwent y'm Aryframan, maybe he had to pay so much for it that no-one else from Caradward will be able to buy another. You can see he wants to have the best in everything, he'll want Salfronardo to be the only woman who ever wore two amber eardrops.'

Ardeth smiled a little ruefully. 'The two of them make a handsome couple. Their children will set new standards for beauty.'

Fosseiro smiled back: his sombre mood was lifting. She took his hand. 'Maybe, but they'll have yours to look up to. I have a wedding gift for *you*, Ardeth. Our first child will be born next spring.'

The early sun slanted through the window, falling on a faded drawing, a simple scene of hen and chicks that Ardeth had scribbled on the white-washed wall in his boyhood. He slid down in the bed and pressed his face against Fosseiro's silver-fair hair, too happy to give his joy words. But four years came and went, years in which Fosseiro miscarried twice; and after five years Numirantoro, daughter of Salfronardo and Arythalt, was born in Caradriggan.

CHAPTER 3

Arythalt

Rain hushed against the windows of Arythalt's house in Caradriggan. Salfronardo was almost glad it was raining; the dark evening and the gloomy weather seemed right on a day when her heart was so heavy with bad news. She heard voices and steps in the courtyard as Arythalt came in from the street and crossed quickly to their private quarters. Dishes clattered in the kitchen and there was a burst of laughter from the cook and the pot-boy in which she heard the giggling of Numirantoro, now five years old. A few moments later, the door opened and Arythalt entered the room, dressed now for evening in his indoor clothes although one or two drops of rain still rested on his dark hair, flashing as they caught the lamplight. Salfronardo smiled a welcome to her husband, but the smile was bleak. After ten years of marriage her heart still lifted at his presence, but somehow today not even that could light her sadness.

'A messenger came this afternoon from Ardeth,' she said. Arythalt, adding water to his wine, turned at the catch in her voice. 'The baby only lived two days. That's the third they've lost. Fosseiro must be heartbroken, she and Ardeth were made to raise a family. Ardeth is past his third ten years now, he should have sons already at his knee.'

'My brother's sorrow is a grief to me,' said Arythalt formally, making the sign. He sat down before the hearth, not quite able to hide his pleasure at the comfort and warmth. 'There is time yet. Ardeth and Fosseiro will surely know the joy of sons.' He sipped his wine and glanced swiftly at his wife. Salfronardo was staring blankly into the flames, her own fires dimmed although sparks of light as ever winked about her hair and her amber eardrops. Arythalt wanted a son himself, though he judged that this was not the time to speak of it. Numirantoro was a beautiful child, so lovely that people would smile and say she was as fair as the Starborn; but she could be strange at times and although much like him in looks, he detected more of her mother's kin in her than he would have liked. And she was already five years old, with still no sign of a brother.

They sat on in silence for a few more moments until the servants brought in the evening meal. Numirantoro entered the room with them, and ran to her father. Arythalt drew the child to him, caressing her hair. She's been spending time in the kitchen again, chattering with the pot-boy, he thought; but though this angered him, he hid his dark mood. He and Salfronardo had differed on this, as they had on many other points, for his wife was not one to give way on matters she cared about. Arythalt disliked her easy way with servants, even though he could not fault her bearing before his family or her dignity towards his councillor friends among Tell'Ethronad. Maybe young Vorynaas was right, he thought with an inward smile. This man was something of a protege of Arythalt, ten years his junior but already making his mark in the council. He hailed from the southern provinces of Caradward, where the Red Mountains neared the Outlands, but his ideas were very forward-looking and he had little patience with the farmers of Gwent y'm Aryframan and what he called their old-fashioned ways. Not that he was so rash as to say anything openly in front of Arythalt, whose wife after all was from Framstock and acknowledged as the fairest flower of her land. But Arythalt was a man of the world, well-travelled and highly placed among his own folk: he could read men's thoughts and hide his own.

So he said nothing now to Numirantoro or Salfronardo, but listened kindly to the little girl's chatter and praised her skill in serving him his wine, and to Salfronardo he suggested that she might invite her brother and his wife to visit them whenever the seasons' work allowed them to travel from Salfgard. And she, knowing well how unlikely it was that Ardeth would come to Caradriggan, brightened nonetheless at the thought that maybe Fosseiro might be persuaded to visit at midsummer, if Arythalt would send a fast horse-gig for her; and she talked too about whether they might go again to Framstock or even Salfgard, as they had done once or twice in earlier years. Numirantoro was all ears at this, and begged tales of Gwent y'm Aryframan from her mother which Arythalt encouraged her to tell after the meal was done. And later, when the child was asleep, Salfronardo and Arythalt went to their marriage bed, she melting to his caresses as she had ever done and he no less ardent for her. But afterwards they lay alone with their thoughts in the darkness, and though Arythalt said to himself, tonight my strength has made a son, Salfronardo knew in her heart that she would not conceive again, so great was the fire that had waked Numirantoro into life.

A surprising friendship

Indeed the child was as striking in looks as Ardeth had predicted, with promise of greater beauty as she grew. She had Arythalt's dark hair, and from him also she got her grey-blue eyes; but sparkling in them were tiny glints of Salfronardo's amber, and her dark locks too carried a secret burnish of gold which sunlight could unlock. She was tall already for her age and likely to stand taller than both her parents eventually: steadier than Salfronardo but just as open of face and nature, pensive and rather grave in demeanour sometimes like her father, but without his way of veiling his heart before men. Her smile was like them both, but kinder than Arythalt, less bright than Salfronardo, sweeter than either of them with a hint of tenderness and understanding far beyond her years. Sometimes her words and deeds seemed over-wistful or wayward to Arythalt, but if Salfronardo found her curled up on the window-seat when she should have been in bed, her face turned north-west to where the last daylight lingered, she would pick her up and kiss her.

'Tell me the answer to this riddle,' she would say with a smile. 'Is Numirantoro named for the sigh of evening, or is *numir y'm antor*, the breath of sunset, named for Numirantoro?'

Sometimes the little girl would ignore the question and play with her mother's amber ear-drops as they swung before her; or child-like she would give one answer and then another as Salfronardo rocked her in her arms. But sometimes she would turn back to the north-west and gaze again through the window, knowing that this was the direction in which lay Gwent y'm Aryframan.

'What lies beyond the mountains of my uncle Ardeth's home?' she asked one evening to her mother's surprise. 'Is that where the As-Geg'rastigan live?'

Salfronardo laughed softly. 'Ah, you've been listening to kitchen tales again! The Starborn have no dwelling place in the world now – and who knows if they ever did? Don't go chasing rainbows, my own little star. Come on now, bedtime.'

She laid Numirantoro gently down and drew the covers up to her chin. The child looked up into her mother's face, her dark hair spread on the pillow and her eyes too seeming dark in the dusk.

'I know why you tell me not to think about the Starborn,' she said. 'It's because daddy doesn't like me to talk about them. But Arval doesn't mind if I do.'

Salfronardo was completely taken by surprise. Deciding to ignore Numirantoro's unexpected insight into her father's thoughts, 'When you have you,' she asked, 'been talking to Arval the Earth-wise?'

'Lots of times,' said Numirantoro. 'Sometimes when he's going past on his way from Tellgard to the council, he sits down on the steps of the porch if he sees me in the courtyard and I go out and sit beside him. Arval says I can ask him anything I want. He says' – the child's voice took on a solemn tone unconsciously picked up from the old man – 'he says that learning is the only thing a man can never regret.'

'No doubt he's right,' said Salfronardo, 'but there are plenty of other things in this world that men can regret, and do.' She gave her daughter's hand a little shake. 'Now that's enough of all this. Remember you're only seven years old. Don't be in a rush to grow up! You should be playing with your friends, not debating with old greybeards like Arval.'

Numirantoro smiled up at her mother, that sweetly tender smile that so belied her years. 'If we can't talk about the Starborn here, could we go to visit Ardeth and Fosseiro at Salfgard?'

'We'll see,' said Salfronardo. 'Now go to sleep.'

She went out of the room and closed the door softly. Downstairs in the main living room, she lit the lamp and sat down with her embroidery. Arythalt was away again on business with his friend Vorynaas; they were developing more mining interests away south in the foothills of the Red Mountains. Salfronardo was quite glad to have the evening to herself, to think over the conversation she had just had with Numirantoro. The child was mature beyond her years, a result possibly of spending so much time with adults – but imagine her talking with Arval! Did Arythalt know of this, wondered Salfronardo. He had (without much success) tried to keep Numirantoro out of the kitchen, but somehow Salfronardo felt a friendship between his daughter and the most revered sage in the land would be almost equally unwelcome to him. It was difficult to say why this should be. Numirantoro's behaviour was, so far as Salfronardo could tell, completely unaffected by any of the friends she made. She chattered happily with their servants, was well-mannered to her friends' parents, deferred politely to visitors to the house and now, it seemed, engaged in weighty converse with Arval the Earth-wise, and yet was still the same Numirantoro they had always known. Maybe that was the problem: her character had seemed formed from an unusually early age, perhaps Arythalt felt excluded in some way by this, unable to mould his daughter in the image he wanted. Salfronardo knew how he had yearned for her to produce a brother for the child; now she suspected that his possessiveness with Numirantoro and his lack of a son were somehow bound up in his friendship with Vorynaas. At ten years younger than Arythalt, he was almost the deferential junior partner in their ventures that a son would have been. At any rate, thought Salfronardo, that is how he used to be: he has grown haughtier at a faster rate than his years have increased. Suddenly she felt a wave of relief that Vorynaas was already married these four years and more. He had been young to wed, in a hurry with this as in most other things; but at least it meant that Arythalt could not bind him to them any more closely. A flash of unwelcome insight had revealed Numirantoro to her thought as maybe Arythalt now saw his daughter: as an asset to be guarded, a bargaining-piece to be used in his plans for ever more ambitious advancement. Salfronardo sat with her embroidery forgotten in her lap. Perhaps a visit to Salfgard would be timely indeed.

Travel plans

Some days later, Arythalt returned to Caradriggan. Numirantoro was in the courtyard, engrossed in some story of her own imagining, when she heard the sound of horses in the street. She came flying down the steps as Arythalt dismounted, throwing herself into her father's arms and laughing in delight as he swung her aloft. Salfronardo hurried out too, sunshine glowing about her as she welcomed her husband. Vorynaas paused briefly to greet them before he rode on to his own home. A strongly-built young man, he had glossy, chestnut hair and dark eyes which swept over the family group before him, lingering slightly on Salfronardo. It occurred to her, not for the first time, that he would be a most unpleasant man to cross. However he was perfectly civil, as always, and after arranging a last item or two of business with Arythalt, he clattered off to his house in the south-eastern district of the city. Arythalt was in relaxed mood that evening, more forthcoming than usual about his travels and his ideas.

'Vorynaas tells me Morgwentan may be interested to join our partnership,' he told Salfronardo, 'and I'll speak to Sigitsar also – and possibly Valafoss. I'll talk to them tomorrow in the council hall, but I'd like to invite them to eat here one evening soon. We can ask the wives to come too, it will make it less of a business meeting. If the weather holds, we might even serve the wine in the garden beside the fountain.'

In due course the dinner party took place and passed off pleasantly enough. Morgwentan's wife was from Framstock and Salfronardo chatted to her over the meal. It seemed that she had inherited her parents' estate and Salfronardo was surprised to learn that Morgwentan was negotiating to buy more land in Gwent y'm Aryframan to add to this holding. Vorynaas and Valafoss (who had been included after all, despite Arythalt's ambivalence towards him) had their heads together rather more than was strictly polite, and the wives of the two younger men seemed a little left out at first, being clearly not well used to such social occasions; but Sigitsar made conversation in his slightly stilted Outland way, and Salfronardo's quicksilver laughter eased their shyness, and soon everyone was merry and companionable. Salfronardo had inspired the kitchen to impressive feats of catering, and she noted that Arythalt was offering some of his best-quality wines; the room was decked with fragrant flowers and delicate summer lanterns swung in the trees beside the fountain in the garden. Arythalt was obviously pleased with the way the evening had gone and afterwards he and Salfronardo sat on in the summer dusk, watching the jewel-bright fish catching the light from the lamps as they darted to and fro in the pool. Salfronardo judged the moment was ripe, and using her conversation with Morgwentan's wife as her introduction to the topic voiced the suggestion that she might take Numirantoro to visit Ardeth and Fosseiro at Salfgard.

Arythalt leaned his head back on the seat and stretched out his long legs. 'Why not?' he said easily, to Salfronardo's silent astonishment at this ready agreement.

Since her marriage twelve years before, she had been to Salfgard twice only: the first time, Arythalt had travelled with her and she had been embarrassed to realise, although nothing had been said openly, that Ardeth believed his wedding pledge to them was being checked. Ardeth had made a very brief visit to Caradriggan after Numirantoro had been born. Fosseiro had miscarried twice by then and Ardeth had seemed much older than his twenty-seven years; he had rocked the baby gently in his strong farmer's arms and stroked her dark hair with tender fingers. Salfronardo had thought that Fosseiro would not want to see Numirantoro, but Ardeth had begged her to travel home with him, saying that children ran in and out of their house all day long and Fosseiro would love Numirantoro as her own – and would surely in time bear a child of her own. For some reason Arythalt had been against this idea, but when Numirantoro was two years old he had agreed that Salfronardo should go to Framstock to let her parents see their only grandchild. He himself had gone off on business, leaving the house in Caradriggan in the charge of a steward, and Salfronardo had travelled on from Framstock to Salfgard, spending a month or more there before journeying back to Caradriggan. Since then she had not seen Ardeth, but Fosseiro had come down to stay for a while after losing her third child. Fosseiro's family came from the Rossanlow, the central uplands of Gwent y'm Aryframan, and she had not been fostered in Caradward like Ardeth and Salfronardo. She was entranced by Caradriggan, delighted by everything from the way Arythalt's horses had swept her swiftly across the miles to the bright little fish in the ornamental fountain pool.

That was almost three years ago now, but Salfronardo remembered well how Fosseiro and Numirantoro had taken to each other, walking through the streets together as Fosseiro made no secret of her wonder and admiration at everything she saw in the Caradwardans' chief city and the little girl skipped beside her, tugging at her hand, wanting to show her yet more marvels. She remembered too how Vorynaas had hinted, by a lift of the eyebrow here and a curl of the lip there, both carefully underplayed, that Caradwardans such as he found Fosseiro's naivety amusing. Fosseiro, fortunately, was too good-hearted and wholesome to notice such meanness; but it was after this that Arythalt had started trying to dampen Numirantoro's enthusiasm for her mother's kin and homeland. The child talked constantly of Gwent y'm Aryframan, the names of its rivers and mountains tripping off her tongue with a fluency unusual in one so young; its stories, which she had never tired of hearing from Fosseiro, became the stuff of her dreams and imagination. She had insisted that she could remember Framstock and Salfgard, though she had been but a toddler of two years when she saw them, and indeed she confounded her elders by recounting incidents and conversations from that time which none of them could recall. More than all else, she loved the old legends telling of the Starborn. After Fosseiro had gone home to Salfgard, Numirantoro would try to wheedle more of these out of her father's servants.

'Please tell me the one called *Maesell y'm As-Urad*, please, please,' she begged in the kitchen one day; but the cook valued her position in Arythalt's household and was not about to put it at risk.

'Love you, my duck, you don't want to be filling your head with sad old stories like that!' she said, helping Numirantoro along with a little shove and a piece of apple-cake to eat in the garden.

Now Salfronardo found herself listening as Arythalt told her that he meant to travel to Framstock himself, having a mind to investigate the purchase of land there as Morgwentan was doing, and he suggested that they all journeyed together.

'If Ardeth will arrange it, you and Numirantoro can go on to Salfgard for a while,' he said, 'but I will return here directly, after my business is concluded. We'll send a message tomorrow and if all goes well, we can travel at the end of summer; that will still give you time for a few weeks' stay before the roads are mired with winter weather.'

'Numirantoro and I could come back to Caradriggan in the wagons, when they return from leaving this year's foster-kin in Framstock,' said

Salfronardo. 'If we arrange everything beforehand, you could bespeak places for us.'

Arythalt sipped his wine for a moment or two before he spoke. 'Yes, I suppose we might do that,' he said, 'although I'm not sure it would be really suitable. I've heard that only one sleeping-wagon is making the journey this year, so its provision and appointments may not be what I require for my wife and daughter.'

Salfronardo turned to him. 'Why only one?' she asked in surprise. It was too dark now to see his face, but she heard the studied tone in her husband's reply.

'Well, it seems not so many families keep up the foster-kin traditions these days.'

'Not from Caradward, you mean. I notice no falling-off in numbers from Gwent y'm Aryframan,' said Salfronardo. She kept her voice level, but a spark leapt in one ear-drop as the lamplight caught it, and Arythalt knew she had moved abruptly.

'True, true,' he said smoothly, 'and may they bring some other lucky young man a bride as beautiful as mine! Send a message to Ardeth tomorrow, Salfronardo.' He moved close to her in the summer darkness of the garden, his lips to her cheek, his voice dropping to an intimate murmur. 'We can be in Framstock to celebrate the return of our wedding day. But let us go in now.'

So Salfronardo wrote to Ardeth, and Numirantoro haunted the porch steps daily, waiting for the messenger to return. Ardeth's letter told them he would meet them in Framstock and that he and Fosseiro were counting the days until they saw Numirantoro again in Salfgard.

'You will see many changes here,' he wrote. 'Fosseiro miscarried of another child in the spring of this year, and it seems now that we will have to think again about the future, but I'll tell you more about that when we meet.'

At Salfgard

Salfronardo thought, as she and Ardeth sat one evening in the porch of his house at Salfgard, that he and Fosseiro had themselves changed very little, in spite of the sorrows that the passing years had brought them. Steadfast as ever, Ardeth had not moved an inch in his love for his land and his wife, and Fosseiro seemed serene and contented. The changes to Salfgard of which Ardeth had written were mostly in the way the farm and household were set up. Seeming now resigned to childlessness, he and Fosseiro had welcomed other youngsters into their home and since both were rightly well-regarded for their skills in husbandry, crafts, livestock rearing and all other necessities of farm life, families all over Gwent y'm Aryframan had jumped at the chance to send their sons and daughters to Framstock. Ardeth had extended the dwellinghouse and built extra sleeping-places over some of the byres and barns, and the whole farm buzzed with an air of purpose, enterprise and industry, its daily round lightened with young voices and laughter. Many hands made light work as they learnt, and those families who could afford it sent a gold piece or two towards the cost of upkeep – for the fresh upland air of Framstock made for healthy appetites, and Fosseiro's cooking, renowned far and wide, was generous to a fault. Numirantoro was enchanted by everything she found at Framstock, running from one new delight to the next from dawn to dusk, heedless of the way in which her own delicate beauty and winning ways worked their bewitchment in return. Salfronardo could see her now, deeply engrossed with her latest love, a litter of fourteen squealing, wriggling piglets.

'Just look at her!' she laughed to Ardeth. 'Trust Numirantoro to make a bee-line for the last thing anyone would expect! The other little girls want to play with the kittens, or help Fosseiro with the baking, but she has to dirty her smock on the sty door talking to the pigs!'

Ardeth chuckled in reply, pouring out more ale for himself; Salfronardo was enjoying a goblet of Fosseiro's herb-flavoured mead, yet another favourite product of her famous ways with food and drink.

'I remember predicting on your wedding-day that your children would be renowned for their beauty, but Numirantoro is more than fair to look at. Her loveliness is of the heart as well as the face.' He paused and looked down at his hands; Salfronardo noted with a small stab of poignant memory that he still found it difficult to speak of things dear to him. 'I hope,' he continued, still fixing his eyes determinedly on his hands, 'that there's no need to ask whether or not she will spend her foster-years here with Fosseiro and myself.'

'Are there Caradwardans at Salfgard now?' asked Salfronardo, in turn looking hard into her mead cup.

'A few,' answered Ardeth. 'Three from the year before last; none last year; and I expect one lad only this autumn. There are others in Framstock, girls mostly I believe; and a scattering in the villages of the Rossanlow.' He put down his cup, straightened his shoulders and turned to his sister. 'Our youngsters make the journey as they always did,' he said, 'but each year the numbers from Caradward fall, and fewer still return when their foster-years are over. Yet it seems their rich men are happy to buy their way into our land. I hear Morgwentan of Caradriggan is now lord of many acres at Framstock and the new owner of two wayside inns on the drove roads southwards.'

Salfronardo noticed that Ardeth had not mentioned Arythalt, although he must surely know that her husband was thinking of following Morgwentan's example. Our parents are old now, she thought, and Numirantoro is their sole heir. What will happen to the home-place in Framstock when they can no longer manage it for themselves? It is too far from Salfgard for Ardeth to take on, childless as he is.

'Have you nothing to say, Salfronardo?' said Ardeth, his tone hardening slightly in spite of all he could do to prevent it.

Salfronardo raised her head and the fire sparked in her eyes. 'I have this to say. You need fear no move from Arythalt towards possession of our father's fields. When the time comes I shall make no claim upon them and nor shall Numirantoro. You may make what arrangements you will without hindrance from me.'

Ardeth ran his fingers distractedly through his hair, making it stick out at all angles. Salfronardo's mood softened immediately, quieting as quickly as it had flared. She saw her brother still had something of his old boyish look, something that lingered still on his man's face under the lines of care and weather that the years had drawn on it.

'I'm sorry. I didn't mean... I just... it's just that...' he gestured vaguely with his arm, then picked up his cup again and drank, evidently giving up the attempt to put into words what he wanted to say.

'It's all right,' said Salfronardo. 'I have married into Caradward, I must live in Caradriggan. But I have never forgotten my homeland and it seems to me that your love for Gwent y'm Aryframan lives again in Numirantoro. When she is thirteen, she shall come to Salfgard and learn its lore and ways from you and Fosseiro.'

Ardeth stood up, pulling his sister to her feet with him. His embrace held a fierce love far beyond the need of words. He held her from him by her shoulders and they looked into each other's eyes.

'Numirantoro shall be as a daughter to me. When she was new-born I told you that Fosseiro and I would love her as our own. I promise that again now, before the As-Geg'rastigan: let them be witness to my words.'

They sat again, as once they had done long ago in the garden at Framstock. The sun was almost gone, soon it would be time to go indoors and light the lamps. Delicious cooking smells drifted through the open door behind them and a few late swallows swooped overhead. Salfronardo could hear voices from the kitchen, where Fosseiro was no doubt showing her young helpers the right way to stir a sauce. Numirantoro was apparently deep in conversation with the piglets: probably passing on pearls of wisdom from Arval, thought her mother with a smile. Salfgard seemed home to her already, with its quiet fields and coppiced woods and the young waters of the Lissad na'Rhos flowing by down the valley. In the distance she could see the mountains: to the north-east the Somllichan Torward and far, far away to the west the high peaks of the Somllichan Asan. No wonder Ardeth called so readily upon the As-Geg'rastigan; if the Starborn still walked the earth then surely they would linger in a place of beauty such as this. A lad came out from one of the byres and crossed to shut the sow and piglets in the sty for the night, then turned for the house-place with Numirantoro trotting at his heels.

'That young fellow's from Caradward,' said Ardeth. 'He's been here three years now, he's a good boy. His family's from somewhere near Staran y'n Forgarad, so he's a long way from home.'

Salfronardo patted her brother's knee. 'However much he misses his home, he'll remember this for the rest of his life. You and Fosseiro have made something really special here. Families in Caradward should be clamouring to send their sons and daughters to you. I don't know why it should be that the custom seems to be no longer followed as it was in our time. Arythalt did say something about it to me once, but now I come to think about it, I was a bit sharp with him and he dropped the subject. Although when I look back further, I have the feeling that the cooling-off started about five years or so ago – yes, I remember! When Fosseiro came to see us in Caradriggan, I remember noticing Vorynaas smirking behind his hand. I just hope she never saw him.'

'Vorynaas?' said Ardeth vaguely. 'Do I know him? I don't seem to recall the name.'

'Lucky you,' spat Salfronardo with a little shiver of distaste. 'I wish Arythalt had less to do with him. He's quite a bit younger than us, too young to come to my wedding, that's why you've not met him. He's a young man on the make, and in a hurry. Arythalt seems to think he has good ideas, and they've done a lot of business together. He has a way of being very correct but with a sneer hidden in the courtesy, if you know what I mean. Not that he's ever been anything other than perfectly pleasant to my face at least, but I'd hate to get on the wrong side of him.'

'Mm.' Ardeth's brows drew down into a frown. He hated the idea of anyone belittling Fosseiro, although she had said nothing and he was sure she would not have cared, even if she had noticed. People thought of Fosseiro as all gentleness and grace, but though she was mild she was anything but meek. Sure of Ardeth's love, and secure in her place among her own people, she had a serene confidence and self-reliance which sorrow had only served to strengthen. 'But this Vorynaas is only one man. Where do his ideas come from? Are there more in Caradward who think like him?'

'I couldn't say,' said Salfronardo. 'Arythalt is well-travelled in Caradward, but it is rare for me to leave Caradriggan, especially in the years since Numirantoro was born. You say you have foster-kin here: do you hear nothing from them?'

'No, not really,' said Ardeth. 'But I have noticed that some among them seem unfamiliar with old lore regarding the Starborn, at least when they first arrive here.'

Salfronardo dug him in the ribs as she used to do when they were children together. 'A few stirring recitations of the *Temennis* from your storyteller here at Salfgard put that right soon enough, no doubt! And, by the way, I meant to tell you! Numirantoro has apparently been discussing the Starborn with Arval the Earth-wise, no less! What do you think of that?'

Ardeth put his head back and laughed heartily. 'Never! But you know, in a way I'm not surprised. Numirantoro is a deep one, no question of that, and you could rely on Arval to see into those depths sooner and further than anyone, even than you or I. I'd love to see Arval again,' he continued more reminiscently. 'He and old Ironsides are the two people I miss most from my time in Caradward.' Suddenly his voice dropped and the laughter left his face. 'I will miss you every day when you leave Gwent y'm Aryframan, Salfronardo,' he said.

'Yes,' she said quietly. 'I have not regretted the choice I made, yet I hope Numirantoro's heart will never be pulled two ways as mine has been.'

Fosseiro appeared in the doorway, ladle in hand. 'Are you two going to sit out there all night?' she demanded with mock severity. 'If you want to eat, you'd better come in before I feed it all to Numirantoro and all these strapping great lads we seem to have about the place.'

Numirantoro came running out onto the porch, reaching for her mother's hand. 'Auntie Fosseiro's baked a *whole ham*,' she announced in tones of deepest respect, 'with parsnips in honey, and roast onions! And,' breathless with excitement, 'and an apple pie that I helped to make!' She tugged her mother from her chair and Salfronardo entered the room, exchanging amused glances with Fosseiro over the little girl's head. Ardeth stood and stretched, gathering up the drinking cups and pausing to glance round the outbuildings in the dusk.

'Uncle Ardeth,' said Numirantoro, and he looked down with a smile.

'What is it, sweetheart?'

Numirantoro gazed up at him. 'Arval the Earth-wise says I should be very careful when I make a wish, because sometimes wishes come true in ways we can't foresee.'

Ardeth was rather disconcerted to be confronted with this sobering, if no doubt true, piece of wisdom from an eight-year-old's lips. At a loss for an answer, he raised his eyebrows encouragingly.

'But I wish I could come and live here with you,' finished Numirantoro. Her face suddenly lighting with a smile, she added, 'With mummy as well, of course.' Ardeth ruffled her hair and chivvied her through the door in front of him. As he turned to shut out the night, he felt an unexpected pang of sympathy for Arythalt. Himself, he had known the pain of having his children taken from him in death; it occurred to him now that losing them in life might be no less bitter to bear.

Later that evening, after the meal was done and cleared away and the youngsters all gone to rest, Ardeth went out with a lamp to do a round of the livestock and the two women chatted for a while beside the wide hearth. Fosseiro was delighted to hear that Salfronardo had agreed to let Numirantoro come to them for her foster-years. 'But will Arythalt agree?' she asked, rather awkwardly.

'I have promised Ardeth,' said Salfronardo, 'and Arythalt won't press me to break my word, although you're right, I can't see him being exactly overjoyed at the idea. But he's too protective of the child. It will be the best thing for her, to see some more of the world and spread her wings a little. She spends too much time at home either with adults, or playing by herself. I want her to have young people around her – I've just been telling Ardeth, the child has made friends with old Arval, of all the people to choose! But oh, I'm going to miss her so much while she's away. Five years is a long time. Maybe we'll be able to welcome a foster-child from Gwent y'm Aryframan into our home in Caradriggan in exchange, but I don't have high hopes of persuading Arythalt to agree to that.'

A silence fell in which both women reflected sadly that if things had turned out differently, it would have been Numirantoro's cousins whose laughter and pranks brightened the life of Salfronardo's house, five years of their clamouring to see Caradward which would have dented Arythalt's dignified reserve. The small fire settled lower with a sigh of soft ash and Fosseiro started as the latch suddenly lifted with Ardeth's return.

He crossed the room and sat down between them, holding his hands out to the warmth. 'Getting a bit chilly already out there at night now,' he observed. 'Why the long faces? What do you say Fosseiro – shall I mull some wine? You'd like a little nightcap, wouldn't you, Salfronardo?'

'Get on with you! You mean you'd like one yourself,' smiled Fosseiro, getting up and organising goblets and utensils. Gradually the spicy aroma filled the room. Ardeth lay back in his chair, beaming happily at his wife and sister; Salfronardo was struck again, as so often in the past, by how well suited her brother and his wife were, how homely and welcoming a dwelling-place they had made at Salfgard.

Ardeth dislodged a dog with his toe and moved his chair nearer to the fire. 'Now, I'll tell you what I'm going to do,' he said. 'As soon as I find a likely lad who I think will be reliable, someone who wants to learn, a steady sort of fellow who I can trust, I'm going to keep him by me and train him up a bit. Have him work with me, you know, so I can talk to him and we can get to know each other man to man; and then when the time comes, I'll put him in as steward down in Framstock. That won't be for a few years more I hope, but if I start now, we'll be ready when my old man does eventually have to ease off. It will save mother and father any worries – and save me from them, too. And I think I'll put a new window in the room upstairs where the girls sleep, one that faces west so Numirantoro can see the mountains when she's here. And tomorrow, how would it be if a few of us went up to Gillan nan'Eleth with our bows and nets and bagged a few partridges and hares? Might even get a duck or two. You could use them in the kitchen, couldn't you?' He directed an innocent look at Fosseiro, who burst out laughing.

'So you think a game pie would look well on the table! Don't think I can't see right through you, Ardeth of Salfgard!' she said, wagging a finger. 'Now, I'll tell you what you're going to do. You're going to put these dogs out in their kennel, where they belong; and then we're all going to bed. And another thing: not a word to Numirantoro about coming to stay here. She's got five years yet before that happens, the poor child would waste away with excitement if she knew about it too soon. Come on, come on, shift these dogs!'

'Am I not the most hen-pecked husband in this village!' lamented Ardeth, rolling his eyes and giving Fosseiro and Salfronardo a step or two of his bandy-legged *Aryfram ac Herediro* routine.

Nonetheless, next day they all agreed that Fosseiro's advice to say nothing to Numirantoro was good; for when the time came for Salfronardo and her daughter to return to Caradriggan, the little girl turned back to wave and wave again, until even Fosseiro's apron, flapped out of an upstairs window, could no longer be seen as the long road wound away down the valley. Then she clung to her mother for comfort and Salfronardo, whose own eyes were misted with tears, promised herself silently that she would say nothing to Numirantoro until she turned twelve. That gave Arythalt four years to get used to the idea.

Chapter 4

A council meeting

Arythalt was indeed displeased when he found that a promise had been made without his knowledge, a pledge which could not now be easily broken and to which he was most unwilling to accede. He was a quiet man and his anger was cold and silent, causing a chill to fall when his presence was felt in the house. But time gradually did its work and smoothed his ruffled pride: besides, in his own way he loved his wife and daughter dearly and he knew in his heart that Salfronardo was right. Not only would Numirantoro be wild with delight at the thought of the wide skies of Gwent y'm Aryframan, but it would be good for her to go, to stretch her limbs a little so that they matched the range of her mind. For as she grew, she became ever more studious and eager for knowledge. She had long been able to read and write fluently, Salfronardo seeing to it that she learnt early at home; but now, with others of her age, Numirantoro went daily to Tellgard for instruction from Arval, and when she returned it was Arval this, and Arval that, from her, with any who would listen. However Arythalt was relieved to hear that Numirantoro knew nothing of the promise her mother had made to Ardeth, and he praised Salfronardo's judgement in saying nothing of it; keeping his thought to himself in his usual way he reflected that a lot might happen in four years. Meanwhile he was much occupied with business, paying close attention to the shifts of influence in the council.

Vorynaas was a voice to be reckoned with these days in Tell'Ethronad and he had collected quite a following of those who found his ideas and opinions to their liking. The most forceful of these was Thaltor, younger than Vorynaas by about the same margin as he in turn was younger than Arythalt, who considered him a brash young hothead, not at all the congenial companion he found Vorynaas to be. Morgwentan tended to agree with whatever view had the majority, and Sigitsar, the Outlander in the council, would sit and listen inscrutably, saying little. Arval often asked him for his opinion none the less, and showed that he valued what counsel he had to give. When Salfronardo and Numirantoro had been two years back in Caradriggan, matters came up in discussion which were of particular interest to Arythalt: for the talk turned first to the custom of fostering, and then to the mineral wealth of the Somllichan Ghent; and since both touched him closely, the one in his standing and the other in his purse, he listened carefully as the debate unfolded.

'For some years now, the number of foster-kin travelling from Caradward to Gwent y'm Aryframan has been falling,' said Arval. 'There could be many reasons, and I suggest that we discuss these and so discover what lies behind the decline. It seems the reluctance is on our part, for young Gwentarans still come to us as they ever did.'

Valafoss stood up to speak. 'There's no mystery there, at any rate,' he said with a quick glance at Vorynaas and Thaltor where they sat together. 'They do very nicely out of the bargain: free lodging for five years, plus skills and knowledge to take back at the end of it that they'd not find at home.'

Thaltor nodded with a smirk, but Vorynaas, who had recently let his beard grow, put up a hand so that his mouth was hidden.

'Are charges made in Framstock for bed and board?' said Arval. His face showed no emotion but his displeasure was there for all to hear in his voice.

Now Forgard got to his feet. 'Surely, the exchange of expertise is a reason for the fostering,' he said. 'Not the only reason, certainly; but the exchange is not one-way, as Valafoss seems to imply. I count of equal value the crafts and learning which our youngsters gain at first-hand in Gwent y'm Aryframan.'

Thaltor rose and inclined his head deferentially towards Arval. 'May I speak, Arval na Tell-Ur?'

Sigitsar the Outlander kept his eyes downcast to the table before him, but unnoticed by any they narrowed darkly under their wide-spaced, heavy lids.

'No doubt in ages past the exchange of foster-kin was devised as a way of binding our two lands together, and was of benefit to both,' said Thaltor smoothly, 'but we should ask ourselves, is this still necessary or true today? The world moves on, times change, men alter. There is no value in continuing with old customs simply for the sake of tradition. Keep what is worth keeping, of course. But Gwent y'm Aryframan stays the same while Caradward progresses. Why lose our children for five years of their youth, when they could be here at home learning the ways of their own land? Caradward has wealth to spare: we could pay for others to do the tasks which are all the Gwentaran have to teach.'

Valafoss jumped up again. 'Well said!' he cried. 'What good did my time in Framstock do me? Sheep-shearing, cattle-herding, practice with the bow and stave, endless re-telling of tedious legends! It would have been better to stay here, to gain experience in directing others on my father's land, to work on my sword-skills! Thaltor is right, the wealth of Caradward grows daily; we would do better to organise in defence of it rather than sit sighing over old stories whose truth no man can prove.'

Arval turned to Sigitsar, although the Outlander had made no discernable sign that he wished to speak. 'I see that Sigitsar would address the council.'

Impassively, Sigitsar looked around the faces of his colleagues as he rose to his feet. 'We Outlanders have our own tales of the Starborn, with which I will not weary Valafoss. But he speaks of defence. From whom does he sense a threat?' His Outland accent intensified slightly. 'From the west, or the north? *A'Torilmar*, where Gwent y'm Aryframan lies, or *ap Aestron* and the wasteland? From the wide east, *a'Magaran* whence you came yourselves before Caradward was settled? Or does he fear an army of Sigitsaran massing in the south?'

The chair scraped as Valafoss thrust it back, banging the table with his fist. 'I fear nothing, Outlander!' he shouted angrily. Forgard half-rose with an exclamation of dismay and Arythalt turned his gaze aside, glancing through the tall windows of the chamber; he found such confrontations distasteful.

'Gentlemen, gentlemen, this is unseemly.' Arythalt looked up as Vorynaas spoke. 'Let's calm down, we are all friends here.' Sigitsar's eyes, now lowered again, narrowed a second time. 'Arval invited us to discuss the exchange of foster-kin, and there are those among us who have close connections with Gwent y'm Aryframan. Let us hear what Morgwentan and Arythalt have to say.'

Arythalt was momentarily taken aback at the direction in which Vorynaas had turned the debate. Wishing to see how the mood of the council might shift, he deferred politely to Morgwentan as the older man, who now stood to speak.

'I have to say, I do not feel my own years in Gwent y'm Aryframan were waste of time,' began Morgwentan weightily. He was as broad in the belt as he was in acres, and an expansive tone was his style. Many words, little substance, thought Forgard privately, preparing to be bored. 'However, they were long ago and perhaps I grow out of step with the times. There again, it was through the exchange of kin that I met my wife, something I have had no cause to regret!' He chuckled in a self-satisfied way and several of the older members of Tell'Ethronad chortled indulgently along with him. Thaltor raised his eyebrows at Vorynaas, who shook his head very slightly in reply. 'It has been through my wife's connections in Framstock that I have had the pleasure of doing business with many of its leading men,' Morgwentan droned on, 'and as you know, I have extended my holdings to include several inns. I hope to expand this network further; the drove-road *gradsteddan* in particular seem profitable ventures.' More indulgent laughter greeted this; Morgwentan was a noted consumer of wines and ale and it seemed more than likely to several of them that he was probably contributing from one pocket to the profits he put in another. Morgwentan cleared his throat, staring glassily into the far corner of the ceiling, preparing to speak again. He's certainly calmed things down, Forgard thought. Much more of this and we'll all be asleep. 'Perhaps others will follow my lead; maybe I have unwittingly shown the new direction in which our two lands will choose to go. Of course, my wife and I have not been fortunate enough to raise children of our own, so it is difficult for me to say whether or not, had we done so, we would have sent them to be fostered. My wife's cousins, and my brother, all made the exchange with their children when the time came, so maybe we would have done the same; but what we might have done in years gone by is perhaps not necessarily what we should do today, were we young again....'

On and on he went, while his audience stopped listening, each man attending to his own thoughts. He spends so much time sitting on the fence, he must have a dent in his backside, Forgard thought impatiently. Suddenly he could take no more. Rising in his place, he addressed Arval.

'We are all indebted to Morgwentan who has spoken words of wisdom, as always. I have very little to add, but I wish to say this before Tell'Ethronad. I am unusual among you in that I have no kin-connections with Gwent y'm Aryframan; all my family are Caradwardan. Yet I spent my foster-years there, and when I have children of my own, I shall send them in turn, welcoming also any youngster from that land who wishes to exchange with them. I believe the custom is good and should be upheld. Whatever others may do, I shall keep to that tradition; and,' he added with a glance at Valafoss, 'the As-Geg'rastigan will always be honoured in my house.'

He sat down again to a subdued murmur in which approval gradually gained the upper hand. Wisely, Forgard had spoken no word against Thaltor, nor criticised Sigitsar for rising to the bait that Valafoss had dangled, and he had even managed to mollify Morgwentan after abruptly interrupting him. But he himself had spoken so briefly, so simply and so directly that he swayed the general mood of the council. Arythalt sensed this, as he took his own turn to speak, but it did not help him decide what to say. His mind had been in turmoil since Vorynaas had unexpectedly turned the focus onto himself and Morgwentan. While the older man was rambling on, Arythalt's thoughts had been spinning furiously. Clearly, Vorynaas and Thaltor had planned their moves in advance: why had he not been included? He felt sure privately that in the end the views of the younger men would prevail in the council; they were bound to be numerically stronger, as time gradually weeded out the elders from among them, and Arythalt could see that the hardliners were likely in the end to get more support than traditionalists like Forgard. But today, now, when he would have to find something to say, Forgard had spoken well and it would be foolish to seem too deeply-dyed a modernist. He noted that Thaltor had alluded to Caradward's growing wealth. That must mean he knew something of the potential of the new mines that he and Vorynaas were developing. Had he got his information from Vorynaas himself, or from some other source? Somehow he was going to have to keep a foot in both camps until he saw how matters fell out when the debate turned to the rich deposits of the Red Mountains.

'I think you would not expect me to speak against the exchange of foster-kin, which brought me the hand of Salfronardo of Framstock?' he said, with no clear idea of how to follow this up. Faces lit all around the table as men saw in their minds' eyes the beauty of Arythalt's wife. 'Of course, my daughter is not yet of age to make the journey,' he went on. Suddenly an idea came to him: he could give them an account of Ardeth's work in Salfgard, with luck he could make it as boring as Morgwentan's speech had been and no-one would notice that he had evaded the issue being debated. 'The council might be interested in some details…' Here he broke off, for there was a scratch at the door and it opened to reveal his house-steward.

'I apologise for the interruption, gentlemen,' said the man, 'but may I speak for a moment with Arythalt?'

They conferred aside in low voices, and then Arythalt turned to the council again. 'I must ask to be excused,' he said formally. 'It seems I have an unexpected visitor: my marriage-brother Ardeth of Salfgard has arrived in Caradriggan.' He bowed slightly and left the chamber with his steward. Sigitsar noted how Vorynaas stared after him, and his unreadable Outland eyes narrowed a third time.

Silver daisies

Ardeth, having no idea of how timely his arrival had been, was pleasantly surprised at the warm welcome he received from Arythalt. All was going well at Salfgard, so leaving Fosseiro to run things he had decided on a fair-weather trip down to Caradward.

'I've often thought over the talks we had, the last time you and Numirantoro were with us in Salfgard,' he said to Salfronardo that evening as they sat on after supper. 'Remember I said I'd love to see Arval again, and old Ironsides? Well, if a man wants something, wishing won't make it happen. So here I am, and I'm going to go on in a couple of days to Staran y'n Forgarad. I'll be back in time for the Midsummer Feast, which if you're agreeable I'll celebrate here in Caradriggan with you; and then I can be back in Salfgard for harvest time.'

Numirantoro and Salfronardo lit up with delight at this, and Arythalt poured more wine, enquiring politely after Fosseiro and life in Salfgard.

'Got a great young fellow there now,' said Ardeth, smiling happily. 'Geraswic. He's only a lad yet, but shaping up really well. I think he'll be the man I need to help me run things at Framstock and maybe take over for me there as steward eventually. We'll see how things go, but give it a few years more and then we'll know. He's actually some kind of second cousin twice removed of Fosseiro's, hails from up towards Gillan nan'Eleth and,' he leaned forward grinning mischievously at Arythalt, 'he tells me his great-great-granny or some such came from

Caradward! Anyway, unless anything goes seriously wrong, I think he's the fellow I've been looking for, young though he is. Can't teach him much he doesn't know already, around the farm, and coming from where he does, he can often show me a thing or two when we're out in the hills. Fosseiro thinks the world of him.'

'I wish auntie Fosseiro could have come to Caradriggan as well,' said Numirantoro, looking up at Ardeth from where she sat on the floor against his knee.

'Yes, so did she,' said Ardeth, stroking the child's dark hair, 'but she's sent some things from Salfgard for you, so would you like to come and help me unload them?'

Numirantoro jumped up at once and ran from the room with her uncle. He came back with the house-steward, both of them bearing all kinds of sacks and parcels, and Numirantoro trotting along beside them holding two very small packages. The bulky items were mostly stores sent from the farm: preserves, jars of honey, roasted nuts, plenty of Fosseiro's specialities including her herb-flavoured mead; salted beef, bacon and ham, and several sacks of grain. Numirantoro's eyes shone as she delved into each item in turn, remembering the golden days in Salfgard and anticipating the treats to come as all the good things which Ardeth had brought found their way onto the table in her father's house. Eventually, all was opened and the only things left were the two small packages, which she handed up to her uncle.

'No, both those are for you,' said Ardeth. 'This one,' shaking it so that a tiny rattling, rustling noise came from it, 'is from auntie Fosseiro; and this other one is from me, something a little bit special because you're ten years old now and I don't see you as often as I'd like.'

Numirantoro took the packages back from Ardeth, looking round at her parents with wide eyes. Salfronardo was all eager impatience; Arythalt smiled quietly as he watched his daughter. How like both of them she was, thought Ardeth. She opened Fosseiro's package first, and from it spilled two dozen or more smaller packets. Gathering them up from the floor, Numirantoro looked at the writing on the labels. *Hollyhocks*, she read on one; *marigolds, snapdragons, daisies, poppies, wallflowers, larkspur.* She looked up at her parents again, her face solemn rather than smiling.

'Auntie Fosseiro has sent me seeds from Salfgard,' she said, 'and she has remembered all my favourites.' She turned to her uncle again. 'Now I can have flowers from her garden here in Caradriggan!' Her voice shook a little, but she kept her gaze on Ardeth's face. 'Please tell auntie Fosseiro I will sow her seeds at the right time, and look after them like she showed me to, and I will think of her every day when I see the flowers. May I open your present now, Uncle Ardeth?'

'Of course, of course,' said Ardeth rather gruffly, clearing his throat to rid himself of the lump that had somehow formed there, knowing as he did what his own package contained. Numirantoro unwrapped a slender silver circlet, bearing on it a dozen or so small daisies of even finer and more delicate craft than the narrow band of smithwork on which they were set. Each had a tiny river pearl from the foaming waters of the Lissad na'Rhos at its centre. The child sat dumbstruck on the floor, holding the beautiful thing in her hands.

'Oh, Ardeth!' breathed Salfronardo. 'Did you make it yourself?' Her hands went to her throat, to the golden circlet that had been Ardeth's wedding gift to her.

'Well now who do you think made it? I learnt a thing or two in my time with old Ironsides, I've told you before.' Ardeth picked up his goblet and then set it down again, noticing that Numirantoro had still not moved from where she sat. 'Come over here, sweetheart,' he said, and taking the circlet from her, he settled it onto her head, arranging the dark locks so that the silver daisies nestled among them. Arythalt marvelled silently that his big hands, their fingers thickened by hard outdoor tasks, could achieve such delicate work. 'Now! Don't you look just beautiful? To your health and long life, my lady Numirantoro!' Ardeth made his niece a courtly little bow, and then raising his goblet to her with a smile, drank from it.

Salfronardo went to the chest in the corner and took her hand-mirror from it. 'Look, you can see yourself,' she said to Numirantoro, who stared speechlessly at her reflection. 'Now, what do you say to Uncle Ardeth?'

Numirantoro looked up. 'I will keep this for solemn days and high feasts, uncle Ardeth,' she said. 'I will be Numirantoro of the silver daisies, and no matter how many other jewels I may be given, I will not mix them with your gift to me. Its beauty is too great to share.'

Arythalt and Salfronardo exchanged surprised glances, but Ardeth laughed merrily. 'Well, well!' he said. 'So it's true what I've heard, that my little niece has a way with words! And I hear you've a talent for design too, so you must show me some of your patterns and I'll see if I can work them into my gold and silver work in the winter-time. But now' – and he tousled his hair – 'will you be the maiden, if I'll be the farmer?' He got up, a hand to his bent back as he faked a grimace of rheumatic pain, and held out a hand to Numirantoro, who pranced and twirled around him, giggling happily now, her daisies shining in her hair.

Summer shadows

Twice Numirantoro sowed her seeds and tended her flowers, and the spring of the year in which she would be twelve drew on. The garden was enclosed now at the heart of a greater household, for Arythalt had bought up the properties adjoining his house in order to have his offices and business premises conveniently to hand. That business had expanded many times, for the mines he had developed in partnership with Vorynaas had proved ever richer and more profitable, and he had agreed in the end to include Thaltor in some of their ventures. Others had followed their lead, as lodes were opened up both northwards and southwards in the Somllichan Ghent: Sigitsar the Outlander spent more time these days away in the south, and Morgwentan had added a mine-share or two to his inns and fields in Gwent y'm

Aryframan. New settlements were growing up all along the eastern side of the Red Mountains, and the chief of these was Heranwark; for Valafoss and Thaltor had gradually persuaded the council that it would be well to put the mining district into defence. Heranwark was set upon a bluff with a wide view all around and its citadel had been fortified. Rigg'ymvala it was called, and the young men of Caradward vied with each other to be chosen for its garrison of trained warriors.

One afternoon between May-tide and the Midsummer Feast, Numirantoro was working in her garden. Her parents were indoors, Arythalt in his office with the clerk of works, and Salfronardo entertaining two or three friends. The fountain played as sweetly as it ever did, and the small bright fish still flashed and glinted in the pool beneath. From the open door in the colonnade Numirantoro could hear the familiar sounds of the kitchen: chopping, pounding, water being poured, someone stoking the brazier, voices murmuring, a yelp as the cook clipped the pot-boy round the ear for some piece of cheekiness. She sat back on her heels and surveyed her flower-border. Something seemed wrong with it this season. Last year it had blazed with colour, a mass of flowers to rival Fosseiro's gardens in Salfgard; but this spring, although the plants were healthy and covered with buds, hardly any of the flowers had opened yet, even though the weather had been good, with warm days and rain enough. Numirantoro put down her trowel with a sigh, and moved to sit on the seat beside the fountain. Despite all she could do to prevent herself, she began to recite again in her head the sad, beautiful words of *Maesell y'm As-Urad* as she had heard them that morning, declaimed in Arval's sonorous tones. Soon the tears swam in her eyes and spilled onto her face. Suddenly she heard her mother's voice in the kitchen; her friends must have left early and Salfronardo was on her way out into the garden. Hurriedly Numirantoro dried her eyes, but Salfronardo saw the trace of tears on her cheek. Reluctant though she was to speak, eventually Numirantoro gave in to her mother's questioning.

'I expect you'll think it's silly of me, and father would be cross, but I'm sad because of the sorrow of the As-Urad,' said Numirantoro. 'Today in Tellgard we talked about it, after Arval recited *Maesell y'm As-Urad* to us. Surely, if these old stories have come down to us, and some among us, especially Arval, still honour the As-Geg'rastigan, then surely, *surely*, the Starborn must once have truly lived, even if now they no longer walk the earth? And if they once did, how could men who met them not love them, if they were like it says in the stories? And then if *Maesell y'm As-Geg'rastigan* is true, and children were born who shared in the heritage of both Starborn and Earthborn, how sad it must have been for them! When they found out, I mean, that there was no place for them to live at peace among either kin.'

Salfronardo put her finger under Numirantoro's chin, and tilted her daughter's face up towards her. 'I've told you before, you take these things too much to heart, my own little star,' she said with a sad smile. 'Whether the Starborn ever walked the earth or not, you will find as you grow older that we of the Earthborn have troubles of our own to bear without sorrowing over theirs. Don't the old stories say that the Starborn loved the earth too much to ever leave it? I think your uncle Ardeth loves the mountains and fields of Gwent y'm Aryframan in the same way, yet he must leave them in the end as we all must leave this world. People say you are as fair as the Starborn – now, now! You know they do,' – this as Numirantoro shook her head fiercely – 'so maybe you take after Ardeth, to feel things deeply like this.'

Numirantoro looked down at her lap, and clenched her hands. 'Oh, I wish I could see one of the Starborn! If I could have just one wish, that would be the one.'

Her mother put her arms around her. 'Ssh, now,' she said. 'Remember what Arval told you when you were a little girl: be very careful what you wish for, because sometimes wishes come true in ways you least expect.'

Numirantoro leaned into her mother's embrace and drew a deep breath with a small catch in it. Salfronardo rested her chin on top of her daughter's head and they sat silent for a moment or two. As the quiet was gradually invaded by the sound of a troop of young recruits for Rigg'ymvala, tramping along the street outside keeping step with the shouts of their leader, Numirantoro sighed again and sat up, looking dolefully at her mother.

'What's wrong with my flowers this year? Auntie Fosseiro's garden will be all in bloom by now, but hardly any of my buds have opened. I think it seems sort of gloomier here than in Salfgard; as if the light is not so bright or something. Do you think so?'

'Maybe it's just that the garden is more overlooked by buildings than it used to be, or perhaps the spring is a little later this year. Don't Ardeth and Fosseiro say patience is the most valuable gift in a gardener?' Then, as a sudden clashing of arms and much stamping and yelling was heard from the street, Salfronardo's own patience abruptly gave way.

'I *hate* all this strutting about with swords and spears, all this stamping and shouting and *noise*,' she hissed vehemently. '*Heranwark*! *Rigg'ymvala*! What ridiculous names! I can't think what possessed the older men in Tell'Ethronad to give in to those young hotheads in the council. Valafoss and that Thaltor are at the back of all this.'

Numirantoro stared at the fish in the fountain pool. 'No, I think Vorynaas started it,' she said thoughtfully; and before her mother could reply, she added quietly, 'and father agrees with his ideas – some of them, anyway.'

Salfronardo made a small noise of exasperation, waving her hand in a dismissive gesture and shaking her head so that her hair swung and sparked and then settled again, rather like a bright bird ruffling and then smoothing its feathers. She had an uneasy suspicion that Numirantoro had overheard her disagreements with Arythalt, that their differences of opinion on the direction Caradward was now taking were matters for discussion in the kitchen. It was time to talk of other matters.

Sigitsar's warning

Numirantoro's twelfth birthday came and went, and brought her the news that when she had turned thirteen she was to go to Salfgard with the foster-kin. This seemed beyond belief to her: every day when she woke there was a heart-stopping instant when she feared it was all a dream, and then she would remember it was real and the day would light up with gladness, however gloomy the dawn outside the window might be. So she walked in a fever of happiness and when midsummer arrived, she wore her silver daisies in her hair at the feast. All Caradriggan was decked with lights for the festival, but there were many there who thought Numirantoro shone brightest of all. Half-child though she still was, the loveliness of the woman she would become was there to see; and as Vorynaas drank deeply of the strong fair-day wine, his dark eyes watched her over his cup ever more hotly as the evening wore on.

Some months later, Numirantoro returned home at mid-day after her morning's studies in Tellgard under the supervision of old Arval. She loved the hours she spent there and would soak up like a sponge all the knowledge that he and his fellow-instructors could impart. Today an idea had come to her for a new pattern, a complex interweaving of lines and curves which she thought would look well in gold- or silver-work, or even set down in coloured inks on the page. She needed time to work out her design and hoped for leisure that afternoon. Luck was with her; when the meal was over, Salfronardo left to visit a friend and Arythalt too prepared to leave the house.

'If I'm needed urgently, you can send a runner over to Vorynaas' house for me,' he said, 'and your mother will be back long before evening.'

Numirantoro took her pens and charcoal and settled herself in the courtyard. She preferred to work outside when the weather was dry, finding the light better for intricate tasks; but today even in the courtyard it seemed too dark and dim. Fetching a lamp from the house and lighting it, she set it in the corner where it reflected the white walls and was soon engrossed in mapping out an interlacing forest of stylised leaves, flowers and beasts.

She looked up as footsteps approached from the house. One of the house servants came down the steps towards her.

'Lady Numirantoro, Sigitsar the Outlander is here to speak with your father,' said the man. 'Shall I ask him to wait while I send a runner?'

Numirantoro hesitated. The house-steward must have gone out with Arythalt; had he been in the house when Sigitsar arrived, he would certainly simply have explained where Arythalt was, leaving it up to the visitor to go on himself or not. But now Sigitsar had been invited in and left to wait while the servant sought instruction; she felt it would not be courteous to turn him away without speaking to him.

'Show Sigitsar through to me here in the courtyard,' she said, 'and please bring us wine and a dish of almond biscuits.'

Sigitsar emerged from the house, followed by the servant who set down a tray of refreshments and then left them. Numirantoro stood and indicated a chair.

'Welcome, Lord Sigitsar,' she said. 'My father is with Lord Vorynaas, but if you will let me pour you some wine while you wait, I will send a runner for him.'

Sigitsar nodded briefly, sitting down and glancing with interest at the work which Numirantoro had put aside. 'My business is not urgent, there's no need to send. But if I may, I will accept your offer of wine.'

Numirantoro poured his drink and then served a small measure for herself, filling up the goblet with water as she had been taught, and offering the visitor the dish of small round almond-flavoured biscuits. Sigitsar sipped his wine appreciatively: one always enjoyed the best in Arythalt's house, he thought.

'I have heard about your talent for design, Lady Numirantoro,' he said, 'and I see the reports are not exaggerated. May I look closer at what you are working on today?'

His face was as impassive as ever, but he nodded several times as his eyes took in the half-done sketches and swirling templates. 'You are a niece of Ardeth of Salfgard, I believe? I have seen both you and your mother wearing his gold and silver work. It's plain that he learnt much from Sigitsar Metal-Master, but learning is nothing without the inborn gift, which it seems lives also in you.'

'You share your name with the famed Metal-Master then, Lord Sigitsar?' asked Numirantoro in surprise.

Sigitsar gave a short bark of sardonic laughter. 'Don't you hear my homeland in my voice? No Caradwardan can get his tongue around the Outland speech, so our names remain for use among ourselves alone and to men of this land we are all *sigitsaran*, men of the south. And,' he added, his voice hardening with displeasure, 'you mustn't call me *lord*. Such titles are not for Outlanders, but only for true-born Caradwardans. So it was resolved in Tell'Ethronad, at the suggestion of *Lord* Morgwentan.'

Feeling rather out of her depth, Numirantoro nibbled on a biscuit, not knowing what to say. 'My mother's family are from Gwent y'm Aryframan,' she ventured at last, 'so I suppose my uncle Ardeth would not be Lord Ardeth in Caradward. But I don't think he would care very much. Everyone knows him as Ardeth of Salfgard.'

'I met him only once, at your parents' wedding,' said Sigitsar, 'but I have heard Sigitsar Metal-Master and Arval na Tell-Ur speak of him. I hold him to be a wise man who knows that honour is earned by deeds, not claimed by titles.'

Numirantoro looked into her visitor's face. It was as ever difficult to read, but she thought she saw a relaxation in its broad features. Suddenly her own cheeks coloured slightly. 'You must think me bad-mannered,' she said. 'I haven't thanked you for your praise of my work. I do so now, and I value your judgement of it.' She smiled at Sigitsar, whose hooded black eyes crinkled suddenly into wrinkles of laughter.

'Lady Numirantoro, it's a good thing that I am already an old man! You are as fair as the Starborn, there will be broken hearts in plenty when it is time for you to wed.' He took her hand and kissed it with a sort of quaint gallantry. 'I'd better be on my way.' Suddenly as he drained his wine, there flashed into his mind the picture of Vorynaas as he had noticed him during the Midsummer Feast, staring greedily at Numirantoro over his cup. Setting down his goblet sharply on the table, he blurted out the words without pausing for thought. 'Take my advice: keep away from Vorynaas!'

Numirantoro rose to her feet, completely taken aback. Sigitsar stood also and they stared at each other. Numirantoro could see that Sigitsar was aghast at what he had said; he was stammering, trying to take back his words. He is afraid, she thought suddenly. He knows something, he thinks I may repeat what he has said to me.

Indeed Sigitsar's mind was racing. He dared not hint at what he knew. Vorynaas had long ago tired of his wife, whom he had married in early youth and who had given him no children. She languished at home in Caradriggan, wan and disregarded, while he took his pleasures elsewhere. Tales of his boorish behaviour in the far south had reached Sigitsar's ears: people said Vorynaas had forced a young woman of the Outlands, whose desperate attempt to abort the child she carried had resulted instead in her own death, whereupon the young man to whom she had been betrothed had vowed vengeance. Vorynaas, fearing that his deeds might tarnish his reputation at home, had enlisted the aid of Thaltor who had waylaid the wronged Outlander and disposed of him, making his death look like the result of an accident, and so between them they had snuffed out the risk of a scandal. But Sigitsar felt he could not speak of this to Numirantoro, and Vorynaas tightened his grip on Tell'Ethronad daily. The Outlander stood appalled at his lack of caution.

'I, I should not have... Please forget what I said, I know Lord Vorynaas is a friend of your father's, I do not mean to...' he faltered to a standstill.

Numirantoro looked directly into Sigitsar's eyes. She smiled slightly, a rather grave, unworldly little smile that melted his fears away. Making sure that he saw her words were carefully chosen, she spoke formally.

'I will remember what you have said, but I know how to be discreet. There is no need for concern, for within the year I shall be leaving Caradriggan to spend five foster-years in Gwent y'm Aryframan with my uncle Ardeth of Salfgard and his wife Fosseiro. But,' and she took his hand, inclining her head and speaking again with deliberate emphasis, '*Lord* Sigitsar, I heed your warning; and I will indeed be wary of Vorynaas, welcome in my father's house though he may be.'

CHAPTER 5

Word games

Snow lay deep on Salfgard, and in Ardeth's homestead paths had been trampled through it from door to door as folk made their way to and fro between barns and byres, logpiles and larders, workshops and washhouse. Darkness had fallen early and stars were burning brightly above; and as the door of Ardeth's house opened a brief glimpse appeared of firelight and golden warmth. Two figures emerged, darkly silhouetted before the door banged shut against the searching cold. Laughing and slipping as they shoved at each other, their footsteps crunching on the evening's new frost, the two lads hurried across to the farm buildings, eager to finish their turn at checking that all was well for the night and to get back to the merrymaking indoors.

'Harvest! Harvest! Come on, somebody give us harvest!' shouted a voice from within. Quite a crowd was gathered in the main living-space: Ardeth and Fosseiro and the young man Geraswic; one or two elders from Salfgard village and some family groups, friends of Ardeth and Fosseiro; shepherds, wheelwrights and other workers from the farm; the village smith and his apprentice; and a noisy throng of boys and girls, both locals and foster-kin, among whom was Numirantoro. She was turned fifteen now; this would be her third Midwinter Feast in Gwent y'm Aryframan. As she looked around the room at the faces of all those she had come to know and love, she teased herself by trying to work out which of the holidays she had enjoyed the most. The first year had been the best, she decided, because it was all new to her and every day had brought fresh delights: but no, maybe it was better to know what to expect, so that she had the pleasure of anticipation. Dreamily she mused, stroking gently at the cat lying curled on her lap. Suddenly she was jolted by an elbow.

'This should be a good one!' whispered the girl who had nudged her, pointing at Ardeth who was getting to his feet with a groan of protest, putting down his spiced ale. They were playing a favourite winter game, vying with each other in beating out speech-patterns on a given word. Some of them were better than others at this, and the smith in particular was notorious for trotting out hoary old chestnuts that had been doing the rounds of Midwinter Feasts time out of mind. But they set great store by eloquence and originality in word-play, as indeed men did in Caradward, yet this particular game had been new to Numirantoro when she first came to Salfgard. It was old Gradanar who had been shouting out his suggestion of 'harvest', and she leaned forward to hear what Ardeth would say.

'Harvest,' declaimed her uncle, sweeping the rafters with his gaze. Seeming to take sudden inspiration from the nets of onions and bunches of dried herbs hanging there, he gestured expansively with his arms and continued, 'Harvest, heavy and hearty, hauled home in happiness!' A mixture of approval and laughter greeted this, in which Fosseiro could be heard remarking that you could count on Ardeth to come up with something to do with food. Hearing this, he raised his cup to her with a grin. As he often remarked, he might have grey in his hair these days but there was nothing wrong with his stomach, and Fosseiro had excelled herself this year with seasonal fare of every kind. Ardeth cracked a nut or two from the bag of filberts on the bench beside him. Chewing thoughtfully, he pretended to ponder, a finger at his lips. Then he suddenly he pounced on the smith with a gleeful yell of 'Oak!'

'Oh no, not again!' Amid a babble of good-natured derision, the smith rose ponderously, wiping his mouth with the back of a massive hand. Clearing his throat, he gave them what they'd heard a hundred times before.

'Oak. Old, older, oldest: outlasting oathtaking, outliving ourselves.' He stood there, smiling sheepishly while the lads whistled and cat-called. Numirantoro, laughing with the others, nevertheless enjoyed his effort on behalf of the oak. She wondered just how old the words were, maybe as old as the oak itself, going back through the generations to a time when the world was new to men's eyes. But the game was going on. With a look of great craftiness on his face, the smith hit back at his tormentors with 'Kestrel!'

The room quieted as people racked their brains, staring around them for inspiration. This was a difficult one, thought Geraswic. Scarcely seeing them, his eyes ranged over Fosseiro rocking her cousin's new baby, Gradanar's knotted old hands resting on his stick, the flames dancing on the wide hearth, the log-pile in the corner into which someone had stuck sprigs of holly, the tankards and jugs on the table, the hunting nets and bowstaves hanging on the wall away in the shadows. As the firelit faces swam before him, a movement caught his attention. Numirantoro had raised her head, her face alert with a sudden idea. As she began to speak, it was as if Geraswic saw her then for the first time. The colour rose in his cheeks; his throat contracted.

'Kestrel,' said Numirantoro shyly, as everyone looked up at her. 'Keen sighted, knife-footed, kitted out for killing.'

Shouts of approval at her cleverness rang out and Numirantoro smiled happily, her confidence growing. Then before she could choose another word in her turn, the door flew open with a crash as the two youngsters returned from their rounds and tumbled back into the room, locked in a noisy struggle to force snow down each other's necks. Half a dozen dogs who had been snoozing by the hearth leapt up barking madly and their various masters yelled in turn to subdue them. Amid the hubbub, Geraswic slipped out from the hall. Hurrying round the corner of the carpenter's workshed he leaned against the wall, barely noticing the cold biting into his feet as his heart hammered and his breath smoked on the night air. Resting his forehead against the rough wall, Geraswic smelt the sweet woodshavings within and knew instinctively that for the rest of his life, the scent of freshly-sawn timber would instantly evoke this moment. His stomach twisted in a pang of longing such as he had never known before as he looked up into the darkness above and whispered Numirantoro's name to the silent, starry sky.

Fosseiro's wisdom

Midwinter was not the only time for feasting in Salfgard, for the year in Gwent y'm Aryframan was measured out by the turning seasons so that May-tide gave way to Midsummer, and Harvest-home brought them back again to the festivities which brightened the shortest, darkest days of the winter. And there were many other activities and diversions too which all enjoyed; but the young folk especially were expected to keep up their skills with bow, stave, sling and sword. Everyone in Gwent y'm Aryframan was taught the use of the bow and the sling, for a good eye and an accurate hand were as useful in the hunting field as in battle, and both girls and grown women often joined the menfolk on a stalk or drive, bringing back a hare or wildfowl for the pot. The boys worked also on their prowess with the sword and stave, although the sword was more favoured by those who hailed from Caradward where the use of the stave was almost unknown except occasionally in sport. Sometimes young lads from Caradward would complain at being set to square up with the stave, thinking it too rustic an activity for their dignity, and their fellows of Gwent y'm Aryframan would retaliate, saying sword-play was unnecessary where all were friends and taunting the Caradwardans with fear of the unknown; but if Ardeth got wind of these disagreements, he would say that a man from a civilised country should be able to defend himself, feed himself and express himself, which was the end to which all their efforts should be working: they would be telling him next it was not worth their while to be able to read and write, or to learn the history and legends of their forefathers! Then they would shuffle their feet and mutter, and turn back again to the task in hand. But as time went on, Geraswic noted that not all of the Caradwardans seemed convinced by Ardeth's reasoning. Some of them would smirk, or apply themselves only so long as he was there to see, and several times Geraswic heard heated arguments from shadowy corners where the lamplight was dim.

Hoping that there was no more to all this than a typical tendency for young men to work off spare energy in aggression, he found more for them to do around the farm and said nothing to Ardeth or Fosseiro. Indeed Geraswic, who had always been of a sunny and open nature rather like Ardeth himself, had become somewhat quiet and withdrawn into himself since the time of the Midwinter Feast. As the months of autumn passed, Numirantoro worked with Fosseiro and the other women on apple-picking, meat-curing, preserve-making and the other tasks of the season and she noticed that if one of them called to Geraswic for help with a ladder in the orchard, or joked with him as he passed through the dairy with a milk pail, or asked for his opinion on what games to include in the forthcoming Harvest-home holiday, he would avoid meeting her eyes and turn slightly away from her while talking to the others, making his answers brief and moving off again as quickly as he could. She wondered what was wrong. When she first came to Salfgard, he had been friendly and approachable, showing her the use of the throwing-stick he had developed and praising her skill with the sling. She had enjoyed his way with a story, and he had admired her talent for drawing and design, and each had been able to tell the other of this without awkwardness. Now it seemed the merry days were over; Geraswic scarcely spoke to her and she hesitated to say anything to him, fearing that she must have annoyed him in some way.

All this was not lost on Fosseiro, whose shrewd eye missed very little of what went on at Salfgard. As she and Ardeth prepared for rest one night shortly before the day of Harvest-home, she decided to speak.

'Has Geraswic said anything to you about Numirantoro?' she asked Ardeth as he sat on the edge of the bed, unlacing his boots.

She could tell Ardeth wasn't really listening. He pulled off his tunic, shivering slightly as he drew his nightgown over his head and swung himself into the warmth of the bed. 'What sort of thing?'

Fosseiro sighed. 'Men! Don't you notice anything strange about him, all this year since midwinter?'

'Don't think so,' mumbled Ardeth, snuggling against her contentedly. 'He seems all right to me.'

'Well of course he's not all right!' said Fosseiro, pinching Ardeth to make sure he didn't go to sleep when she wanted to talk. 'Do you mean to tell me you've never noticed how he can't put two words together, how he sits right on the edge of every gathering, how he peeks at Numirantoro all the time when he thinks no one's looking? He's madly in love with the girl, ever since the Midwinter Feast!'

'Really?' said Ardeth, astonished. 'Come on, he can't be – she's only sixteen and he's only, what, eighteen, nineteen?'

'Ardeth of Salfgard,' said Fosseiro severely, leaning up on one elbow to look down at her husband; he realised belatedly that she had not snuffed the lamp. 'I honestly do think you must be getting old, your memory seems to be going. What age were we, when you asked me if I'd wed you and I promised I would?'

A big, reminiscent smile began to dawn on Ardeth's face. 'Point taken, I suppose we were about fourteen. By the Starborn! Thirty years ago, as near as makes no difference. I'll tell you another thing, I don't feel any different either,' and he began to caress her slowly. But Fosseiro caught him by the arms.

'No, listen, Ardeth. I think we should do something about this, bring things out into the open with Numirantoro and Geraswic.'

'Oh, I don't think so,' said Ardeth, settling back down into the bed and resigning himself to talking, instead of doing what he wanted to do. 'Geraswic's a grand fellow, but somehow I don't think he and Numirantoro were made for each other like you and I were. He'll get over it in time – he'll have to, she won't be here for ever.'

'That's where I think you're wrong,' said Fosseiro. 'Geraswic's not the straightforward yeoman type everyone takes him for, there are hidden depths in him. Laugh if you want to, but I can tell! If he pines for Numirantoro in secret, it will turn him in on himself, his life will be spoilt. And she needs to act her own age more, or else in a few years' time she's going to fall for someone completely unsuitable and get hurt. I think we should bring the two of them together now, while there's still time enough: time for them to enjoy an innocent little romance here in Salfgard, time for it to run its course, time for them both to grow apart again without bitterness so that he can settle down here at peace with himself and she can go back to Caradriggan with only sweet memories to enjoy.'

There was a long silence. Eventually Fosseiro nudged Ardeth. 'You're not asleep, are you?'

'No, no, I'm just thinking,' said Ardeth. 'You're probably right, you usually are. It's amazing how women pick up on this kind of thing.' He squeezed Fosseiro's hand as she chuckled softly. 'Well, you're the one who seems to have thought it all out. You tell me what you think we can do.'

'Well,' said Fosseiro, 'this is what I thought of doing. In the evening time, at Harvest-home, we'll have storytelling; and then I'll arrange it so that…' and she whispered her plan into Ardeth's ear.

'Sounds fine to me,' he murmured at last, having just about managed to listen to everything she had to say before sinking sleepily into dreams conjured by happy memories of his fourteen-year-old self.

Harvest-home

In the final few days before Harvest-home itself, Fosseiro and Ardeth worked from dawn till dusk to complete all the preparations which

Fosseiro had planned. Ardeth took the farm carpenter off the fencing job he was working at, and gathered together a team of lads to help him. Together they set up a skittle run and short-flight archery butts within the main yard; Geraswic, much to his surprise, was instructed to take the two-mule cart and hurry off to Framstock with a request, backed up by the promise of many winter stores, that the most renowned storyteller of the town would come back with him to spend the holiday in Salfgard. Numirantoro was given a list of jobs and was soon running about with the other girls putting up hop bines and autumn garlands to decorate the main hall; and Fosseiro, first making sure that everyone in the kitchen was far too busy to come looking for her, spent a couple of hours in the brew-house making some preparations of her own.

At last the actual day of the feast arrived. After a sharp early frost, the sun rose into a clear blue sky; and as the morning opened out the air became warm enough in the enclosed space of the yard for spectators to sit at ease on the benches against the walls. Those taking part in the fun were more than warm, for Ardeth and Fosseiro had put together a strenuous programme of activities for everyone to enjoy. The boys hitched up two little dog-carts to a couple of donkeys, and took it in turns to race each other in pairs along a twisting course marked out with saplings: not that the donkeys were very co-operative, and no clear winner of the event ever emerged, but it caused a great deal of mirth among the onlookers and large quantities of ale were consumed as wagers were made on the outcome. A couple of young Caradwardans gave a demonstration of sword-play with blunted foils, and were warmly applauded; they sat down flushed in the face and looking more pleased with life than usual. Ardeth challenged all comers with the stave, and when he proved unbeatable, offered to take two opponents on at once. They took their mid-day meal out of doors, since the day was fine, enjoying the grilled meats and sausages that had been cooking over a large brazier. In the afternoon there were contests of skill and marksmanship with the sling and bow, and a pastime which was a speciality of Salfgard in which those taking part stood with their backs to a man who fired a weighted decoy into the air from a catapult, shouting as he did so. On the shout, the contestant whirled around and attempted to hit the decoy with a sling-stone before it fell, not an easy thing to do as the weights were sewn in off-centre and the outer skin was decorated with feathers so that its flight was unpredictable. All the winners were rewarded with small prizes and acclaimed with much cheering and good-natured teasing, and plied with a selection of drinks. The winner of the decoy-shoot was Geraswic, and Ardeth clapped him on the shoulder and gave him a new leather sling-stone bag. Fosseiro stepped forward smiling, with a steaming jug in her hand.

'Well done, Geraswic!' She held out a cup to him. 'You deserve some of this, it's my special harvest ale. Guaranteed to warm you up, keep your fingers supple and your reaction-time lightning fast! And talking of warming people up, shall we go inside now? The sun is almost gone, I'm getting quite cold standing about here.'

A confused babble of shouts greeted this suggestion, for (as Fosseiro knew perfectly well) they had not yet held the game of skittles for which Ardeth had put up the prize of a piglet. She raised innocent eyebrows at her husband. 'What's the matter?'

'The skittles,' called Ardeth with a grin he hoped was not too obviously conspiratorial. 'We haven't done the skittles yet, woman! There are people here who only came today because they want to win one of my pigs!'

More joshing broke out at this, several voices being raised in protest and maintaining that Fosseiro's catering was the big attraction; and Geraswic, to his own surprise, called out to compliment her on her harvest ale, of which he was now drinking his second cup. It was warm and highly spiced, so that he detected nothing strange about the heady glow which was spreading through him, making him feel unusually confident and relaxed.

'Yes, come on!' he called out. 'Who's going to have a go at the skittles, then? Is it teams, or every man for himself?'

'Now can you explain to me, young Geraswic,' slurred the smith, who had been imbibing freely for quite a time, 'how a piglet would be any good shared among a team? 'S up to each man – or woman, o'course,' he added gallantly, noticing Numirantoro lining up with the other hopeful contestants. She looked round and smiled at them, and Geraswic found it suddenly quite easy to smile back. After that … well, afterwards he was rather vague about what happened next. He remembered that quite a crowd took part in the game, and that after a few rounds only himself, Ardeth, some friend of Fosseiro's, and Numirantoro were left. Something seemed to have gone wrong with his hearing: sometimes he felt as though he was moving about in complete silence, but then the rumble and rattle of the wooden ball down the skittle alley, and the crash of the pins as they fell, would beat upon his ears like thunder. Then it was down to Ardeth, himself and Numirantoro. He stepped up for his turn, and after his three throws, five pins were down. Numirantoro demolished seven. Ardeth squared his shoulders amid much laughter and encouragement. Geraswic suddenly found himself being pushed forward; unbelievably Ardeth, whose usual prowess at the game was a source of much resigned groaning, had only knocked down four pins. Now it was between Numirantoro and himself. His head swam: belatedly he wondered what had been in his drink, but everyone else seemed perfectly all right. His first throw took down two pins. The second hurtled down the course and missed every single one, to a groan of sympathy from the onlookers. The third hit one skittle, which collided with another as it fell, but failed to topple it. Only three, then: to his surprise, he didn't feel stupid, as he expected to. Easy to beat that. He stepped back, smiling again at Numirantoro.

Everyone craned to see, as Numirantoro, concentrating hard, took aim. Three pins went down and a fourth wobbled without falling, but her second shot fired straight through the standing group of skittles, just as Geraswic's had done. Competing shouts came from the onlookers, some calling for Geraswic to win, others for Numirantoro.

She stepped back and looked carefully at which pins were still standing, and then moved forward and pitched in one fluid motion. The ball flew down the course and with a tremendous battering noise, demolished what remained of the formation: skittles ricocheted in all directions, one even flipping up and over the wall of the alley.

'Nine, nine! I've won, I've won the piglet!' Numirantoro jumped up and down with excitement and then impulsively hugged Geraswic, who looked completely stunned.

Ardeth punched the air and then grabbed Fosseiro in an embrace of his own, muttering into her hair. 'How on earth did you manage all this, you amazing woman! Just you wait till we're alone!' Then, turning to the two youngsters, he hoisted the squealing piglet from its pen and held it out to Numirantoro. 'May I present your prize pig?'

Numirantoro laughed happily. 'Oh, I love pigs! But what am I going to do with it? I know – Uncle Ardeth, can she stay here with you? Not to be eaten though, I mean,' she added anxiously.

'I'll tell you what,' said Ardeth, 'we'll install her in my very best sty, and breed her with the best boar I can find, and then she can be the mother of generations of prize piglets. How would that be?'

'Oh, yes! Geraswic will look after her, won't you?' said Numirantoro, seizing his hand and completely forgetting that there had ever been awkwardness between them.

Fosseiro took charge. 'Well, now that we've settled that, come on indoors everyone. I need some help setting up the tables for the supper, so you three,' grabbing some youngsters as they passed, 'and you two as well, can get started; and Ardeth, I want you to…' She took her husband by the elbow and steered him slightly away from the crowd, speaking into his ear. 'Well, that all went as planned! Now don't forget what you've got to do after everyone's eaten.'

The storyteller from Framstock had been well primed, as well as well paid, by Ardeth. When the harvest supper was all cleared away, after the customary hearing of the *Temennis*, he gave the company

Warriors of the Sun. This was a favourite in Caradward, but seldom heard these days in Gwent y'm Aryframan, and the man made sure he delivered the tale with all the expertise at his command. By the end it was not only the young Caradwardans who were enthralled: the entire company were hanging on every word, their emotions swayed this way and that as the story wound to its end. It was applauded enthusiastically, several of the listeners getting up from their places to shake the man's hand and add their individual thanks for his performance. The storyteller took a short break, soothing his throat with the warm honey and water drink he used when professionally engaged, and then launched into one of the oldest tales in his repertoire, *Lords of the People in Starhome*. When it was over, Ardeth proposed that a member of the company might like to take a turn while the visitor rested his voice. Various suggestions were made: some of the women wanted *Numir ap Aldron Ancras* and one or two of the foster-kin from Caradward called for *Carad y'm Inenellan*. Fosseiro gave Ardeth a surreptitious dig in the ribs.

'What about something a bit lighter to give us some variety?' he said, turning to a table where the older men were drinking together.

'Good idea – not that we can't guess what's coming next,' laughed Gradanar.

'Yesh! C'mon now Ardeth, you 'n Fossheiro do *Aryfram ac Herediro* for ush,' mumbled the smith.

Rubbing his hair, Ardeth stood up slowly. 'Well, if you're sure you want us to do it *again*', he said, with every sign of reluctance, beckoning Fosseiro out into the middle of the floor. But she stood her ground.

'No, no! Ardeth, for goodness' sake. People must be sick to death of seeing us go through our old routine. Let's have *The Farmer and the Maiden*, by all means, but let's see some new blood in action! Come on, Numirantoro: *you* be the maiden for me this time, and Ardeth, get one of those young fellows over there by you on his feet.'

Before either of them quite knew how it happened, Numirantoro and Geraswic found themselves in the centre of a ring of smiling faces, as friends called out to them to get started and some of the lads stamped on the floor and whistled. Fosseiro and Ardeth exchanged conspiratorial glances as the two young people self-consciously began to enact the tale to old Gradanar's recitation. Geraswic's head was feeling steadier now, after he'd lined his stomach with supper, but the fumes of Fosseiro's secret harvest concoction still twined around his thoughts and took away his usual inhibitions. As he entered into the spirit of the occasion, he became more animated and had everyone in fits of laughter with his enactment of an old boy wooing a delicate and retiring young maiden. Not that Numirantoro seemed all that reluctant, for she laughed too and flashed Geraswic many a sparkling glance, and at the end of the tale when they joined hands and turned to face their audience, he pulled her to him in an embrace and she moved willingly into his arms. For a second they stood there, Geraswic's heart pounding. I will never forget this moment, he thought, the first time that I held Numirantoro in my arms.

And so the evening wound on to its close: gradually those who lived nearby took their leave and returned to their own homes, the storyteller bade the company a gracious goodnight and retired to his guest-bed, Fosseiro did a bit of general tidying before going upstairs, and Ardeth went out as he always did, lantern in hand, to do a final check around the farm buildings before sleep. Numirantoro had slipped up to the girls' room, hoping the others would think she was asleep when they found her in bed. Some of the lads sat on downstairs, hoping for fun at Geraswic's expense and disposed to tease him unmercifully; but he, muttering about helping Ardeth, grabbed another lantern and dashed out into the dark yard leaving them disappointed, and soon they too tramped off to their beds, yawning and stretching. Night settled over Salfgard, but not all slept. Numirantoro lay with her thoughts in a whirl, re-living the moment when she had stood in Geraswic's arms. She had looked into his eyes and seen that he loved her, and this seemed to her a huge responsibility for her to bear. Did she love him? How did people know when they were in love? Her mind ranged over famous lovers in old tales, and married couples such as Ardeth and Fosseiro, and her own parents, but there were no clues to help her there. Geraswic was grateful that his standing with Ardeth meant that he now had a small room to himself. Unable to lie still, he tossed and turned, wondering now how soon he would hold Numirantoro again, now what to say to her next time they met, now whether he dared hope that one day they might be betrothed. Fosseiro and Ardeth lay in each other's arms, she delighted with her match-making, he full of admiration for her cleverness, and each as tenderly loving of the other as they had ever been. The storyteller was wakeful also. He often found it difficult to sleep after a performance and tonight his stomach was troublesome too. It had not been a good idea to eat that second piece of venison pie. He sat up and sipped at some water, seeing again the young couple who had enacted *Aryfram ac Herediro*. And now a new story began to form in his mind, but this time it was a tale of young lovers parted by fate and doomed to misfortune.

Unsettling news

Before winter closed in, shutting down the roads and bringing the new season's round of tasks to farm and field, Ardeth and Geraswic paid a brief visit to Framstock to settle arrangements for the home-place, and for Ardeth to attend a meeting of Val'Arad, the general council of Gwent y'm Aryframan. It was agreed that Geraswic should begin spending a few weeks at a time in Framstock, starting the following spring, gradually taking over the running of the family farm from Ardeth's father. The old people were pleased with the arrangement, having been fond of Geraswic ever since he first came to Ardeth in Salfgard, and they looked forward to having a young fellow more often about the place again. The news in council was not so pleasing, for many, including Ardeth's father, had plenty to say about Caradwardans such as Morgwentan and others buying their way into Gwent y'm Aryframan. It was affecting trade, they claimed, with the prices they were offered for their goods always falling, while the cost of imports always rose: ores from the Somllichan Ghent, finished metalwork from Staran y'n Forgarad, seedcorn from the Ellanwic, lamp oils from the Lowanmorad, all became ever more expensive.

As they travelled back up the valley to Salfgard, Ardeth and Geraswic passed the time in talking matters over while the mules plodded steadily along the road.

'I'm not surprised the Caradwardans drive ever harder bargains,' said Geraswic. 'They have to find some way to pay for all the new building at Heranwark and the fortifications of Rigg'ymvala – not to mention the upkeep of the garrison which I've heard is quartered there permanently now. What's it all for?'

'Well, as far as I could make out from what I saw and heard last time I was in Caradriggan, the official reason is to protect the mines in the Red Mountains,' said Ardeth. 'My marriage-brother Arythalt runs a huge enterprise there, even though he has lands and other interests elsewhere in Caradward. At one time the whole metal industry was concentrated in the south and the Outlanders more or less controlled it, but once Arythalt and others began prospecting, the mines began to spread north and the *sigitsaran* have got rather left out of things, or so I gathered. Funny lot, the Outlanders, though. They don't seem to care much about what the Caradwardans get up to, but I think all that rubbish about who could be addressed as *lord*, and who couldn't, riled them a bit.'

'Do you think the Caradwardans fear that the Sigitsaran might try to take over the mines, then?' asked Geraswic. 'I mean, who else would? Surely they don't think we'd come storming down the road from Framstock? Mind you they might be a bit worried if *you* were at the front, brandishing your sparring-stave!' He ducked with a laugh as Ardeth aimed a playful cuff at the side of his head.

'No, I don't see how anyone in Caradward could genuinely detect a threat from the Outlanders, and certainly not from our side of the mountains,' said Ardeth, 'although who knows what *they* imagine they see. Certainly I find they grow haughtier and more touchy as the years pass, and more inclined to turn away from the old ways. Do you know, last time I visited Salfronardo and Arythalt, a few years back at the time of the Midsummer Feast, I never heard the *Temennis* recited once, except with Arval in Tellgard. And I'll tell you another strange thing, I heard them talk about it at the meeting of Val'Arad. Carstann was saying he'd been over to a market near Heranwark, there's a merchant there he's been dealing with for years, buying his oil in return for wool and hides. This time, it seems he had a real job on to persuade the fellow to trade at all – first he said oil stocks were low, then he wanted a ridiculous price, even asked for river-pearls, which of course Carstann doesn't deal in anyway; then it came out, when Carstann had plied him with wine for a bit, that he's not supposed to trade in oil at all any more, because it's all needed in Caradward! What do you make of that?'

'Did Carstann get any oil in the end?' asked Geraswic.

'Couple of dozen large jars,' grunted Ardeth, 'and he reckoned he paid well over the odds for that.'

'Well,' said Geraswic slowly, 'I can see how they might need all the oil they can get in Caradward, because I, well, I heard that …' he broke off, seeming suddenly rather tongue-tied.

Ardeth glanced round at him. 'Yes?'

'Well, they maybe need it for lamps, and lights generally,' said Geraswic, looking hard into the middle distance with the air of a man wishing he'd kept his mouth shut. 'I heard that, I mean, people say that there seems to be something a bit odd about the weather in Caradward these last few years – bit dark and gloomy, not much sun, crops not growing well and that sort of thing.'

'Don't see how even Caradwardans could light up whole fields of wheat, if that's their problem,' said Ardeth. Then something jogged at the edge of his memory. 'But hold on, now you come to mention it, I remember hearing Numirantoro saying, when she first came up to Salfgard this time, that she'd had difficulty getting the plants in her garden at home to come into flower, and that she thought it was much brighter here than in Caradriggan. Maybe there's something in it, after all. And,' he gave Geraswic a friendly barge with his shoulder, 'that's where you heard it too, eh? "They say", "people say"! Numirantoro says, that's more like it, isn't it? How are you two getting on these days?'

Geraswic, blushing and wishing Ardeth would leave him alone, mumbled something non-committal, and Ardeth decided not to press the subject. He tickled up the mules and they put on a bit more speed for the last couple of miles before the next *gradstedd,* a wayside inn situated on the edge of a hamlet between the road and the waters of the Lissad na'Rhos and a favourite stopping-point with Ardeth when travelling back home from Framstock. Later on, after evening had fallen and their meal had been taken in the common room of the inn, Geraswic and Ardeth sat on for a while around the glowing embers in the paddock firespot. It was warm for the time of year, and Ardeth had encountered some friends who were also spending the night at the inn, travelling in the opposite direction. They sat at ease with their drinks around the fire, talking and laughing; and Geraswic lingered too, exchanging a word now and again with the watchman who would tend the fire through the night, safeguarding the wagons and the pack animals turned out to graze. The watchman was taking his wine well-watered and in the way of such men was not particularly talkative, and Geraswic found himself left alone with his thoughts.

Love declared

Since Harvest-home, it had been easier for him to talk to Numirantoro and to spend time in her company. Once his interest in her had been openly acknowledged, it had been more natural for him to sit beside her, or to ask her to partner him in games, or to walk with him in the village at Salfgard and on hunting trips in the hills. She seemed fond of him, but he could not hide from himself that she did not burn as he did. He thought back over the last time a group of them had gone up into Gillan nan'Eleth with their bows and nets. It was a part of the country which he knew like the back of his hand, for his childhood home had been in one of the wider, south-facing valleys and his aunt still lived there, alone since the death of her husband some years before but with the rest of her family near at hand for support. It had been easy for him, while apparently following the chase, to draw Numirantoro a little apart from the others, up into a high, wild little dale where a tiny, reed-fringed tarn reflected the intense blue of the autumn sky. A small group of silver birches grew there, leaves tinted golden and trembling slightly in the mountain air. The view was open to north, east and south and the quiet was broken only by the gentle lapping of water on the shore and the piping of wading birds.

Slightly out of breath, Numirantoro scrambled up the last slope of rocks and stood, eyes wide as she took in the scene before her.

'Oh, how lovely!' she exclaimed, looking all around her. The noon-day sun shone down on the reeds as they swayed, edging every ripple of the tarn with gold and sparkling on the distant snows of the Somllichan Torward away to the east. 'You know, I'm quite sure I'm right. The light *is* brighter here than in Caradward, or at least in Caradriggan. Before I came to Salfgard, sometimes I had to light a lamp even when I was outside in the courtyard. Sit down here, and let's have our food now, before the others catch us up.' She moved across to some wide flat rocks and settled herself, patting the stone beside her and smiling up at Geraswic.

'Right.' He sat down and opened the small pack he was carrying, taking out bread, cooked sausage, cheese and apples, with a knife and two horn cups. 'I'll just go over and get water, there's a spring across there where a little stream goes down to the lake.'

He came back as she was dividing up the food. 'Shall I light a fire?' he asked.

'Oh, no,' said Numirantoro. 'It's a warm day, we don't need one. And anyway, this little valley looks as though no-one ever came here before from the beginning of the world, we should leave it like that and not spoil it with smoke and mess. But *you've* been here before, haven't you?' she added, seeing Geraswic smiling slightly at her words.

'Yes, often,' he said, 'but I've never been here with anyone else before. It's a secret place of mine, but I wanted to share it with you.'

Numirantoro smiled at him, the smile that made his heart turn over. He must speak! He must make her understand the depth of his feeling for her, must ask her if there was any way, any chance at all, any hope… He must do it now, today, while they were alone in this wild place whose beauty reached out to touch them both, there would never be a better moment…

'Numirantoro, I, I'll be going down to Framstock in the spring, to look after things there for your grandparents,' he said, hearing his own voice as from a great distance and realising that this was not at all what he had meant to say.

'I know,' said Numirantoro, 'but I'll still have another whole year here after that, we'll see each other every time you come up to Salfgard. Come on, let's eat!'

Geraswic gave up and turned his attention to his share of the food. He was young and they had made an early start, he was ravenous. There would be time to talk afterwards. He bit into one of Fosseiro's spicy sausages and followed it with a big chunk of cheese bread.

Numirantoro was gazing into the distance, looking at the high peaks of the Somllichan Torward, the Mountains of Sun's Abiding. 'Did you know that in Caradward, they call them the Somllichan Stirfellan?' she asked. 'I wonder why.'

'I suppose our name is because the sun rises over them, if you're looking at them from Gwent y'm Aryframan,' said Geraswic. 'From Caradward, they'd be more to the north, maybe that's the reason – although I don't see why that would make them the *Deadly* Mountains. But the Caradwardans live more in towns and cities than we do, don't they? Perhaps they don't feel comfortable with wild places. Ardeth used to say he wondered why they were afraid of the forest; he said it looked quite harmless to him when he passed by it, journeying from Framstock to Caradriggan.'

'You don't think of me as being from Caradward, do you?' said Numirantoro with a laugh.

Geraswic selected an apple. 'No, I suppose I don't, in a way,' he said, 'because you seem to me to belong here more than there.' He waited, hoping her reply would give him the opportunity to turn the conversation, but he was completely unprepared for what she said next.

'Geraswic, tell me about the Starborn. Are there any in the world now? Because if there are,' she said thoughtfully, 'I think they would be found in places as beautiful as this, or maybe away in Ilmar Inenad, west of the Somllichan Asan. Don't you think that's why the mountains in the west are called the Star Mountains? Does anyone live in Ilmar Inenad? You're lucky, here in Gwent y'm Aryframan, you still keep the old stories alive. *Temennis y'm As-Geg'rastigan ach Ur, Maesell y'm As'Urad, Carad y'm Ethan nad Asward.*' She spoke the names slowly, seeming to savour them. 'In Caradriggan, people don't bother much any more, except in Tellgard with Arval – he still teaches us about them.'

'What makes you think I know anything special about the As-Geg'rastigan?'

'Not anything *special*, I just want to hear what men say in Gwent y'm Aryframan, and what you think yourself.'

'Well, we keep the memory of them alive and honour it, as you've seen and heard for yourself. We believe they once walked the earth, but left this world long ago and will never be seen here again. But we think they still live on, somewhere, somehow – I can't explain that to you. Myself, I wish I could believe they will come back one day, but I don't really think they will. I think they loved the earth too deeply to return again.'

Numirantoro had been listening intently and now took Geraswic's hand. 'But why did they go, if they loved it here so much?'

'Doesn't Arval's teaching tell you why?'

'He says that something bad happened to the world, long ago. Really long ago, thousands of years, so we don't know now what it was, but it was after that when the Starborn began to leave us.'

Geraswic gripped Numirantoro's hand and pulled her to her feet beside him. 'Come over here,' he said, heading round the end of the tarn towards the northern rim of the little valley. They jumped over the stream and skirted the reed-bed, climbing up beyond the birch trees until they stood looking down a long, barren slope leading away to the north. A pair of wagtails fluttered away from their scrambling feet and a buzzard swung in a wide arc high above. Bleak, bare and desolate the land stretched away before them, fading into a featureless distance.

'What do you see there, Numirantoro?' said Geraswic.

Numirantoro shivered a little. 'Is this what people mean by the wilderness?' she said; it seemed much colder here on the ridge.

'Yes, Na Caarst, the wilderness where men cannot live. And beyond it is Na Naastald, the Waste. It's rare to hear it spoken of, yet not naming it doesn't make it not to be. The centre of the earth is dead. I can't believe it was always like that, and I think that's why the Starborn left us.'

They stood in silence for a moment or two before climbing back down to the warm rocks where they had sat to make their meal. Numirantoro began to pack away the remains of the food, but Geraswic caught her arm and pulled her to face himself.

'Numirantoro, you are more beautiful than the Starborn, and more to me than the As-Geg'rastigan. I love you, I will love you all my life. Do you, could you, love me in return? Do you think your parents... if Ardeth spoke for me... Numirantoro, could we be wed?'

A startled second or two passed, then Numirantoro sat down again, not looking at Geraswic. She scarcely knew what to answer, and after a moment was almost surprised to hear herself speak quietly. 'Geraswic, I don't know why, but I think I may never be married.'

'Oh, don't say that!' said Geraswic, slightly taken aback but relieved not to hear an outright dismissal. He took her hand and raised her to her feet again, and then put his arms about her. 'I love you, Numirantoro! Do you not love me, not at all?'

'You are my dearest friend, of course I love you, I love you dearly,' said Numirantoro, smiling at him. Geraswic knew she would not tease him, that was not her way. He saw she meant what she said, but he saw too that her words of love meant something different from his. But his heart was wrung within him again, and he kissed her for the first time there beside the birches under the open sky, while a little flock of finches swung and twittered in the branches above them.

A stranger in the wilderness

After he and Ardeth got back to Salfgard from their trip to Framstock, Geraswic waited his chance and went back one day up to the little valley where he had spoken with Numirantoro. It was late in the year now: small drifts of snow were already lying in hollows on the north side of rocks and slopes, and the birches were bare. He had brought a few daffodil and iris bulbs with him, and hoping he had not left it too late in the season, he dug down into a soil pocket among the rocks and set them where they would be sheltered from the keen spring breezes. He went down to the tarn to rinse off the dirt from his fingers at the water's edge, and then walked slowly up the northern slope of the little dell, pulling his sleeves down over his hands to warm and dry them. Deep in thought, he gazed out over the wilderness, where suddenly a movement caught his eye. To his amazement, he saw a man walking towards him, heading not south for the gap between Gillan nan'Eleth and the Somllichan Torward where the headwaters of the Lissad na'Rhos began, but more south-east as if making for the mountains themselves. The man was still far off; so quickly retreating below the skyline Geraswic moved to his right and downhill as fast as he could, every so often creeping up to a vantage point to keep an eye on the mysterious stranger. Quickly though he ran, he was not swift enough to intercept the traveller, whose steady pace was deceptive in the way it ate up the distance. Geraswic formed an impression of a tall man, plainly dressed, whose dark hair blew back from his face as he strode along. Soon the increasingly broken ground into which he was walking hid him from view. Slowly Geraswic retraced his steps to where he had left his pack, pondering what he had just seen. He felt uneasy: in any other place he would have openly hailed a stranger, but what sort of man could come out of Na Caarst, on foot too, and without either weapons or gear? He put his trowel and water-bottle back into his pack and hoisted it to his shoulder. Looking down at the ground, at the spot where he had planted his bulbs, he imagined flowers blooming every spring for years hence, marking the place where he had first kissed Numirantoro. Smiling at the memory, he set out for home, never suspecting that the happiest moment of his life was already behind him.

CHAPTER 6

Winter worries

The door to the kitchen opened and Numirantoro came into the room; but without smiling, or greeting her uncle and aunt, she crossed to a chair near the window and dropped heavily into it, staring out at the drizzle falling from a leaden sky. Ardeth was making steady progress at mending various small hand-tools; as the weather was so miserable he had brought his work into the house and spreading a hide out to catch the shavings and splinters, was passing the time companionably with Fosseiro, who was busy as usual, today stitching around the edges of a pile of blankets she had woven earlier in the winter. Listlessly Numirantoro watched them, occasionally sighing dolefully. Eventually she pulled her chair nearer to the table.

'Is there anything you'd like me to do?' she asked Fosseiro.

'You could check to see whether the dough's risen yet,' said Fosseiro, 'and if it has, you can knock it back. And you can start heating up that broth now ready for when everyone comes in at mid-day, if you like.'

'Good!' said Ardeth, straightening his back and rubbing his hands. 'Is there anything I could eat now?'

'Honestly, I don't know where you put it,' said Fosseiro, but she rose with a smile at her husband and went over to the larder. Rummaging about on the shelves within, she returned with a small cup of ale and an onion pasty.

It was all too much for Numirantoro. Slumping down at the table again, she looked from one to the other.

'How can you *bear* it when the weather is so miserable for so long?' she wailed. 'It's awful! All that rain, for weeks and weeks after midwinter, and then the floods, and now this horrible *drizzle* for days on end, and it's so *cold!*'

'Well sweetheart, there's not a lot I can do about it, now is there?' said Ardeth with his mouth full. 'When you're a farmer you're at the mercy of the weather, you've just got to make the best of it and hope that it all evens out over the seasons. Patience! I've told you before, it's the greatest gift a gardener, or a farmer, can have. The floods have gone now, and one of these days we'll have a week or two of windy weather, things will dry up, and we'll be sowing seed before you know it. Then we'll be so busy you'll wish these days were back, when all we could do was sit indoors in the warm and catch up with little jobs like these.'

'Where is everyone else today?' asked Fosseiro, wondering how it was that Numirantoro was hanging about the kitchen on her own.

'Oh, the girls are upstairs. They're not really doing anything much, just talking about the boys and teasing me about Geraswic.' Numirantoro scowled: the effect was actually quite comical on such a lovely face. 'And the boys are by the fire in the hall, mostly arguing. They're having wagers on how late in the year it will be before this year's two from Caradward can go home, with the bad weather closing the roads.'

Ardeth clicked his tongue and Fosseiro, picking up on something else Numirantoro had said, encouraged him to go through to the hall and find work for idle hands to do before more bickering broke out.

'You're not worrying about Geraswic, are you?' she said to Numirantoro.

'Well yes, I am, a bit,' admitted Numirantoro. 'I mean, I'm sure he's all right, but it would be nice if a message came. And I wish we knew about granny and grandpa, too. When I was going to Tellgard, to Arval, we had instruction from other teachers as well, and some of my favourite lessons were the ones we had about medicine and remedies for illness, and that sort of thing. We even looked at dead animals: you know, ones that had been cut up, and there were charts to show how to set broken bones, and we learnt about what to give sick people to drink to make them sleep and not feel pain. It was so interesting! And we heard all about how it often happens that when it's really cold and snowy, and then warm for the time of year, and then very wet, just like it was here this year, people get ill, and sometimes so many of them are ill at once that it's difficult to treat them. Old people and children often die when that happens, and it's almost three weeks now since the last cart came through from Framstock and the driver said nearly everyone was ill there. I know he said then that Geraswic was getting better, but I feel so sorry that all this had to happen just when he'd gone to start up at Framstock! He didn't say anything, but I know he was anxious to do a good job, so that grandpa would be pleased, and he'll be bothered that he was ill straight away, and now he might be having to look after the old people too. I wish I was there, I could help with granny and grandpa for him.'

'Dear, dear, what a tale of woe!' Fosseiro moved round the table to sit beside Numirantoro, putting her arm around her and giving her a little cuddle, marvelling privately at her niece's account of her studies in Tellgard. She was a deep one, all right! Fosseiro remembered laughing years earlier at Salfronardo's tales of Numirantoro's friendship with old Arval when she was just a little girl. 'Do you miss Geraswic, now he's gone to Framstock?' she asked.

'Mm, a little bit.' Numirantoro picked at the edge of her sleeve, not looking at Fosseiro. Then, suddenly confiding, she turned to her again.

'Auntie, I don't know what to do about Geraswic! He says he wants us to be wed, but I've told him we can't, well not for ages yet anyway, and I don't want to hurt his feelings, and I do like him, but, well…' She tailed off.

'You know he loves you, don't you?' asked Fosseiro. Numirantoro nodded silently. 'Do you love him?'

There was quite a long silence. The warm kitchen began to fill with the smell of the new bread batch as it baked.

'I, I don't know quite how to put it,' began Numirantoro. 'Now he's not here, I miss him. I like talking to him, and being with him, and sometimes when I think of him, or suddenly catch his eye, I feel sort of funny inside. I *do* love him, in a way. But I can't imagine being wed to him, or living with him all my life, like you and Ardeth.' She stopped herself at the last possible moment from adding that another thing she could not picture in her mind was herself and Geraswic as the parents of children. She felt the sorrow of Fosseiro and Ardeth at their childlessness and in a moment of insight she saw that if she and Geraswic were wed, and lived in Gwent y'm Aryframan, their children would be like grandchildren to the older couple. 'And there's something else. I know Geraswic says he loves me and I can see he means it. But somehow, I don't feel he sees me as a real person. He sort of makes too much of me, thinks too highly of me, or something – I can't explain it properly. It's as if he doesn't really see me as myself, as an ordinary person.' She was too embarrassed to say what would have explained exactly what she meant: Geraswic gave her a kind of devotion from afar, as if she were not Earthborn, but Starborn.

'Well, look, there's no need to worry about all this,' said Fosseiro. 'You'll be here for another year yet, a bit more even. And Geraswic will be up and down the road from Framstock. Both of you may feel differently in a few months' time. If he meets another girl in Framstock, you'd wish him well with no hard feelings, wouldn't you? And if he doesn't, and the two of you decide you do want to tie the knot, then where's the problem with that?'

Numirantoro looked out at the falling drizzle again. 'I don't want Geraswic to be hurt,' she said. 'I expect you'll think this is silly, but I told him once I don't think I'll ever be wed – I don't know why. And where would we live? I can't see Geraswic coming to Caradriggan, can you?'

'He'll have to if he wants to ask your parents if you can be wed, won't he?' said Fosseiro. 'Who knows – he might be so impressed with Caradriggan that he wants to stay! He's never been there before, you know. But we're running too far ahead. You're just moping because of this miserable weather. By the time May-tide comes around, we'll all feel better.'

Ardeth came back into the room, shaking his head. 'These lads from Caradward!' he said. 'To be honest, I'll be glad to see the back of the two who're going home this spring. They're turning into a real pair of trouble-makers.'

Numirantoro stood with her back to him, stirring the soup over the brazier. Ardeth tilted his head in her direction, with a lift of his eyebrows to Fosseiro: she shook her head slightly in reply. 'Do you know yet if we're expecting any newcomers in their place?'

'Not yet.' Ardeth began to clear away the mess from his tool-mending so that the mid-day meal could be set. 'Maybe there'll be some news when the next messages come through from Framstock. Right, let's get to it. Numirantoro, give everyone a shout, will you, and tell them it's time to eat?'

She ran upstairs, smiling to herself and feeling more cheerful already. Ardeth was so, so nice! She knew he was worried about his parents, and although he never mentioned it, she knew he wished too that her mother had stayed in Gwent y'm Aryframan; he'd taken on all these fractious lads from Caradward, and he had no children of his own to help him, but he was always so even-tempered and good-natured. Numirantoro suddenly knotted her fists. I want Ardeth always to be happy, she thought fiercely. I don't want anything bad to happen to him, ever again.

Numirantoro's promise

The year turned, and as Ardeth had predicted, the spring winds blew, the clouds lifted, and the farm sprang into life as the fields were sown and the animals turned out to graze again. One day there was a rumble of approaching wheels, and much shouting in the yard, and there was Geraswic, arrived from Framstock to report to Ardeth on how things went at the home-place and with tidings for everyone on events in the town. To Ardeth's enormous relief, his parents, although they had been laid low for weeks, were now well again and getting about.

'In fact,' said Geraswic, 'bad though things were at one time, everyone pulled through in the end except three or four very old people and a baby. I'll tell you who was in Framstock, though! Morgwentan's wife had been over to visit her family, and took ill, and had to stay in Framstock and be nursed there, because she was too ill to be moved and in any case there was no hope of travelling back to Caradriggan in all that terrible weather. It's as well she recovered or we'd never have heard the last of it from *Lord* Morgwentan, next time he comes to town to count his gold. You can be sure it would all have been our fault for poor care of his good lady. Anyway, as soon as the roads were open again, he sent a fast carriage and she couldn't get away soon enough. Took one of her cousin's grand-daughters back with her, poor little thing. But no word came through yet about whether any foster-kin are coming up to Salfgard this year, I asked particularly.'

'Time enough,' said Ardeth. 'If any are coming, it won't be till the autumn. Now, tell me how you're getting on down there, Geraswic.'

'Tomorrow,' said Fosseiro firmly. 'It's late, he's had a long journey. You can go through things in the morning.'

A couple of days later, when the mules were rested from the outward trip, Geraswic was off again down the road to Framstock, accompanied this time by the two youngsters from Caradward who were due to travel home. It was slightly too early, but Ardeth had lost patience with them and for the sake of a couple of weeks was glad to take the chance of transport for them.

'You can put them up at the home farm until the wagon comes from Caradriggan for them,' he said to Geraswic, 'but watch they don't give trouble or cheek to the old folk. They can work for their keep, and they're to respect my father and be civil to mother.'

May-tide came and went with the usual merry-making, though Geraswic was too busy in Framstock to come to Salfgard and Numirantoro was secretly surprised at how disappointed she was; but when early summer came in and brought her seventeenth birthday, he clattered into the farmyard on a horse with a big grin on his dusty face. Fosseiro set tables under the evening sky for a festive supper, and Ardeth proudly brought out some new little bronze lanterns he had made. They winked around the eaves like stars, and Numirantoro wore her silver daisies in her hair. She was much taller than Ardeth now, indeed he thought she would stand taller than Geraswic before she was done. Not that such things mattered to that young man, whose soul shone in his eyes as he gazed at Numirantoro and pledged her as the evening ended. They spoke together alone for a few moments as the last glimmer of sunset still showed green in the north-west sky.

'Numirantoro, I miss you so much in Framstock! It's as well I'm kept so busy every day, or else I don't think I could bear it. Can't you give me an answer yet? Can we be wed, one day?'

She looked at him and saw he was thinner in the face; he seemed a little older than when she saw him last. Pining for her, and missing Fosseiro's good food, and shouldering new responsibilities, were changing the set of his features but had not touched the desire of his heart. She took his hand in both hers, speaking solemnly.

'I promise that next time we meet, you will have your answer.'

The spring sickness

So matters stood, and the days passed with hard work for all in Salfgard, as they strove to make up for the lost time of earlier in the year. By about two weeks before midsummer, Ardeth was well pleased with their efforts. He said he thought they had almost overtaken the seasons, for the spring had been so late that even now the hawthorns were still laden with blossom; in every hedgerow around the farm and village, down the valley and up the hillsides as far as the eye could see, clouds of white flowers almost hid the new green leaves from sight. Birds sang from every thicket, the cuckoos called from the higher slopes where the grass was thinner and the sheep grazed, and the river, contained once more between its proper bounds, burbled loudly over the stony shallows in the twilight. In the early afternoon of a perfect summer's day, Ardeth sat with his back to an old ash tree at the edge of one of his far fields. It sloped down to a small river, a tributary of the Lissad na'Rhos, flowing down from the north-east to join the main stream. About a quarter of a mile to the south, there was a ford where a road crossed and went up to Salfgard. It was not much used, except locally and when moving stock, for most travellers to Salfgard passed through Framstock first and then came up the main road in the valley.

Ardeth had been up since dawn, and had worked all morning. He had brought food with him for mid-day, to save having to go back to the farm, and had eaten it in the shade of the ash tree washed down with water from the stream. Half an hour to rest and watch the world go by will do no harm, he said to himself. It was one of his favourite places; he loved to listen to the water babbling over the pebbles, to watch the swallows hawking for insects low over the fields, to smell the scent of flowers and herbs all around him. You could almost hear things growing, he thought, sliding lower against the tree and closing his eyes. By and by he realised that he could hear something else, a sound on the edge of hearing but growing louder. Sitting up, he noticed a cloud of dust away to his left, and shading his eyes he saw a small two-horse gig coming as fast as the road would permit down the valley of the little stream, heading for the ford. Who in the world would drive horses at that speed in the heat of the day, he wondered. As the horses splashed through the water, the wheels rocking in the ruts of the ford, he pushed himself to his feet. The driver turned as if for Salfgard, and Ardeth came out from beneath the tree, waving his arm with a shout.

The traveller reined in, and Ardeth walked down to meet him. He did not recognise the stranger, but surely this was Arythalt's carriage? Now he had left the shade of the tree, he felt the full force of the sun's heat on him and wished he had not left his hat on the ground with his meal-bag and tools. The driver was climbing down now, and seemed to be alone. Surely he could not be bringing foster-kin up to Salfgard? But no, however few they might be this year, a larger wagon would be needed and in any case they would follow the main road with its inns and forges. Ardeth's heart leapt with a sudden idea: was Salfronardo coming to visit? It was not thought quite proper for parents and children to meet during the foster-years, but Salfronardo had come to Framstock to stay at the home-place for a short while when Numirantoro had been two years in Gwent y'm Aryframan. Now he was only a few paces away: he could see the dust sticking to the sweaty horses, see that this was indeed Arythalt's gig, light-built for speed but now showing several scrapes and splintered bumps where the paint was the worse for wear. The driver moved to the horses' heads and Arythalt greeted him cheerfully.

'Hello there! Driving's no joke in dust like this. Are you making for Salfgard?'

'Yes, I have a message for Ardeth of Salfgard,' said the man, who seemed ill at ease. Ardeth realised he had not smiled in response and was rather pinched in the face; perhaps he was ill or feeling the effects of the heat?

'That's me,' said Ardeth. 'Look, pull up a bit further, you can get yourself and the horses into the shade. I'll get you some water, you look as though you could use it! Message from Arythalt, is it, or from Salfronardo? I'm sorry I don't know your name.'

'I was not in service with Lord Arythalt, the last time you were in Caradriggan,' said the man, who was some years younger than Ardeth as he now saw. 'I am Merenald, chief driver and relief yard-manager to Lord Arythalt.'

'Oh, right,' said Ardeth, inwardly rolling his eyes up at the Caradwardans' fondness for titles and formality. 'So, welcome to

Salfgard! This is all my land you can see here, the farm is just over the brow of that rise and the village beyond it. Shall I get my things and we can go on up together?'

'I think it would be better if we spoke now,' said Merenald, his face set and his eyes not quite meeting Ardeth's. What on earth could be the matter with him? Ardeth shrugged easily and gestured for him to continue.

'There was sickness in Framstock early this year, after the Midwinter Feast,' began Merenald. 'You may be aware that the wife of Lord Morgwentan of Caradward, who has kin in Framstock, was herself very ill. I am glad to say that she made a full recovery and returned to Caradriggan when the roads were open once more.'

Suddenly Ardeth saw where the man's words were tending. He knew what was coming, as surely as the ox knows when it sees the butcher raise the poleaxe; and he stood like the ox stands, mute and staring, helpless for all its strength in the face of the ruin descending upon it: rooted to the spot, unable to move out of the way, unable to avoid the blow. Merenald was still speaking.

'She brought her cousin's grand-daughter back to Caradriggan with her and soon afterwards the child took ill. The sickness spread like wildfire and cut a swathe through our city: many have died. The child herself, servants in almost every household, Lord Thaltor's sister, Lord Forgard's eldest son ...'

Merenald continued, but Ardeth had almost stopped listening as the sorry tale of those who had fallen to the spring sickness went on. It was as if he had become two men. One Ardeth was wondering with cheerful exasperation why he was standing there in the open fields, the sun baking down and already burning the back of his neck, imagining himself at home with Fosseiro, telling her later all about meeting Merenald and how for a moment he'd been quite alarmed when the fellow said he brought news. The other Ardeth was icy cold, seeing in his mind's eye himself and Salfronardo sitting on the old bridge in Framstock during her last visit, watching the autumn leaves floating away; and knowing now that a river of time was flowing past, a river he would never be able to cross, dividing yesterday from tomorrow in the tale of his life. He realised that Merenald, maybe disconcerted by his blank, sightless stare, had faltered into silence. Their eyes met, this time in the contact of shared understanding. Merenald stood a little straighter and squared his shoulders. He raised his hand in the ancient, threefold gesture of comfort, warding and acceptance.

'Ardeth of Salfgard, your sorrow is a grief to me. Your marriage-brother Arythalt bids me tell you that your sister Salfronardo is dead.'

Ardeth just stood there, speechless. It seemed there must still be two of him. One Ardeth had senses that still functioned, hearing the summer song of a skylark high above in the blue, noticing the sweaty smell of the horses overlaid with that of the polish on the metal of their harness, feeling the stones of the track through his boot soles, which had worn thin and were overdue for repair. The other Ardeth, this strange, numb person who seemed unable to think or move properly, as if his mind and body were slowed down by some invisible substance that mired him like a wasp in syrup, now felt his frozen lips form words. He heard himself speak, as from some great distance.

'Come over to the barn there in the far corner of the field. We can put the whole outfit in there for a while, there's water for the horses and straw for bedding; I'll have someone come down from the farm to rub and feed them.'

Greatly relieved that Ardeth had at last said something, even though it was not the grief-stricken enquiry he had been expecting, Merenald sprang into action. Together they walked the horses slowly along the lower edge of the field, passing the ash tree where Ardeth had sat such a short time before. They went into the cool darkness of the old stone barn and worked together silently to uncouple the horses and lead them into the stalls. The gig was backed into the far corner where the floor was clear, and Merenald pulled out some bundles, working his arms into a pack and slinging what looked like a heavy bag across his shoulders. Ardeth was leaning on the half-door now, looking out over the field. His brain was slowly beginning to function again.

'Do my parents know?'

'No, I travelled by the quick route straight here to Salfgard: Arythalt judged that if he sent the gig, it would be light enough to pass the rougher road and he felt it best that the old folk did not hear the news first from a stranger.'

'Yes, I'll go down to Framstock and tell them myself.' Ardeth turned to Merenald, who was standing behind him in the barn, loaded down with his luggage. He had been staring into the bright sunshine and as he turned into the shady barn, his eyes were slow to react and for an eerie moment Merenald was quite invisible to him, increasing the sense of unreality he still felt. 'When did it happen?'

'The sickness began in Caradriggan some days before May-tide,' answered Merenald, 'and before two weeks were gone, it had raged through the city like a plague.'

Ardeth stirred some loose straw on the floor with his foot. When he looked up again, his face had changed as grief began to pull at his features. 'But in two weeks' time it will be the Midsummer Feast. Why did word not come sooner?'

'My journey has taken me nine or ten days at most; I have travelled much quicker than news will take to reach you by the longer road through Framstock, but I had to wait until we could be sure no more would fall ill. Lord Arythalt sent me to you once a week had gone by after we, after…' He began to falter, his voice trembled. He cleared his throat, gripping the strap of the bag he carried until his knuckles whitened. 'After we buried Lady Salfronardo. She was the last person to die.'

There an old cattle-trough in the corner, upturned and festooned with thick, dusty cobwebs and dry leaves. Ardeth sank on to it without a word. He looked at his hands, burned brown by the sun as usual in summer, and then put them to his head, running his fingers through his hair. He looked at the dust on the floor. Salfronardo lay in dust now: her bright hair, her amber eyes, gone for ever; all her fires quenched. Salfronardo dead, buried, these two weeks and more, while he went about the farm unknowing. Dead, buried: the words tramped through his head like the heavy tread of armed men. And she'd been the last to die! She must so nearly have escaped, how bitter it was to know that. Uselessly, he wished Merenald had not told him. He looked up again, out through the door, noticing vaguely that the shadows had barely moved. It must be no time at all since Merenald had arrived, although to Ardeth it seemed that a lifetime had passed since he walked out from the tree to greet the stranger. There was no point in hiding in the barn. There was no point in wondering what the right words were, no words would do any good. It was unfair of him to blame Merenald for what he'd said, the young fellow had been given a difficult task to do, he'd done his best. He stood up again, took a deep breath, forced some sort of smile onto his face and gripped Merenald by the arm.

'Sorry. I just ... well, you can imagine. Now, we'd better think about what to do. I'll send someone down to the horses, and you can come up to the farm with me. My wife's there, she'll get you some food.' Suddenly he thought of Numirantoro and wondered whether she was in the house or not. They would need to keep Merenald out of her way until she had been told about her mother. He supposed he would have to do that. Searching for anything to block that picture from his mind, he turned again to Merenald.

'Here, let me take that. I shouldn't have left you standing there weighed down with all this stuff.' He lifted the long bag from the younger man's shoulders onto his own, surprised at how heavy it was. 'Whatever have you got in this?'

'Mostly things for the return journey, for Lady Numirantoro,' said Merenald, taking a step back, startled, as Ardeth dropped the bag and whipped round on him.

'There is almost a year yet, before Numirantoro must return to Caradriggan,' he said.

Merenald swallowed, looking down at his feet. He was hot, tired and sweaty; his throat was full of dust and his stomach was empty. He was desperate for a drink, for some food and rest; his head ached with fatigue, sorrow, and the effort of dealing with this strangely quiet man who he sensed was barely in control of his grief. But it was no use returning to Caradriggan alone, he might just as well stay here and learn to till the fields. Setting his jaw, he raised his head and spoke.

'I have a letter for you from Lord Arythalt. He requires that Numirantoro should return to Caradriggan with me, without completing the final year of her fostering here. He thanks you for your care of her but he instructed me to say that she is his only child and her place is with him, now that Lady Salfronardo is gone. I must take her home to her father as soon as she can be ready to travel.'

Ardeth stared at the man blankly. Dead feet, in a procession of the dead, were marching brutally through his head again. Abruptly he seized the bag and set off up the field, noticing vaguely that once more he was icy cold, untouched by the burning summer sun. Merenald hesitated for a moment, and then trailed slowly after him.

CHAPTER 7

A bitter blow

Fosseiro sat alone in the living-hall of the old home-place in Framstock. It was mid-evening of a day when late winter hovered on the edge of earliest spring: the evenings were a little lighter now, the first blackthorn flowers were breaking in the most sheltered spots, but bitter winds still blew, sending searching draughts through windows and under doors. Fosseiro was cosy enough however, sitting quietly before the fire in an old chair, in the homely, familiar surroundings she had known all her adult life. She could hear little noises all around, the rustle as a log slipped in the fire, the usual creaks and groans of an old house settling as the temperature dropped outside, the purring which started up each time the sleeping cat awoke briefly and curled into a more comfortable position. Occasionally sounds from outside the house made themselves heard, the distant barking of a dog, gusts of wind in the garden, once a sudden shout and then laughter from two men passing in the street. Fosseiro was spinning, working some especially soft, fine wool that she planned to make into a shawl for Ardeth's mother. The old lady had failed visibly since her husband died: poor man, he had never got over the news of Salfronardo's death and when winter came he had simply given up, faded quietly away in the night like a little bird in the frost. Beside Fosseiro on the hearth were the ingredients for a warming posset which she would give her marriage-mother before they all retired for the night; meanwhile as she worked, she kept an ear out for any movement or call from the box bed in the ingle.

She was waiting now for Ardeth and Geraswic to return from a meeting of Val'Arad, the main assembly of Gwent y'm Aryframan. Rumours were running that momentous affairs were up for discussion and in some ways Fosseiro was glad to hear this. Provided the news was not bad, of course, she felt it would be a good thing for her menfolk to have something different to occupy their minds. It had been a hard time for them all, since Numirantoro had left Salfgard so suddenly, and so sadly, but Fosseiro thought Ardeth had borne the heaviest burden. He never spoke about Salfronardo now, but she knew his sister's untimely death had hurt him beyond words and he had endured the further sorrow of breaking the news to the old folk in Framstock, followed by the death of his father only half a year or so later. Geraswic had been inconsolable when he heard that Numirantoro was gone back to Caradriggan; he had moped round the place for months, casting more gloom when Ardeth was already missing her keenly enough himself. Fosseiro sighed; the girl had been like a daughter to them, it was no use pretending: that was how she and Ardeth had come to look on Numirantoro. And why had no news come from her? Ardeth was in his mid-forties now, and for the first time he looked his age: sorrow had taken away the boyish look he had kept up until then. He could do without worrying about whatever reasons Numirantoro might have for not keeping in contact.

Footsteps and voices sounded again from the street outside, and then again. Wondering whether this meant the meeting had finished, Fosseiro got up and mended the fire and then brought food and drink through from the pantry. Yes, here they were: she heard the latch lifted on the garden door and then the bang as it closed. She had to smile: Ardeth always came in that way, even on brief visits to the town he took every chance he could of walking in the garden. To her surprise, when the house door opened it revealed not just Ardeth and Geraswic, but Gradanar of Salfgard also and another man only vaguely known to her. Gradanar came forward and embraced her fondly, claiming an old man's privilege.

'Lovely as ever, my little heart,' he smiled, 'and generous as ever too, I see!' He'd spotted the bread and ale and other samples of Fosseiro's art on the table. She smiled back at him, but had eyes only for the other three. Ardeth was wearing a black frown such as she never remembered on his face before, while Geraswic and the other man, flushed in the face, looked as though they were spoiling for a fight – but not with each other at least, she noted with relief, as Geraswic took the older man's cloak and hung it on a peg.

'This is Carstann, merchant of Framstock,' said Ardeth, introducing his wife in turn. 'He has news which I want you to hear first-hand.'

'Welcome, Carstann,' said Fosseiro. 'Will you have ale, or wine, and eat with us?' She hurried through to the pantry again and returned with plates and cups, the remains of some ham with cold sausages, a larger choice of cheeses. They settled themselves around the table, Fosseiro first mixing the old lady's drink and putting it to warm. She directed a glance at Ardeth. 'Your mother's resting,' she said, 'so we need to keep our voices down, if we can. I don't want to disturb her too soon.'

'Right,' said Ardeth, his black look lightening a little as he met his wife's eyes, but his fist tightening its grip on his eating knife. 'I'll just put you briefly in the picture. Carstann here, his business is in trade. He's back and forth to Caradward these thirty years: metalwork, hides, oil, grain, timber, stock, you name it. He's got contacts all over Caradward, right over to Staran y'n Forgarad, up in the Lowanmorad, south in the Ellanwic and with the Outlanders, been in Caradriggan more times than I've calved cows, set up new networks in the Red Mountain mines and even in Heranwark. Everybody knows him, he knows them. Now, last autumn, he's over in Staran y'n Forgarad, doing a deal takes longer than he expects, winter closes in, he decides to stay. Come the turn of the year, there's a break in the weather, he makes it over as far as Heranwark, spends two or three weeks in and around the city, his business is finished, so, fair enough it's cold all right but seems likely to stay dry, he decides he can risk the journey home to Framstock. You tell her the rest, Carstann.'

'Well, with hindsight,' said Carstann, leaning back in his seat, 'I can see maybe I should have read more into one or two things I noticed. For instance, when I stayed in Caradriggan, the welcome seemed a bit lukewarm, even though I've been using the *Sword and Stars* for as long as I can remember. Paying up cheerfully, too, even though they know how to charge you there. Then Heranwark, well, it was like an ants' nest that you put your spade through. Young fellows marching up and down all the time from Rigg'ymvala, and you should see that these days. It's well-named, a regular fort all right, walls and gates all round the top of the hill, if you go near enough you can hear them yelling passwords and practising sword-drills. Not that they're keen for you to get too close, or to ask questions. One cocky young so-and-so actually told me to mind my own business, when I asked him about it over the trading-counter, so I told him I'd do just that and he could look somewhere else for the hawking glove he wanted, and good luck to him if he could find one of half the quality of mine.' Carstann snorted derisively into his wine cup. 'The ordinary folk seem to have swallowed the idea that it's to guard the mines from the Sigitsaran, but that's rubbish. The Outlanders are the same as they ever were, they keep to themselves – don't give much away about what they think, as you know, Ardeth – but it seems to me their attitude is, if the Caradwardans are such fools as to waste their energies, let them get on with it. Anyway, I'm getting off the point.'

Carstann lifted his cup, saw it was empty and put it back on the table with a glance at the bottle. Fosseiro took the hint and poured him a refill.

'Oh, many thanks. Excellent wine, this. Well, as you'll have gathered, I must have been in Caradward for about four and a half months all told, from mid-autumn last year until just about a week ago. When I get near the crossing into Gwent y'm Aryframan on the way back, I can't believe what I'm seeing: earthworks all across the gap between the Red Mountains and the forest, and patrols from

Rigg'ymvala stationed along it. I drive up to this sort of ramp that goes across, and there's a building there, all new since the time I went through in the opposite direction. I thought at first it was some kind of *gradstedd*, if rather grim-looking for an inn, but no such thing. It's for the members of a patrol to live in, while they're on duty there, and four of these fellows came out to me. "What's all this about?" says I. "Checkpoint," says one of them, "the council have decided that we need to mark out an established border, regulate the traffic that comes in and out. Things have been far too informal in the past, we can't have travellers not knowing whether they're in Caradward or not, using that as an excuse for getting up to who knows what. Four wagons? That'll be five gold pieces each, plus five more for a permit to trade. Twenty-five gold pieces, payable now, and we'll issue you with the permit for use in the future."

'Well, I was stunned, but I wasn't going to take nonsense like that lying down. I'd got down from the wagon, big mistake, as I was about to find out, but I laughed in the fellow's face. "Permit be damned!" says I. "I've been trading up and down this road since before you were born, and you'll get no gold piece out of me except at sword-point!" On the word, another man came out of the door of the building; it was open, he must have been listening just inside. He had a drawn sword in his hand and he strolled right up to me. "Have a good look at this, *gwentar*," he said, raising the sword-point up to my nose-end, "and then get your wallet out and pay up the gold like a good boy." "Who are you?" I said, but I knew rightly I'd have to do what he said. "I'm Lord Thaltor," he said. "My men here will check the coins and complete the paperwork. Have a pleasant onward journey." I tell you, I could have spat in his face, and so would you, if you'd seen the evil smirk on it.

'Anyway, there was nothing for it, I had to go into the building and give them the gold. I will say, in fairness, I could see that some of them didn't like what this Thaltor had done and said, although it was obvious they were afraid to cross him. I got the permit, and they said to keep it handy, I'd need to show it again at the end of the ramp on the far side of the earthworks – it's a double ditch, pretty deep when you take into account the rampart thrown up from the digging. The fellow at the second checkpoint was younger than the others and seemed uncomfortable with the whole set-up so I had a few words with him while he looked at the document. He told me that the men in the patrols from Rigg'ymvala have signed on for a set number of years and they get pay, with their board and equipment provided. But the others there, like himself, well they get food and lodging but no money, it's another new regulation they've got now in Caradward. Every second son in a family has to serve for a year. So I said to him, "But why? What's the idea? Why do all this, now, what was wrong with how things have always been before?" And he said it had started when somebody got up in the council and persuaded Tell'Ethronad that the spring sickness last year came to them from Framstock. They put the blame for their misfortune on Gwent y'm Aryframan and they mean to make us pay for it, or at least to make sure they control who comes and goes in future.'

Carstann finished speaking and a heavy silence fell in which Fosseiro looked from one to the other. 'What happened in Val'Arad, when everyone heard about this?' she asked at last.

'For one thing, there was a first-class yelling match the like of which I've never seen or heard there before,' said Ardeth. 'Half of them outraged at what Carstann had to report, half of them suggesting what to do about it, mostly fairly wild ideas as you can imagine, and everyone shouting at once before things calmed down a bit. But basically it boils down to three options: do we strike back at the Caradwardans with some equally ridiculous posturing of our own; do we turn our backs on them, rely on ourselves in future and settle down to life this side of the mountains; or do we meekly accept what they've done, pay their tolls and hope they don't think up any more little games to play with us.' Ardeth's teeth showed at this: his anger had risen again as he was speaking.

Geraswic had been moodily pushing crumbs about on his plate with the end of his knife. He spoke quietly without looking up. 'Some of them thought we should fight, or at least threaten that we would.'

Alarm registered in Carstann's eyes as he imagined the effect this would have on any hopes of good trade. Without being invited, he helped himself to more wine to steady his fears. But Fosseiro drew a sharp breath and reached for Ardeth's hand. 'Oh, no! Not fighting, surely! Who would want that?'

The merest ghost of a grin appeared on Ardeth's face as he caught Fosseiro's eye. 'Well, the bold Gradanar here, for one.'

Fosseiro turned on the old fellow. 'Gradanar, never! I can't believe you meant it!'

Gradanar stared round belligerently. 'Why not? I wasn't always old, you know! When I was younger, I could manage a sword as well as any of these strutting Caradwardans. And, by my right hand! If it comes to it, I'm ready to sharpen up the old blade again, and you can take my word there's plenty of others who would feel the same. At least we ought to show them, down in Caradriggan there, that if they want to play games, as Ardeth puts it, they should remember it takes two to make a contest!' He thumped his fist on the table and the plates and cups jumped and rattled. There was the sound of movement from the corner where Ardeth's mother lay; she had woken and called out.

With a cluck of exasperation at Gradanar, Fosseiro rose from her place, but Geraswic stayed her. 'It's all right, I'll do it,' he said, going over to the hearth to lift the warmed posset and taking it into the ingle where the box bed was built. He had grown fond of the old woman during his time in Framstock and she doted on him.

'Well, anyway,' said Ardeth, as those around the table settled down again, 'threatening the Caradwardans, or establishing little Heranwarks and Rigg'ymvalas of our own – well, we might as well go ahead and attack them. They would think that's what we meant to do, and get their own blow in first; so the end result would be the same. In fact that was a point which Inenar made at the meeting. Maybe it would be best to have a look at our side of the Somllichan Ghent. It seems more than likely to me that ore deposits are there for the finding. Why should they be on only one side of the Red Mountains? Food, we can grow or raise that for ourselves. If we had metal too, we'd want for nothing and could go our own way without let or hindrance from outside.'

'But it's not just a question of trade,' put in Carstann, for whom of course this was indeed of overriding importance. He'd had time to think, however, and was anxious not to seem as if he rated nothing more highly than his own affairs. 'We might well be able to make Gwent y'm Aryframan sufficient to herself, but what about all the ties that bind us to Caradward? I know the foster-kin exchange seems to be almost a thing of the past now, but nearly every family in the land is bound to another in Caradward in some way or other, going back centuries. If we cut ourselves off, there'll be partings and sorrow, and needless separations to cause more pain.'

Geraswic came back in time to hear the end of what Carstann had said, and exchanged a glance with Ardeth. Both of them knew more than enough about the sorrow of parting, thought Geraswic. Then he saw a faraway look steal over Ardeth's face: Geraswic knew him well enough to recognise the dawning of an inspiration. The talk rumbled on for a while, but Ardeth scarcely contributed more than a nod or an exclamation here and there. He was doing some hard thinking, turning over the ideas that had formed in his mind.

'Did Ardeleth have anything to say in Val'Arad?' asked Fosseiro. 'He has a reputation for wisdom as well as his way with words and the skill of his hands.'

'Oh, the sage of Framstock, yes, he spoke all right,' said old Gradanar dismissively. He really is fired up tonight, thought Fosseiro; I'd never have thought he had it in him to be like this. 'I'll say he has a way with words! You'd think he must be one of the As-Urad. "If we do nothing and pay up, they'll make us pay more next time. If we turn our backs on them, we hurt ourselves. On the one hand this, on the other hand that.

Yes, but then again, no." And so on. We need a leader, we need action! We shouldn't take this lying down, we should …' In spite of themselves, they had to smile as Gradanar ranted on, spots of high colour showing in his thin cheeks, the veins standing in his scrawny neck as he poked an arthritic finger into his palm to emphasise his points.

'So, what did Ardeleth have to say about your idea of fighting?' enquired Fosseiro with a hint of mischief.

'Uh, not much,' mumbled Gradanar, suddenly subsiding and disappearing into his ale cup.

'I'll tell you what he said,' Ardeth put in with a smile. 'He said why didn't we come back to that at the end of the meeting, when everyone else had had their say. Then he asked for a show of hands from all those in favour of joining Gradanar's army, and about half a dozen young hotheads volunteered. So he suggested that they should meet tomorrow morning in the square, and Gradanar as their officer would put them through their paces with the sword. After that, they seemed to go off the idea quite quickly.' They all laughed as Gradanar muttered mutinously into his drink; good humour was restored.

'He was right about one thing, though,' Geraswic said, as they began to move away from the table and the visitors prepared to leave. 'If we pay now, and accept these permits and checkpoints, that won't be the end of it. The Caradwardans will come up with another way of lording it over us, if we let them do it once.' Gradanar looked up hopefully and Carstann, in the act of taking his cloak from the peg, turned as tension crept back into the room.

'Well, well, we've talked enough for tonight,' said Ardeth, 'and there'll be more than one more meeting of the council before it's all settled. Let's sleep on things now.'

Later, when he and Fosseiro were alone, she smiled at him and said, 'When are you going to tell me? I know you're thinking up some plan.'

'As usual, you're right,' he said, 'but this time, I need to think a bit more before we talk. I told the others to sleep on things, and I'm going to do the same. We'll talk tomorrow.'

Ardeth's idea

Next morning after breakfast Geraswic went out with a farmhand or two to get on with the day's tasks, and Ardeth, after spending a while sitting staring into the fire, and a while more staring out into the garden, wandered around the house for half an hour or so. Then fetching his thick winter jacket, sewn with the wool left on the leather and turned to the inside, he stood for a moment looking down on his mother where she nodded in her chair. Raising his collar up round his ears, he turned to Fosseiro as if he'd made some decision.

'I'm just going out for a bit of a stroll round the town. I don't know how long I'll be, but I'll be back by mid-day at the latest.'

For some time he wandered up and down the familiar streets, exchanging a greeting now and again with passers-by. Eventually he found his feet had brought him to the old bridge over the Lissad na'Rhos and he leaned on the stonework, looking down into the rushing water. His mind ranged over the years of his life: his childhood here in Framstock, his young promise to Fosseiro, their life together in Salfgard; the years spent in Caradward, the day of his home-coming, the news Carstann had brought to Val'Arad last night; all the joys and sorrows which time had brought. His thoughts returned again and again to those dearest to him: Fosseiro, Salfronardo, Numirantoro, his parents, Geraswic. I cannot include my children, he thought sadly. They were lost to me before I ever knew them, and now my sister and my father are gone too. Tears stung his eyes as he remembered that it was on this very bridge that he had last talked with Salfronardo. They had sat in the little wall seat in the parapet, watching the bright autumn leaves float downstream, while Numirantoro played with her friends in the water-meadow and hunted for chestnuts. Roughly he passed his hands over his eyes: this wind's cold, it's making my eyes water, he thought angrily, refusing to give in to the pain he still felt. As his vision cleared, he noticed a little clump of snowdrops low on the riverbank, almost at the water's edge. Frail and delicate they seemed, trembling in the wind, yet they survived frost and flood and bloomed every year, a sign of hope and better days to come. Ardeth looked up at the sky. It was overcast but the cloud had thinned and he could see the sun, pale and chilly-looking but nearing the noon. His mind was made up: it was time to go home now and talk to Fosseiro about his plan.

'But what about Arythalt? He won't want her to leave Caradriggan, and he won't want to come with her, you can be sure of that!' Fosseiro had listened with bright eyes to Ardeth's ideas, but, ever practical, could see where his schemes were most likely to come unstuck.

'I know. But look, it's still winter and it will take time to arrange things here. We'll get on with all that, and then by the time Geraswic makes the journey, Numirantoro will be turned eighteen when he arrives in Caradriggan and if it turns out to be necessary, she can go against her father's wishes. I hope she won't have to and I'll make the offer that he'll be welcome here too. Arythalt's not so bad, I can't say I've ever *dis*liked him, he's a bit stiff and reserved for me and just a bit *too* good-looking, if you know what I mean – you can laugh! – who knows, it might do him good to get away from Caradward, the way things seem to be going there.'

Ardeth looked at Fosseiro and she smiled back at him. His face was eager and his manner more animated than it had been this long while; he was alight with enthusiasm. Fosseiro knew very well that in spite of his words, Ardeth had never really liked Arythalt. There was no warmth between them, no point of contact between their minds: they had nothing in common. Except Salfronardo, of course. It was a measure of what his sister had meant to him that Ardeth was prepared now to offer her widowed husband a place in his own home. Ardeth was speaking again, going over his idea again, elaborating its points.

'I'll speak to Geraswic first, ask him how he feels about it. But *I've* no doubts, and you haven't either, have you?' Fosseiro shook her head, and he continued. 'You couldn't ask for a nicer, more hard-working, worthier fellow: we think of him as one of the family already, have done for years. I'll have everything made out formally, and ratified in Val'Arad, so that he stands to inherit after me. That way, when he arrives in Caradriggan to ask for Numirantoro, he'll have status of his own. It will be the same as if he was my son, not my steward; he'll be a man of property in his own right, which should go down better with Arythalt. When they're married, they can live here or up at Salfgard with us – it won't matter, as long as Numirantoro comes home to Gwent y'm Aryframan. It's where she belongs, where she should be. She made it clear enough when she lived with us, from what she said to you and me, and to Geraswic as well from what he tells me, that she felt happier here. I'm not easy in my mind that she's sent no word since she went back. But anyway, think of this! She's my niece, and Geraswic is from your family: it's a distant connection I know, but still – if the two of them were wed, their children would be related to both of us! And mother will be pleased too, you can see she loves it when Geraswic calls her *is-iro* and why not, she has been like a grandmother to him.'

'Well, you and I have long thought of Geraswic and Numirantoro as like son and daughter,' said Fosseiro, 'but Ardeth, remember, whatever we think or feel, Arythalt is the girl's father. I don't want either you or Geraswic to get too carried away, because I'm quite sure that Arythalt will make difficulties of some sort.'

'Oh, yes, I'm sure he will too,' said Ardeth, waving a hand, 'but as I said before, by the time we've got everything signed and sealed here, and Geraswic all kitted out and fitted up, Numirantoro will be eighteen anyway. We'll make sure he's got new clothes, and suitable gifts for Arythalt, and I'll have the wagon re-fitted and freshly painted. I'll give Geraswic gold as a wedding-present from us, and he can drive down to Caradriggan with the mules, then stay at the *Sword and Stars* while he sells them and gets a nice pair of horses in their place. Take it from me, when he arrives in style like that, and papers with the Val'Arad seal on them in his hand, Arythalt will come round quick enough!'

'Well, I certainly hope so,' said Fosseiro, smiling delightedly at the picture Ardeth painted of Geraswic cutting a dash in Caradriggan, which she remembered with pleasure as almost like a city out of old tales. 'I just want you both to be prepared, in case things don't go quite as smoothly as you expect.'

'Yes, I know, I know, but look,' and Ardeth put his arms around Fosseiro and lifted her up, twirling her around and laughing, 'now which of us has their feet on the ground, eh?'

'Put me down!' Fosseiro hugged her husband happily; at last, it seemed the gloom was lifting and she had her old Ardeth back again, full of life and laughter.

A sad homecoming

In Caradriggan, the days had dragged by for Numirantoro since her return from Salfgard with Merenald. He had treated her sympathetically, but with exaggerated deference, all down the long road, when she longed for a friendly face or warm arms around her. She sat staring in front of her as the days went by, unable to make her mind understand that her mother was gone for ever, unable to imagine what she could say to her father. When they arrived and she saw Arythalt, she was shocked at his appearance. He was thin and drawn and had aged visibly, his black hair showing an almost metallic sheen of blue-grey when it caught the light, so many strands of white were now spreading through it. He stood at the steps, unsmiling, his eyes dull and yet fixed with yearning on his daughter.

'Daddy…' The old childish name came to Numirantoro's lips, as she ran to embrace him. Arythalt held her in his arms silently; he could not trust himself to speak. He was glad that as she grew she had favoured him more in looks, but there were those sparks of Salfronardo's amber in her eyes and he shut his own against them, setting his thin cheek against his daughter's dark hair. After a few moments he stepped back, nodding to Merenald to deal with the baggage.

'This is a sad homecoming for you.'

'Yes. Daddy...' Numirantoro made to take his arm, but he had turned away and was slowly climbing the steps, going back into the house, shut in with his grief. Numirantoro followed him, gloom settling on her like a black cloud, silently entering the silent house, noting with dismay that all signs of her mother's presence had already been removed, her heart sinking further and further as Arythalt closed the door of his room behind him without another word, leaving her alone with her thoughts, oppressed by the atmosphere of sorrow, stricken by her sense of loss, appalled at the prospect of the days that stretched ahead in this cheerless place she had once thought of as home. Her bags and belongings had already been brought in, and she sat on her bed, wondering at how much smaller her rooms were than they had appeared in her memory, how the toys and other treasures of childhood which had been left behind in the playroom now seemed relics of another life, as if her own younger self had died too. She moved across to the deep window seat and looked out. How dark it was everywhere, even the house seemed lifeless. Suddenly she remembered how she would sit on this seat as a child, gazing into the summer nights, half-hoping that her mother would come to check on whether she was in bed or not. The memory brought back with painful intensity the sound of her mother's voice, the scent of her hair, the tiny sparks that waked in her amber ear-drops when she laughed. Numirantoro caught her breath; she felt as if a merciless, iron-fingered hand was squeezing her heart, tightening with each word that formed in her mind: I will never hear my mother laugh again. She jumped to her feet, gripping the sill as she fought off tears. I will be strong like Ardeth, she thought; I will go to Tellgard and talk with Arval, and find something new to learn; I will lighten my father's sorrow, and bring life to this house again. Ardeth had spoken truly, looking into her heart when she was still a child: she had a hidden strength of character under the beauty that was there for all to see. She left the room and went down the stairs to Arythalt.

Days, weeks, passed in Caradriggan: long, difficult and dark they seemed in Arythalt's house, where Numirantoro strove with her own grief in an effort to ease her father's loss, where Arythalt sat silent for hours with no interest in his work or the affairs of the council, where the servants moved about with downcast eyes and even the kitchen seemed subdued and cheerless. Numirantoro discovered that Salfronardo's had not been the only death in the house: a young lass who helped the cook had also died during the spring sickness. The old woman paused in her tasks to wring her hands and then wiped her eyes on her apron, leaving a dusting of flour on her face.

'Poor little thing, she was my cousin's youngest,' she told Numirantoro, who was sitting on a stool beside the workbench; at least in the kitchen there was some company to be had. 'She was mad for my tales of the city, nothing would please her but to come and work here with me. She was at me every time I went back home of a feast-day, "Auntie, speak for me in Caradriggan!" And so I did, and your mother was that generous, your father too of course, and they said bring her back with you, we'll find a place for her, and now she's dead! Ah, if only I'd not spoken, she'd be at home today, alive in the village as she should never have left, it's all my fault.'

She dabbed her eyes again and Numirantoro bit her lip; this was not turning out to be the brighter morning she had hoped for. 'Look, I wanted to talk to you about things,' she said. 'Has daddy been like this ever since, since,' she swallowed hard, 'since my mother died? He sits in front of his papers and accounts, but he's not doing anything with them, the pages are never even turned. Does he never go out on business, or receive his friends here at home any more?'

'Love you, my little duck, don't you know how many people died here in the spring? There isn't a friend of your father's that hasn't lost someone: sons and wives, mothers, grandfathers, babies, servants and all!' And a fresh storm of weeping broke out. Numirantoro gritted her teeth and stood up; she took the cook by her shoulders and gave her a little shake.

'Now, come on! This won't bring anyone back, we've got to try to do something for those who're still here with us, and I'm going to start here at home with daddy. If I can persuade him to invite a few friends to come for supper one day, you can still manage to put together something special for them to eat, now can't you?' She smiled encouragingly at the old woman, who managed a wan and watery reply.

'Ah, you're a good girl, I know it must have been hard for you to come home to all this. We'll not let you down, if you can persuade the master; but mark my words, my little duck, you'll not find it easy.'

Numirantoro did indeed find it difficult to pierce Arythalt's armour of grief, but she would not be deterred, and gradually his frozen silences thawed a little. She would sit with him in the evening, and talk to him in the morning-time about how his enterprises went; ask him about his plans, and seek his opinion on small matters about the house. Eventually time and her persistence did their work, and he began to pick up the threads of his life again; he was out and about once more, and the day came when he sent for his various stewards and deputies and they were shut up together for hours, catching up on how business went. By autumn he had even made a short trip south, and one day when he had been to a meeting of Tell'Ethronad she heard men's voices in the porch; glancing from the window she saw Vorynaas and Thaltor taking their leave of her father. They seemed animated and Thaltor set off down the street with a swagger to his step, but Arythalt was once more preoccupied and morose when he sat with the wine she brought him. Numirantoro decided this was the moment to speak.

'Daddy, I have an idea I wanted to ask you about. Why don't you invite some of your friends round one evening, to eat with us here, like you used to do?'

Arythalt smiled bitterly. 'There would be many empty places at the table, not least beside me.'

'I would sit beside you,' said Numirantoro, looking steadily at her father. He returned her gaze, his features softening a little. She was very like him, and he was still a fine-looking man, for all the marks that sorrow and time had left upon him. Now he found he could bear to notice the likenesses in her to Salfronardo: he found himself looking for the little amber sparks in her grey-blue eyes, the bright sheen in her dark hair which the lamp sometimes waked.

'Well, I will think about it,' he said, 'but Thaltor is away to the border-lands now, it will be some weeks before he returns.'

Privately Numirantoro would have been more than happy to do without Thaltor's company, but now was not the time to spoil things. She smiled at Arythalt. 'We can wait, can't we?' she said. 'Decide on who you would like to be here, and I will make the arrangements; and when Thaltor comes back, you can speak to him then.'

A real smile stole on to Arythalt's face, shyly as if it felt it had no right to be there. 'Would you really do this for me? Will you sit beside me as the hostess, and wear your silver daisies in your hair?'

Numirantoro crossed the room and embraced her father. 'Daddy, of course I will. I would do anything for you, if it would make you happy again.'

Grief that blinds

During the days of the Midwinter Feast, Arythalt was a guest at Vorynaas' house and the two men sat late into the night, talking over their drink. Arythalt, who had always been impressed by the younger man's energy and enterprise, and had been flattered by his early deference, taking him first under his wing, then into his confidence, and finally making him his business partner, now felt they had even more in common, for Vorynaas too had lost his wife to the spring sickness. He sighed a little, shaking his head.

'This has been a sad year for us, Vorynaas. Did either of us think for one moment, as we sat here at last year's feast-time, that both of us would be alone now?'

Vorynaas sighed in return, getting up and taking Arythalt's empty cup over to the table in the corner of the room. Checking that the older man was still gazing into the fire, he poured full-strength for Arythalt and well-watered for himself.

'I am indeed alone. It's a bleak view for a man, when he looks into the future as I do, with no wife at his side and no children to comfort him.'

'You know, I always wanted a son. I waited, and hoped, but the years passed and I was left disappointed. And now, well, it will never be.' Arythalt felt the wine warming him; his habitual reserve was evaporating. 'There have been times, this past year of sorrow, when I've wondered what meaning there is in my continuing with the business. What point is there, when I have no one to come after me?'

Vorynaas put a friendly arm across Arythalt's shoulders. 'Ah now, don't say things like that. Believe me, you still have plenty to contribute. You show the way to us younger fellows, you know.' He dropped back into his chair, giving Arythalt a little man-to-man nod and smile.

There was a moment or two of silence. Then Arythalt spoke again. 'It's well for you, Vorynaas. You still have time to start again. Late thirties, that's nothing. You're well set-up in business, a rich man these days, you've your health, you're good-looking – you can marry again. You'll have sons, and grandsons, yet.' Arythalt was becoming maudlin as his wine took hold. Now he repeated himself gloomily. 'I have no-one to come after me.'

Vorynaas could scarcely believe his ears. Just wait till he told Thaltor how things had gone! Better than either of them would have dared predict, when they had laid their plans after the evening they had spent at Arythalt's house earlier in the year. He set down his cup on the table and turned to Arythalt with an air of sorrowful deliberation. He was indeed a handsome man, of middle height and strongly built. He kept his hair cut short; it was thick, glossy and chestnut-coloured and he suited the close-trimmed beard he now wore. His eyes were very dark, and he kept them steady as he looked at his senior partner and spoke in a serious tone.

'Listen, Arythalt. It's not right for you to say you have no-one. There's many a man would forego all hope of sons, if he could have such a daughter as you have in Numirantoro. She is lovelier than the Starborn, a credit to yourself and poor Salfronardo if I may be permitted to say so, and it's plain to see that she is devoted to you. She was an enchanting child, and now she is a beautiful woman; believe me, you are more fortunate than you know.' He picked up his cup, sighing again, and leaned back in his chair, apparently staring straight ahead but watching Arythalt out of the side of his eye. The older man's reactions were slowing down as the wine-fumes wreathed in his head, but he sat up sharply, turning to look at Vorynaas, as if a sudden thought had struck him.

CHAPTER 8

Conspirators

The *Sword and Stars* was an expensive inn, and not really lively enough for Thaltor's taste, but Vorynaas used it a great deal these days and if he was prepared to pay, Thaltor was more than ready to meet him there. They sat together in a private corner one evening, talking quietly, Vorynaas with the best wine that the house could provide before him on the table, and Thaltor with a flagon of ale. The serving-man came over when Vorynaas beckoned, and listed the evening's fare: grilled chicken, spiced beef, venison stew. Vorynaas chose the chicken, requesting mushroom sauce, bacon and red beans with it, and raising his eyebrows in enquiry at Thaltor. Rubbing his hands with anticipation, for the *Sword* was renowned for its catering, he settled on venison stew with thyme dumplings and flatbread. When the orders had been taken, he turned to Vorynaas.

'What's all this about? Not eating at home these days?'

Vorynaas smiled. 'Not often, if I can help it. I get a better meal here, if I'm not asked out, that is. Little Sigitsiro isn't much use as a cook, in my opinion – but she has other talents, I've discovered, so I've kept her on.' He directed a meaningful nod at Thaltor, who smirked knowingly.

'But you do get asked out quite often, I believe? Everything going to plan, is it?' Thaltor leaned forward, his elbows on the table. He had been away for a few weeks, checking matters up and down the border between the Red Mountains and Maesaldron, and he was avid for news. He drained his ale and pointed at the wine Vorynaas was drinking. 'What about some more of that, to go with the meal?'

'It's strong, you'd best not mix it with ale,' said Vorynaas. Thaltor's brows came down as his temper immediately rose.

'You wouldn't be implying that I can't hold my drink, would you?'

'All right, all right! But be careful, keep your voice down.'

Vorynaas turned with a genial air to the serving-man who was now approaching with their food. 'Keep us topped up with this wine if we run low, would you? And bring another cup now, so that my friend here can join me.'

The man murmured his thanks for the coin Vorynaas slipped into his hand, returning very shortly with the fresh cup and a second bottle of wine from the cellar. The two began their meal, not speaking again until after he had gone back to deal with other customers in the main room.

'There's no sense in attracting undue attention,' said Vorynaas, 'but since you ask, everything is going very much to plan. He's eating out of my hand. I guarantee you, in no time now he'll be begging me to do what I fully intended to do all along.' He smiled complacently. 'Amazing, really. And do you know, I'm beginning to rather look forward to it. The girl's not as cool as her father, I'm sure of it. Now she's older, I can see her mother in her. Now *there* was a woman! If I'd had half a chance… But anyway, I have a feeling that when the time comes, I won't miss little Sigitsiro too much at night.'

Thaltor took a long drink of his wine. Somehow, Vorynaas was really irritating him this evening. It wouldn't do to annoy him publicly, seeing he was so keen to maintain his standing in Caradriggan – and was footing the bill: Thaltor was hopeful that another bottle of wine might be produced eventually. But wiping that smug look off his face would be very entertaining, and he knew just how to do it, too.

'Excellent!' he said heartily. 'But I wouldn't delay too long, if I were you. You might not be the only person in the running, from what I hear.'

'Meaning just what, exactly?' Vorynaas spoke coolly, but Thaltor noticed the flicker in his dark eyes with satisfaction.

'Meaning I've a young friend up on the border who's in the Rigg'ymvala garrison now, but spent his foster-years in Salfgard with Arythalt's marriage-brother Ardeth. Nearly went mad with boredom, by his account: Harvest-home feasts were about as exciting as it got, I gather. But anyway, the point is, what really galled him most was being ordered about by the farm steward, a fellow from the hill-country not much older than himself who was well in with Ardeth. So well in, in fact, that everyone about the place assumed that when the time came, he'd be cementing the bond by marrying Ardeth's niece.'

'By my right hand! If you think I'll be made a fool of by a yokel from Gwent y'm Aryframan, you have seriously underestimated me!'

Vorynaas gripped the edge of the bench under the table, fighting his own temper down. 'I'll not be stopped! By this time next year, I'll have Tell'Ethronad, including Arval and his new friend Arymaldur, and that insufferable Forgard, just where I've got Arythalt now: where I want them! And remember,' thrusting his face close to Thaltor over the table, he spoke in a venomous undertone, 'remember we're in this together.' He was cooling down now, enjoying striking back at Thaltor. He gave him a calculating look, pausing to take a drink. 'I hope you're not neglecting your practice with the sword. I don't suppose anyone on the border has dared to break the news to you, but you're not the best swordsman in Caradriggan any more.'

The colour rose in Thaltor's cheeks. Though boiling with rage, he remembered to keep his voice down. 'That's a lie! Nobody has ever been better than me! I was the best when I was a boy, and I'm the best now!'

Vorynaas shook his head, smiling in a manner calculated to infuriate Thaltor further. 'You *were* the best, true, but that was before Arymaldur arrived. He's been helping out with the drills, while you've been away. Take it from me, he's not just good: I'm telling you the truth, he *is* better than you.'

Thaltor pushed his plate away from in front of him with a violent gesture. Why was Vorynaas going out of his way to rile him like this? All he'd done was warn him how the wind was blowing in Salfgard; he should be grateful. Then he recalled Vorynaas reminding him that they were in things together. That was true enough, each knew too much about the other to risk a quarrel: they stood together, or they fell together. Maybe Vorynaas had picked a fight in a public place deliberately, to see how he could control himself. He looked up with an unpleasant smile.

'Well, I'm glad to hear that Arymaldur has more going for him than eloquence in the council and an even larger store of proverbs up his sleeve than Arval. Don't you fret: my sword-play is as good as it ever was. All I'm saying is, I've heard this rumour from Salfgard, so why wait for Arythalt to show his hand, when by your account you could nudge his elbow a little?'

'I know, I know,' said Vorynaas. 'I'm grateful for the information and you can rely on me to act on it.' He grinned at Thaltor, raising his cup to him and then draining it. 'Another bottle of this wine for us, if you would, please,' he said to the serving-man, beckoning him over again.

A made man

'Off you go now! And remember, the details aren't important: I mean whether you and Numirantoro are wed in Caradriggan before you come back, or whether you wait and tie the knot here. Just get that girl home to Salfgard! We'll organise a feast-day to remember either way, when you're both back, isn't that right, Fosseiro? The main thing is, just bring Numirantoro home. And Geraswic, take care: have a safe journey, my son.'

Ardeth gave Geraswic a rib-cracking hug and the young man hid his face, biting his lip hard. He could still scarcely believe the events of the last few weeks, but here he was, about to set out from Framstock on his journey to ask for Numirantoro. The neat little wagon was all freshly-painted and stowed inside it were a set of silver harness ornaments and some brightly coloured silk pennants which Geraswic intended to tie on when they neared Salfgard on the return journey. He had new clothes, finery such as he had never possessed in his life, packed away for wearing after he arrived in Caradriggan; and best of all, carried in the leather wallet which never left his side, the documentation which proved that he was now officially Ardeth's heir and effectively his son. How many times already had Geraswic taken out the small scroll to feast his eyes on the words it contained, ratified by the seal of Val'Arad. In the end it was only the thought that he wanted it to be still clean and clear, with the ink bright and the seal uncracked, when he presented it to Arythalt, that had made him roll it carefully away and tie it up. Ardeth's son! In a way that made him already a sort of cousin to Numirantoro, and soon she would be his wife. As he set out, showing off just a little by keeping the mules to a spanking trot for the first few furlongs, unable to suppress the wide grin of delight and anticipation which shone on his face, he felt as if the world and all it contained was his and his alone.

Watching and waving until the dust-cloud of his wheels had dispersed, Fosseiro turned at last to Ardeth. 'When do you think he'll be back?'

Ardeth looked down at his wife. To his eyes she seemed hardly to have changed at all from the girl who had married him when they were both so young, the girl who had come to Salfgard with him to begin life together there, who had shared the years with him: her hair was so silvery-fair that the beginnings of grey were almost invisible. She looked so bright-eyed, so happy, that he felt almost as if he was waiting for his own wedding-day once again. He put his arm around her as they began slowly to walk back towards the garden door.

'I'd like to say six weeks, but that's just wishful thinking. He might be delayed by bad weather, or at these border crossings; or there might be problems with the wagon, or anything – best not to expect him too soon.'

'I wonder why your mother wasn't more enthusiastic about things?' said Fosseiro as they entered the garden; she could see the old lady sitting in the kitchen, looking out at the birds where they foraged for food in the sun-warmed soil. 'Geraswic told me she held his hand and kept on saying "Don't go, I don't want you to go, don't go to Caradriggan," over and over again.'

'Oh, I blame myself for that,' said Ardeth, pausing to dead-head a few spent daffodils. 'She heard too much of what we said, that night I brought Carstann and Gradanar back from the council meeting. She's just fretting for Geraswic, she dotes on the lad. It'll give her a whole new lease of life, when he comes back again with Numirantoro.' He straightened up and saw his mother watching him through the window. Waving cheerfully at her, he headed for the door. 'There she is now. Come on, let's go in and eat and then you can wrap her up snug and I'll take her out into the garden for a little walk this afternoon while it's warm and sunny like this.'

Hopes dimmed

As the year turned in Caradriggan, life gradually returned to Arythalt's house. He was busy once more, occupied with his own affairs, attending regularly at Tell'Ethronad, occasionally travelling to Heranwark and the Red Mountains. His friends and associates called at his home more frequently, there was a bustle in the kitchen again and activity in the offices and stores around the courtyard. Numirantoro was often called upon to deal with visitors if he was away, or to act as hostess beside him when he entertained friends; and yet strangely, the busier she was and the less time for reflection she had, the more she seemed to miss her old life in Gwent y'm Aryframan. For one thing, there could no longer be any doubt about it: something strange was happening to the weather, or the climate, or the sky – she was unsure how to describe it – in Caradward. The light seemed dim even in the daytime, not helped by the smog overhead as folk in the city strove to lighten their streets and homes with ever-increasing numbers of lamps. Arythalt was a wealthy man and could afford the best filigree-work lanterns and lights; they were beautiful, almost works of art in themselves, and they shone like fallen stars indoors and out, for he had them placed all around the courtyard and porch and in the gardens too; but Numirantoro would have gladly exchanged them all for the wide skies and bright dawns, the windy uplands and sunny noons of Gwent y'm Aryframan.

Something else she missed was the cheerful, happy atmosphere of Salfgard. Much though she loved her father, and glad though she was to see him shaking off his crippling sorrow, she found it difficult to talk to him. She saw now the resemblance between Ardeth and Salfronardo, the sanguine air and bright spirit they shared even though they were different in character. How she wished she could have talked to her mother about Salfgard, and about Geraswic. For whatever reason, she found she could not tell her father about her relationship with the young man. It seemed to her now like something from an old story, perfect and unsullied but somehow already over and long gone by; when she remembered the day they had talked together in the little upland valley, the scene with the birches and the blue waters of the tarn trembling under the clear autumn sky was like a jewel set in a ring or a brooch: flawless and beautiful, but fixed immovably without possibility of change or future. And she felt there was no help either in discussing things with the old cook or her other friends among the household staff; she knew they would simply tease her or be over-sentimental – in the nicest possible way, she conceded to herself – and not really understand. Arval the Earth-wise would understand; she talked with him as often as she could, holding him in a respect that bordered on reverence, but, she thought with a shiver of embarrassment, she could not discuss a boy with him, understand though he might. There was another aspect of her new life that brought her an unease that she had not known before. Her father's friends seemed strangely chosen, for a man who was himself so reserved and correct in manner. These days, the visitors to his house rarely included Arval, or Sigitsar or Forgard, or even boring old Morgwentan. Valafoss, and Thaltor when he was back in the city from whatever he did on the borders, and Vorynaas, these were the faces most frequently seen at Arythalt's table. Especially Vorynaas, thought Numirantoro, suddenly remembering how Sigitsar the Outlander had once warned her to keep away from him. Small chance of that, when the man was so close with her father, a welcome and ever more frequent visitor.

A quarrel at the border

As Geraswic's journey took him down towards the gap between the Red Mountains and the forest, he began to meet other travellers on the road who were wending their way towards Caradward. When he stopped at a roadside inn one night, he discovered that a merchant with three wagons, a family party, two stockmen with a small flock of sheep and a couple of lone travellers like himself were all heading towards the nearest border crossing. After what he had heard back in Framstock from Carstann's tales, Geraswic thought it would be a good idea to join up with these travellers so that they all arrived at a checkpoint together. He was afraid that if he was alone, he might say or do something to show what he felt about the new regulations that the Caradwardans were enforcing, and he wanted nothing to go wrong that might delay his progress towards Caradriggan. It seemed, when the talk got going at the inn during the evening time, that his feelings were generally shared; and so, a couple of days later, he arrived at the crossing as part of a substantial cavalcade of wheels, hooves and trudging feet in the midst of a cloud of dust.

As he waited, he looked around him at the earthworks which the Caradwardans had made, and marvelled at their depth and extent. The stockmen with the sheep were admitted through the outer gate first, and the sheep led into a holding pen within the double ditch while the men went into the building on the far side. After a few moments, they came out again and moved the sheep through, and then it was the turn of the merchant. This took longer, but eventually, his permit checked and payment made, his three wagons creaked off into Caradward. The young man on the outer gate had been watching for the signal, and now he beckoned Geraswic forward. He clicked his tongue to the mules, and drew up beside the ugly-looking patrol station at the inner ditch. A few faces glanced out of the window but he was concentrating on the man who halted him with raised hand and asked him to get down from the wagon.

Geraswic showed the man his documentation, giving his name as Geraswic of Salfgard and his errand as visiting Arythalt of Caradriggan. 'He is marriage-brother to my adoptive father, Ardeth of Salfgard and Framstock,' he said. The man glanced without much interest at the papers and then over the mules and wagon. 'Three gold pieces, payable now,' he said. 'One for yourself, one for the wagon and mules, and one for the pass token to be shown on return.' Doing his best not to let any expression filter on to his face, Geraswic had begun to dig in his pouch for the coins when out of the corner of his eye he saw someone come out of the door of the building on his left; the man who was dealing with him looked up.

'Time for your break now, I think,' said the newcomer, 'I'll take over from here.'

The man shrugged and turned away, leaving Geraswic and the second man facing each other.

'Well, well, well. Geraswic of Salfgard. Fancy seeing you here, so far away from the pigsties of home. It's been quite a while, hasn't it?'

Geraswic nodded curtly, determined not to lose his temper. 'Valestron. Yes, must be about a year. All well with you, I hope.'

A year, he thought, a year since I brought you down early from Salfgard to Framstock because even Ardeth, with all his patience, could stand no more of your arrogance; a year since you were so insulting to an old lady who'd shown you nothing but kindness that I turned you out of the home-place in Framstock and made you wait for the wagons from Caradward in the inn. You young scoundrel.

'Very well indeed, no thanks to you or anyone else in Gwent y'm Aryframan,' said Valestron, while the travellers held up behind Geraswic craned to see what was causing the delay, and his fellow-patrol members stared from the door, sniggering. 'Fortunately I'd not forgotten all my skills with the sword, and now I'm part of the permanent garrison in Rigg'ymvala, currently on secondment to the border. A pleasant change from chopping turnips, I must say.'

Geraswic could not trust himself to speak, but something of what he felt must have shown on his face, for Valestron narrowed his eyes and stepped forward a pace. He spoke quietly but with a noticeable air of menace.

'My colleague here is new to the patrols, he made an unfortunate mistake just now. The charge is ten gold pieces: two for yourself, three for the wagon and mules, and five for the permit – if I find you're entitled to one. I'll need to see your documentation myself before I can be sure of that. And the wagon will need to be checked; you may need to pay tolls on the contents.'

'I'll see you in Na Naastald before I pay you more than three gold pieces, or let your thieving fingers anywhere near my goods or papers,' said Geraswic through his teeth; in his whole life, he never remembered feeling anger like that which coursed through him now. 'Get out of my way before I drive the wagon over you.'

Valestron adjusted his sword-belt pointedly and looked quickly towards the door of the building; Geraswic saw that the men grouped there were all also armed. Valestron, who had noticed Geraswic's glance, smiled with an air of elegantly studied insolence. 'Oh, *not* a good idea.' The smile vanished. 'You stay, you pay – *now*. If not, back to your dung-heaps, farm boy.'

White to the lips with fury, Geraswic backed the mules and turned the wagon, heading back into Gwent y'm Aryframan and looking neither at the sheepish glance of the outer gate-guard nor at the popping eyes of those still waiting to cross. He drove straight back up the road; it would be no good to go along the border where he could be seen from the earthworks: Valestron would simply make sure that he was watched and prevented at the next gate. The only thing he could think of to do was to go back to the *gradstedd* where he'd joined the other travellers, and then take a completely different route down to the border so that he arrived at a distant checkpoint where, with luck, Valestron was neither known nor his orders obeyed. It was obvious that the man was going far beyond official regulations, but who was going to know, or to stop him? Ah, let the Waste take him! But in the meantime, precious days were being added to Geraswic's journey time. He cracked the whip at the mules, feeling a sweat of apprehension break out on his forehead.

Twice Geraswic turned again for the border into Caradward, twice he tried to cross, at two more different checkpoints, and at both he was blocked in the same way. Valestron's orders had been swiftly conveyed both north and south and everywhere he went, Geraswic was ordered either to pay the ten gold pieces or return whence he came. Having wasted a good two weeks in fruitless travelling up and down, tiring his mules and wasting money on feeding both them and himself, Geraswic finally bowed to necessity and paid up. He vowed to himself, as he saw the gold change hands, that he would take it out of the gift Ardeth had given him and say nothing. After all, he still had money to put towards trading the mules for horses, when he arrived in Caradriggan; and no search was made of the wagon's contents, so that all his own belongings, and the gifts for Arythalt, were still intact. How fortunate, thought Geraswic as he hastened to make up lost time now that he was at last within Caradward, that either the guards had ignored that part of Valestron's orders, or else his malice had not extended so far. There was no way he could know that, no sooner had the dust of his going settled on the road back into Gwent y'm Aryframan, than Valestron had issued his orders, left the patrol in the charge of his second, and ridden off at top speed for Caradriggan. Something told him that Thaltor might pay him handsomely for the news that Geraswic of Salfgard was on his way to visit Arythalt of Caradriggan.

Geraswic in Caradriggan

Unable to sleep, in spite of the comfort of the bed, Geraswic lay in his room at the *Sword and Stars* with thoughts chasing each other through his head. Thank the Starborn he had finally arrived with no further mishaps; no one had given him a second glance as he passed the city walls and there had been no problems at the inn, although, he thought anxiously, Carstann had not been exaggerating when he said they knew how to charge. What with the stabling and livery costs, and the bed for himself, there would be precious little to spare. He had taken the precaution of choosing the plainest meal on offer and wondered now if he should have sold the mules as soon as he arrived. But no, he would get a better price for them once they were rested up from the journey and anyway, somehow he felt it was tempting fate to buy horses before he had even seen where Arythalt lived. It had been almost dark when he arrived in the city and he had gone straight to the inn.

Geraswic refused to admit it to himself, but his first impressions of Caradriggan had been more than a little daunting. Tomorrow he would have a walk around, get the lie of the land, ask someone for directions to the right street, and have a private peep at Arythalt's house before he had to face actually presenting himself there. Then he would check the horse market, get an idea of prices, come back to the inn and think over what words to use when he spoke to Arythalt. Yes, he could afford another night there, to get himself composed for the coming ordeal. He grinned with delight into the darkness. Numirantoro! Now he would be seeing her again so soon, he almost wanted to prolong the anticipation. He thought he would rather they were wed in Salfgard or Framstock, but it would be no matter if her father insisted on the ceremony being held in Caradriggan. He stretched his toes out in the bed; it was so good to lie in soft, clean blankets after the privations of his journey, to be clean himself after a prolonged session in the bath-house of the *Sword and Stars*, to have arrived in Caradriggan at last. He'd just take tomorrow to steady himself, and then the day after that ... His eyes closed as sleep finally washed over him.

When the moment arrived, Geraswic walked up the steps to Arythalt's door, his heart hammering in his throat. He had decided not to trade the mules, having concluded during his previous day's wandering around Caradriggan that to drive up the street to the house would be somehow too ostentatious. He would present himself quietly first, the flourishes could come later. If the truth were told, underneath a painful mixture of nerves, excitement and sheer fright, Geraswic was somehow much less elated than he had expected to be. He had been impressed by Caradriggan, as who could not be: the stories he had heard from Fosseiro and Ardeth had not been exaggerated. And yet, as he wandered the streets, marvelling at the goods for sale in the shops and markets, staring at the fountains and lamps, the carved masonry on the arches and steps, astonished at the sheer size of the place and the numbers of its people, he was slightly downcast. He felt threatened by the noise and the hurrying crowds, and irritated by the way the frequent passing patrols expected everyone to clear a path for them through the throng. He had never seen so many armed men before and supposed they must be from this Heranwark place everyone was talking about, or at least from Rigg'ymvala he thought, remembering Carstann's tales.

Above all, he had been depressed by the lack of the clear skies and bright light of Gwent y'm Aryframan. There was brightness here in plenty, but it came from the lamps and lanterns that hung everywhere to lighten the gloom. Numirantoro had often remarked on this contrast between her home and Salfgard. He glanced apprehensively at Arythalt's house. It was so elegant, with its steps and porch in honey-coloured stone, its many windows with their elaborate tracery, its carved lintel over the door. If this was what Numirantoro was used to, how could he think of bringing her away to Salfgard, or even Framstock? For the first time, Geraswic doubted himself. He felt out of place, rustic, ordinary: he wished he were better-looking, more confident, more sure of his errand. With still the last few yards to go, he paused in the shelter of a colonnade across the street, taking deep breaths, trying to steady himself. I am a man of standing in my own country, he told himself firmly. I am steward, heir and adoptive son to Ardeth of Salfgard, the worthiest man I know: I am the son of his heart, if not of his body. Geraswic glowed with pride at the thought. I can till the earth and tend my stock, I can read the sky and the seasons as well as words written in a book. I can make and mend, sow and reap; I can ride and drive; I am skilled in fieldcraft. I have been admitted to Val'Arad; I can defend myself and my own; I can feed myself and provide for a wife and family.

With that, Geraswic crossed the street, walked resolutely up the steps of Arythalt's house and rapped at the heavy door with the twisted-bronze ring. In truth, he was not so ordinary-looking as he thought himself. When the house-steward opened the door, he saw a broad-shouldered young man, blue-eyed, with a strong, open face tanned by outdoor air; his hair was thick and brown, its natural curl held in check by its short-cut style. He was clean-shaven and well-dressed, if rather plainly by the standards of Caradriggan. He wore a russet-coloured gown, high collared, with silver buttons, which fell to just below his knees, and over it a sleeveless waist-length coat of quilted leather that showed off the pleated sleeves of the gown. On his feet were light, calfskin boots with tassels and at his belt was a matching pouch. Geraswic smiled and bowed slightly; his cap, brimless and pointed in the style of Gwent y'm Aryframan was in one hand; the other rested on the pouch as if on a touchstone, for it contained the precious document from Val'Arad and a gold arm-ring for Arythalt, a small earnest of the other gifts which Geraswic had left in bond at the *Sword and Stars*.

'Good day to you, and good health,' he said. 'May I speak with Arythalt?'

'Lord Arythalt is away on business,' said the steward, 'but the master is within, if you would speak with him instead? May I know your name?'

Geraswic gave his name, biting his lip with annoyance at having omitted through nervousness to give Arythalt his title and quite forgetting in his embarrassment to ask who the master might be. He looked around the room into which the steward had shown him to wait; it gave onto a small courtyard at the foot of a short flight of steps and he could see the tops of shrubs over the walls as if a garden might be beyond. He felt like kicking himself. Why hadn't he asked first how long Arythalt was going to be away? Maybe he was only at a meeting, he might be back later. And who was this other man who was going to talk to him? Surely Arythalt was the master in his own house, but the steward had not spoken as if this was so. Geraswic made up his mind to say nothing of his true errand, until he had a better idea of the situation. He heard footsteps approaching and turned as a man entered the room: more heavily built than Geraswic and older. Late thirties, early forties, thought Geraswic, taking in the rich clothes, the handsome face with its dark eyes and high colouring, the glossy hair, the neatly-trimmed beard.

The man approached with his hand outstretched, smiling. 'Geraswic of Salfgard, welcome!' he said, indicating a seat and beckoning forward a servant who hovered behind him with wine and a selection of light refreshments. 'Arythalt will be so disappointed not to see you, and to miss the news from his marriage-brother Ardeth at first-hand.'

Geraswic sat uneasily; there was something about this man, his easy manner, his proprietorial air, that was starting little voices of warning within him. 'Arythalt will be away for some time, then?'

'Unfortunately, yes; two or three weeks probably. He is on a visit to Heranwark and the Somllichan Ghent. But never fear; if you can't wait in Caradriggan, I will make sure he receives any message you may wish to leave. And I believe congratulations are in order? You are now heir, as well as steward, to Ardeth? To your success and good health!' He raised his cup and drank from it, while Geraswic flushed in surprise and sipped at his own.

'How do you… I mean, I didn't expect that…' He faltered to a stop; the man's smile was unnerving him.

'It seems news travels more quickly to Caradriggan than it reaches you in Gwent y'm Aryframan,' the man said now, smiling even more broadly, 'so I see that I must have appeared most unmannerly to you. I failed to realise that I needed to explain and introduce myself. After all, we are almost kin now: marriage-cousins at least, maybe. I am Vorynaas of Caradriggan, business partner and now marriage-son to Arythalt.'

Geraswic felt the sip of wine he had taken slide down into his stomach like an icy drop of poison. Vorynaas put his hand up and stroked his beard, hiding his mouth; his dark eyes disguised his savage satisfaction at the other man's obvious distress.

'Yes, Numirantoro and I are just recently wed,' he said, 'I'm a fortunate man. But, I regret to say, I have little leisure to enjoy her company as a new husband should: the demands of my business take me away more often than I should like. Arythalt relies on me a great deal, you know; he's not the man he was before his wife died. Indeed when you called I was just about to leave; we are opening a new shaft at the mine and I have promised to be there. But, not to worry!' He rose and clapped Geraswic heartily on the shoulder. Going to the door, he put his head round it into the corridor and spoke to someone outside. 'My wife will join us directly,' he said, 'I've just sent to call her. You're not drinking, man! Help yourself, don't stand on ceremony.'

The door opened. There stood Numirantoro, staring as if she had seen a ghost. 'Geraswic.' It was the merest whisper.

Geraswic felt as though the muscles of his face would never move again; if Vorynaas had held a knife to his throat, he could not have smiled. But somehow, words came to him to cover the dreadful moment. He stood, formally.

'May the Starborn keep you, Numirantoro,' he said, his heart breaking as his voice spoke her name. 'I am in Caradriggan to buy horses for Ardeth, and called to pay my respects to yourself and your father.' Geraswic had never told a lie in his life until that moment; how bitter it was to him that the first untruth should be told to Numirantoro.

Vorynaas had been watching under his eyebrows as he swirled the wine in his cup. Now he spoke again, still smiling: he had enjoyed this encounter. 'Well, Geraswic, you and my wife are cousins now, and I'm sure you will have much to say to each other. Now, if you'll excuse me, your very good health.' He drained his cup and strode from the room.

His elbows on his knees and his head in his hands, Geraswic sat staring sightlessly at the floor. From a great distance, as it seemed, he heard footsteps and laughter from the courtyard, a door banging, more footsteps in the corridor, the sound of hooves in the street outside, voices in the porch, someone running down the front steps, more laughter. Then the hooves clipped smartly down the street and faded away, and still he and Numirantoro sat in silence. At last he spoke without raising his head.

'I'm not here to horse-trade: that was a lie. I came to ask for your hand. I have gifts for your father and messages from Salfgard. Ardeth has made me his heir and adoptive son. It was ratified in Val'Arad. I have the document with me as proof. Ardeth and Fosseiro want me to bring you back with me. Ardeth would have welcomed your father too. He gave me money, he has been more than generous.' Geraswic's voice shook a little, but he paused and mastered himself. 'He has had the wagon painted and refitted, and bought me new clothes. I was to sell the mules and buy horses after I got here. The patrols held me back, I was delayed at the border. When were you married.'

The sorry tale came out flatly, in a series of short, lifeless sentences; even his question failed to lift his voice, though his head came up at last. Numirantoro was still looking at him as if he were not really there.

'Two weeks ago.'

Geraswic cried out in anguish. 'I could have been here before then! Valestron, you must remember him, he's on the border now, he wouldn't let me through. May the blindworms of Na Naastald suck his life out!' He slumped back in the chair and buried his face in the cap he still clutched in his hand, his voice dropping to a broken murmur. 'I have a set of silver harness ornaments for our homecoming.'

Numirantoro flew across the room and took his hand. 'Ssh, the walls are thick but someone will be listening to our voices, Vorynaas has put his own servants in the house. Geraswic, listen to me. Nothing would have made any difference, it's as if Vorynaas has bewitched my father. You don't know what it's been like here since I came back, after mother died.' The tears that had gathered in her eyes began to roll down her cheeks but she kept her voice calm. 'It's as if father has no mind of his own any more – he agrees with everything Vorynaas suggests, and does everything he wants. They were in partnership anyway, and Vorynaas' wife had died too, and he was never out of our house. He has no children of his own, and I know daddy always wanted a son, and now he's brought Vorynaas into the family itself in the hope of a grandson' – she broke off as Geraswic pulled his hand away – 'oh, don't, I'm so sorry you had to find out like this! But Vorynaas is really the one in charge now, he gives the orders, and everyone does what he says. It was all rushed through before I came of age, so that my consent was no matter. Father can't see it, but he will pay for it in the end with bitter regret, somehow I know it.'

A long silence fell. Eventually Geraswic stood up slowly. He felt weary to the point of exhaustion, as if he had spent hours toiling at the hardest task he had ever tackled on the farm. He was still in shock, immune from the pain he sensed was lurking in ambush, waiting to spring upon him with rending claws as soon as his guard was lowered. He turned to Numirantoro and even managed a small smile, mirthless though it was.

'The last time I saw you, I remember that you promised me I should have my answer the next time we met,' he said. 'I thank the Starborn that I never for one moment expected such a meeting as this, or such an answer. Numirantoro, I promise you again, I will love you as long as I live; but however soon death finds me, my life will seem over-long to me now.' He picked up his cap and opened the door, causing the servant who was standing too close to it to jump back, and without turning or speaking again walked out of the house, down the steps and into the busy street, leaving Numirantoro standing stricken in the porch.

In the fountain garden

Back at the *Sword and Stars*, he spoke with the ostler and arranged for the mules to be ready by early afternoon and then negotiated with the storeman for his goods to be taken out of bond and loaded into the wagon. He went into the inn and up to his room, returning the friendly greeting of the parlour-maid who was mopping just inside the door. As he took off his fine new clothes and changed into his old travelling gear, he wondered a little at his ability to do all these normal, everyday-seeming things as if nothing had happened. Nothing seemed real to him, it was as if he was enacting some story on a feast-day, trying hard to make his actions as convincing as possible to the onlookers. With everything packed away, he went back downstairs into the common-room. During the day, the kitchen was looked after by a cheerful, stout woman who looked as though she enjoyed her own cooking. She peered at him with motherly concern as she recited the various dishes he could choose from.

'Are you all right, my duck?' she enquired. 'You're as white as a sheet, sure you don't want a drink first?'

Geraswic smiled that small, mirthless smile again. 'No, I'm fine, thanks. I'll have the beef stew, please, with some bread. But maybe I will have a drink, I've a long journey before me. Make it a flagon of small ale, please.' He sat staring in front of him while he waited for the food. It was still quite early and the few other customers left him alone. When the woman came back, she set his meal before him and then, with a glance around her, sat down at the table.

'Look, I don't want to butt in on anything you want to keep to yourself, but are you quite sure you're all right? You look terrible, is there anything I can help with? You're here from Gwent y'm Aryframan, right?' She spoke with the accent of his homeland, Geraswic noticed now. He looked up at her wrinkled, homely face.

'Yes, like yourself, I think,' he said. 'I'm from Salfgard. Where's your home place?'

'I was raised in a *gradstedd* between Framstock and the Rossanlow,' said the woman, 'but I've lived here in Caradriggan these thirty years, ever since I was wed.'

A spasm of the pain to come flashed across Geraswic's face. 'You've been very kind,' he said, 'and I'll remember it. I'm going back to Gwent y'm Aryframan this afternoon.'

The woman stood up, still looking rather concerned. 'Right then, my duck, safe journey to you. Eat up now, there's a good lad.'

Geraswic got right through the meal, although it was an effort, and was in the stable checking the mules before he gave in to necessity and threw the whole lot up in a corner. It had seemed sensible to fill his stomach before the journey, but evidently this had not been such a good idea after all. More money wasted, he thought grimly, as he fetched water and sluiced the mess down the channel and into the drain. Well, it was no matter; he had provisions with him. He went back across the yard, fetched his bag and settled his account. As he came out again, there was Numirantoro waiting for him.

'I must talk to you,' she said desperately. 'Surely you're not leaving already?'

'What is there to wait for? I am ready to leave now. If you're seen with me publicly, people will talk.'

Numirantoro stood her ground. 'You forget, Geraswic, by virtue of your new status with Ardeth and Fosseiro we are cousins now. I may walk with my cousin as and where I will.'

Geraswic felt a second, worse, stab of pain run through him. 'Cousins, yes. Your *husband* was explaining that to me. All right then, tell me where to meet you, and I'll follow, once I've explained the delay about the mules and the wagon.'

They sat together on a seat beside one of the many fountains of Caradriggan, in a small formal garden slightly set back from the street, which sloped away down from them. Geraswic stared blankly at the scene before him, the flags and cobbles of the street, the stone and timber of the houses, the people passing by, the carving of the seat under his hand: every detail of it would be indelibly imprinted on his mind. Talking was difficult, as Geraswic had known it would be and as Numirantoro soon found. Across the street there was a lantern hanging from a wrought-iron bracket in the stone wall of the houses opposite the fountain; it swung in the breeze and sent spangles of golden light spattering across the street. Geraswic watched without seeing as the splashes of light moved and danced.

'You told me once you thought you might never be wed,' he said dully to Numirantoro. 'How wrong you were, and how I wish now you had been right.'

'Geraswic, don't say things like that, things you will wish afterwards you had left unsaid.' Numirantoro spoke quietly, determined not to let their parting be even more bitter than it was. 'Do you count mine a marriage, when it was against my will? At least Vorynaas cannot possess my mind, my thoughts are my own...' Her voice changed suddenly, strangely, as if her throat had closed; she swallowed, and finished, '...and can roam where they will.'

Hearing the new note in her voice, Geraswic glanced quickly at Numirantoro and saw her eyes wide, fixed on something or someone across the street. His head turned. A man was coming up the street towards them, walking uphill with a steady, purposeful stride; he was dressed plainly and carried a cloak over one arm. The light from the lantern fell on his face, showing dark hair blown back from a high forehead. Something about him caught Geraswic's eye and nudged at his memory.

'Who is that?' he asked Numirantoro.

She looked away. 'Why?'

'I'm sure I've seen him somewhere before,' said Geraswic slowly.

'His name is Arymaldur, he's a member of Tell'Ethronad.'

Geraswic looked at Numirantoro, but she was still turned away from him. He stood up. The time had come: he must go, go now, get away while he still had the strength of will to do it. He had had his fill and more of Caradriggan, with its shadowy air and dim skies, lit by the light of many lamps though it was.

II   STARBORN

CHAPTER 9

Arval the Earth-wise

Arval sat gazing out of a window high in the tower of Tellgard. The window was open, even though autumn was drawing on and it was late in the day. Outside in the corner of the exercise ground there was a cherry tree whose reddish-gold leaves were illuminated by the lantern that hung in its boughs. Somewhere hidden among the leaves there must be a robin; Arval could hear its song, plaintive and wistful, the voice of the dying year singing on into winter when all else was silent. That was one unconsidered benefit of the lamplight, thought Arval. Game little cock-robin sang on and on long after he should be at roost in the ivy. He fetched a jar of crumbs from its shelf in the alcove and scattered some on the outer sill of the window, looking forward to a closer view of the little bird's soft feathers and the cheeky, head-on-one-side consideration of its bright, beady eye. Then a movement caught his attention and he looked down to see a figure crossing towards the colonnade that ran along one side of the square. Numirantoro, slowly heading for home. She must have come out from the workroom next to the silversmith's workshop.

The old man shook his head sadly. Home! He hardly expected that was how Numirantoro thought of it. Her father's house, or her husband's? To Arval, it seemed as though something had died in Arythalt with the loss of Salfronardo: certainly she would never have agreed to the mismatch of Numirantoro with Vorynaas and now it was an open secret in Caradriggan that the younger man was the master in his marriage-father's house. Once his position was strengthened by marriage to Numirantoro, he had somehow persuaded Arythalt that it would be better to combine their households; he had sold his own property in the city and moved his own servants with him into Arythalt's home, paying off most of the existing staff. At first he had made a show of obtaining Arythalt's agreement for what he did, but seeing that this, or at least acquiescence, was readily forthcoming, he soon abandoned all semblance of deference and now it was Vorynaas alone who gave the orders.

Arval wondered how Numirantoro stood in this. When first she returned from Gwent y'm Aryframan, she had come to Tellgard and sought him out, begging for instruction, knowledge, anything he could teach her, quoting at him his old precept of learning being the one thing no man could regret; and it had been a pleasure to work with her, seeing her quick mind and ready intelligence absorb all he had to tell, watching her gradually wake from her sorrow and loss. But as her efforts to ease Arythalt's grief bore fruit she was busier with her father, coming less often to Tellgard; and then in the early spring of that year had come the tidings that had stunned Caradriggan, that she was to be wed to Vorynaas. The marriage had been arranged and performed with unusual speed, and like most people Arval had heard rumour of the young man from Salfgard who had called on Arythalt and been confronted instead by Vorynaas. The old day-cook at the *Sword and Stars* had been regaling all who would listen with her tales of how Geraswic left the inn one morning, jaunty in his smart new clothes, and returned by noon like a man whose soul had died within him.

Since that time Numirantoro had begun to visit Tellgard again but now she seemed to Arval to be avoiding his company, spending time rather with the craftsmen and artisans who specialised in wood-carving and metal-work, withdrawn into herself and working on her designs with few words for anyone. Maybe I should be the one to make the effort, thought Arval, try to make her talk, to lift the burden that she bears in silence. He sat on in the darkened room, his silver hair and sharply defined profile illuminated by the light from the lantern outside although his dark eyes remained in shadow. How still and close it seemed this evening, too warm for the time of year. He half stood, pushing the window wider to catch a breath of air, and his eye caught a swift movement from below, a quick wing-beat of white. Then he heard the first notes of the mistle-thrush, competing with the robin from the rowan tree beyond the colonnade. He could just see its dark shape as it sat in the leafless, barely swaying branches. The storm-cock folk call it, he mused. Suddenly a shiver ran through him, for a strange thought came to his mind. Surely, if the world were about to end, this was how it would be: not in sound and flames, tempest and fury, but creeping on unawares, as the robin warbled sweetly to men unheeding, and the storm-cock sang defiantly, hailing the ruin to come, knowing more than they. Arval shook himself to dispel his foreboding mood. Yes, I must seek out Numirantoro, he said to himself, and then paused, listening. He heard footsteps in the room below: Arymaldur must be there.

The opportunity Arval sought arrived, strangely enough, as a result of Vorynaas' high-handed dealings in his marriage-father's house. Arythalt's cook had been one of the servants turned off by Vorynaas, and she had found new employment in Tellgard, where feeding the youngsters who came there for instruction, and the adults who worked and studied in the house, needed experienced hands in the kitchens. When Arval discovered this, he requested Numirantoro's presence in his private study, first arranging things so that the old woman should knock with refreshments after the two of them had begun to talk. When she and Numirantoro saw each other, the tears and embraces, and the words of sorrow and regret which went with them, exposed such an abyss of loss and longing that it would have been useless for Numirantoro to deny it, or for Arval to ignore it, now. But though Numirantoro yielded a little to Arval's gentle questioning, and gradually words came easier to her, not for the world would she reveal anything of what had passed between herself and Arythalt on the subject of her marriage. Shamed and degraded though she felt, and burn though she might with anger at how she had been used, still she would not betray her father by speaking.

A father's betrayal

But, as Numirantoro sat beside Arval, her sadness assuaged a little by his kindness and quiet sympathy, she was hiding an immense bitterness. I will not betray my father, she thought; for the sake of my mother's memory I will keep silent, but he has betrayed me, his only child. And I tried so hard to help him, I was so glad when he began to take up the threads of his life again! Never, never would she forget that evening when he returned from Vorynaas' house. She had risen to greet him and take his cloak, drawing him to sit beside her at the fire, for the spring night was raw and cold. Fetching mulled wine to warm him, she had enquired whether he wished to eat, and asked whether he had spent a pleasant evening.

'Yes, most agreeable,' Arythalt had smiled, and she had smiled back, happy in his happiness. 'I ate with Vorynaas, thank you; adequately enough, though not particularly well. Poor fellow, I believe he mostly dines at the *Sword and Stars* unless he has company.'

'Vorynaas is well, I hope?' enquired Numirantoro politely, knowing this would please Arythalt further.

'Yes, he's going about his business again like myself. We have much in common, especially this last year,' said Arythalt, shaking his head sadly. After a moment or two he went on. 'He has been a great support to me in my work these many years, and even more so now. He has always been a vigorous man, full of new ideas, and now I find it a great reassurance to know that I can rely on someone young like Vorynaas if I feel unable myself to travel so often to Heranwark and the south.'

To Numirantoro, Vorynaas scarcely seemed young at all. He had been a grown man when she was still a child, a vaguely disquieting presence among her father's friends and business associates. Searching for a suitable reply, she came up with something mildly positive on the subject of his work at the mines. After a short silence, Arythalt raised his head and looked at Numirantoro. She saw something in his face that made her suddenly alert with foreboding. He seemed to come to some decision; clearing his throat, he spoke.

'When a man suffers a loss as great as I have done, it causes him to think deeply about what is left of his life. I have no sons, and Vorynaas also has no child. Vorynaas has been colleague and partner to me for some years now; he is my friend, but I wish to bind him to me more closely. I have agreed that you and he will be wed.'

The sheer unreality of this momentarily numbed Numirantoro's mind. 'But Vorynaas is too old!' was all she could find to say, desperately.

Arythalt chuckled dismissively. 'Not at all! He's a man in his prime, not even twenty years your senior: you will enjoy parenthood together. That's the child in you speaking, you know nothing of the world yet.'

Numirantoro could feel cold horror settling on her now: she felt as if she had been traded for breeding, like a beast at the mart. Suddenly she saw Geraswic in her mind's eye: so young, so true, and now lost to her forever, for she knew instinctively that it was useless to speak of him. The bargain was already made with Vorynaas, that was plain, and her father was a man of his word. She would not have Geraswic's name dragged into this, but she would not give in without a fight. Jumping to her feet, she confronted her father.

'Enough to know that Vorynaas is not the man you take him for! He will deceive you and disappoint you, he will tighten his grip on you until you are helpless in your own house. Enough to know that my mother would not have wanted this!'

Arythalt rose in turn. Anger, his cold, implacable anger, was growing in him. Suddenly he saw the resemblance to Salfronardo in his daughter's face, the little amber sparks that waked now in her wide, pleading eyes, the hair which lifted a little from around her face.

'Your mother? If I had not yielded to her when you were a child, you would have stayed here and not run wild in Gwent y'm Aryframan, filling your head with nonsense and learning nothing but rustic ways and disobedience. Your mother would be alive today, if sickness had not been brought to this city from Framstock! But I, I am a man of standing in Caradward and you will do what is fitting for my daughter.'

Numirantoro felt herself beginning to tremble slightly with shock and a sick, horrified dismay. She turned away and leaned against the wall, her shoulders sagging as if bowed with an intolerable weight. The anger drained from Arythalt, to be replaced by a wave of mixed emotion in which love for his daughter was confused with an overwhelming pity for himself. He clung stubbornly to his wishful thinking, to his vision of the future in which he, Numirantoro and Vorynaas lived in harmony, blessed with his grandsons.

Now Numirantoro turned to him again and in spite of himself he quailed before the look in her eyes. 'You knew well that I would never consent to wed Vorynaas; that's why you have made this move before I am of age, when you can compel me to do it, willing or not. You have given him your word, I know it.'

'It's not so long since you told me you would do anything for me, if it would make me happy again,' said Arythalt in a wheedling tone, reaching for Numirantoro's hand; but she snatched it away as if his touch stung her.

'Yes, and that is more than you have done for me,' she said bitterly. 'You have bought your happiness by selling mine; and you will live to discover that the trade was no bargain, for the price will prove too high in the end.'

Words of comfort

'Tell me about Geraswic, little daughter.'

The deep, gentle voice broke into Numirantoro's unhappy reverie; she looked up in surprise, seeing Arval's dark eyes upon her. Lost in her thoughts, she had forgotten where she was and who sat with her. She wondered how long her silence had lasted and then smiled a little to think he called her *is-gerasto*. A small kindness such as that, reminding her of childhood days with her mother, or sunny hours with Ardeth and Fosseiro, settled like balm on her wounded spirit. Arval smiled back at her, and suddenly it was easy to talk to him. She told him about Salfgard, about what Ardeth and Fosseiro had made there, about Framstock and her grandparents' house, about Geraswic's loyalty to Ardeth and its reward, even about the piglet she had once won at the harvest games. She told how Geraswic had become like a son to Ardeth and Fosseiro, how they had treated her as their own daughter, how Geraswic had wanted to wed her; and then she faltered to a halt. When Arval spoke, his words were not what she had expected.

'You yearn for the open skies of Gwent y'm Aryframan, for its windy dawns and starlit evenings,' he said, and it was not a question.

She nodded without speaking, acknowledging to herself that he was right: much though she longed for the faces of her loved ones there, it was the hills and the skies that called to her heart. Arval was indeed *Tell-Ur*, the Earth-wise. Now he spoke again, and this time her eyes flew to his face.

'I was myself born in the high valleys of the Somllichan Asan.'

'You … But I've never heard men speak of this in Caradriggan! Oh, please tell me of Ilmar Inenad, away west beyond the Star Mountains, and why it is that you are not a leading voice in Val'Arad, but rather make your home here in Tellgard?'

Arval smiled again. 'Numirantoro. You have never heard this spoken, because I have never told it before. As for Tellgard, this is where I have chosen to live these many years, these very many years. It is where I think; and where, when I can, I teach. I do not call it home.'

Numirantoro bit her lip. Then she bowed her head, dropping her eyes as she saw in memory the little upland valley where she and Geraswic had sat and talked of the Starborn. She heard again the lapping of the tarn against the white rocks of the shoreline, smelled again the sweet springing turf underfoot and the yellow autumn birch leaves overhead, saw again the snowy peaks of the Somllichan Torward shining in the sun, the finches fluttering in the branches, remembered Geraswic's words and the embrace they had shared high on the open hillside under the wide blue sky. Suddenly the memory struck at her heart with a stab of pain: how perfect that hour had been, how innocent the love between herself and Geraswic, how pure the air, how clean the earth, how unstained the day, how clear the future! And now, how sullied she felt, brought low, her wings clipped, treading from one dark day to the next, endlessly and without hope. Tears sprang at last as she turned blindly to Arval.

'I wish I had never gone to Salfgard, it would have been better if I'd never seen it. Ardeth and Fosseiro, and Geraswic too, would have been happier without me. But now, I wish I could have stayed! Oh, if only my mother hadn't died, if I could have stayed, I wish I had never come back here, I wish I had never seen...' She brought herself up sharply, caught her breath a little, and went on, 'I wish I was far away from the gloom of Caradward, back in the sunshine in the hills, I wish I could have my old life again.'

Now she wept as she had never done, not for Salfronardo's death, not for the news that she must wed Vorynaas, not even for her last sight of Geraswic walking away down the street from the lamplit fountain, away and out of her life for ever. Arval sat beside her and stroked her hair, his old heart wrung with pity. He let her tears run their course and then spoke gently to her again.

'*Is-gerasto*, your sorrow is a grief to me. No man can turn back time, although how many have wished they could, as you do now. Dry your tears, little daughter. Listen to me now, and let me see if I can give you something new to think of. You are right to feel for Ardeth: it will have been hard for him when Geraswic returned to Salfgard alone. He is a worthy man, a bright spirit like your mother; he does not deserve the heavy blows which fate has dealt him, of which this is by no means the first, is it? And yet he has tried to turn his misfortunes to good account, to bring joy from sorrow, even though the wait may have been long. Think how bitter the seed of the peach tree is, yet how sweet the blossom and how rich the fruit. Ardeth will lift his head in the end, he will find some new ideal to work towards; his hands, with all their lifetime's skills, will be set to some new task: and Fosseiro will help him, and Geraswic will stand beside him. In the same way, I will help you, and stand beside you, Numirantoro. Together we will bring something good out of our present trouble.' He paused. 'I have told you things about myself today that none have ever heard before. Why do you think I did that?'

Numirantoro looked up, and a hint of life returning showed in her face. 'I don't know, but I am deeply honoured that you trust me, Arval the Earth-wise.'

'That is one reason: to show you that I trust you. I see something in you, Numirantoro, which makes me think it was for you that I have waited in Caradward so many years. I sense that momentous times are almost upon us and afterwards, if men still walk the earth, your name will be remembered among them.'

'But why, why me?' Numirantoro gazed at Arval, utterly perplexed at his words. Into her mind came memories of her childhood teaching from Arval about the ancient disaster which had befallen the world, and Geraswic saying "The centre of the earth is dead" on the day he had made her climb up to look into the wilderness. A further thought struck her.

'Arval, how long have you lived in this world?'

He raised a finger with a smile. 'Not now, little daughter,' he said, 'but I promise, we will talk of this again: that is, if you will come to Tellgard and seek me out, as you used to do?'

'Oh yes, I will,' said Numirantoro, 'and Arval, thank you for the comfort you have brought me today.'

Arval watched her from the window as she walked across towards the colonnade. She seemed to tread with a livelier step, but he noticed that her walk slowed as she went, and before she left Tellgard she paused and turned, looking around her as if she hoped to see someone.

Hands and heart

After Numirantoro had gone, Arval sat on alone for some time. He searched back in thought for his earliest recollections of her, from the days before she went to Salfgard, to the time when she and her contemporaries were daily attenders at Tellgard; and his mind ranged back further, to the time when, as a small child, she would talk to him earnestly as to an equal. He remembered clearly her thirst for knowledge, her skill with words, her quest for beauty, her desire to seek out the essential heart of any matter or topic. An idea struck him, and he went out from his rooms, across a corner of the exercise ground where, he noticed, Arymaldur was now putting some youngsters through training in sword-drills watched by Thaltor, and into the range of workshops. Passing the wood-turning bay, with its humming wheels and pole-lathes, he entered the finishing room. As he opened the door, a few shavings swirled around the floor in the draught, and heads turned from the benches where youngsters and experienced craftsmen alike were at work carving, polishing, staining. Neat lines of tools, their handles smooth and shiny from use, hung in racks on the walls and the smell of linseed and beeswax was strong in the air. Arval requested words with the master-craftsman, and was shown into a small private space off the main workroom. The man followed, wiping his hands on his apron.

'Arval, good health to you! Is there anything we can do for you today?'

'There is, indeed,' said Arval. 'Have you any work by Numirantoro, either finished or in progress, which I might look at? Don't worry,' he added, as a bothered look came over the man's face. 'If there is anything she's unwilling for people to see, or work which she prefers should remain private, of course I shall respect her wishes.'

The smile came back immediately to the fellow's face. 'Oh, right,' he said. 'Actually yes, I have something here which I'm finishing off for her. You can see this, no problem: here it is on the stand, look.'

He indicated a carving which rested on the turntable; clearly he had been oiling and smoothing it. Arval looked at it closely, turning it slowly so as to view it from all angles. Several different types of wood had been used, so that the shadows and light made by deep cutting and surface burnishing were echoed and imitated in lighter and darker grains. The work was an unusual blend of the abstract and the representational: Arval's eyes saw shapes and textures, but his mind saw forests, flames, even faces.

'It is as though the earth itself awoke and reached up towards the sky,' he said at last.

'Well, anyone could trust you to see straight to the heart of it, Arval,' said the man, applying an oily rag to the work with a touch as gentle as a mother tending a child. 'Lady Numirantoro, she said to me, that this is how she sees the world – or at least, how she did see it when she was a youngster away in Gwent y'm Aryframan. Not that she's only a young girl still, poor lass. She does the designs, you see, and I do the heavy carving first, with her looking on, and then we work together on the finer stages. I can tell you, it's a rare treat for me to have any part in something as beautiful as this, even though my contribution's only the hard labour, as you might say. Lovely, isn't it?' He looked at it fondly, his head on one side. 'But, you know, you won't get her to agree. She's never satisfied with her work, that's why there's lots of stuff here she doesn't like folk to see. She says to me, Woody, she says – that's her name for me – Woody, why won't my hands make what my heart sees? Ah, she's a way with words as well as with the wood, has Numirantoro. She's a lovely lass, like her poor mother before her; how her father could have married her off to that Vorynaas – well, I know, that's none of my business.' He fell silent with an embarrassed air; Arval had an easy manner and those in Tellgard spoke freely before him, but he hadn't meant to be quite so forthcoming.

Arval gripped his arm with a quick smile of reassurance. 'No need to worry.' He paused, looking again at the carving. 'I wonder what it is that Numirantoro sees in her heart.'

'Oh, that's no secret. "It's not worthy of the Starborn" she'll say, if it's a reject; or, "I want this one to reveal the Starborn" when she begins something new. This one here now, from what she says it's meant to have the Starborn in it, somehow. As I was telling you before, she's not satisfied with it herself, but I don't know. Sometimes when I look at it, I think I can nearly see what she's trying to do. Yes, it's the As-Geg'rastigan she keeps in her heart, and you wouldn't wonder. She's as lovely as the Starborn herself, is Numirantoro – always has been.'

'She is indeed,' said Arval. He looked again at the work on the turntable, moving it into and out of the light, applying to it the insight he had just been given and viewing it now with eyes that saw more deeply and clearly than before. He straightened up and stood a moment in thought.

'You've been kind to Numirantoro,' he said, 'and I'm deeply grateful for it. There's companionship and warmth for her here. She needs friendship: I hope she'll always have it from you.'

The man beamed with pleasure. 'She will, right enough, Arval. All my lads would do anything for her, it's a bright day for us when she comes in to the workshops for an hour or two.'

'Good man!' said Arval, heading back across the darkening square towards the ground-floor door of the tower. His mind was made up. He must talk to Arymaldur, tonight.

At the main meal of the day, that evening in Tellgard, Arval was unusually silent, but his pensive mood was respected by those around him, who left his musings uninterrupted. There were thirty or so people present: instructors, teachers, artisans, all masters of their various crafts who were either permanently or temporarily housed at Tellgard, sharing their knowledge and expertise with like-minded visitors, or passing it on to the new generation. There were guests at table also, and some youngsters whose homes were in far corners of Caradward and who were therefore quartered in Tellgard while they studied. Arymaldur was seated at the top table and Arval's dark, deep-set eyes occasionally rested upon him as the meal progressed and conversation flowed about him; then, excusing himself early from the company, he left the gathering with a request that Arymaldur should join him later for private discussion.

The pledge renewed

Arval climbed to his study room in the tower, deep in thought. Closing the door behind him, he lit three lamps, one in a small alcove to each side and another that he placed on a high stand behind his own chair, which faced the entrance to the room. On the table was a heavy flask of plain crystal containing the spirit used only on occasions of particular significance or solemnity: Arval alone knew the secret of its making. He poured two small measures now and sat down to wait, meditating on the man who would be joining him shortly.

Two years before, a man had arrived at the doors of Tellgard, giving his name as Arymaldur and requesting speech with Arval. It soon appeared that Arval was glad to welcome him as a colleague, for he was a man who seemed deeply versed in all that was taught or discussed in the house. If his help was sought in the smithies, his metalwork surpassed that of the *sigitsaran*; if the raw material was wood, or inks and paint, he was equally skilled. In matters of lore, his learning seemed inexhaustible: legend, law, life of plant and animal; medicine, minerals, mysteries of the mind, in all these his speech was subtle and his reasoning profound. With the bow, his aim was unerring and his eye true; he was tireless in exercise or the chase and with the sword he had no equal. And yet his manner was unassuming and quiet, his demeanour modest and reserved; he would willingly help any who requested it, but never put himself forward unasked. It was not long before Arval had introduced him as a member of Tell'Ethronad, where his observations were always to the point, if not always what men wished to hear; his renown spread beyond Tellgard until most in Caradriggan acknowledged him as a man of rare worth. But there were also those to whom his presence was unwelcome: men such as Thaltor, who burned with resentment at no longer being supreme swordsman of the city; Vorynaas, who foresaw a curb being applied to his secret ambitions; men such as Morgwentan and Arythalt who, being too easily led, had been seduced to Vorynaas' party; and Valafoss, who shied from integrity, having none of his own.

Arval heard a footfall on the stair and steadied himself, striving to empty his mind so that he would be fully receptive to whatever impression was to come. There was a soft knock at the door, and then Arymaldur entered the room. He saw Arval before him, his deep, dark eyes seeming blacker than ever as the pupils dilated; his thin face, framed by its silver hair and short, pointed beard, was fixed and expressionless. For a few seconds of silence, they remained thus: Arval seated and Arymaldur poised with his hand still on the door, a couple of strides into the room. Arval kept his eyes unfocused and knew immediately that his intuition had been correct. There could be no mistaking the way the lamps burned brighter, their flames more intense at the heart of a radiant nimbus which flared against the darkness; no mistaking the change in the air of the room, which tingled with a fierce, unearthly energy. Now he concentrated his gaze as Arymaldur sat opposite him. He saw a tall, long-limbed man, lithe and lean, spare in face and body; the face was strong-boned yet curiously serene in expression, with dark hair flowing back from a high forehead and grey, unflinching eyes. Arymaldur always dressed simply and tonight his plain attire was dark and unadorned; yet he had an aura of elegance and understated power that went far beyond dress or appearance and was almost visible to Arval's heightened perception.

Their eyes locked and held, then Arval spoke quietly. 'Lord Arymaldur. In all my years, I have never thought to see one of the Starborn face to face. Will you tell me what brings you now among the Earthborn?'

'You are versed in lore, Arval; you must know how deeply the Starborn loved the earth long ago.' Arymaldur's voice, deep and resonant, held no carrying tone; yet somehow, as he listened eagerly, Arval knew its strength was banked down, that if Arymaldur wished, he could make his words ring out so that men would follow him wherever he led. 'Ages have passed, but that love has never faltered. At last it had begun to seem to us that, as the earth might renew herself to flourish once more, so we might return to love her anew. We come to try the truth of that hope, and my journey brings me to you here in Caradward.'

'But Caradward falls away from its ancient wisdom, as you will know without my telling. How else could it be that though many welcome and respect you, some whisper against you and none revere you for what you are? Why do you suffer the ignorance of fools and the folly of the ignorant? Why labour unthanked for our youth, and advise our elders without praise?'

'Among men, we must play whatever part the Earthborn put upon us; if that be evil, we will warn but not ward: beware of what may follow, if you drive the As-Geg'rastigan away again.'

Arval bowed his head and a short silence fell in the room. 'Lord Arymaldur, may that day never come! I am ashamed that only I have seen who is among us, and that it has taken so long for my eyes to open. I am called Earth-wise, but the name is not deserved.'

Arymaldur's smile transformed his austere features as if a light shone within him. 'Arval, look up! Truly, your wisdom has borne fruit: you are not alone. As I walk in Caradriggan, I feel a secret touch upon my heart, a silent call from an unknown voice. Someone else in this city knows me for what I am.'

He picked up the small glass vessels and handed one to Arval, holding his own up before his face. The crystal flashed in the lamplight as the liquid moved. 'For their sake and yours, I renew the pledge of the Starborn with the earth.'

The fiery spirit coursed through Arval, its strength as potent as the joy he felt to hear the sweet words of the *Temennis y'm As-Geg'rastigan ach Ur*, spoken as he had never thought to hear them, from the very voice of the Starborn.

They talked for a little longer before parting, but Arval, though he extinguished the lamps, did not retire to rest. For a long while he leaned on the sill, staring into the darkness. All was blank above these days, where once stars would have shone to his gaze; but late though it was, the small sweet song of the robin floated across from the tree under the light. Gradually his mood quietened from exaltation to something more like foreboding. So Arymaldur had felt the power of someone's thought on him, the force of a yearning heart. And now into Arval's mind came Numirantoro: Numirantoro chained against her will to Vorynaas, Numirantoro cheated of Geraswic's love, Numirantoro starved of the light she needed. Numirantoro looking back as she left Tellgard, Numirantoro weeping against his shoulder, stopping herself revealing the name of someone she wished she had never seen: Numirantoro, who kept the Starborn in her heart.

Secrets

Across the city, in the spacious, elegant dwelling that had once been Arythalt's house and Numirantoro's home, Vorynaas ran down the stairs that led to the range of buildings where the live-in staff had their quarters. That morning, he had chaired a meeting in which he had seen to it that Arythalt was despatched on yet another extended business trip to Heranwark; in the afternoon, he had spent time talking privately with Thaltor and Valafoss in his own office, discussing ideas which were as yet known only to the three of them; he had then dined at the *Sword and Stars*, having previously told Numirantoro that the sight of her long face was enough to put a man off his food; and now he was bathed, slightly flushed with wine, and about to enjoy a few hours of pleasure with Sigitsiro. A particularly good day, he thought to himself, shoving past Sigitsiro as soon as she opened the door.

The girl's welcome was genuine enough in its way. She felt no affection for Vorynaas, and in fact was slightly scared of him, but there was something about his confidence, his ruthless air and suave manner, which she found exciting; and it was flattering that he still sought her out frequently. She had not expected this, once he was married to Numirantoro, and had been surprised to be included among the staff brought over from his own house. But she was shrewd enough to say nothing, to ask no questions: it gave her a certain status among her fellow-servants, who all knew the master was sleeping with her; and who would be fool enough to refuse the money and jewellery which Vorynaas occasionally gave her? She was keeping these secure, and taking all the care she knew to avoid pregnancy, in the hope that one day she would be able to go back to her own people in the south. How good it would be to get away from the stifling city, from its haughty people and from her intimidating employer! But Vorynaas was already pushing her impatiently onto the bed, his mouth at her neck; she giggled and responded, licked by flames of unwilling desire.

Meanwhile Numirantoro was huddled on the narrow bed in the rooms that had been hers in the happy days, now lost for ever, when she had been a child and Salfronardo was still alive. She slept in here whenever she could, and recently had been retreating here during the day too, treating it as her sanctuary. She knew Vorynaas was with Sigitsiro but could not bring herself to care about it. At least it meant she did not have to endure his presence; but, Vorynaas, you won't get the son you want from Sigitsiro, she thought with a vicious little flare of hate, quickly replaced by apprehension as worry gnawed at her again. This was the second month now, and – no, I won't think about it, I won't, she told herself: think about something else, anything else.

But that was no good either. From the moment she woke until sleep took her again, she had one thought only, an obsession that fed on itself so that one face, one voice, one name alone filled all her mind. For the thousandth time that day, she gave up the struggle to think of other things, yielding to the power of the strange, frightening emotion that gripped her.

She had not been back in Caradriggan for long after her mother's death when she began to hear a new name mentioned: the name of a stranger who had come to Tellgard, who worked with Arval, who spoke in the council. As Arythalt began once more to attend Tell'Ethronad, she gathered that the man had exasperated her father and infuriated Vorynaas. Then she noticed that the servants whispered his name too, this time with respect. Her curiosity piqued, she made a point of looking out for the newcomer on her visits to Arval in Tellgard. At first, she saw simply a tall man of full age, dignified and reserved in bearing. Yet somehow, even from that beginning she had been unable to keep him from her thoughts; and then had come the Midwinter Feast.

By then, Arythalt had risen a little from his decline after Salfronardo's death and had begun to move about socially once more. He had spent the evening of the feast itself at Vorynaas' house, and Numirantoro had been free to attend the ceremonies at Tellgard where Arval maintained the ancient traditions she loved. They had all gathered in the great hall of the house: Arval, the students and apprentices, the artisans and learned men, and many from Caradriggan who were free to join the company whenever they wished and were always welcomed by Arval. The time had come to dim the lamps and douse the lights; and then in the darkness the flame had waked once more as the *Temennis* was recited. The familiar words lodged in her heart as if they flew on silver-flighted arrows, for the voice was Arymaldur's; the new-born light fell on his face, slightly upturned, solemn and exalted, casting shadows under the high cheekbones and filling the grey eyes with brightness: to Numirantoro those eyes seemed to fall on her alone as she stood in the throng, unable to tear her own gaze away. She saw him lift his hands in the ancient sign and involuntarily she took a step back, appalled yet fascinated by the power at his command.

Numirantoro sat now on her bed, staring before her, breathing quickly. The memory was so vivid, the scene played itself in her head so often; even thinking of it now, her heart hammered within her, she trembled and her hands felt cold. She had returned from the ceremony, her mind in turmoil. It could not be possible that she loved a man she had never met, a man she did not know! She loved Geraswic, it could not be, she would not let it be, that she loved Arymaldur. But the voice within her would not be stilled, and it told her what she had known from the first instant she saw Arymaldur. For months, she had tried to hide the truth from herself, until the very day of her bitter farewell to Geraswic, when Arymaldur had come walking up the street towards them and her own voice had betrayed her. She smiled hopelessly to herself, alone in her room. It was words that were the problem, there were no words to describe fully how she felt. Yes, she had loved Geraswic and nothing would ever touch or change that now. But she loved Arymaldur too, yet how differently. She loved him from the depths of her loss and despair, without reservation or end, but without hope and in sorrow. She longed to be in his presence, yet felt so unworthy that she would not have wanted him to yearn for her. Her heart cried out to him, willing him to hear the silent voice, to turn, to look at her; but she was afraid for this to happen. I love him more than I can express in words, she thought, but it is deeper and more dreadful than that. I love him more than I am able to, for I am Earthborn, Ur-Geg'rastig; and he is one of the Starborn, and I cannot help myself.

Vorynaas

Vorynaas lay beside Sigitsiro in the darkness of her little room. He moved to sit on the edge of the bed, feeling unsuccessfully for the lamp.

'Get some light on, will you?' he said. 'I need a drink and I don't want to spill the wine in this infernal blackout.'

Sigitsiro dithered. She was almost out of oil and had thought to save what she had until she was next paid. 'Sir, I'm sorry, there is only half the crock left and I can't afford to buy more this week.'

'Oh, we can't have that! I want to look at you while I drink my wine,' said Vorynaas indulgently. 'Light the lamp, there's a good girl, and I'll make sure you have the silver you need before I go.' He ran an intimate hand over the girl's body as he sipped his drink. 'I'll say one thing, Sigitsiro. You certainly know how enjoy yourself in bed, and that's a pleasant change for me, I can tell you.'

Sigitsiro giggled and moved up against him; she decided to press her luck while he was still in this generous mood. 'Oh, sir! But I think the Lady Numirantoro maybe is not feeling too well at the moment?'

Vorynaas made a derisive gesture with his free hand. 'Always drifting miserably about the place, it's enough to drive a man to drink.' He refilled his cup, laughing at his own joke, then suddenly registered something significant in the tone of the girl's voice. 'How do you mean exactly, "at the moment"?'

Oh, thought Sigitsiro, he doesn't know! If I'm the one to break the news to him, I might get even more from him than the silver he promised. She gave him an experienced caress and a knowing look. 'Well sir, it's been talked of among the staff that Lady Numirantoro's been sick often recently... and mostly first thing in the morning, it seems.'

The following day, Numirantoro sat listlessly on the window-seat in her room, thinking about Salfgard. They would be getting ready for Harvest-home there now. She saw the laden apple-trees in her mind's eye, the familiar faces of the village folk and farm-hands, the homely living-hall of Ardeth's house. Suddenly she heard quick footsteps in the corridor outside, and the door burst open to admit Vorynaas. Richly dressed as he was, ready to leave the house to go about his business in the city, he looked a vigorous, impressive man; and yet as he crossed the room swiftly and stood over her, there was an air of menace and aggression about him. He looked down at his wife, and addressed her curiously formally.

'Are you with child to me?' he asked.

Numirantoro rose to her feet. She was taller than he, and she saw how he hated that. She looked into his dark eyes and answered him with a single word.

'Yes.'

Chapter 10

Children's voices

The courtyard rang to the sounds of children at play, shouts and laughter and shrieks such as had not been heard there for a good twenty years. Small children tumbled about Numirantoro's feet as she sat in the corner with a toddler lying beside her. After a while, she was joined by Ancrascaro, who being the only girl often felt herself too grown-up to join in boys' games and liked to talk to Numirantoro. Swinging her legs as she sat on the wall-seat, she looked up into Numirantoro's face hopefully.

'Could I hold the baby for a while?'

'Of course, if you'd like to. He might not want to sit on your knee though, now he's crawling,' said Numirantoro, putting down her reading and going to pick up her son Ghentar, now almost eighteen months old.

'No, I want to hold Isteddar, not Ghentar!'

Ancrascaro's earnest little face held pleading eyes; no-one could be cross with her, it was so obvious that she had no idea her words might upset a young mother. Numirantoro smiled slightly and hoisted Isteddar from his blanket instead, placing the child carefully in the little girl's arms.

'There! Got him all right? Tell me if he gets too heavy against your arm, and mind him if he wriggles. We don't want him to fall off, do we?'

Ancrascaro sat gazing down with rapt attention at Isteddar, who stared solemnly back, apparently quite happy to be cuddled and petted rather than pushed and shoved by his seniors or trodden on in the course of Heranar's still shaky progress. No wonder Isteddar was such a favourite, thought Numirantoro. All his young life he had been handed from one pair of arms to another, set down in a different corner each day, and he had learnt early to take such changes calmly, knowing that comfort and food were more likely to come his way thus than if he cried and refused to settle. He was the grandson of the woman who looked after the household's laundry, whose daughter now worked in the kitchens of the *Sword and Stars* during the day: no place for a baby. Numirantoro had welcomed his presence in the house, thinking he would be company for Ghentar, but it seemed her own son preferred other playmates.

She watched him now, determinedly raising himself to unsteady feet and hanging on to the edge of the flowerbed wall, frowning in concentration as he watched Heranar tottering rather erratically after his elder brother Valahald and Forgard's son Heretellar. The children were spending the afternoon with her while their fathers attended a meeting of Tell'Ethronad: Forgard had lost his first child to the spring sickness which had taken Salfronardo, but Heretellar was the same age as Valahald. The two older boys had pulled woody stalks from the garden and were playing at sword-fighting: Valahald was gradually pushing Heretellar back, but though he was giving ground, Numirantoro thought she could see whose style the boy was trying to imitate. How many times had she watched Arymaldur on the exercise-ground at Tellgard, while apparently engrossed in work of her own! He would be at the council meeting now. She imagined his voice, wondered what he would say, whether her father and husband would speak of it when they returned for the evening meal.

'What are you reading about?' Ancrascaro, though carefully rocking Isteddar on her knee, was gazing now at Numirantoro rather than at him.

'It's a story called *Spirit from the Free Forest. Numir ap Aldron Ancras*: that's a good story for both of us, isn't it? It's nearly got both our names in it.'

Ancrascaro digested this in silence for a moment, still looking steadily at Numirantoro with a child's unabashed curiosity. 'What's it about? Where did you get it? Can I read it?'

'Oh, lots of questions! You *will* be able to read it, when you've grown up a little bit and learnt to read. I borrowed it from Arval, when I was talking to him in Tellgard. When you're bigger, you'll be able to go there every day with your friends like I used to, and learn all kinds of things, not just reading and writing.'

'What kind of things?'

'Things about the world, and the men and women that live in it, and about the As-Geg'rastigan.'

'How many people live in the world?'

Numirantoro laughed, remembering the endless questions of her own childhood. 'Well now, I don't know exactly, but there must be thousands and thousands mustn't there? Because just think how many people there are here in Caradriggan, and that's only one city in Caradward, before we've even started adding up the people in Gwent y'm Aryframan and the Outlands.'

'I can count a bit, already,' said Ancrascaro. 'I'll count how many people there are here: there's me, and you, and cousin Heretellar, that's three; and then there's Valahald and Heranar, that's five, and then Isteddar, that's six!'

'You've missed somebody out, haven't you?' asked Numirantoro, smiling. The little girl looked crestfallen. 'Oh, I forgot Ghentar! So that's seven people. I forgot because I was thinking about something else.'

I know only too well how that can happen, thought Numirantoro, I who think constantly of Arymaldur even at moments like this. 'What were you thinking about, *is-gerasto*?' she said.

Ancrascaro turned right round to face her. 'I was thinking about the As-Geg'rastigan, and about Gwent y'm Aryframan. You used to live there, didn't you? Tell me about it, and about the Starborn!'

For a moment Numirantoro considered fobbing the child off with some easy answer: there was nothing she could say that would do justice to either the question or the questioner. But no, she must be true to what she loved. She looked down at Ancrascaro and spoke quietly.

'Gwent y'm Aryframan is the most beautiful place I know of on this earth, where the sun still shines in the daytime and where, when the night comes, there are stars in the sky. The people there remember the old stories of the Starborn, and look for them to walk in the world again; and if the As-Geg'rastigan ever did return, they too would find no place more lovely than the hills of Gillan nan Eleth. Although I tell you now, Ancrascaro, that no-one can know when or where the Starborn may come among us, and we should watch, so that our eyes are open when they do.'

The little girl looked into her face silently, touched by the solemnity of the moment. Grown-ups did not usually speak to her like this, and instinctively she stored the words away in her memory, to be mulled over when the time came that she would be old enough to understand them better. But before she could even begin to think of her next question, a piercing wail rang out. Heranar had tumbled over, in his efforts to catch up his older brother, and Ghentar was sitting on him, preventing him from getting up, and jabbing at him with a rough piece of stone that had fallen from the wall.

'Ghentar, stop it!' Numirantoro jumped up and waded in, fending off Valahald who was yelling that Ghentar had pushed Heranar, and Heretellar who, flushed in the face, was shouting equally loudly that he had done no such thing. Ancrascaro looked on silently, sucking a finger and rocking Isteddar, and he lay placidly, ignoring the tears and tantrums, the raised voices, the sulking and stamping. Eventually it was all sorted out, Heranar was cleaned up, he and Ghentar were pacified with milk, and the older children settled to a selection of nibbles and the promise that Numirantoro would have the quoits brought out for them to play with. The afternoon passed, and in due course everyone was collected and taken off home when the council meeting broke up; Ghentar was brought indoors by his nurse and Numirantoro went up to her rooms with a sigh to prepare for spending the evening with her father and husband. But throughout all the games, the stories, the rough and tumble, the childish prattle, the questions and the squabbles, her mind and heart were filled with one voice, one face, one name: Arymaldur.

A loveless family

She sat now in front of the mirror in her room, brushing her dark hair. The past two years had left her a little thinner in the face: the sorrow of her mother's death, the loss of her happiness in Salfgard, the shock of the forced marriage to Vorynaas, the pain of the separation from Geraswic and, above all, the stress of her all-consuming obsession with Arymaldur, a constant gnawing ache which she could barely understand or explain to herself, all these had left their mark. But Numirantoro was only twenty years old; and although she had lost weight and was paler than in happier times, her youth still triumphed over her misfortune, so that her face seemed lovelier than ever now that its fine bones were revealed. She twisted her hair up into a loose knot and sat back, looking at her reflection. As long ago as she could remember, people had been telling her she was as fair as the Starborn. And yet when a lord of the As-Geg'rastigan walked among them, they seemed unaware of it! She tilted her head slightly from one side to another. *Was* she beautiful, as people said? Arymaldur seemed beautiful to her, beyond words to describe; but his beauty came from within, from what he was.

She wondered whether he had ever seen her, so as to be aware of her. When she was in his presence, her eyes never left him: she could hardly bear even to blink, unwilling as she was to allow anything to impede the printing of his image indelibly upon her mind and heart. Restlessly she stood up and moved over to the window, kneeling on the seat and looking out into the gathering night, the darkness spangled with hundreds of lamps. She watched Merenald cross the courtyard below her and smiled a little. It had taken no time at all for her to commit to memory all the times and places where she was likely to catch a glimpse of Arymaldur. She knew exactly which street to be walking in, which window to be looking out of, what time to go to the market, which day to cross the park. How glad she was that all her life she had been a frequent visitor to Tellgard and was well-known to be a friend of Arval, so that now it was easy to be present at all the ceremonies or to sit where she could see the exercise-ground from her work. Yet in some ways she dreaded the moment of setting out, would almost have welcomed it if circumstances had prevented her from going to Tellgard. She did not dare to join any group that was instructed by Arymaldur, or to risk her skill on any craft at which he too might work. Always she hung back, standing in the shadows or mingling with the crowd, wishing to be noticed yet afraid for this to happen. She felt that if once his eyes met hers, there could be no going back: he would see straight to her soul and though she was desperate for him to know the innermost secrets of her heart, she feared that these would be unworthy, that she would be found wanting.

There was a tap at her door: a servant had come to tell her the evening meal was being served. As she went to take her place at the table, her husband and father looked up from their conversation. Numirantoro had always tended to dress very plainly, but now she cultivated a simple elegance in emulation of Arymaldur's style. Tonight she wore a dark-blue robe, high at the neck and low-waisted with fitted sleeves that flared out towards the wrist, caught back to the elbow with pearl buttons and showing the ivory-coloured silk lining. She saw the look in Vorynaas' hot, dark eyes as he watched her and could read his thought. He was more attentive to her recently, clearly thinking it was time Ghentar had a younger brother to lord it over. As ever, she spoke little during the meal, but listened to the men's conversation, hoping to hear something of what had passed at the meeting of Tell'Ethronad and marvelling a little inwardly at her newly-acquired skill of listening, talking, living on one level yet all the while thinking constantly of Arymaldur with a different part of her mind. But tonight his name was not mentioned, although it seemed the meeting had been well-attended.

At last the meal was done and the dishes cleared away; and the nurse brought Ghentar in to them for a few moments before his bed-time. Vorynaas lifted his son to his shoulder and the boy crowed with glee as his father swung him round and then settled him into the crook of his arm.

'There you are then, my little warrior! Here, let me feel how strong you are.' Vorynaas put up the index finger of his free hand before the little lad's face, and Ghentar gripped it with his fist. 'Ready? Now, can you push me down?'

Ghentar frowned with concentration and effort, striving to force his father's arm back. He was just beginning to talk, no more than a word or two, but understood much more that was said to him, and this game was an old favourite. Vorynaas grinned with pleasure, his white teeth showing in his beard and his arm-rings catching the light where his sleeve had fallen back. He never tempered his own strength to the child's efforts until the boy was almost in tears of frustration and disappointment, then he would relax a little and let his arm be pushed back slightly.

'Well, that's not bad. But you'll have to do better than that if you're ever going to make a swordsman. And you'll have to be quick on your feet, too! Show me how clever you are at walking tonight.' He set the child on the floor and retreated to a chair. 'Now! Come on, my son, run!'

Ghentar set off unsteadily, but fell after a few paces. Before he could wind himself up to a full-scale wail, his father hoisted him to his feet again. 'Oh, not like that. Come, try again.' This time Ghentar fell more heavily, catching his shoulder on the leg of a chair, and loud howls rent the air.

Numirantoro took him on her knee, wiping his tears and hushing him. She glared at Vorynaas. 'Now see what's happened! He's tired, the other children were here all afternoon and he's been playing with them. You shouldn't try to make him do more than he's capable of yet, making him excited and upset right at the end of the day when he should be quiet before bed.'

'Oh, nonsense,' said Vorynaas, 'he'll have to learn not to cry at a little knock like that. You're a big boy now, aren't you, Ghentar? You're going to be strong and tough like me, aren't you?'

Here we go, thought Numirantoro. Now for all his favourite leading questions. The child was already over his tears, reassured by his mother's caresses; but he turned towards his father, instinctively attracted by the new face and voice, the rougher style of play. He wriggled to get down on the floor, and Vorynaas held his hands, holding him steady so that his feet walked weightlessly across to his father's chair. Then he sat the lad on his knee so that he leaned into the curve of his shoulder and looked down at his son.

'You like daddy's games, don't you?' said Vorynaas, and Ghentar shoved his thumb in his mouth and nodded vigorously. 'Do you want me to let you ride my horse?' More nodding. 'Shall I buy you a little sword, and get uncle Thaltor to teach you how to use it?' The child's eyes were wide and shining; he removed the thumb from his mouth. 'You don't want to play at home with little girls and read stories, do you?' Ghentar shook his head. 'Shall daddy teach you proper boys' games? Would you like that?'

Predictably, the boy bounced on his knee with enthusiastic agreement.

Vorynaas hugged the lad; the love-scene was being played to its end. 'You know daddy loves you, don't you?' Numirantoro noticed the slight emphasis he put on *daddy*. 'Who do you love most in all the world?'

'Dadda.'

'That's my boy! Now, daddy has to go out for a while, so you be good now and then when you're older we'll go to the *Sword and Stars* and have a drink together!' Laughing, he lifted Ghentar on to

Arythalt's knee and stood up, looking down on Numirantoro.

'I'll be a couple of hours at most.'

Progressive schemes

She ignored him and he turned on his heel abruptly, striding from the room. She knew what it meant when he gave her notice of his return. Sigitsiro was the lucky one tonight, she'd be left in peace to her own dreams. For a while she watched Arythalt holding Ghentar on his knee, smiling at him, talking back to his baby's babble, letting him play with the silver buttons on his sleeves. He dotes on the child, thought Numirantoro, indulges his every whim. He was not like this with me: what a difference a boy makes. Truly, Arythalt was enchanted by his grandson, the more so as the child was so unlike himself. Indeed he took after Vorynaas far more than Numirantoro, being big for his age and strongly-built, with a tendency to bully his playmates and to sulk and throw tantrums if he failed to get his own way. His temper seemed likely to match his hair, which was thick and strong like his father's; the chestnut tints of Vorynaas and the fiery sheen hidden in Numirantoro's dark locks had combined into a rich, dark red in Ghentar. He had a high colour to go with it and Numirantoro thought Vorynaas had named the lad more accurately than he knew. Giving way to him, and pandering to his every wish, was the last thing the child needed, and yet this was all he got from his father and grandfather. No wonder little Ancrascaro preferred to nurse Isteddar. Eventually she got up from her chair and lifted Ghentar into her arms to take him up to bed. He immediately began to struggle and scream, the wails and protests gradually receding from Arythalt's ears as he sat on beside the hearth and the mother and baby climbed the stairs.

When she returned, Arythalt was standing beside the small wine-table in the corner alcove. Declining his offer to pour for her, she sat down, staring into the fire, and after a moment or two he resumed his own seat. Arythalt cleared his throat and broke the awkward little silence.

'Anyone can see that Ghentar loves you too, Numirantoro. He favours his father now, but that's only natural in a boy. All he wants now is action and excitement but when he's a little older, it will be important that he learns also what you can teach him. You have a way with children, I've seen the way his friends like to come here, and I know he too will respond to you.'

She shrugged indifferently. 'Do you really think anything I do or say will make any odds? His father has already half taken him from me. You and he have the boy you wanted. You will do with him as you will, whatever my wishes may be, as we all know perfectly well.'

Arythalt's fingers tightened on the arm of his chair; he took a sip of wine to calm himself and disguise the frustration he felt. His daughter was withdrawn from him, into some mysterious inner world of her own where he could no longer reach her. He remembered with a pang how she would run to him as a child, flushed with happiness if he approved some little childish achievement; how her beauty increased as she grew, and people would say how alike she was to both himself and to Salfronardo; how close the two of them had been when she tried so hard to lift his spirits in his bereavement. Stubbornly he closed his mind to the painful memory of their bitter words over his bargain with Vorynaas, the demeanour of frozen disdain she had brought to her wedding day.

Casting about for someone, something, other than himself to blame, he remembered Numirantoro's radiant delight when she heard she was to be fostered with Ardeth and Fosseiro. She couldn't wait to get away, to leave her home and parents to run off and live with yokels, he thought angrily. And here she is now, daughter to a leading man of the greatest city in the world, married to another who looks likely before he's finished to be richer and more powerful than I ever was, with a strong healthy child at her knee, and she can barely acknowledge our presence! As if I have not endured sorrow enough already, I must put up with this cold disregard, and this from my only daughter, who not long ago promised to do anything for me, if it would make me happy again. No wonder I indulge Ghentar, to have the pleasure of his high spirits and laughter. He took a deeper pull at his wine, breathing hard in agitation. But little by little, Arythalt regained his self-control. He had always been able to hide his thoughts when necessary, to dissemble if he thought it prudent; and now, glancing across again at his daughter's closed face, he tried once more to cajole her into conversation with him. He crossed to the wine-table, and taking down a small silver goblet from the shelf, he filled it and carried it across to her.

'Look, it's your favourite wine; you used to say you really enjoyed this one. Join me now, I've poured you just a little measure. I think you'd be interested in the plans we talked of this afternoon in the council. Would you like to hear about the ideas which were discussed?'

Numirantoro raised her head, her attention immediately engaged; and he was pleased, not knowing that it was the hope of hearing Arymaldur's name which filled her face with life. She listened carefully as Arythalt outlined a scheme to pipe water from the Red Mountains through a huge new network of growing-houses which were to be built in the south of the country, in the Ellanwic to the north-west of Staran y'n Forgarad. He explained how contracts were to be put out to tender in that city for the making of special ducting and glass panels for the buildings, and for the manufacture of thousands upon thousands of lights to hang from their beams. Many names were mentioned in his account, *sigitsaran* who would oversee the foundry-work and forging, engineers who would be in charge of the building and water-management, agriculturalists and researchers. She heard the names of Morgwentan, of Thaltor; and it seemed Valafoss too was a leading light of the new development, but clearly the main impetus had come from Vorynaas. Arythalt was bringing his account to a conclusion, obviously deeply impressed by his marriage-son's enterprise.

'…so while it's true to say that all will play a part, it needed Vorynaas to show us how to go about it: it took his vision to see how we could use all Caradward's resources of men and materials, and put them together so that we can overcome the problems which the recent change in the climate has caused. When the growing-houses of Cottan na'Salf are completed, they will be lit day and night, and their production will fill the markets once more with fresh fruit, and vegetables, even flowers; and seedsmen will work there, to develop new strains of plant more responsive to the new conditions in the growing-houses, so that in time maybe trees too can be planted there. A modern method for today's tasks, so that the future holds opportunities rather than problems: that's the slogan Vorynaas urges us to adopt.'

He finished, animated and enthusiastic, looking across at Numirantoro and waiting for her response. She frowned a little.

'This scheme will tear up broad swathes of land which families have tended for generations, time out of mind. Is everyone in Tell'Ethronad happy to see their acres built over like this? And what of those without land of their own, who sell their labour to buy their bread?'

'Simple: they'll work for the owners of the growing-houses instead. As for land-owners, those with sense will throw in their lot with the development of the Cottan na'Salf. Those who can't see the potential, and I concede that there are a few… I myself was disappointed with Forgard's response, I have to say… well, if they insist on being stubborn, they may find themselves being bought out. A foolish option, in my opinion, but no doubt their sons will find employment in the cities, or in Rigg'ymvala if their abilities are up to it. And, it has to be said, their loss will be other men's gain, for those who buy will be making a shrewd investment.'

'But however many growing-houses you build, you cannot light whole fields of crops. What of the farms that will remain in the Ellanwic? There are acres of wheat and roots which struggle to grow there now; how can we produce enough corn for bread, or fodder for beasts? How can grass grow for stock to graze on if the days continue dark, or darken further?'

'Listen, if we need wheat or barley, or our flocks and herds decrease, we will buy what we need to make up the shortfall. In Caradward we have wealth to spare. We can afford to purchase whatever we want, from the Outlands or from Gwent y'm Aryframan.'

'So, Morgwentan will increase his holdings again, adding to what he already has here and has grabbed in Framstock! And I can imagine who the other main beneficiaries will be. More lands, more money for yourself and Vorynaas: more recruits for Thaltor and Valafoss, to swell their delusions of martial grandeur. Though maybe it has occurred to them that threats may well be needed to back up our purchase power, now that their strutting border patrols have so angered those who used to be our friends, and are still our kin, in Gwent y'm Aryframan. What does Arval have to say of the new plans?'

Arythalt sat back in his chair with a small sound of exasperation. 'Oh, Arval! He's as gloomy as the weather, always negative, always looking for snags. He is out of date: his arguments are not appropriate in today's world, they are based on nothing more than superstition and outmoded ways of thought.'

'So Arval was against the idea?' asked Numirantoro. 'The council would be ill-advised to ignore his words. He's not called Earth-wise without reason.'

Resentment suddenly welled up in Arythalt, so that in his anger he spoke with raised voice, something he was rarely provoked into doing.

'You may run off to Tellgard all you like, sighing over Arval's maunderings,' he snapped. 'But I have told you before, you are daughter to a man of standing in a great country; and now you are wife to another, who has it in him to rise to a position of eminence where none will challenge him! And I tell you another thing now: mope and pine for the rustic life though you may, be sure that Vorynaas and I will see to it that Ghentar stays here and wastes no time labouring as a farm-hand.' Arythalt looked down, and spread his hands on his knees, calming himself. Looking up again, he spoke in a gentler tone, almost pleading with his daughter. 'Surely, any woman in this city would be glad to change places with you, and yet you have no word of affection for either husband or father, and take no joy even in your son! Numirantoro, believe me, I want you to be happy. Won't you wear your silver daisies in your hair for me, and smile again?'

She looked at her father, amazed and saddened anew at the extent to which he could delude himself. 'I promised my uncle Ardeth, on the day he gave them to me, that I would keep my silver daisies for solemn days and high feasts, and I will hold to that promise. I will not wear them as mere adornment here in this house, where such days are no longer honoured. And,' she broke off, with a bitter laugh, 'words of affection for my husband! How many times must you hear me say this before you believe me: I hate him, and I tell you, he will betray your trust.'

Suddenly into her heart with the words came memories flooding back of Ardeth's visit for her tenth birthday, his and Fosseiro's kindnesses to her, the years of friendship and innocence all now gone for ever. Sweeping from the room she went to lie in her cold marriage bed, awaiting Vorynaas' return while her thoughts sought solace in the bright days before all she had to live for was her despairing love for Arymaldur.

Obsession

Much later, she felt Vorynaas slide from the bed. Without kindling a light, he slipped into his house-robe and left the darkened room, treading softly. Numirantoro wondered without much interest whether her husband had found her so unresponsive tonight that he was off to the servants' wing again to seek out Sigitsiro. She dismissed him from her mind and surrendered to the sweet pain of her obsession with Arymaldur, seeing his face against the darkness, allowing herself the indulgence of whispering his name to the night. He always attended the meetings of Tell'Ethronad, she knew that and always saw to it that she caught a glimpse of him as he strode up the street past the house. If Arval had spoken against the new scheme, surely Arymaldur must have agreed with him. She wondered why her father had not mentioned this, when he had named Forgard as a dissenting voice. How much did Forgard say at home about council business? Could she get any clue from Heretellar, or from his cousin Ancrascaro? The little girl's mother was Forgard's sister. But no, the children were far too young. She would have to take her courage in both hands and try to talk to Arval.

A little shudder ran through Numirantoro. What if Arval saw through her interest, saw what lay behind her questions? Admitting to the old man that she had loved Geraswic was one thing, but she was afraid that if he guessed the strength of the hold that Arymaldur had upon her, he would find its power unseemly in some way. She felt her face grow hot, and her heart raced in the darkness as she admitted a new dimension to the turmoil of emotion that lay suppressed within her. Now that she was a grown woman, she understood more fully many aspects of life that had been a mystery to the child of earlier years. Looking back on Salfronardo and Arythalt, and on Ardeth and Fosseiro, she recognised the magnetism of her parents' mutual attraction, which could spark to life even when they disagreed; and she saw the warmth of the others' physical bond, still able to ignite between them after so many years of daily companionship. She understood too, now, desire without love: an exerting of dominance, as Vorynaas used her, or a casual coupling like that between her husband and Sigitsiro. A great sadness and regret coloured her memories of Geraswic now, for she saw, too late, that he had loved her as a man loves a woman whereas she had offered him only the love of friendship, affection that was true and enduring, but unripe through innocence.

But Arymaldur! She clenched her fists before her face under cover of the night. For Arymaldur she was consumed by a desire that never slept:

it beat upon her like the force of great wings and twisted in her heart with an intensity that would not be assuaged. While she was still able to, she had refused to admit it to herself, tried to deny that she was capable of such intemperate emotion; but she could no longer pretend. From the first moment, she had been assailed by a yearning that remained unsatisfied, a hunger that raged unabated. Sometimes the longing was so strong she felt almost sick and faint, and at such moments she would wish she had never seen him, that their meeting had not occurred, to wreak such havoc in her life: and yet she was incapable of staying away from where he might be, of refusing the chance to spend time in his presence. A day without him was a wasted day, blacker and darker than the gloom that had settled over Caradward; and days when she saw him were lit with a brightness no lamp could ever achieve, a radiance as if every star in the sky had descended to burn upon earth.

Numirantoro rose and prowled the room in the darkness restlessly, wrapping her arms around herself. She went to the window and peeped round the curtain, but all was black outside except where a light shone here and there in a courtyard or on a street corner. Her mind trod unceasingly up and down its well-worn corridors of thought, as tense and nervy as her pacing of the cold floor. She remembered the old story which had so moved her as a child, *Maesell y'm As-Urad*. If there was any truth in it, then unions of the Starborn and the Earthborn had once occurred, from which children had been born. How could this be? She hated the merest touch from Vorynaas, but that was because she hated him. If Arymaldur… Her hands clenched themselves again. Her body craved Arymaldur, she must acknowledge that, and yet somehow she knew that would not be enough. Unbearable though it was to imagine something she wanted so much, it would still be but a touching here, a straining there, a puny, Earthborn ecstasy. She struggled to define what she really sought. She wanted Arymaldur to possess her totally, and she him, whatever the cost. Though I should be consumed by its power, she thought, yet I would lose myself to the love of the As-Geg'rastigan.

Suddenly her ears caught the sound of footsteps approaching the door. Vorynaas was coming back! She flung herself on to the bed, grasping hastily at the covers, shivering with cold and distaste. It must surely be near dawn, so why was he returning? She heard him remove his robe and throw it over the chest against the wall, then felt the bed yield to his weight as she lay turned away from him. He put out a hand and touched her waist and she flinched in spite of herself.

'No point in pretending to be asleep, then, is there?' said Vorynaas quietly, with a hint of mocking laughter. 'But what's been happening here? You're icy cold!'

'Nothing; I feel slightly unwell, that's all.'

Vorynaas moved nearer Numirantoro and pulled the covers back, running both hands over her as she twisted away. 'Rubbish, woman, don't lie to me. Even your feet are freezing. You've been out of bed! Where have you been?'

He had her by the wrist now, in a grip she could not break, and fury suddenly flared up in Numirantoro. She rarely lost her outward composure, being more like her father than her mother in this, but she spat back at Vorynaas.

'Let go of me! Do I ask you where you have been, when you roam the servants' quarters and come back with Sigitsiro's stale scent still on you? You disgust me. This was my father's house and my family home before ever your filthy footprints trod here. I will not be questioned on my use of it!'

'Oh, so there's a spark or two in my little wife after all,' sneered Vorynaas, releasing his hold on Numirantoro and moving to strike a light and kindle a small bedside lamp. 'We must have a closer look at this.'

He turned her face roughly towards him, so that the light fell on it, and looked down at her, one knee on the edge of the bed. The anger in her expression reminded him of Salfronardo and excitement began to stir in him, remembering how in his youth he had fantasised about encountering the older woman some warm afternoon when Arythalt was safely away from Caradriggan. He smiled slowly and moved fully on to the bed. Looking up at him with hate, Numirantoro felt a stab of panic: what might he do if he ever suspected that she loved Arymaldur? She forced her mind and face to assume blank indifference, schooling herself not to let her husband see behind the guard she kept on her emotions. Vorynaas had noted the hate, he was used to that, but he saw the momentary fear too. That surprised him, but he found he enjoyed it and his desire strengthened. He went about his business slowly at first, his words chosen to wound with contempt, and then growing angrier as his vehemence increased.

'Yes, "was" is the right word, Numirantoro. This *was* your father's house, but I am master here now. You should remember this, you might not like it if I had to remind you too often, I think? And if you prefer me not to visit Sigitsiro, perhaps you should see to it that I enjoy a little more pleasure in your company?' He began to move more urgently, deliberately showing Numirantoro how his strength was so much greater than hers, how he was far too powerful for her to fight off. Her eyes were shut, her face turned aside from his on the pillow, but a small sound of misery and protest escaped her closed lips. Vorynaas moved faster, pinning her down, his own lips pulled back from his teeth as his words came in menacing gasps. 'There are three things you should never try to do, Numirantoro. Never deceive me, never lie to me, and never betray me. Remember that!' At last, it was over; he lay for a long moment with his face against her shoulder and his hands tangled in her hair, his breathing gradually quieting again. Then he heaved himself off the bed and reached for his robe. Pausing as he left the room, he added a final word. 'You're turning into a bag of bones. Ghentar needs a brother: I don't want him growing up alone, turning into an oddity like his mother; but you are too thin to conceive. You should eat more, I keep a generous enough table.' The door banged, and he was gone.

Numirantoro lay where he had left her, bruised in body and mind, feeling used and cast aside like some broken vessel. Refusing to give him the satisfaction of tears, she listened to the small sounds of the household awaking around her: water being drawn, footsteps in the courtyard, stable doors opening, the soft stamp of hooves on straw. She wondered where Vorynaas had been during his absence late in the night, for in spite of her words, she had detected no trace of Sigitsiro on him, although he had smelt strongly of wine. How extraordinary it was, she thought, that new life could come into being from what Vorynaas and she had just done; that life could be conceived as equally in violence and hate as in love and tenderness. Tiredness crept up on Numirantoro, who was worn out with lack of sleep and nervous exhaustion. It was strange that she almost never dreamed about Arymaldur. Maybe she thought of him so constantly while she was awake that her sleeping mind demanded a respite. Yet when she did dream of him, the same scene invariably recurred. She was towards the back of a crowd of people in a slightly darkened room, and Arymaldur was talking quietly with two or three people at the front, with his back to her. Silently she called his name in her heart, willing him to hear, to respond; and suddenly, amazingly, his head turned. It all seemed to happen very slowly: the crowd parted a little, and he moved to face her. The darkness at the edges of the scene increased, but now it was globed around a strange radiance that lit the noble lines of Arymaldur's face. It seemed that he and she were left alone in the room, and now their eyes met. But either the dream always ended there, or else she remembered nothing else: for just as events trembled on the very edge of understanding, all became dark, and try as she would, Numirantoro could never recall anything more.

CHAPTER 11

Forgard pays a call

The buzz of background chatter, drifting out to Numirantoro from the house, became suddenly louder and more animated and she heard a man's laugh mingled with the women's voices. The months were turning once more towards spring, and she was in the courtyard working at the raised bed she had made, hoping that she could maybe adapt the principles of the new growing-houses for her own use. She had been setting seeds and arranging a row of silver lamps to hang from hooks in the wall behind, but now she straightened from her task and looked to see what was happening. To her surprise, Forgard was chatting with the women who worked in the kitchen. He had been bending down, looking to see what little Isteddar was doing, and was glancing up at the boy's grandmother with a smile as she paused in her passage through the room with a pile of folded linen. Numirantoro saw that he had his niece Ancrascaro by the hand and now he left her to play with the toddler and came out into the courtyard towards her. The day was warm, so she invited him to sit and wait for her, showing him her hands all dirty with earth, and hurrying in to wash them.

It turned out that Forgard had called in the hope of seeing Vorynaas and Arythalt, but had found both of them to be out of the house. However the steward had told him that Arythalt was only to be briefly in his office to sort out some query, and had said he would return very shortly, so Forgard had decided to wait for him. Numirantoro relaxed in her chair, pleased to chat to Forgard in the meantime. She liked him and was fond of both his son Heretellar and his niece Ancrascaro; she wished that he was an associate of her husband, rather than Thaltor. Forgard was slightly younger than Vorynaas, but his hair had begun to turn grey when he was still in his twenties and now it was almost completely silver, although thick and strong. His eyebrows however were still black, as dark as his eyes, and his skin was slightly sallow; his unusual colouring made him recognised everywhere and he would say with a laugh that it was no good his trying to get away with any kind of trickery, for everyone would know him immediately. Not that Forgard was ever likely to be involved in anything at all underhand, being a man of principle who kept his word and spoke his mind in the council, unwelcome though this was to some of his colleagues.

Numirantoro remembered now that her father had mentioned Forgard as being one of the members of Tell'Ethronad who had spoken out against the establishment of the Cottan na'Salf. The work on their development had proceeded apace ever since the previous autumn and from what she had heard since, during discussions at table or over wine between her husband and father, it seemed unlikely to her that Forgard had changed his mind. She was amazed to find him actually seeking Vorynaas out like this, but before she had the chance to find out anything further, Ancrascaro came running from the house with Isteddar behind her, trying his best to keep up.

'Where is Ghentar this morning?' asked the little girl.

'He's not here today,' said Numirantoro. 'He's gone to play with Valahald and Heranar, over at their house.'

'Oh. Well, it's all right if I play with Isteddar in the kitchen, isn't it?'

'Of course, and tell the cook I said you could have some milk and a piece of spiced bread each,' said Numirantoro. The little girl skipped and turned to run back inside with the good news, then turned suddenly, remembering something important. She pulled at Forgard's sleeve.

'Uncle Forgard, don't forget to ask, will you?' she said, looking up at him with anxious eyes which then slid to Numirantoro and back again.

Her uncle laughed and ruffled her hair. 'No, I won't forget, I promise,' he said. 'Now you play nicely and don't make a mess in the kitchen with Isteddar.' He laughed again, shaking his head, and had just begun to speak to Numirantoro when the door that led from the courtyard to the various out-offices and business premises opened and Arythalt came through it with a preoccupied air. It was obvious to Numirantoro that he was disconcerted to find Forgard there, but he welcomed him politely, if rather formally, and sat down to join them.

Forgard, who had risen courteously in deference to the older man as Arythalt entered, resumed his own seat and enquired for his well-being.

'I am in good health, thank you,' said Arythalt, 'though if I were to tell the truth, I find myself sad at heart at this time of the year, remembering the loss of my dear wife. Although time dulls the pain, it cannot heal the wound.'

'True,' said Forgard, remembering with a surge of sorrow his own son who had also died in the spring sickness. He would never forget cradling the little lad, feeling the last tiny flicker of life gutter out in the small body as he held it in his arms. 'Yet I hope that young Ghentar has brought warmth to your heart again, as Heretellar has brightened my own home.'

Arythalt's thin face lit up slightly and he spoke with more animation. 'Ah, indeed yes, Forgard! The boy is a delight, so strong and active! But he needs others of his own age, his father dislikes him to be cooped up here with women and servants, and I am too old now to give him the companionship he should have…'

He tailed off, and for a moment all three were silent. Privately Forgard thought the last thing Ghentar needed was to spend time with Heranar and Valahald, two little ruffians who were likely to grow up even worse men than their father. He stole a covert glance at Numirantoro, wondering how she felt about the dismissive tone Arythalt used. Her face was expressionless, although he noticed that her breathing had quickened slightly. She was thinking of the scene earlier that day, when Vorynaas, as he prepared to go out himself, had instructed Ghentar's nurse to take the boy over to Valafoss' house. Ghentar had been sulky and badly-behaved, twisting away from his grandfather's attempt to embrace him and stamping his foot in a temper when told he could not accompany his father. Vorynaas had simply grinned, making no attempt to correct the boy or to chastise him for his rudeness to Arythalt; handing him over to the long-suffering nurse he informed his marriage-father without further explanation that he was off to a meeting with Thaltor and Valafoss. You are making a rod for your own back there, Vorynaas, thought Numirantoro. Your indulgence is turning your son into a brat, but he will not grow to love you for it. And as for you, my father, I warned you that Vorynaas would betray you and now you see already how he pushes you aside and goes his own way.

Forgard decided to press on with what he had come to say.

'Lord Arythalt, forgive me for correcting you,' he began, 'but you do yourself a disservice. You are not an aged man! You are still hale and strong, you should not speak like this or you will indeed make yourself old before your time. You are a respected voice in the council, a voice, if I may be permitted to say so, which should be heard more often. You grieve still for Salfronardo, I know; yet don't all of us, whether we remember lost loved ones or not, feel downcast at heart today as men should not, in the springtime? Arythalt, rethink your support for the Cottan na'Salf! I readily agree that in itself it may succeed; it is ingenious and inventive, a tribute to the fertile minds of the men of Caradward, but it will cause more problems than it solves. Surely you can see that Arval and Arymaldur are right when they say we are treating the symptoms of the disease, not the cause. The remedy must lie with us, in us, or why else does the gloom lie only on Caradward when the sun still shines in Gwent y'm Aryframan?

I have come here today in the hope of talking quietly with yourself, with Vorynaas and Thaltor. I regret the divisions that are widening in Tell'Ethronad, which are harder to close in open debate where many men look on and pride is at stake. Let us put our differences aside, we are all true sons of Caradward. We all want the best for our homeland, but I tell you Arythalt, I am afraid that if we continue on our present road, we shall all go down into the dark.'

Arythalt and Numirantoro looked at Forgard in astonishment. Numirantoro's heart had leapt when Arymaldur's name was mentioned and she fought to appear calm as she waited to hear what her father would say. Arythalt was taken aback by the urgency of Forgard's words and demeanour, and his mind wavered. He was impressed by the younger man's sincerity, by the fact that he had been prepared to risk being treated with contempt by holding out the hand of friendship to his adversaries. He knew well enough what the reaction of Vorynaas and Thaltor would have been, had they been present. But for himself... Could it be that there was some middle ground, maybe, which he could make his own?

'Forgard, you are a man of integrity. It can't have been easy to come here today, and I honour you for doing so, and acknowledge the strength of your views. Arval's wisdom is deep, he has been revered in this city for as long as men can remember, and rightly so. But don't you think that in his age he becomes out of step with the times? How can progress be wrong? You say yourself that you are impressed with the enterprise now going forward in the Ellanwic, and as you know there are other schemes and ideas ready for test or already in trial. We cannot turn back time, yet all Arval can advise is negative: don't do this, don't do that, hold by the ways of our fathers, and their fathers before them!'

Sitting back in his chair, Forgard relaxed a little and smiled at Arythalt. He had been worried that he would be dismissed out of hand and was encouraged to be met by a more measured response. 'No, no,' he said now, 'I see I have not explained myself clearly. I'm all for progress, and I think you'll find that Arval is, too. In any case, as you've said, life moves on whether we will or no, and no-one can stand against the march of years. No, I think it's not so much what we are doing, but the *way* we are doing it, that may be the problem. Or maybe, the way we have started to think, as if the men of other lands, or even some from among ourselves, are of no account. What will be the good of the food produced by the Cottan na'Salf, if their building is forced through regardless and men are made homeless by it? Why antagonise our friends in Gwent y'm Aryframan by harassing them with armed men along the border? The risk is that they will retaliate with tolls and tariffs of their own. What if we find that for all our wealth we cannot afford the price they ask for grain? Surely, our most urgent task is to find out why the light has failed; and for that, Arval bids us look within ourselves.'

Arythalt sat silent. Forgard's words had touched more than one raw nerve within him. During the winter months, he had noticed men hanging about on the street corners of Caradriggan, groups of them jostling at the markets when there was a hiring fair, knocking on doors looking for work, scrounging for food at inn yards. Sometimes now there were women too, with hungry faces and thin children. And hide it from himself though he would, he knew without thinking about it that if the price of imports became too high, men like Thaltor and Valafoss would simply take what they wanted by force. Yet, he thought, folk flock to the old ceremonies for the Starborn: even in these modern times, there has been quite a resurgence of that kind of superstition. Tellgard is crowded for all the festivals, Arval can have no complaints there, but the darkness still deepens. Who knows what is right?

An old memory suddenly came back to him, of the debate in Tell'Ethronad when he had had to leave the council chamber because Ardeth had arrived in Caradriggan unexpectedly. Forgard had spoken out that day, had spoken against the trends the younger men were already setting, and had swayed the majority to his own views. But

Arythalt remembered thinking then that time would weed out Forgard's supporters, and he had been right: men of his own age were the seniors now, and most of them voted with Vorynaas and his party. Forgard and Arval stood almost alone, except for the few Outlanders who had been admitted to the council, and for Arymaldur. And there was something about Arymaldur, something he had never been able to put his finger on... Arythalt felt a slight shiver run through him, as if the hair had risen on his head. It occurred to him also that Arval's support in Tellgard came mostly from the common people with no voice in the council, or from those whose loyalties were suspect because they had too many ties with Gwent y'm Aryframan. He had wavered, but he felt his resolve strengthening. It was too late to change sides; he must hold to Vorynaas now.

He looked up, found Forgard watching his face intently, and tried to strike a breezy tone. 'Oh, this will be just a run of bad years such as must surely have happened before,' he said. 'In times to come, old folk will look back and bore their young people with stories of when days were dark in Caradward. How can men possibly either influence or change the weather? We'll get through this, and be better off for it: don't we say necessity is the mother of invention?'

Forgard's shoulders sagged a little. For a moment or two he had thought he was making some headway with Arythalt, but it seemed he had been mistaken. He spoke quietly, almost sadly. 'Arythalt, use your eyes, man!' he said, pointing up at the leaden sky and the lamps which shone in the courtyard. 'Can you remember when you last saw the sun? Your lanterns are masterpieces of the silversmith's art, and they shine out in beauty: but their light cannot bestow life. The leaves wither, flowers fail to open, fruits do not ripen. Daily the clouds above us are deeper and darker. If we cannot halt them as they lour upon us, sooner or later the light will go out also in our hearts.'

Momentarily he rested his forehead on his hand, his eyes downcast and his brow furrowed with concern. Numirantoro noticed little Ancrascaro peeping at the open door of the kitchen, her finger in her mouth and her eyes round with surprise as she watched her uncle, her game with Isteddar forgotten. Forgard sighed and then looked up again, spreading out his hands in appeal to Arythalt.

'Could we talk of this further? You had no warning of my visit; perhaps you would prefer to think over our words together, and then meet again? I would be pleased if Vorynaas too would join us. I understand your marriage-son isn't at home at present, but do you expect him back soon, or should I seek him elsewhere and talk to him alone first?'

How do I know when Vorynaas will be back, when I do not even know his errand, thought Arythalt angrily. He sent the boy to Valafoss' house with his nurse, so clearly he has not gone there himself; but he and Thaltor are meeting Valafoss, and I am not included. A tiny voice within told him Numirantoro's warning had been well-founded, but he dismissed it. Abruptly rising to his feet, he addressed Forgard haughtily.

'There is no need to speak to Vorynaas separately; you will find that he and I are at one in our opinions. He is my business partner as well as my marriage-son and if, when I have considered what you have said to me, I feel that he should know of our conversation, I will tell him of it myself. Now, if you'll excuse me, I have much to attend to and I regret that I can spare no more time for leisure.' He held out his hand to Forgard, who stood to shake it, acutely conscious of the chill that had fallen on the gathering, and then left the courtyard through the door to the offices by which he had entered.

Not realising his words had probed too deeply into what was becoming a festering wound, Forgard was surprised by the coldness of Arythalt's reply. 'I'd better go. I'm sorry, I seem to have upset your father,' he said, looking after Arythalt with a baffled expression. 'I don't know how it happened, it was quite unintentional.'

Numirantoro smiled at him. 'Don't worry,' she said. 'You have made him think about something he would prefer to ignore, that's all it is. Sit down again, doesn't Ancrascaro have something she wants you to ask me about?'

'Oh, yes! It had gone quite out of my head,' said Forgard, smiling back at Numirantoro. By the Starborn, he thought, she is wasted on Vorynaas! 'Come over here, Ancrascaro,' he continued, drawing the little girl to him and setting her on his knee. 'Now, I have promised my clever little niece here that I will ask you whether you would be willing to take her with you sometimes, when you visit Tellgard. She has been working hard at home, all winter, and now she can read and write, a little; and though she is a year or so younger than the usual age, nothing will satisfy her but to have a taste of the rarefied air of Arval's kingdom. I have told her that when you go there, you will be at your studies, or busy in the workrooms, and will have no time to spare for children; but she promises me she will be as quiet as a mouse and do whatever you tell her, so long as she can come with you, perhaps once or twice a week. Have I got all that right, *is-gerasto*?'

'Yes, uncle Forgard,' said Ancrascaro, her eyes fixed on Numirantoro's face. 'Please, I swear I will be good, and only look at the books you allow me to use, and only ask questions when you say I may.'

Faint colour stole into Numirantoro's pale cheeks and her face brightened as her sad heart spread its wings in a little flight of unaccustomed happiness. 'It will be a pleasure to take her with me,' she said. 'I remember Arval telling me, when I was probably younger than Ancrascaro is now, that learning was the one thing men could never regret; and I have found that he was right.'

Behind closed doors

Meanwhile, across the city in a house near to the wall at its east gate, three men were deep in discussion behind closed doors. Thaltor was unmarried and could now afford to indulge his tastes; these were dubious in many ways, but his cellar was well-stocked and his servants discreet: they had been left in no doubt about the price they would pay for loose talk about their master and his business. Vorynaas had been outlining a risky new scheme and was becoming exasperated by the slowness of his companions' approval.

'Look, trust me, it's foolproof! Who's going to stop us? If you think I won't have the nerve to pack the old fellow off, you're much mistaken.'

Thaltor and Valafoss exchanged glances and after a pause Thaltor spoke. 'It all sounds well enough, provided we can trust you. But let's face it, we all three of us know that's a big *if*.'

Vorynaas raised his eyebrows and gave the two men a hard stare. 'Well, they say it takes one to know one, I suppose.' He laughed sardonically. 'Honestly, you two haven't got the brains you were born with. I've trusted you enough to tell you the plans, haven't I? If you don't come in on them with me, where does that leave me? Going it alone, knowing you can tell tales behind my back to anyone who'll listen? Not to mention what I might do, if I let things drop and then found that you two had gone ahead without me. Come on, have sense. Either we do it together, or not at all.'

'Yes, count me in. I want to do it.' Valafoss, greedy and unscrupulous, was keen to attach himself to Vorynaas' party, seeing him as the rising star in Caradward. 'What do you say, Thaltor?'

The other man brooded for a moment or two in silence. He had known Vorynaas for longer than Valafoss and had every reason to know his untrustworthiness from first-hand experience. Thaltor was not a particularly subtle or intelligent man and although he enjoyed throwing his weight around, he was inclined to laziness. He wanted money and power, because then he could do as he wished and take what he wanted. Bullying the new recruits in Rigg'ymvala, cutting a dash riding up and down the border, ordering the patrols about and intimidating travellers… yes, he was happy with all that; but this scheme of Vorynaas' sounded complicated and ambitious, he was damned if he was going to be stuck in some office with piles of paperwork to oversee. He decided to temporise.

'It's just that I'd be keener if we knew more about the background. Can you be quite sure your information is reliable?'

His hand at his mouth, stroking his beard, Vorynaas hid his satisfaction. Really, Thaltor had walked into this one! He threw a warm smile of approval at Valafoss and then gave Thaltor a friendly pat on the arm. 'Good man, Valafoss. I have to hand it to you, though, Thaltor: you've put your finger right on the crucial point.'

Thaltor's face registered surprise, gratification and bafflement in equal measures, but it quickly darkened as Vorynaas continued.

'My contact is your young friend Valestron, up on the border patrols. He's a bright young fellow, one to watch, I'd say. Anyway, it seems his cousin is still in his Tellgard years, but found Arymaldur's swordsmanship instruction rather difficult to stomach, so he took himself out of the drills and enrolled for metalwork instead: his family are from away south, so it seemed a sensible thing to do. Then one thing or another that he heard piqued his curiosity, and he started digging around, asking a question or two; Arval was a bit terse with him he said, and he wasn't going to take that from the old buzzard; so to cut a long story short, he watched his moment and managed to 'borrow' a couple of volumes from the locked cupboard in the library. I've gone through them thoroughly, and don't worry, I've done it carefully with the household safely abed, and now they're back all snug on the shelf in Tellgard with no-one the wiser. It was all there: the whole story of what happened in the old days up at the headwaters of the Lissa'pathor, where Maesaldron meets the wilderness, set down in the official reports by those who were actually involved at the time. *That's* my source of information: couldn't be more reliable than that, could it?'

Valafoss was open in his admiration. 'You've got contacts everywhere! How did this youngster get away with it? Can we trust *him*? Is he in on the idea?'

Vorynaas inclined his head modestly. 'I like to maintain a healthy network. The lad doesn't waste his time in classes, he can pick any lock you choose. I've got him on a retainer, he'll be working for me once his studies are over, but as far as he's concerned, I just had an interest in a little-known episode of ancient history.'

There was a sharp scrape as Thaltor's chair was pushed suddenly back. He jumped to his feet, jabbing a finger at Vorynaas. 'Contacts, I'll say! A finger in every pie!' He began to pace up and down. 'By my right hand! I hate Arymaldur! Who does he think he is, setting himself up in Tellgard with Arval, and the two of them so sanctimonious in the council as well. What wouldn't I give to send him packing, back to Gwent y'm Aryframan!'

'But he's not from there,' said Valafoss in surprise, 'he doesn't bear the sign of the springing corn on his arm.'

'So what! Maybe he's not a native born, but that's where he came from, through the gap between the Somllichan Ghent and the forest before the patrols were set up. There's got to be some sort of connection between him and those stupid peasants, look at the way they all go on about the Starborn, for one thing.' Thaltor spat viciously into the hearth in passing; Vorynaas curled his lip in distaste, but at least they were meeting in Thaltor's house. If he wanted to behave like an oaf in his own home, it was his own business. He moved to calm things.

'Now gentlemen, we're getting off the point. Thaltor, simmer down and come back here. You've yet to tell me whether you're with me, so what's your answer?'

Thaltor sat again and brought his clenched fist down onto the table. 'Yes! Yes, let's get on with it, what's the first move? Wait, I'll get some more wine, we need to drink to this.'

He went to the door and shouted for a servant. While they waited for the bottles to appear, Vorynaas chuckled to himself inwardly. Really, Thaltor wasn't too bright! As soon as he'd lost his temper over Arymaldur, he lost the battle to think rationally too, and he was ready to agree to anything. But, thought Vorynaas, I owe him for one thing, though...

He lifted his replenished cup. 'Well, the first thing is for you to back me when I propose to Arythalt that Valafoss should formally join our partnership. The second thing is for us all to vote together after that, so that he either has to agree with us, or do what we want regardless. And given what we know now about previous events in the valley of the Lissa'pathor, I have a feeling that the old boy could soon find himself nominally in charge up there. So, here's to our future success!' They drank, laughing, and Vorynaas gave Thaltor a conspiratorial grin as he raised his cup to him. Thanks, Thaltor, he thought: you probably don't realise it, but you've just given me another very interesting little idea to play with.

At the *Sword and Stars*

Much later, Vorynaas settled his account in the *Sword and Stars* and headed for the door. Earlier, he had stayed on after Valafoss left for his own house, and Thaltor had sent his steward over to the *Golden Leopard* with money and a message for its proprietor. The *Leopard* was an inn much frequented by on-leave members of the Rigg'ymvala garrison and soldiers from the border patrols. Thaltor was well-known there, and although Vorynaas, conscious of his standing in the city, avoided it, he was not at all averse to the company of the two girls whose services Thaltor paid for. The four of them spent a few hours in varied and decadent pleasures of the kind not available to Vorynaas under his own roof, before he left to dine alone at the *Sword and Stars*. Estimating that he had left it late enough to avoid the necessity of either dealing with Ghentar or spending too much time with Arythalt, he left the inn to make his way home through the lamplit streets of Caradriggan.

As he passed the wide gateway into the inn yard, his attention was caught by movement within, and as he glanced over he saw a woman who, silhouetted against the light spilling from the back door of the inn, seemed somehow familiar. He stepped inside the gateway and realised that he had been right: the woman was Sigitsiro, hurrying over to the far corner carrying a bulky bundle and looking about her fearfully; all her actions had a furtive air. Vorynaas saw now that there were people huddled together under the arcade that ran around the courtyard, crammed in between the straw stacks and the parked wagons, gathered into one or two mixed parties and a few of men only. Sigitsiro went to one of the larger groups and crouched down, opening her bundle. Hands reached out to her and a murmur of voices broke out, in which a baby's cry was mingled; but quickly the voices were stilled as the people began to eat what she had given them. Faces in the other groups looked on sullenly.

Vorynaas crossed the yard swiftly and silently and caught Sigitsiro roughly by the arm, spinning her round and pinning her against one of the wooden uprights that supported the eaves of the arcading. She cried out in alarm and then fell silent as she saw who had confronted her. Now she felt the full force of the menace that had always been latent in her sexual relations with Vorynaas, but this time she experienced no frisson of excitement or desire. Her employer's face was thrust close to hers and fear twisted within her.

'So,' said Vorynaas very quietly. 'You are creeping out from my house to give my food to this riff-raff. How long has this been going on?'

Sigitsiro could hardly speak for fright. 'Sir, I mean no harm,' she faltered. 'It's for the children, they're so hungry, I just wanted to help…' She shivered with fear, unable to finish the sentence. Vorynaas moved very slightly closer and she flattened herself against the rough wood of the support, unable to get any further away from him.

'There is a child in my house, is there not? You are taking his bread, to give to beggars?'

'Sir, no! They are from the south, made homeless by the building of the Cottan na'Salf, they have come to the city in search of work. And see, the bread is stale, you would not eat it at your table, it is only scraps, just waste the cook would throw out…' Again she stammered to a halt, unnerved by what she saw in his face.

'You have been stealing from me,' he said, tightening his grip on her arm painfully as she made to protest. 'You have been stealing my substance to feed these worthless peasants. From the south, are they? Maybe *sigitsaran*, like yourself? Well then, no doubt they'll have a welcome for you. You have clothes on your back which I have provided. You may keep them, but make sure you never come near my house again.'

Sigitsiro sagged against his arm, in despair as she thought of the gifts he had given her from time to time, the small hoard of gold and silver coins so carefully stored in her room to give to her family. It was wealth so pitiful, yet so dearly bought, and she would lose it all if he would not permit her to return and collect her meagre belongings. Desperately she began to plead with him.

'Sir, please, I'm sorry, I'll go if I have to, but please, let me get my things…'

Vorynaas smiled. He almost thought that frightening her like this was better than dominating her sexually. 'Surely you're not deaf, as well as dishonest?' he said. 'I repeat: if I see you at my home again, or hear that you have been in the house, you will regret it. Now, I suggest you join your friends here before they eat everything you have stolen.' He stepped back, yanking her viciously by the arm so that she staggered towards the group who looked on in frozen silence, and then with a contemptuous glance around him he left the courtyard.

There was a murmur of sympathy among the huddled people, and a woman moved to put a comforting arm around Sigitsiro's shoulders as she sat slumped on the ground at the edge of the group.

'What a bastard!' A man's voice spoke, keeping it low but his tone full of venom. 'If that's how they treat their own folk, no wonder us newcomers can't find work!'

'No, you heard what he said, she's an Outlander,' said a woman, young-sounding by her voice, from the far side of the group. 'What street's his house in? There'll be a place for someone there tomorrow, if they go round early in the morning. Tell me what your duties were. I might be from the south, but I'm Caradward through and through: maybe he'll take me on.'

'More fool you, to go to a house where he's the master,' said a young man from the shadows at the back of the arcade, sitting separately from the larger group. 'If he's like that in public, what do you think he'd be like to deal with behind closed doors?'

A sob broke from Sigitsiro at this, and the other woman persisted. 'Look, just because he had a problem with her, it doesn't mean I wouldn't get on well. Come on, you, Sigitsiro is it? Dry up now and give me an idea of what work you've been doing. Beggars can't be too choosy, even if him over there hasn't realised yet.'

'Oh, just, just general duties,' mumbled Sigitsiro. 'Household things: cleaning, and a bit of cooking, errands to the market and, well, just whatever, really.'

A quick burst of whispering was heard, followed by a knowing snigger.

'Especially whatever, eh? Was that how it was?' The young woman laughed again and spoke with a harder edge to her voice. 'Well Lord High and Mighty can forget that with me. But my friend here tells me that from what she's heard in the city, if you're stuck for ideas, you should go along to the *Golden Leopard* – always pleased to see a girl with a bit of experience there, she says.' She tittered again with her friend, who was hidden in the general darkness, and Sigitsiro drew a ragged breath and sobbed again. Oh, not the *Golden Leopard*, she thought, please, not that; yet she knew she might have to go there in the end. Meanwhile scuffling and angry voices had broken out among the group she had tried to help.

'By the Starborn! You should be ashamed of yourself!' hissed a man's voice. 'I hope you do get this young lassie's place tomorrow, it would serve you right! You shouldn't speak like that to someone who's just been treated like she has, someone down on their luck because they tried to help us. And *that* for true-born Caradwardans!' He spat out into the channel. 'Who forced us off our land and from our homes? Yes, I don't need to remind you, do I? And when we got here, who helped us? The storeman, who's from Framstock; a woman from the kitchens who's married a Gwentaran, and this poor girl from the Outlands who's just lost her own livelihood for it.'

'I'll tell you something else,' came another, younger, man's voice. 'If I was on my own, I'd try my luck in Framstock, or over the border somewhere. But it's no good even thinking of a long road like that with the baby so young, and my wife here with two other youngsters still at her skirts. We've been here at the *Sword* for two nights now, we can't bank on them letting us sleep here much longer. If my luck doesn't change very soon, I'm going to try at Tellgard.'

'Oh, listen to him! Didn't know we had an intellectual in our midst. Going to help that old fossil Arval with his poetry, is that the idea?' This time the laughter from the cynical young woman and her friend was greeted by voices raised in real anger. It seemed the man who had chided her earlier took exception to her scathing remark about Arval, while an older woman, possibly his wife, and various others in the group attemted to damp things down. The woman with the children tried to calm them again when they roused up, and moved to quiet the baby. Meanwhile sounds were heard too from the darkness at the back of the arcade, where the young man who had spoken out against Vorynaas had made a small refuge against the straw stack. A child awoke and cried out in confusion, while an old man's wheezy coughing persisted for a few moments. There was a murmur of voices as the young man reassured the others, who eventually settled to sleep again.

When morning came, the lanterns in the yard showed an old man sitting in the straw beside a lad of eight years or so, both of them thin and watchful-looking. Beside them on the ground were four bundles tied up in blankets. They looked up as a young man came out of the stables and crossed towards them. He squatted down to talk to them, holding his father's eyes with his own.

'Dad, I've made my mind up. I've just sorted things with the storeman and the yard-manager. They'll give me three days' work, and they say I can pick around and see what suitable wood and other bits I can find. We'll have to share my food, or else you and Cunoreth will have to try to beg for some more. I won't have time, because I'm going to make a barrow, if I can find an old wheel – if not, it'll have to be a cart on runners. Then you can ride in it, with some of the stuff, and I'll carry the rest. Cunoreth will help when he can, and I can carry him too if I have to, but once we're ready, we'll be off. I'm going back to Ardeth in Salfgard.'

The old man's eyes filled with tears and his hands shook slightly. 'It's too far for us, son. The boy and I would never make it. You go, you can make it on your own, you take the chance.'

'Listen! Either we all go, or none of us do. But how long do you think we'd last here? Once we get into Gwent y'm Aryframan, we'll be all right. I know it's a long way, but I know how to set snares and find food, and we can stop if we have to and I'll work on a farm or in a *gradstedd* or something. But we'll manage! And believe me, if we make it to Salfgard, Ardeth won't let us down. He'll remember me, I know he would help us.'

He looked round as someone pulled at his sleeve, and saw Sigitsiro. Unable to think straight about what to do, when the others dispersed in search of work or food she had simply sat on and had overheard the talk of Salfgard.

'I will get food for you, during the three days you stay here,' she said. 'Ardeth is my mistress's uncle, I have heard his name spoken before. Would you let me come with you to Salfgard?'

'It's Sigitsiro, isn't it? Look, it's really kind of you to help: I appreciate it, and don't think I'm just turning you away, but … well, my father here is right: it's a long way to Salfgard. A very long way, further than you probably imagine. And you'd have to walk, because you see how we are: I might have to carry the lad, and I can't make a barrow big enough for you and the old man as well as our gear. I'd be afraid that you'd get part of the way, and have to give up, and what would we do then?'

Sigitsiro looked down at the ground, fighting despair. Suddenly an idea came to her, suggested by the taunting she had received the previous night. She had been accused of stealing and of having no honour left to lose. Well then! Would three days be long enough to steal some stout shoes, and to earn enough at the *Golden Leopard* to buy a donkey?

'I can see what you're bothered about,' she said. 'But if I can show you in three days' time that you don't need to worry about me holding you back, can we talk about it again? What's your name?'

There was a long pause. 'I'm Mag'rantor,' he said. 'All right, we won't set off until we've talked some more.'

Chapter 12

Things left unsaid

A quiet born of deep concentration filled the room, disturbed within only by the small sounds of pen on paper, a sleeve rustling, chairs creaking, the occasional turn of a page; and without by the distant noise of arrows thudding into the target, a voice calling the shots, the echo of footsteps. Numirantoro glanced up from her work. This was her favourite place in Tellgard, the quiet, airy room on the ground floor next to the library. It was in the middle of one of the three ranges grouped about the courtyard, with the colonnade fronting the street on the right side and the various workshops to the left. There were four windows, large but narrow in proportion to their height, with deep wall seats below. In brighter days they would have admitted a flood of light to those who worked within, for although filled with delicate tracery, they were glazed with clear glass; but today the room was lit by lamps. Numirantoro loved its studious atmosphere, the air of dedication, the feeling that those who had worked there over the years had somehow contributed to its invisible patina of learning. She loved being next to the library, with its stored riches of wisdom; she loved the smell of books, of ink and paints, of polished wood and leather cushions; she loved the refuge it gave her from Vorynaas' crassness, from Ghentar's incessant demands, from her father's morose indifference.

The room was kept free for any to use, who did not need the specialist tools or materials which were provided by the various workshops; and Arval often sat in there himself, reading or simply thinking, yet available if any wished to talk or debate with him; but today Numirantoro and Ancrascaro had the room to themselves. The little girl had kept her promise of perfect behaviour as the price of being allowed to come to Tellgard, and was sitting now at a table, looking carefully at a picture before her, and slowly making a list on a loose piece of paper. She will be ahead of her classmates, when the time comes for her to attend Tellgard daily, thought Numirantoro; I hope she will not be teased for it. The child reminded her of herself at that age, with a thirst for knowledge and a cast of mind too studious for her years. But they made a companionable pair, and though Numirantoro had to admit inwardly, if she was honest, that she was only too pleased to have an extra reason for spending time in Tellgard, it was nevertheless true to say that she did genuinely enjoy the child's company and it had been a pleasure for her to see the little girl blossoming under the informal teaching she was able to impart.

For the hundredth time, Numirantoro swiftly checked the view from the windows. From this room she could see all who came and went in Tellgard, while the window tracery obscured her from the view of any outside who might look in. Some time ago, she had seen Arymaldur enter the goldsmith's workshop and he had not yet come out; another instructor was working with the youngsters at the archery butts today. She wondered whether he was making something, or sharing the teaching duties. Recently he had been spending time with the silversmith too. The numbers who could work at one time in those rooms were too small for her to risk joining them, long to though she did: her eyes would betray her within minutes. She wondered whether to suggest to Ancrascaro that they should go down and see Woody, so that they could walk right along that range of buildings. Strangely, she had no qualms about being seen with Ancrascaro, although she had avoided Tellgard while pregnant with Ghentar. She looked down at her work, frowning. She would never forget the despair of knowing that she was carrying the child of a man she hated, while aching for the loss of Geraswic and suffering the torment of her obsession with

Arymaldur. When her pregnancy began to show, she had felt gross and unclean, yet ashamed of this antipathy to the life growing within her. Ghentar was so like his father, she could not help but regard him rather as the pipit must view the alien cuckoo it has unknowingly hatched.

She shifted in her chair, putting down her pen and flexing her hand. Ancrascaro looked round, and seeing that they were still alone, spoke in a careful whisper. 'What letter are you on now?'

'I've gone back to A,' said Numirantoro. 'I think I'll try to do them in order after this, now that I've finished the ones that were already in my head.'

She was working on a project which had suggested itself to her as a result of Ancrascaro's desire to come to Tellgard, and for which she was drawing on her memories of the favourite old word-game they had played in Salfgard. Generations of children in Caradriggan had learnt their letters in Tellgard by turning the battered pages of the 'C is for Cat, D is for Dog' booklets, but she wanted to make something which would do the same job yet at the same time open wider dimensions to those minds agile enough to leap beyond the page, to resonate with the associations conjured up by the words – and the pictures, for she planned to illustrate what she was writing. She had begun by including *Oak: old, older, oldest: outlasting oathtaking, outliving ourselves*, as she had heard it from the smith at midwinter in Ardeth's house, for no-one knew who had thought up that one, it was traditional, handed down from time out of mind. Also on the list was her own effort from the same occasion, the *Kestrel: keen-sighted, knife-footed, kitted out for killing*, which had impressed the company. There were others from Salfgard she thought she might also include, but she could remember nothing for 'A' which really suited, and she'd been turning over various new ideas for it in her head. It would be the first entry in the book, so she wanted it to be right.

Outside in the courtyard, the archery practice was over and the youngsters who had been taking part were chattering as they worked together to carry the targets into the store. The instructor checked the bows as they handed them over, tallied up the arrows to make sure all were accounted for, and then unlocked the armoury to replace them. Within a moment he emerged and turned to lock the door again behind him, but a hail from across the exercise ground made him look over his shoulder to see Arymaldur walking towards him, obviously gesturing for him to leave the door unlocked. They met and exchanged a few words, then Arymaldur took the key from him and went into the armoury. After a few minutes he came out again: Numirantoro's throat tightened with suppressed excitement as she watched him. She saw that he had brought several swords out of the armoury, which he placed in the wall-rack behind him. Then he selected one for himself and turned to stand, balanced lightly on widely-planted feet, hands clasped before him, his back to the far wall, directly facing the windows of the room where Numirantoro watched.

After a few moments, Arymaldur was joined by about half a dozen men, mostly youngsters in their late teens by the look of them, but to Numirantoro's surprise Forgard was there too, and among the younger men was one who by his build and colouring looked as though he could be an Outlander. It was a practice, then; the swords would be foils. They each took one from the rack, and then all smeared the points and edges with chalk from a basin that stood beside the wall. All of them were dressed like Arymaldur, in quite closely-fitting clothes of plain dark grey cloth without adornment of any kind. Numirantoro knew this was part of the new technique of practice that Arymaldur had introduced, which she had heard ridiculed by Thaltor in conversation with Vorynaas. Thaltor was indeed a dazzling swordsman, even she could see and appreciate his skill; but his whole philosophy was aggression. Attack, attack, he would urge his pupils, keep going forward. But while this was well enough for someone of his strength and ability, many were not skilled enough to bring off the feats he could perform, and some youngsters had been hurt. Arymaldur on the other hand emphasised defence. He advised his opponents to watch each other's eyes, to parry the strokes, to keep their balance, conserve their energies, wear down their adversary until his concentration lapsed, then pick the right moment to pierce his guard. To enable a tally to be kept of progress, he had his classes wear dark clothes and their foils rubbed with chalk, so that hits would show up immediately.

Now Numirantoro saw him pair up with one of the youngsters, and go through the short ritual he always observed. First he stood, absolutely still although poised on the point of movement, the sword held before him, his expression withdrawn, as if rapt in some inward vision; then his head came up, his eyes swept the scene before him, suddenly alert: his whole face lit up with life, his body tautened with controlled energy, and he began to move with a balanced, elegant economy of effort which only served to heighten the impression of a power within, kept in check until its moment came. Suddenly Numirantoro realised that he had already taken on two or three opponents while she watched, fascinated, and she wondered with a quick flurry of panic whether Ancrascaro had noticed. Earlier, she had given the little girl an outline sketch in ink of a scene to go with the entry in her list under O, and had asked her to make a list of all the things in the picture she could see which also began with that letter, and another list of things that could be included in the final illustration. She turned now to Ancrascaro and asked her how many she had come up with.

'Well, there's the oak, of course,' said the child, 'and I can see oxen in the field beyond it, and if I'm allowed to include things like this, then there's the open door of the house, and the old man standing in the doorway, and that could be an oil-lamp he's holding. The crop in that second field is oats, and there are onions in the garden of the cottage. Then behind the garden, I can see a small orchard. But I can't think of many more things that would look right in the picture. You could have an oast-house in the farmyard, or put a stream in so as to have an otter; but I think that would be too much. If you wanted, though, you could add some oxeye daisies in the field with the oats in it, and I think it would be nice if an owl sat in the oak tree.'

'I like the owl,' said Numirantoro. 'We'll definitely have him. What do you think of this for A? *Apple-tree, ancestor of all our autumns*?'

'Yes, that's good,' said Ancrascaro, 'it makes you think about more than just apples.' She hesitated a moment as if considering, glancing out of the window. 'I thought you might want A to stand for Arymaldur.'

Numirantoro had to decide in a split-second how to deal with this, and settled on a matter-of-fact approach, saving for later her worries about what the child might have heard, seen or suspected. 'Well, I don't think so,' she said as casually as she could, 'because it's someone's name, and none of the other pages will have names on them.'

'So you wouldn't even include the As-Geg'rastigan then?' asked Ancrascaro.

Numirantoro relaxed slightly, although her smile was rather sad. 'I'd love to, *is-gerasto*,' she said, 'but who would have the skill to make a picture of the Starborn?'

Ancrascaro swung her legs as she sat on her high chair at the table, sucking the end of her pen. 'Numirantoro, can I ask you something?'

Wondering with dread what might be coming next, Numirantoro dug her nails into her palms under the table as she nodded agreement. Ancrascaro paused for a moment or two, then she looked straight into Numirantoro's eyes. 'Is Lord Arymaldur one of the As-Geg'rastigan?' she said.

The two of them looked at each other for what felt like an eternity to Numirantoro, who was completely taken aback by the question and at a loss to know how she should answer. Eventually, she pulled herself together and spoke. 'I think you should ask Arval the Earth-wise about something like that, not myself.'

Just as Ancrascaro was about to answer, a commotion started up outside; they heard ragged shouting and yelling, apparently coming from the street, and then running footsteps and the sounds of scuffling. The child slid down from her chair and ran to climb onto the window-seat in the wall, but Numirantoro was before her, flying to the window to see what was happening. Arymaldur's head snapped round towards the colonnade and he stood poised for an instant, his right arm outstretched with the sword, his left hand held high in counter-balance. Then things happened very quickly. Calling out instructions, he threw the armoury keys to Forgard, who gathered up the foils and equipment from the youngsters and chivvied them off towards the tower door in the corner. They moved off too slowly for Forgard, who shouted at them to hurry as he tipped everything into the armoury and re-locked the door. But Arymaldur had not hesitated: foil in hand he ran across the exercise-ground, up the steps, into the colonnade and disappeared from Numirantoro's view. He moved so lightly, so swiftly, his dark hair blowing back from his face, that to Numirantoro it seemed he was gone before she had time to catch her breath. Now Forgard too was running, doors were slamming, she heard footsteps within the corridors of the house and saw people hurrying out of the workshops to the left, shouting questions as they hurried after Forgard.

Numirantoro and Ancrascaro looked at each other, wide-eyed; the little girl was pale with fright and Numirantoro picked her up and cuddled her for reassurance. She rocked her gently, as much to calm herself as the child, who pressed her face into Numirantoro's shoulder. Some kind of affray must be happening, for the noises from the street had grown louder and uglier.

'Is it a fight?' whispered Ancrascaro.

'That's what it sounds like,' said Numirantoro, 'but don't be frightened, little daughter, no-one will come in here.' But her heart was in her mouth: whatever was happening, Arymaldur had run to meet it bare-headed, with only a foil in his hand; he was so lean and spare, so unprotected in his simple dark fencing clothes, how could she bear it if he was hurt? Suddenly they heard a great voice rise above all the others, a voice that rang out clear and fearless. Numirantoro knew immediately that this was Arymaldur, though she had never heard him cry out to men like this before: there could be no mistaking the authority of command, the dignity of reason, in its tones, even though she could not make out the words. Gradually the sounds of struggle died down and after a few moments most of those who had run out from the workshops returned; Numirantoro saw her old friend Woody cross the courtyard, deep in discussion with the master-goldsmith and several others. Then after a long pause, Arymaldur returned, accompanied by Arval and others from Tellgard, and with them was a group of about twenty people, both men and women, some stumbling and limping, some with bloodied heads, who stared about them and seemed ill at ease. Forgard was there too, but when the others made as if to enter by the door that led to the main hall, he left the group. Arymaldur had handed him his foil and Forgard now unlocked the armoury once more, eventually emerging after a few moments. He must be tidying up all the gear that was thrown in there in haste before all this started, thought Numirantoro.

She sat down under the window, with Ancrascaro on her knee, breathing a little easier now all seemed over. After a short time, the door opened and Forgard entered the room, looking concerned but smiling with relief when he saw the two of them together.

'There you are!' he said, taking his niece from Numirantoro and swinging her into his arms. 'You weren't frightened were you, *is-gerasto*?'

'No, Numirantoro was with me and we stayed in here,' said Ancrascaro, 'and anyway, Lord Arymaldur spoke to the people, didn't he?'

'That's right,' said Forgard. 'Now, are you ready to go? Arval has sent me to you,' he added, looking rather pointedly at Numirantoro, 'and has asked me to take Ancrascaro home, and to escort you also to your house, Lady Numirantoro. I will wait for you in the gate-lodge, if you have work to put away.'

For a few moments Ancrascaro helped Numirantoro to sort out which papers were to be taken home with them, and which could stay on the shelf in Tellgard; they tied up the separate bundles of pens and charcoal and made sure all the inks were securely capped. Just as they were about to leave the room, Ancrascaro stopped and looked up at Numirantoro.

'I have made my mind up about Lord Arymaldur,' she said.

First signs

By evening, the whole city was buzzing with talk: rumour and counter-rumour being hotly discussed and disputed in homes, on the streets, wherever men gathered, be it in market or inn. But nowhere in Caradriggan were there any meetings with such far-reaching consequences as those that took place in Valafoss' house, and later in Tellgard. Valafoss lived in one of the older parts of the city, in a house that was becoming rather too small now that two boisterous children formed part of the household. However at the end of its narrow rear garden there was a little building which no doubt in sunnier days had been used by previous occupants as a summer-house. This Valafoss had converted for his own private use, with three very small rooms within. There was a privy at the back with a separate entrance, a tiny galley fitted with store cupboards and a wine rack, a charcoal burner and a water supply, should he require food to be freshly prepared and served; and a sort of snug where he met his cronies if the talk was to be completely confidential. He sat there now with Vorynaas, discussing the day's events. Suddenly the door burst open and Thaltor came in, slamming it behind him.

'I was out on exercise with Valestron and a few friends. What happened?'

'There's been an interesting little skirmish involving your friend Arymaldur,' said Vorynaas, grinning as Thaltor's brows immediately drew down blackly at the name. 'Apparently a whole gang of disaffected idlers were milling around, claiming to be starving and homeless, desperate for work; should have taken the offer of employment down at the Cottan na'Salf, shouldn't they? Anyway, some of them took umbrage at the sight of Gwentarans with full bellies working in the horse-market, insults were exchanged, tempers rose and then a few fists started to fly. Before anyone had time to think, a regular brawl broke out, more men joining in without knowing quite what they were fighting about, and the whole lot of them surged down towards Tellgard. Where, it seems, the wonderful Arymaldur managed to calm everything down more or less single-handed.'

Thaltor snorted with derision. 'Anyone hurt?' he asked.

'A few cuts and bruises, nothing too bad,' said Vorynaas. 'One or two sore heads and a black eye here and there were the worst of it, I think, except for a youngster who got pushed over and broke his arm, and a fellow who was kicked when a mule got loose. He might have a couple of cracked ribs. Walking wounded, anyway.'

'And it couldn't have happened in a better place, could it?' added Valafoss, smirking. 'Because now they're all snugged up in Tellgard being looked after by Arval's devoted band of wet-nurses.'

Vorynaas put his finger-tips together as he leaned his elbows on the table between them, looking up into the far corner of the room with a judicious air. 'Mm, well, that depends on how you look at it,' he said. 'You know, even that old bore Arval surely can't be expecting to live too much longer. I wouldn't be at all surprised if he wasn't hoping that Arymaldur would be just the man to take over from him, eventually. Such a shame,' he went on in heavily loaded tones, 'that he should spoil his chances of that by rushing out of Tellgard this afternoon waving a drawn sword about.'

Much though he hated and envied Arymaldur, in his heart of hearts Thaltor acknowledged a fine swordsman when he saw one. Now he shook his head dismissively. 'No, he wouldn't do that. He'd have been in a class, it would only be a foil. They're blunted on both edges and at the point, you couldn't chop nettles down with them.'

Vorynaas laughed in his most patronising manner. 'You know, Thaltor,' he said, 'your biggest problem is a complete lack of imagination. You don't make any allowances for the power of suggestion! Now, Arymaldur's an impressive man, in an odd sort of way: there's no denying he can give you a bit of a shiver when he gets that look in his eye and he's tall, as well; so here's a struggling mass of sweaty peasants, and the first thing they know is some fellow comes leaping on them through the colonnade brandishing a sword. Do you think they stopped to look whether it was real or not? Even more to the point, how many people will believe it wasn't, after the rumour that it was has gone the rounds two or three times? Suppose some of the cuts were sword cuts, wouldn't that be unfortunate? Funny how the ones who ended up injured are all Caradriggans, no? Unarmed, defenceless against the best swordsman in the city? Some people might think it looked rather as though the bold Arymaldur was coming to the assistance of his Gwentaran friends. Bit hasty of him, don't you think, to show his true colours like that?'

Valafoss punched the air with glee. '*Yes*! Trust you to think of it! A word here, a hint there… and no-one will ever know where the story started!'

'Well, it's a means to an end,' said Vorynaas smugly. 'One, discredit Arymaldur. Two, tar him and the Gwentarans with the same brush. Three, pile poor old Arval's plate so high with problems that he won't have time to spare to get in our way – and take it from me, there are going to be big problems, soon. Four, unveil our audacious scheme which will, how fortunately, bring much-needed employment to our own riff-raff and clear the streets of unwanted scroungers from elsewhere. So magnanimous of us! And with Arymaldur and Arval either out of the way or out of action, no one to stop us.'

'What about Arythalt?' asked Valafoss. 'I'd say he could be a bit old-fashioned if he chose. Does he know about all this? What happened, by the way, when you voted me into the business? The old boy was all right about it, was he?'

'Oh yes,' said Vorynaas easily: no point in letting Valafoss know how reluctant Arythalt had been to admit him to their partnership, how he and Thaltor had had to argue with him at length and eventually had simply overridden his mulish opposition to the idea. Best to keep that item of information up his sleeve; who knew, it might come in handy at some later point if Valafoss made himself annoying in some way. He gave Thaltor a quick warning glance. 'But of course he doesn't know about the rest of it: that's between the three of us. Valafoss, do give Thaltor something to drink, it might cheer him up a bit. What's the matter with you, man?'

The black look which Thaltor always wore when Arymaldur's name cropped up had not lifted from his face. 'What do you mean about problems? What problems?'

Valafoss, rummaging about in the next room, returned with a couple of dusty flagons and three goblets. He was just in time to hear the end of what Vorynaas said.

'Just you wait till the price of corn imports goes sky-high, and people go hungry because they can't afford to buy. Then you'll see more than just a street brawl or two.'

Thaltor brooded for a moment or two. 'Have you got agents in Framstock too?' he asked eventually.

'Naturally,' smiled Vorynaas, 'but in this case, they're hardly necessary. My dear Thaltor, you're up and down the border with the patrols, you must know that even nowadays there's still a fair amount of traffic in and out. A well-placed pair of ears at a crossing here and there can pick up all kinds of interesting conversations. I guarantee you, Val'Arad will slap a levy on supplies any day now. In fact, imagine if they were meeting even as we speak here – now there's a thought!'

Forgard meanwhile was hurrying through the streets, carrying Ancrascaro in his arms so as to make faster progress, touching Numirantoro's elbow and guiding her through the crowds, parting them as courteously as he could while keeping up a swift pace. Everywhere they saw people muttering in twos and threes, arguing forcefully, milling about at corners casting sullen looks around them. Eventually they reached Numirantoro's home and she turned to thank Forgard for his escort. To her surprise, he interrupted her, holding her eyes with a direct stare.

'Perhaps we could go through to the courtyard for a moment?' Without waiting for a reply, he led the way and then set his niece down on her feet.

'I apologise for rushing you home before I have had the opportunity to wash or change. May I impose upon you further? Maybe Ancrascaro would fetch me a drink of water from the house.'

The little girl ran off and Numirantoro, registering for the first time that Forgard was sweaty-faced from his exertions and still wearing his fencing clothes, with a cloak hastily thrown over them, began to stammer her regrets at her lack of hospitality. Again, Forgard brushed aside her words.

'No matter, Numirantoro, there's no time: I don't want to be overheard, that's why I suggested the courtyard and sent Ancrascaro for water.' He took a nervy pace across to the corner and back, and then spoke quietly but urgently. 'There is something rotten in this country, something that eats into the heart of our city. The spring sickness that took my little son will be as nothing compared with what gnaws us now from within: today's unrest is merely an early warning. We have allowed this canker to take hold, we have allowed it to grow and spread: but how are we to cut it out? Who can help us now?'

Numirantoro had often felt fearful for her herself when she contemplated the bleakness of the years ahead, but now she knew a sudden surge of new alarm when she heard Forgard's words and saw the worry etched on his face. Then into her mind came the words of Arval, uncomprehended at the time and still mysterious: *I will help you, and stand beside you, Numirantoro. Together we will bring something good out of our present trouble.* She looked up at Forgard.

'Arval will help us, but we cannot expect him to stand alone. We ourselves must help him.'

Forgard was pacing back and forth but as her words registered in his mind his face lightened. Renewed hope grew in his heart. He poured water from the jug which Ancrascaro now carefully carried from the house, and raising it to Numirantoro he spoke as solemnly as a man who pledges himself in strong feast-day wine.

'Lady Numirantoro, your steadfastness puts me to shame. I promise you I will be true to Arval, as I know that you yourself will be.'

Casualties

In Tellgard, Arval was supervising the attention of those who had been hurt in the skirmish. Medical training formed an important part of the work that went on in Tellgard: Arval encouraged as many students as he could to take an interest in at least the basics of medicine and first-aid and there were several specialists among his colleagues. The establishment also maintained a staff of auxiliaries: general orderlies, some of whom also performed other duties; nurses and pharmacists. By tradition the Outlanders were renowned for their knowledge of the medicinal uses of plants and their skill in blending herbal remedies, and several *sigitsaran* were to be found on the medical staff in Tellgard. Most of the superficial injuries had by now been taken care of: cuts and bruises cleaned and dressed, twisted knees and sprained ankles strapped and supported, black eyes bathed and soothed. In spite of what Vorynaas had claimed to his cronies, the injuries were not all to Caradwardans, but in any case all who were hurt were treated alike in Tellgard. Two middle-aged men sat side by side, wincing as the split lip of one and the broken nose of the other received attention. One was a shopkeeper of Caradriggan, who had joined the affray late on as it spread down the street outside his premises; the other was a man from Framstock who, caught up in the crowd as he returned from the Lowanmorad, had tried to calm things down by separating the struggling antagonists. The two of them had ended up punching each other without any clear idea of why, and were now having their wounds dressed by an Outland woman. They had the grace to look sheepish, and when all was done, they thanked her politely and shook each other's hands before they left.

The most serious injury was to the young lad whose arm had been broken. He sat white-faced on a bed, his pain dulled by the draught he had been given but apprehension clear to see in the way his eyes darted this way and that, flickering over his strange surroundings. A man stood beside him, twisting a Gwentaran cap round and round in his hands. He was still dazed by what had happened, by the speed with which things had turned ugly. He'd been trading in the horse-market for years, ever since his marriage to a woman from Caradriggan. His hard work had paid off and now he ran his own business, specializing in supplying mules for travelling merchants. The lad was his brother's son, raised in a *gradstedd* on a southern drove-road in Gwent y'm Aryframan; being handy with animals he had jumped at the chance to come and work in the business, dreaming of making his way in the world as his uncle had done. The day had been like any other, himself indulging in some good-natured banter with a muleteer, the boy polishing up some harness fitments, when with frightening suddenness a mob had spilled around the street corner into the horse-market, some hungry-looking fellow had pointed at him with a wild scream of hate and envy and the whole gang had surged towards them, shouting and brandishing fists. The next thing he remembered was a yell of pain as the boy had been pushed off balance and disappeared under the feet of the crowd. After a period of confusion in which he was vaguely conscious of voices hurling insults and accusations, the turmoil had moved on leaving him battered but otherwise unharmed and his nephew on the ground, his arm dangling uselessly.

Arval and Arymaldur were both helping to tend the lad. The mule-trader shifted his feet a little, catching a breath as he felt his bruises beginning to stiffen up. Arval looked across at him with a quick glance of sympathy and reassurance.

'There's no need to worry about the boy, it's a clean break,' he said. 'You're hurt yourself, you should go through to the treatment room and let them see to those bruises with an arnica salve.'

The man relaxed a little, but made no move to go. He looked round, saw a chair nearby, pulled it over to the bed where his nephew lay and sat down.

'I'm all right,' he said. 'I'll get some salve later, when the boy's been seen to. You've been really kind, all of you, Lord Arval and Lord Arymaldur and all.'

He'd only ever been inside Tellgard for the rites before and felt awkward at the strange surroundings, conscious of his Gwentaran accent, and rather overwhelmed at the personal attention of both Arval and Arymaldur. Looking down at the floor, he fell silent again. He remembered now that it had been Arymaldur who had been mainly responsible for calming things down, although when he first appeared suddenly through the colonnade some people had screamed in fright when they thought he had a sword. Idiots, he thought angrily. Like many of the common folk of the city, he held Arymaldur in deep reverence: look at him now, he thought, doing all he can to help some unknown young lad; he's not even putting himself forward, it's all "Should we try it this way" and "Would you like me to hold that bandage" and I'll wager he knows more about it than all these others put together: he shamed the rioters into calming down just by speaking to them, a man like that need draw no sword to make his authority tell!

They had nearly finished now; the lad's arm was set and splinted and they had placed it in a sling. He looked a lot easier and even managed a wan smile. Worry gnawed at his uncle again. It was his right arm! Suppose it didn't mend properly? He might not be able to work like a man should, what would his brother say? Almost as if he heard the thoughts spoken aloud, Arymaldur now turned to him. The man felt a slight shock as their eyes met, a strange feeling as if the two of them were alone, removed from the everyday world even though all around them stayed as it had been.

'The arm will mend, you need not distress yourself on the boy's account,' Arymaldur said; and then to the lad, 'You are right-handed, yes?'

'Yes sir, I am,' said the boy, suddenly also beginning to worry as his pain and fear subsided. 'Oh sir, it's my right arm! Will I be able, I mean, how long will it…' he calmed down as Arymaldur held his eyes.

'Your right arm will be as good as it ever was, if you are careful to exercise it correctly once the break has healed and the wrapping is removed,' said Arymaldur, 'but a man has two arms and two hands. You should always try to use both equally, even if you naturally favour one. Look on this time of injury as an opportunity to increase the skill of your left hand, and the strength of your left arm. See how the muscles of your left arm are undeveloped compared with the right?' He turned to include the lad's uncle in his words. 'Come over to Tellgard again tomorrow, both of you, and I will have one of my colleagues prepare a salve for you, and show the young man here a set of exercises to practise. Now, is there anything you would like to ask? Do you trust my reassurance about the arm?'

The lad slid onto his feet, and his uncle put an arm around his shoulders. Squaring his own, he looked into Arymaldur's face.

'My lord, I believe everything you say, because I see that you would never speak anything but the truth.' He stopped, embarrassed, but Arymaldur smiled.

'Well then, the Starborn keep you.'

The two of them backed away awkwardly, mumbling thanks, the man making an unconscious gesture of almost courtly obeisance with the cap he still held in his hands; but the boy was overwhelmed with a mix of emotions he had never felt before: something proud and fierce was born in him, an intense aspiration to some high, burning ideal which he could never have put into words, a yearning for something unknown, apart, which lay tantalizingly just beyond his reach. It was all too much for him, on top of his fright and hurt. As he reached the familiar surroundings of his uncle's house, he dissolved into unexpected and helpless tears. His aunt fussed over him, appealing mutely to her baffled husband, but though eventually the lad calmed down, he could not bring himself to utter the words that possessed his mind: *Surely, Arymaldur is a lord of the As-Geg'rastigan.*

Words of hope

In the quiet hours of the night, Arval and Arymaldur spoke together in the tower of Tellgard. Arval was overwhelmed by anger and shame for what had happened in the city that day, and for all his wisdom could not help pleading with Arymaldur to intervene, to show his power, reveal himself for what he was.

'You know I may not do that,' said Arymaldur, 'but remember that I renewed the pledge of the Starborn with you. While I am here, we will stand together. Have I not spoken for you in Tell'Ethronad and endorsed your authority? You will always have that support; and I tell you again, you are not alone. There are others in Caradward who have recognized me for what I am. They will remember me and take your part.'

Arval sat silent. Men called him Tell-Ur, the Earth-wise, and his wisdom was indeed deep and long-gathered; and he had secrets and sorrows known to himself alone. But he was old, and now he felt weak and afraid. In his mind he heard again what Arymaldur had said to him when he renewed the pledge: *Beware of what may follow, if you drive the As-Geg'rastigan away again.* There was only one conclusion to draw from that: whatever it was that had happened so long ago, men had caused it, and were in danger if they repeated their error. Arval's intellect, as sharp and enquiring as it had ever been, told him he should seize this chance to ask Arymaldur what had happened. Knowledge was power; if he had that knowledge, maybe he would be able to use it to bring men to their senses in time. But his heart quailed when he thought of putting the question. 'Something bad happened', people said; they called it 'the bad time' or 'the bad thing', as if it was some petty misdemeanour in a children's tale; and yet their eyes slid sideways as they spoke, indeed they avoided all mention of such things where they could. Arval sensed some ancient shame, an age-old reluctance to face a truth too unpalatable for men to live with its memory. What could it be? He shrank from the thought of hearing that truth from Arymaldur. Inwardly, he fought for the strength of purpose to put the question he knew he should ask, but his resolve failed at the last. Instead his dark eyes widened in sudden fear as he looked up.

'While you are here… My lord, do you mean you intend to leave us? We will be lost, without hope, if you leave us!'

'Arval, I have told you before: among men, the As-Geg'rastigan must play whatever part is put upon them by the Earthborn. My time draws to its close.'

Arval inclined his head in bitter acknowledgement, battling a wave of despair that threatened to engulf him. His hand clenched, hidden in a fold of his robes. Fool, to have lost his chance! The moment had passed, he could never ask now. He looked up at Arymaldur: austere, beautiful, other-worldly. It seemed as if this lord of the Starborn was somehow already more remote, removed from him, even though the air of the room still tingled with the life of his presence. Arymaldur's face softened in a slight smile, though the sorrow and pity he had felt as he saw Arval fall a prey to weakness still shadowed his eyes. He spoke gently.

'There is always hope, if men know where to find it. Know that I will leave something of myself with you when I go; but also I shall take something away. Let that which is left seek for that which is taken. When the two are united, hope shall return. Now, the hour is late and the day has been long and wearying. Let us go to our rest.'

CHAPTER 13

Refugees

'Well, you're the expert. I'm quite happy to be guided by your judgement. Any of these three look fine to me. Perhaps you'd decide for me, once you've got them put into training.'

Carstann straightened up from squatting to look closely at the litter of pups, replacing the young dog he had been examining beside its mother, and turned to Ardeth who stood by. 'Is that all right with you? How long will it be before you know?'

The two men began to stroll across towards the hall door at Salfgard. Carstann was spending a few days with Ardeth and Fosseiro, having made the journey up the valley from Framstock to attend to some trade in the village. He wanted a dog that could be trained to guard his goods caravan at night when he travelled into Caradward. With tension high between the two countries and increased numbers of displaced and desperate men on the roads, being a merchant was a hazardous business these days. Some had gone so far as to hire armed guards to escort their wagons, but Carstann was reluctant to do that. Of course he and his employees carried weapons themselves, the times being what they were, but he had mixed feelings about hired swords. He felt it gave out an ambiguous message, it was something extra to worry about and, always a consideration with a canny operator like Carstann, it was an additional expense – something he avoided whenever possible. But a dog, if he chose the right one, could be trained to know the difference between friend and foe, to be docile with strangers if so bidden, and to give the alarm instantly if it sensed anything amiss, especially at night: and so he had sent a message to Ardeth to let him know he was in the market for a suitable pup.

'Give it until the autumn,' Ardeth was saying now, 'say, another three, four months. We're beginning to wean them already and I'll put them into basic training when they're about ten weeks; after that I'll have them started with work around the farm. Once they're reliable around people and animals and responding well to a handler, you'll need to come back and take the job on yourself, so that whichever one is to go with you bonds with you and not me or someone from the farm. Or if you don't want to come up this far, send a message and I'll drop down to Framstock myself. I'm often down at the old place to see Geraswic.'

He glanced up at the sky and paused in his leisurely progress towards the house. 'It's about an hour yet before we eat. Shall we walk up the fields a way, and I'll show you a few tricks of the trade?' He indicated a dog lying in the shade of an outbuilding. 'There's the fellow who sired your pup. I trained him, and his father before him – in fact it's a strain my old man developed years back, down in Framstock. Come on, we'll give him a run out before it gets too hot.'

Carstann agreed readily, and Ardeth grinned with pleasure. He whistled up the dog and they walked up the sloping pastures on the east side of the farm. Within a short time Carstann was sitting on an outcrop of rock beside the top hedge, warm in the sun, watching with admiration as Ardeth put the dog through its paces. The animal completed a manoeuvre and raced back to Ardeth, who stooped to pet and praise it. Carstann's eyes lifted idly over his two companions; he noted, without really seeing, a movement down in the valley where the side-road ran. Suddenly something caught his attention and his gaze sharpened; Ardeth was still wrestling playfully with the panting dog, and he pulled at his sleeve to distract him.

'Look down there. Are they all right, do you think? I can't make out what's slung over the donkey, but I'm sure the fellow on foot is staggering about, and he's carrying a child on his back. Maybe we should go and see if they need help.'

'Now, now, calm down, there's a good lad. Sssh, now, down, stay!' Ardeth wanted to show Carstann how the dog would go from over-excitement to complete obedience at his word, and hadn't really heard what he said; but as the dog lay down, he looked up. 'Sorry, what was that?'

'Down there, look, on the valley road. I think they're in trouble; yes, look, he's just fallen down!'

Pointing with his hand, Carstann began to get up from his seat on the boulder, but he stared in surprise as the colour drained from Ardeth's face. He was not to know that twice already in Ardeth's life, tidings of sadness beyond solace had come to him down that road. Ardeth stood in the summer pasture, seeing again in his mind's eye first Merenald, bringing him the news of Salfronardo's death; and then Geraswic, returning alone from Caradriggan, in despair at the loss of Numirantoro. Foreboding clutched at Ardeth's heart: what new sorrow might now be approaching? As he watched for a moment, the man whom Carstann had seen stagger and fall rose wearily to his feet again and stood leaning against the donkey; then he stooped to a small figure still lying in the road. Trying to lift the burden again to his shoulders, he fell once more. Ardeth made his mind up. Turning to the dog, he raised a finger.

'Home, boy! Home!' he said. 'Fetch Fosseiro!'

The dog streaked off, and the two men hurried down the field, taking the shortest line they could towards the travellers now motionless on the road.

Fosseiro went to the door for the third or fourth time and looked out. Where on earth had those two fellows gone? It was most unlike Ardeth to disappear without putting his head into the house to tell her where he would be working, especially with a meal imminent. Now here she was with good food about to go to waste if he left it much longer to return. She called to one of the farmhands, who told her Ardeth and

Carstann had gone up the fields with a dog. Well, that was something, thought Fosseiro; she knew Ardeth secretly liked showing off with his dogs, but surely he wouldn't keep a visitor from his mid-day meal. Just as she began to go back into the house, she heard frantic barking and turned round, startled, to see Ardeth's dog hurtling towards her across the yard. The animal rushed up to her and pulled at her skirt, ears raised, bright eyes fixed on hers, yelping excitedly, bounding away for a few paces and then hurrying back to her. Fosseiro realised immediately that he wanted her to follow. Oh, what had happened? Surely Ardeth and Carstann could not have met with an accident, or danger of any kind?

She ran back into the house and took her pots and pans off the direct heat, leaving them covered on the hearth, and then dashed back out to join the dog, who was still barking. The commotion had brought one or two curious faces to windows and doors; Fosseiro shouted to one of the farm lads to come with her and set off as fast as she could down the track. A few hundred yards from the last of the outbuildings, they rounded a bend and came face to face with a sorry sight. Carstann, leading a scrawny, mangy-looking donkey burdened with several dirty bundles and an emaciated old man who was tied onto its back, was carrying two more bundles himself. Ardeth had a small boy draped across his shoulders; the child looked about eight years old but was painfully thin, with matted hair and flushed cheeks. Both the boy and the old man appeared to be unconscious. Sweat was beading on Ardeth's face because in addition to the boy, he was supporting most of the weight of a young man who was clinging on to him as if he could scarcely stand, muttering incoherently, his eyes rolling up under drooping lids. Ardeth stopped with relief when he saw his wife, quickly re-organising things. They put the child on the donkey with the old man, Carstann taking more of the baggage himself, while the farm hand and Ardeth took the spent young man between them, carrying him by the shoulders and knees as he sagged, and all of them making better speed. Ardeth managed to impart a few details to Fosseiro as they toiled up the track.

'Carstann spotted them,' he panted, 'coming down the valley road. It's Mag'rantor – remember him? He was with us a while back, must be seven years at least since he left. Comes from way over Staran y'n Forgarad way, the Starborn know what he's doing here, or who the old man and the boy are.' He took a few more paces, getting his breath back. 'But Mag'rantor seems to have been heading for the farm; all we could make sense of before he passed out was some mumbling about Salfgard, and he kept muttering my name, although whether he recognised me is anyone's guess. They're in a bad way, so never mind about us, you see to them first. Carstann and I will help you get them settled and cleaned up and then we'll grab a bite when we can.'

A new beginning

A couple of weeks later, a group of people walked down to Salfgard from the village. It was mid-morning, but they were not dressed in working clothes; their faces were solemn and there was no laughter and little talk among them. As they arrived back on the farm, Mag'rantor wandered off with bowed head towards the outbuildings and Ardeth beckoned the others away.

'Leave him to himself for a while,' he said quietly, 'and let him choose the moment when he wants to talk. Meanwhile, the rest of us have got plenty to do, so let's get to it.'

They dispersed, Ardeth and Fosseiro making for the main house where Ardeth changed back into his jerkin and breeches. As he was pulling on his boots, Fosseiro came into the room and he looked up at her with raised eyebrows.

'Still sleeping, poor little lad,' said Fosseiro. 'He's going to pull through, but I can't make up my mind whether he knows about his granddad or not. It will be better for Mag'rantor to tell him, when the time comes.'

The morning wore on towards noon, and Fosseiro went about her tasks, occasionally checking on Cunoreth who slept on peacefully in the little room that had once been Geraswic's. A regular thump and clatter came steadily from the woodshed where Ardeth was splitting logs with beetle and wedge. She knew why he had retreated in there, into the cool darkness away from the bright summer morning. He was a man who felt things more deeply than people might realise, who only saw the bluff, hearty face he presented to the world; but words did not come easily to him, and it was typical of Ardeth to come back from a funeral and work off by heavy physical labour the angry frustration he felt in the face of death. Fosseiro sighed a little and permitted herself a short rest, gazing out of the window for a moment or two. For herself, she was content so long as Ardeth was happy. Her intuition told her that he was already wondering whether Mag'rantor would stay on, would fill part of the place Geraswic had taken in his heart. Then she thought of the dark tidings about Caradward that Mag'rantor had brought, of which they had heard only a part, as yet, and misgivings stirred in her. She wanted no further sorrows to visit Ardeth of Salfgard.

Next time she checked on Cunoreth, he woke while she was still in the room. His thin arm lay outside the covers, and his hand stroked at the soft wool of the blanket as his eyes wandered over the strange surroundings. He squinted a little at the brightness where sunlight fell on the wall, and licked his dry lips.

'What's your name?' His voice was rusty from illness and lack of use.

Fosseiro came over and sat on the edge of his bed. 'I'm Fosseiro, wife to Ardeth of Salfgard. That's where you are, now. You've not been very well, but you're going to be fine from now on.'

'Are my uncle and granddad in Salfgard, too?' asked the boy.

'Yes, you all arrived here together,' said Fosseiro, settling on a half-truth and hoping the child's questions would turn in another direction.

After a moment, the boy spoke again. 'Why is it so bright in here? You've got no lamp, are there lots of lanterns right outside?' Fosseiro was baffled by this, and Cunoreth gestured to his left. 'There, where all that light is, on the wall.'

'Oh, I see what you mean!' Fosseiro laughed a little. 'That's sunshine, sweetheart! It's nearly noon, and a lovely summer day outside.'

The boy's eyes flew to her face and he tried to raise himself against his pillows. 'The sun is shining? Like in the stories? Can I see it?'

'Listen, Cunoreth. Of course you'll see it, you'll see it most days here. If you're a good boy, and rest today, Ardeth will take you round the farm tomorrow and show you the fields and the river, and all the animals. But you need to take things slowly, you've been ill. Your uncle Mag'rantor only just got you here in time: you were half-starved and then you've had a fever. We need to build you up! Now, I smell today's bread baking. It's nearly ready to come out of the oven. I'm going to go down to the kitchen and bring you some fresh milk, with a little new loaf and some coddled eggs. Won't that be nice? Ah, there, sweetheart, don't cry!' Fosseiro wiped the lad's tears as they sprang from his eyes and trickled onto the pillow. 'There's no need to be sad. Everything will be all right, now.'

She ran downstairs, nearly at the point of tears herself. The poor little mite! It seemed almost worse, to her, to be deprived of the sun than to be starving for lack of food. When the way-worn travellers had first arrived, the old man seemed to rally a little with food and rest, before he began to sink towards death. Fosseiro had seen enough people die to recognise the tell-tale signs and spoke privately to Mag'rantor, thinking it better for him to know the truth rather than cling to false hope, so that he could act as seemed best to him. He had asked for help in moving his father's bed, so that the old man could see as much sky as possible; and then sat by him for hours at a time, talking to him quietly about small matters of daily life on their own farm. Ardeth and Fosseiro knew that this had been a modest holding from which they had been turned as a result of the building of Cottan na'Salf; but every man's home place is highest in his own heart, and

Mag'rantor spoke to his father as if he had been lord of wide estates. It was impossible to know whether the old man realised he was dying in a strange land. At first he had mumbled the occasional response to Mag'rantor, looking out of the window as if he saw his own fields.

'Aye, aye, we must put a hoe along the bean rows, lad,' he would mutter, when Mag'rantor told him the new crops were springing in the summer sun; but as the days went by he became ever more silent.

'The fruit has set well in the orchard this year,' Mag'rantor would say, or 'This year's barley is coming on, look there, dad, you can see it bending in the breeze,' but the old eyes stayed closed, although sometimes he would smile in response. Then on the last day of all, Mag'rantor woke suddenly from a tired doze to find his father watching the sky through the window, all his remaining strength gathered in the intensity of his gaze. It was almost dawn: small clouds in a blue and gold sky were touched with rose as the sunrise came closer. The old man raised his right hand: the gesture was part greeting, part farewell. Glory spilled in a dazzling ray over a high shoulder of the Somllichan Torward and light waked the dewy fields of Salfgard. Mag'rantor never knew whether this was what his father saw, or whether in his mind he was home once more.

'Look there!' the old man cried in a strong voice. 'Sunrise! Mag'rantor, you promised me the sunrise and now I see it, I see the dawn once more! The fields will be warm with life again... the sun... the sun returns!' His hand fell, his eyes closed; he spoke no more and by afternoon he had slipped away.

And now he was buried in the warm earth of Salfgard, leaving the future with all its uncertainties to those who yet lived. That evening Mag'rantor ate with Ardeth and Fosseiro, though he was subdued and had little to say; but afterwards he joined them in the living-hall. Clearing his throat, he began to speak hesitantly.

'You've been so kind to Cunoreth and me, and my father, I'll never be able to pay you back. I was so worried about dad, the journey from Caradriggan was too much for him. I'd never have forgiven myself if he'd died without help by the roadside, although there again, how long he'd have lasted if we'd stayed in the city is anyone's guess. But now, well, thanks to you he died in peace like a man should, and he knew me before he went.'

Mag'rantor bit his lip hard and looked down for a moment or two before he continued. 'And Cunoreth had some solid food today.' He laughed a little, rather shakily. 'He must be tougher than he looks, the little pup! How we made it here with him like he was towards the end, I just don't know. I'd lie wakeful in the nights promising my sister in my heart the lad would be all right, and then I'd promise the boy his mother was watching over him to bring him safe to Ardeth and Fosseiro…' He tailed off again, gritting his teeth.

Fosseiro made a little sympathetic movement towards him. 'Mag'rantor, don't upset yourself about it any more. You kept your word, you've brought the boy to us and he's going to be fine. I've promised that Ardeth will take him round the farm tomorrow, he'll enjoy seeing all the animals. He's still very weak though, he'll probably need carrying – but you can take some time out to show him things, can't you, Ardeth?'

'Of course, of course,' said Ardeth. 'Mag'rantor, I… there's something I wanted to ask you. We don't see youngsters coming from Caradward like we used to, even in your time here, but news comes over the border in travellers' tales and merchants' reports, so we hear bits and pieces of what goes on. And so I just wanted to clear up whether there's anything I should know, about… I'm not sure how to put this.' He ran his hands through his hair in the familiar gesture that left it sticking out at all angles and then gave Mag'rantor a straight look. 'You're not running away from anything, are you?'

Mag'rantor sat back and laughed rather bitterly. 'No, and yes,' he said. 'I've done nothing wrong, and I assure you no-one in Caradward will come chasing after me. I am nothing to those who rule in Caradward now, and if they knew of me, they would be glad to be rid of me. But yes, I'm running from injustice, and unrest, and gathering gloom. I leave behind me the life I should have had: my old hopes for the future are buried there with my mother and sister, lost along with the family fields which should have come to me in time. I bring with me nothing but my strength and my skills. My strength is returning, thanks to you; my skills were largely learnt from you; I see that even the clothes I'm wearing have been provided by you.' He looked down at the plain but well-made garments that had replaced the tattered garb in which he arrived. 'I already owe you debts I can never repay, but if you'll take me on, I will work for my keep and provide for the boy myself. Ardeth of Salfgard, I offer you my service.'

'I am honoured that you would serve me,' said Ardeth. He stood up, facing Mag'rantor. 'Give me your hand.'

Mag'rantor got to his feet and clasped hand in hand with Ardeth, who now spoke again. 'I do not accept your service.'

An exclamation of shock and dismay escaped Mag'rantor, and he took an involuntary step back, but was halted by Ardeth's firm grip. His eyes flew to Ardeth's face, where a smile was beginning to appear.

'Let's have no more talk of service,' said Ardeth, 'but rather of friendship. It means more that you've remembered your foster-years here, and sought me out now when trouble has come to you, even though it meant leaving your own land. Let me rather honour the trust you have shown in me. Until your strength has fully returned, you're welcome here as a guest; after that will be soon enough to arrange things between us so that a place is made at Salfgard for you and the boy.'

Painful memories

Within a couple of months, Ardeth was making steady progress down the main road to Framstock, sitting easily on his mule's back and enjoying watching Carstann's young guard-dog as he sat riding in the little cart or cavorting alongside with the energy of youth. The interruption to the normal routine of Salfgard caused by the arrival of Mag'rantor had meant that Ardeth had missed a meeting of Val'Arad, and now he intended to stay at the old home-place with Geraswic and catch up on the news. He wanted Geraswic to help Carstann put the finishing touches to the dog's training; and also he wanted to explain to Geraswic, face to face, about Mag'rantor and Cunoreth – especially about the boy. The lad was growing like a weed now, thriving on Fosseiro's cooking and the fresh upland air of Framstock, and both he and Mag'rantor had settled in so well that they seemed like natives of the village. As evening approached, Ardeth rattled into the yard of a wayside inn much frequented by the herdsmen and drovers of Gwent y'm Aryframan. Giving the dog the 'watch and guard' signal, he went into the building to make the arrangements for his supper and to explain that he would be pitching a tent beside the picket-line, rather than needing a bed.

Much later, having enjoyed a convivial evening in the *gradstedd* where as usual he had encountered several old acquaintances, he crawled into his little tent and made himself comfortable for the night. The dog was curled in the cart alongside, and the mule cropped the grass quietly, moving around at the length of its tether. A few more pack and riding animals were also picketed there, and cattle and sheep were in the pens; over in the wagon-park lights shone where a party of merchants was getting organised, and the dark shape of the night-watchman showed against his fire. There was a burst of laughter from the wagons, and a clatter as somebody let one of the tail-boards fall; some of the animals moved restlessly and Ardeth's dog sat up and barked. 'Quiet! Friends!' said Ardeth, and the dog obeyed immediately, lying down in the cart once more though remaining alert. This was the dog's first experience of what he was likely to encounter during his life with Carstann, and he was shaping up nicely: Ardeth was pleased, and removing his boots and jacket, he wriggled into his blankets and lay down to sleep, well content with the day.

Yet the hours passed, and Ardeth, who was usually asleep within minutes of his eyes closing, could get no rest. He thought over some of what he'd heard during the evening's talk, tales not unlike Mag'rantor's story: folk from Caradward who had Gwentaran connections being thrown on hard times, turned from their land, laid off from their jobs in favour of Caradwardans in search of work; and many of them now making their way across the border hoping to start anew this side of the Red Mountains. If this sort of talk had reached up-country inns, plenty more rumours must be flying in Framstock, and Ardeth's heart went out to Geraswic. Poor fellow, surely the last thing he would want to hear was constant talk of Caradward. No wonder he had avoided the main roads when he came home, returning alone when he should have had Numirantoro beside him. Ardeth sighed and turned over yet again. He could see Geraswic's homecoming in his mind as if it had happened only yesterday.

He heard again the wheels ring on the hard ground of the yard and again he was running out from the house, Fosseiro not far behind. He should have guessed then, as Geraswic turned his back, trying to warn them of bad news by his stance, and turned again, slowly, unwillingly, as he heard their footsteps falter to a standstill. Fosseiro and he had been lit up with anticipation, craning past Geraswic into the wagon, but their smiles had gradually faded as apprehension took over.

'You haven't used the harness-silver,' Fosseiro had said uncertainly, and then, taking in Geraswic's haggard expression, 'What's the matter? What's happened?'

Geraswic's voice stuck in his throat: no answer came out. Ardeth had been slower to jump to conclusions than his wife. He remembered giving Geraswic what must have been an uncertain, lop-sided grin.

'Come on then, where is she? Where's Numirantoro?' He'd been surprised when Fosseiro squeezed his hand hard, trying to stop him.

Panic had suddenly gripped him and he had grabbed hold of Geraswic roughly. 'Where is she? Say something man, what's gone wrong?' His voice breaking, 'What's happened to her?'

But the worst thing had been the way Geraswic had looked at the two of them, and the words he had used. When he spoke, it had been as if the very words had a bitter taste.

'She's in Caradriggan, already married to Vorynaas. You must take back your gifts and your gold, for I cannot be a son to you now, Ardeth of Salfgard.'

Truly, the journey back to Salfgard had been like a nightmare without end to Geraswic: an evil dream in which all was dark, where effort seemed to bring no forward movement, where horrors seemed lurking ready to seize him when he tried to rest but where waking brought only a return to the black void in his heart. His mind refused to function coherently, to put together any kind of rational thought; he heard only his own voice within him, brokenly repeating Numirantoro's name. Though the noon sun shone down on the road, darkness rose within him like a black tide, and night filled his mind, freezing his senses in the grip of an icy despair. He would not take the main road through Framstock, there were too many there who knew the reason for his journey to Caradriggan. Turning more to the north to follow the direct route, he began to worry about what Ardeth and Fosseiro would say. His return would bring bitter tidings for them, too: they had lavished affection and generosity upon him, and he felt he was throwing it back in their faces, for he would never wed, now. Their grandchildren were lost to them, unborn as their children had been stillborn. His heart wept for them, though not for himself. Nothing can touch me now, he thought: I am invulnerable, for whatever the future holds, it can never bring me hurt worse than the pain I suffer now.

Looking at Geraswic as he sat with him in the old home-place in Salfgard, Ardeth thought he looked ten years older than Mag'rantor, even though he was actually the younger by a few years. He and Fosseiro had done their best with him: eventually she had coaxed the whole sorry story out of him, and Ardeth had refused even to contemplate going back on their agreement.

'You are the son of my heart,' he had insisted to Geraswic. 'Of course I hope that one day you can put this sorrow behind you, but if you will have no-one in Numirantoro's place, still you remain my heir.'

So matters had stood, and Geraswic had resumed his work in Framstock; but there were bitter lines etched on his face, and he had little to say these days, unless it was to Ardeth's mother. The old lady seemed to Ardeth to have taken on a new lease of life by making it her business to comfort Geraswic, and he could see that the two of them took great solace in each other's company.

After staring at the fire for a long time in silence, mulling over the news Ardeth had brought, Geraswic finally spoke.

'So this young woman, this Sigitsiro, you're sure she won't be coming to Salfgard too?'

'No, I've told you,' said Ardeth. 'She only travelled with the others for part of the way. Mag'rantor said she begged to leave Caradriggan with them, even though he wasn't keen, but she got hold of a donkey from somewhere so that the old fellow could ride on that with most of the baggage, and she and Cunoreth took turn about with walking and riding in the barrow that Mag'rantor had made. But eventually, that fell apart once too often, and he couldn't mend it on the road, so they both had to walk: he could carry the boy part of the way, but not Sigitsiro, so when they made it as far as the side road that comes down from the Rossanlow, they had to stop because she couldn't go any further. He begged a few days' work at the *gradstedd* where the roads meet. He says he was at his wits' end to know what to do, because this was exactly what he'd been afraid would happen, if she came with them; but then some fellow said there might be permanent work for her in another inn further up the side road, so he left the boy with his grandfather and took Sigitsiro up on the donkey to find out whether it was true. When they heard that she'd been in service in one of the biggest establishments in Caradriggan, they took her on as a parlour-maid or some such, so Mag'rantor left her there.'

'Right.' Geraswic lapsed into silence again.

Ardeth had thought it best to suppress the more lurid details he had heard about Vorynaas' household affairs and business doings, told to him by Mag'rantor as he in turn had gathered them from Sigitsiro as they travelled. He wanted to spare Geraswic unnecessary distress, but he had had to tell him that Numirantoro and Vorynaas now had a child, the boy Ghentar. He wondered what was going through Geraswic's mind, but hesitated to intrude upon his silence. It was as well that he did not realise he had unwittingly put out the last glimmer of light in the young man's darkness. Geraswic was remembering how he and Numirantoro had sat together beside the fountain in Caradriggan. She had told him then that Vorynaas was childless by his first wife, that this was one of the reasons why he and her father had agreed on the match.

In his mind he heard again the hopeless, dejected tone of her voice, so different from the bright laughter he remembered from the sweet days in Salfgard. 'Maybe,' she had said to him, 'maybe, as he only wants me for the son he expects me to bear, he won't be willing to wait too long. If I disappoint him in this, maybe he'll put me aside.' A tiny seed of hope had taken hold in Geraswic then, for he had refused to imagine Vorynaas as the father of Numirantoro's children; now he knew the seed was blind and would never flower. But then, against his will, memory brought something else to him: the look on Numirantoro's face, the sound of her voice, as she watched Arymaldur walk up the street towards them. A shadow, a strange presentiment of darkness to come fell on Geraswic. Numirantoro, you and I are both lost, his heart told him.

A contentious vote

Next morning, Ardeth took the dog over to Carstann's house. Shortly after he arrived, they heard voices in the hall and the door opened to reveal Inenar and Ardeleth, two of the more senior members of Val'Arad and men whose opinions in council Ardeth had always respected. Good, he thought, now I'll get up to date on the meeting

I missed, and in more detail than I could prise out of Geraswic last night. They were settling with their wine, when Carstann stood up with an exclamation.

'I've something new for you to try,' he said, hurrying from the room and returning after a moment or two with a dish containing small, cream-coloured confections.

'Almond biscuits from Caradriggan?' said Inenar, obviously surprised – this was nothing new to any of them.

'They look a bit like that, don't they?' said Carstann with a chuckle. 'Go on, have one – you'll find they're something quite different.'

Intrigued, they all helped themselves and Ardeth laughed as the expression on each face changed. What looked like biscuits were in fact more like very small cakes; they did have a hint of almond about them, but were mostly flavoured with lemon, a bright, tangy taste that burst on the tongue as the cakes, with their unexpectedly soft texture, dissolved in the mouth.

'These are good!' said Ardeth, reaching for another. 'Come on, Carstann, tell us where you got them. I hope you haven't got a monopoly on the supply!'

'I only wish I had,' laughed Carstann. 'No, apparently they're an Outland speciality. My son set up a contact for me: you know he married a girl from Staran y'n Forgarad and he runs a tannery in the city now. You'll remember from your time there, Ardeth, that there's a thriving Outland community in those parts, and that's where I first came across these little lemon-flavoured bites. They're expensive, even in Caradward, on account of the lemon trees only growing in the far south.'

'Best enjoy these while we can, then,' said Inenar, 'because from what we hear, lemons might not flourish for too much longer even in the south, the way things seem to be going in Caradward. Unless they can get them to grow in these, what do they call them, these seed-house places they've been setting up.'

Ardeleth shook his head with a worried expression. 'Even if they do, they'll not be for sale or trade now we've put the corn price up so high. I have a bad feeling about that, I know it was a majority vote in the council, but I still think it was a mistake.' Noticing the look on Ardeth's face, he added, 'You weren't there – it was passed at the last Val'Arad meeting, the one you couldn't come to.'

'What good will that do?' said Ardeth, all the laughter gone from his voice. 'It will only make things worse for ordinary people in Caradward, and then there'll be more trouble of the kind that's already brought Mag'rantor to me. He tells me any man with connections to Gwent y'm Aryframan keeps his head down these days.' He brooded for a moment or two. 'I wouldn't have voted for it.' The others exchanged glances, but said nothing while Ardeth was still with them.

'Obviously Geraswic's not mentioned it to him, then,' said Inenar after Ardeth had gone.

'No,' said Ardeleth, 'and he was one of the keenest supporters of the motion. Geraswic's changed a lot. It's not so very long since the lad was shocked when old Gradanar was all up in arms about the border patrols – remember that?'

'Yes, I went back home with them that night,' said Carstann, 'and he was very subdued. But I know what did it this time: it was when I reported what I'd seen and heard in Caradriggan, when I was on that flying visit a few weeks ago, about them taking on cheap labour for this new feast-hall they're building.'

'Well, that's not surprising, is it? The developer, Vorynaas is it, he's Ardeth's marriage-brother or something. No love lost there, by all accounts,' said Inenar.

'No, he's married to Ardeth's niece,' Carstann corrected him, 'but you're right, she's the girl Geraswic wanted to wed. That's probably what prompted his support, although to be fair, there were plenty of others shouting for the price rise, too.'

Ardeleth sighed. 'I know, and I hope we don't have cause to regret it. People vote for such muddled reasons. You need look no further than Geraswic, poor fellow. It's not that I don't sympathise with him and although he's never said anything himself, I believe there's more to the story than a thwarted love-affair...'

'By the Starborn, you're right!' interrupted Carstann. 'Ardeth got an eye-opener from what Mag'rantor had to tell him about Vorynaas: a very nasty piece of work, take it from me!'

'Well, that's as may be, but my point is,' continued Ardeleth patiently, 'that it's not good to let private matters, or personal problems of any kind, cloud one's thinking, especially in matters that will affect everyone. *Have a warm heart in the hall, but keep a cool head for the council*: yes, I know it's a proverb that's been trotted out a hundred times before, but that doesn't make it any less true, or less worth bearing in mind. The thing that worries me is what playing tit-for-tat with Caradward, because that's all it is, will lead to. You've pointed out yourself, Carstann, many a time, how careful we should be not to damage relations further in view of all the connections between the two countries. Look at your own family, for one.'

'I know. If I'm honest, I've been more bothered than I've admitted about my son and his family. But so far they've had no trouble, and maybe if more of their wealthy men weigh in with developments that will bring employment, like this Vorynaas seems to have done, things will ease. It does seem to me that they've made their own problems in Caradward, so they should find their own solutions. I don't understand why they ever tried to pin blame on us.'

'Isn't it always easier to blame the other fellow? They're looking for a scapegoat, that's the reason,' said Inenar. 'But Ardeleth, you said yourself when the border checks and trade tolls were first levied on us that if we did nothing, more harassment would follow. And now we keep hearing about trouble for Gwentarans inside Caradward. Remember when Ardeth suggested we should prospect for ore in the Red Mountains? I know we've found none so far, but I think we should keep looking. If we had our own metal supplies, we'd be self-sufficient and they could do what they like on the other side of the Somllichan

Ghent, it wouldn't affect us. But meanwhile, if they're short of grain and want to buy corn from us, I don't see why we shouldn't make them pay through the nose for it.'

Ardeleth still looked doubtful. 'I know that's what I said, but punitive prices aren't what I had in mind. And we can't cut ourselves off completely, life isn't that simple. It's just that I can't help, somehow, having a foreboding of worse trouble in store for us. But there, it's no good me, of all people, getting up in Val'Arad with vague talk like that. Everyone wants a reason, when I speak, and no doubt you all think I'm doom-mongering.'

'No, no, we don't,' protested Carstann and Inenar, although they were discomfited by Ardeleth's words. They had both sided with the majority, and voted against him in Val'Arad, and both still felt they had done the right thing; but Ardeleth's reputation for wisdom was well-founded and they had not found it easy to gainsay him. Their conversation turned now to more mundane topics, and the mood of the gathering became merrier; but when they went their separate ways, unease settled on them again.

Trouble flares

When Harvest-home came, Ardeth wanted Geraswic to come up to Salfgard for the feast; apart from any other considerations, he wanted Mag'rantor and Geraswic to get to know each other, and for Geraswic to see at first hand that the newcomer posed no threat to his status. Mag'rantor and Cunoreth were still living on the farm, but the plan was that Mag'rantor would set up for himself as soon as all was ready. He had made friends easily and with their help had begun building his own place on the edge of the village; he was walking out with the smith's grand-daughter and Cunoreth was learning his letters from the Salfgard storyteller with the other youngsters every morning before lending a hand with the farm jobs in the afternoons. Geraswic had promised to be there, so when he failed to make the journey to Salfgard, Ardeth had been annoyed; but he was apprehensive rather than angry when he discovered the reason.

Carstann's efficient mercantile routine had been severely shaken. One day his comfortable old house in Framstock had been thrown into turmoil, and all work had come to a standstill in his well-ordered warehouses, when without warning his son and marriage-daughter, together with their family and as many of their belongings as they could cram into two large wagons, had arrived. It seemed that Carstann's optimism about his son's affairs in Staran y'n Forgarad had been misplaced: faced with demands that he should turn his production over solely to contracts from Rigg'ymvala, for what he considered paltry rates, the man had sent the agents packing and tried to carry on his business as normal; but the campaign of intimidation which followed had eventually driven him to leave the city.

'I feel sorry for Carstann,' said Geraswic, sitting with Ardeth and Fosseiro around the hearth in Salfgard on a windy late autumn evening, 'because to tell you the truth, although his son has had a hard time of it, he's not the most sympathetic of characters. I know it's easy to sit here and say he should have handled things better: after all who knows what demands might have followed, even if he had agreed to the contracts with the garrison; but digging his heels in like he did has bankrupted him – when he decided to sell up and get out, no-one would buy the business. Some Caradwardan will be running it now, of course. Anyway, he's ruined; and they've arrived in Framstock with whatever bits and pieces they could carry away, taking it for granted that Carstann will sort things out. And as you know, it's his marriage-son who's his partner in the trading set-up, he won't welcome dividing the shares three ways. I don't know whether Carstann's other son will be able to help out at all, I'm not sure what size of a farm he has up country towards the Rossanlow.' He fell silent for a moment or two, swirling his ale around in the cup, then he sat up straighter and began to speak again.

'They've five of a family, the ones who've arrived from Caradward,' he said, 'three lads, and two girls. The girls are still just children, but the boys are older; Rossanell is really a man grown, he must be about eighteen. I hope this is all right with you, but I've taken on the two younger lads to help out at Framstock.'

'Whatever you think, Geraswic,' said Ardeth. 'You know I trust your judgement, and if it's taking a weight off Carstann's shoulders too, then so much the better. Why not the eldest son, though?'

Geraswic paused before he answered. 'I don't really take to him,' he said at last. 'I think he could cause trouble. He and his father have already built up a reputation for heavy drinking in the *Salmon Fly*.'

Fosseiro had said very little, but she had listened carefully in her quiet way, and she sensed that Geraswic had not told them all that was on his mind.

'There's a problem, isn't there?' she asked. 'If there's something bothering you, tell us, Geraswic. Don't worry about it on your own, share it with us.'

Geraswic looked aside into the corner of the room for a moment or two. 'Well, the thing is,' he said eventually, 'I'm afraid I may have brought trouble myself.'

Fosseiro and Ardeth exchanged glances as Geraswic rubbed his hands over his face as if he hoped this might help to sort out his thoughts. Then he turned to face them again.

'It's like this. I felt ashamed of the way I've behaved these last years, since I, since, well, since I came back from Caradriggan: I've been a bit short with you and the Starborn know you don't deserve it after all you've done for me. So in a way that was one of the reasons I wanted to help Carstann out: I thought it was the sort of thing you would have done, if you'd been down in Framstock. But before then, while you were busy up here with Mag'rantor and his folk, I voted in Val'Arad to put up the corn price. In fact, to be honest, I was one of the main supporters of the motion, but I wish now I had spoken against it. It was bound to cause unrest in Caradward and sure enough, after harvest, when the wagons came up to collect the grain from Morgwentan's land at Framstock, there was an armed escort with them "to prevent any unlawful levy being taken", as if there would be any question of that, when it's his own land and his own corn! But naturally, this caused bad feeling in the town, and as ill luck would have it, Valestron was in charge of the escort. As soon as I found that out, I kept well out of the way, but you won't be surprised to hear that he spent plenty of time throwing his weight around in the *Fly*, where he ran up against Rossanell, who's also inclined to shoot his mouth off when he's had one too many. I heard later that one evening they nearly came to blows after he told Valestron it would serve the Caradwardans right if we turned on them like they've turned on us, and how would he like it if Rossanell and his father took over Morgwentan's inns the way their tannery was taken from them – all complete rubbish, of course, but it started a whole chain of rumours flying, each wilder than the last; and the upshot of it all was that when the wagons set off back for Caradriggan, half the town was hanging about cat-calling and jeering at the escort. And that's when the worst thing happened.'

Geraswic's brows drew down and he glared angrily in front of him, re-living the scene. After a moment, he drew a deep breath and carried on.

'It was early afternoon, and they were going down the street outside the house. I was inside with the old lady, and when I heard them coming I decided to stay put. Then I noticed through the window that Gillis, the younger of the two I've taken on, had come through from the garden and was at the gate, gawping with the rest of them. I'd told him to get on with clearing out the border under the damson tree; I just wish the fool boy had had the sense to do what he was told! Anyway, I slipped out to yank him in, and the whole thing happened in an instant. Valestron let his horse swing round, deliberately you may be sure, and Gillis panicked and fell. Next thing, from nowhere, Rossanell appeared out of the crowd, grabbed hold of his brother, and started yelling at Valestron.' Geraswic paused and sighed, and then continued.

'No doubt he'd been in the *Fly* again. Valestron walked his horse slowly right up to him until the idiot was pressed against the wall, rolling his eyes in fright, so I got hold of Rossanell by the front of his tunic and heaved him out of the way as well, into the garden beside Gillis. And then Valestron, may he rot in the Waste, said to me in front of the whole crowd that was standing there, "Ah, Geraswic! My word, that was very direct. But I expect you get plenty of practice here in sorting out street brawls. Let's face it, you'd have been completely out of your depth in Caradriggan."'

Geraswic clenched his fists till the knuckles whitened. 'I wanted to kill him, that's the truth. I was so angry I can't remember exactly what I did say, but I left him in no doubt what I thought about Caradwardans in general, and him in particular, and topped it all off by telling him I'd voted for the price rise on grain and I hoped he'd be reduced to eating acorn flour and that his stomach would shrivel on it. Then I noticed the look on his face, almost as if he was pleased by what I'd said: he was half sneering, half gloating. That brought me to my senses, but it was too late then. He took a long look at the house and said, "So the leavings of Caradward are being sheltered in Ardeth's house? I can't say I'm surprised. And how interesting to hear the way his *heir and right-hand man* thinks." Well, I couldn't have that. I shouted up at him, "None of this has anything to do with Ardeth! He knew nothing about it, he was in Salfgard when the vote was taken!" But the slimy, misbegotten little toad-spawn just sat there smirking, and then he gave an order and they all got under way again, off down the street.'

After a moment or two of silence, Geraswic looked up at Ardeth. 'I'm really sorry I got you dragged into it.'

Ardeth reached across and gave his arm a little shake. 'Don't give it a second thought. Who could know what it is that eats at Valestron? He always was the bad apple in the barrel, even as a young lad. You've done what you thought was the right thing, it's not your fault if the Caradwardans are spoiling for trouble.'

But later, he tossed and turned, wakeful in the night. 'Shall I warm some milk for you?' whispered Fosseiro.

'No, no, I'm all right,' Ardeth whispered back. He put his arms around her. 'I'm sorry to keep you awake. I know it's a waste of time, wishing for what you can't have, but I can't help it. I wish my sister had never married into Caradward.' Then he dropped his head into the curve of Fosseiro's shoulder and when he spoke again his voice was muffled. 'It strikes me as all too likely that it's in Caradriggan they'll soon be needing armed guards, rather than in Framstock.'

CHAPTER 14

Disappearance explained

As she walked back along the upstairs gallery from the nursery to her own rooms, Numirantoro wondered which of the servants she could trust enough to talk to. She considered each in turn, mentally running her eyes down the list. Well, none of those brought with him from his own house by Vorynaas, for a start. That ruled out quite a few, and then there were others who were either unlikely to know what she wanted to ask, or who were too indiscreet to be worth risking: Merenald, for example, who was devoted to her father, or Ghentar's nurse, who seemed to have sawdust where her brain should be. The stable lads and the girls who worked in the kitchen were too young to involve, whereas the fellow who had looked after the garden since before Numirantoro could remember was too old: he was trustworthy enough, but she knew instinctively that he would retreat into silence if she approached him. She got on well with the new cook who had arrived with Vorynaas, although being uncertain where the woman's loyalty would lie if she was put to the test, she paused only briefly at this name. The sound of voices and activity from the courtyard below brought her to a window to look down. One of the lads had been set to work the water-pump, while the laundry-mistress was unlocking a door and calling over her shoulder, telling the girls to hurry: two of them were just coming out from the house carrying big baskets of linen. Of course! That's who I'll ask, thought Numirantoro. Plenty of noise and steam to cover the conversation, no risk of Vorynaas coming anywhere near the wash-house and if he did, there's that door in the corner that connects with the little storeroom where I keep my own things for when I work outside.

She waited until later in the morning, and then, having rummaged for a while in the store, opened the door and let herself through into the hot, steamy atmosphere of Tiranuro's domain. Loud bubbling noises came from the large vat where household linen was boiling in one corner, while across another, drapes and sheets were hung dripping into the draining-channel. Tiranuro herself was busy at the pressing-table, occasionally pausing to go over and add some extra vigour to the washing cauldron with the wooden clothes-dolly. She was an elderly woman, but straight-backed, tough and strong from a hard life of heavy work. As Numirantoro came through the door she looked up, pushing a damp strand of grey hair back from her forehead, and returned Numirantoro's smile of greeting. My word, you can see both her parents' good looks in her, but it's her poor mother she gets her easy way from, thought Tiranuro.

'May I talk to you for a few moments, or is this a bad time?' asked Numirantoro.

'It's not for me to say. You're the mistress, you talk to me whenever you want,' said Tiranuro, folding and pressing as she spoke.

Numirantoro came over beside her. 'Ah now, you've known me since I was a little girl, I don't think of myself as the mistress with you. I know you're busy, but I want to ask you something privately – just the two of us.'

Tiranuro added a couple of towels to the pile and then paused in her work, looking at Numirantoro enquiringly.

'Where has Sigitsiro gone? Has something happened to her? Don't worry' – this as the older woman put a hand to her mouth, clearly disconcerted – 'I know what's been going on between her and my husband. Believe me, I really don't care. But I can see from the way some of the other girls look at me that they know something.'

248

Tiranuro sighed and shook her head. 'It's not right,' she said, 'and none of this would have happened if Lady Salfronardo had lived. There's not a day goes by but what I miss her, and that's the truth. But yes, as it happens I can tell you all about it, on account of my daughter working at the *Sword and Stars*. The way I heard it was …' She stopped suddenly as footsteps approached the courtyard door, which was open. In came the boy, carrying a fresh load of wood for the fire, and a girl with an empty wicker basket. Tiranuro loaded her up with clean laundry, barked at the lad to hurry, and indicated with a nod to Numirantoro that she should help fold up a sheet. They matched edge to edge, corner to corner, and added it to the pile, Tiranuro waiting until they were alone again before she continued.

'… and my marriage-son, he works with the storeman at the *Sword*, and he heard that Sigitsiro asked to go with them, although the young man wasn't keen, but with the donkey as well as the barrow he made, he had to agree. Where she got hold of a donkey, who knows, but my daughter says the word is that she went round to the *Golden Leopard* and it wouldn't take her long there to earn enough. Poor lass, she must have been desperate, but at any rate, she's gone now – set off at least with this young fellow, although whether they ever arrived is another matter what with having an old man and a child along with them too.'

When Tiranuro came to the end of her tale, Numirantoro was silent. She walked over and leaned on the window-sill, looking out into the courtyard, while behind her after a pause she heard Tiranuro go back to her methodical pressing and folding. So Sigitsiro had set off for Salfgard! Numirantoro wondered who the refugees were she had joined, but though she plied Tiranuro with questions, the older woman was able to impart very few details. And other questions crowded Numirantoro's mind: how long would it take them to reach Salfgard, if indeed they succeeded in journeying that far; whether Ardeth would take them in; what Sigitsiro would tell them about Vorynaas, Numirantoro and herself; how Geraswic would react if he heard she had a child; whether any news of all this would ever come back to her in Caradriggan. Eventually she turned around.

'Well, that's the last thing I expected,' she said, 'but I'm glad to know. They chose a long hard road; it's a big risk to take it on foot, even with a donkey. Poor Sigitsiro! She deserved better from Vorynaas, and if she ever reaches Salfgard, she'll get it from my uncle Ardeth: he and his wife are kindness itself. May the Starborn keep them all.' With a sad little smile to Tiranuro, she left the wash-house. And may they watch over you as well, poor child; it's a blessing your mother never lived to see this day, thought Tiranuro angrily, brushing away a tear as she vented her feelings by giving the vat a good pounding with the clothes-dolly.

Unbreakable chains

Restlessly, Numirantoro took a turn or two in the garden and then sat down on the seat beside the fountain. A flash of colour caught her eye as she stared sightlessly down at the fountain pool. The bright little fish still darted and swam in and out of the pebbles and water-plants, reflecting the lamplight. Numirantoro looked up at the beautiful silver lantern that overhung the pool. Vorynaas had bought it from Issigitsar, a younger member of Sigitsar Metal-Master's family from Staran y'n Forgarad. Numirantoro had often heard Ardeth speak fondly of his time with the Outlander during his foster-years, and although old Ironsides, as Ardeth had always called him, was dead now, it seemed that the mantle of metal-master had fallen on his younger relative. Rightly so, thought Numirantoro as she admired the delicacy of the filigree-work on the lantern, the light, airy lines of its design. Issigitsar was involved in Vorynaas' big building project in Caradriggan, having been contracted to produce the decorative items in precious metals himself and to oversee the on-site structural metal-work. She had met him on a recent occasion when he and Poenmorcar, the clerk of works, had been invited to eat with Vorynaas in the evening-time.

There had been several other guests, including Thaltor and Valafoss, no avoiding them of course, and the young man Valestron. Vorynaas had made much of him, to Thaltor's obvious displeasure, and Numirantoro had noted that at long last she and Thaltor had one thing at least in common. She had been resigned to passing the evening with the wives in small-talk about children, but Poenmorcar's wife had come to the rescue with a non-stop flow of domestic chatter which she shared with the wife of Valafoss. Clearly she was glad of the opportunity, for Poenmorcar was a rather quiet man who obviously had no talent for conversation except about his work; but it occurred to Numirantoro several times, as the talk went around the table during the meal, that Ardeth would have enjoyed his company and that of Issigitsar. So she had said little herself, and listened with interest to the two men as they discussed the finer points of their crafts. It was clear from what they said that Poenmorcar had been contracted above all for his skill in tunnelling, vaulting and other forms of underground engineering, for it seemed that the new hall was being raised above vast cellars and undercrofts. But just as Numirantoro was wondering what the purpose of all this was, the name of Arymaldur had come into the conversation.

In response to some complimentary remark from Arythalt on the quality of his work, Issigitsar had demurred politely, citing Arymaldur as the master from whom all could learn. His slight Outland accent caused him to soften the sound of the 'd' in the name, Numirantoro noticed even as her heart leapt within her. Issigitsar, apparently oblivious to Thaltor's black glare and the curl of Valestron's lip, went on to speak in glowing terms of a work in progress which he had seen in Tellgard: '…shape and substance in perfect marriage, the very essence of gold and silver captured in a singular purity, in the form of an arrow. The simplicity of genius.' Poenmorcar was nodding agreement in his quiet way, when Thaltor leaned forward with an ugly expression on his face.

'Generous words, Issigitsar, but let us hope Arymaldur keeps this wonderful arrow to himself. We don't want a repeat of that unfortunate business when he set about an unarmed crowd with a sword.'

Numirantoro felt a white flame of fury run through her. So that was where the malicious rumours had started! She spoke quietly, but Thaltor was taken aback by her eyes, wide in a pale face from which the hair lifted away slightly with the force of her anger.

'That is not what happened. He ran out to a riot with no weapon but a blunted practice foil. I know, I was in Tellgard that day. I saw him go out, followed by Forgard and others; and I saw them return with Arval, helping those who had been hurt.'

Thaltor, although inwardly seething, subsided with some kind of conciliatory mumble. But Valestron was staring insolently across the table at Numirantoro.

'You are often in Tellgard, I believe, Lady Numirantoro?' he asked.

'I am honoured to be a friend of Arval the Earth-wise,' said Numirantoro proudly, 'and though he is kind enough to call me colleague, yet I hold myself to be more his pupil.'

Arythalt shifted in his chair; he found any kind of confrontation disagreeable and deplored the uncomfortable atmosphere that had fallen upon the room.

'I can vouch for that,' he said. 'I remember how Arval would converse with my daughter even when she was a small child; my poor wife often teased her for it.'

He directed his wan smile towards Numirantoro, but she and Valestron were still staring at each other. The young man's eyes were fixed on her throat, where the pulse which had begun hammering at the first mention of Arymaldur's name was still visibly beating.

Valestron raised his wine-cup to his lips. 'Indeed,' he said, lifting one eyebrow as he drank, his eyes never shifting their sardonic focus.

Fighting down the little flutter of panic that started within her at these recollections, Numirantoro turned her thought back to the astonishing news she had just heard about Sigitsiro's flight to Salfgard. Perhaps she too could slip away, run back to Ardeth and Fosseiro! Her mind buzzed with schemes. She would have to wait until Vorynaas was away on business, and she would need provisions, clothing that would disguise her identity: maybe she could hide these in Tellgard until she was ready? The best part of the year was ahead: she could time her journey for the summer months, maybe take the direct route and avoid going through Framstock; that way she would encounter fewer other travellers. But little by little, the excitement which had filled her began to ebb away as she realised the impossibility of any such escape. She could handle the two-horse gig, but there was no question of removing that from under the conscientious eye of Merenald. Yet transport of some sort she would need, and it was no good thinking she could hazard the journey alone: she knew she would not be able to deal with any kind of accident or running repairs. She could not ask anyone to risk accompanying her, knowing the price Vorynaas would exact if they were caught. Then there was Ghentar. He would be an extra liability, but could she leave her own son behind? For a moment her imagination played upon the kind of man he might yet make, if she could only bring him to Salfgard. She saw him, bearded and handsome like his father, but smiling and sunny-natured like Ardeth; taller than both of them, strong and healthy, respected throughout the village, taking his share of responsibility around the farm. Ah, how much better such a future would be than whatever fate lay in store for him in Caradriggan!

With that thought, Numirantoro came back to reality. For her, there could be no escape. Invisible though they were, she was fettered three times over in shackles that could not be broken. In the first place, as Arval had reminded her, no man could turn back time: she could not have again what was lost to her now. Then, as Vorynaas had known from the start, she would never be able to slip his clutches. Look at the way he had left her alone with Geraswic, so sure of himself as to be almost contemptuously casual about it. But there was a third bond, stronger than any other. Suddenly she laughed aloud. Had she not sat on this very seat and told her mother that her dearest wish, even if she could have only one, would be to see one of the As-Geg'rastigan;

and what had Salfronardo replied? She had warned her daughter to be mindful of Arval's precept: take care of what you wish for, lest your heart's desire be other than you expect. Who knows the truth of that better now than I, thought Numirantoro. The distant peaks of the Somllichan Asan, touched with the summer sunset; the upland valleys of Gillan nan'Eleth filled with a noonday glow: it was there I hoped to see the Starborn walking again upon the earth, there that I looked for them in vain. Then sad necessity brought me back here, and here in darkling Caradriggan, it is here that I have looked on a lord of the As-Geg'rastigan. And no matter what may befall, I cannot walk away from Arymaldur while he dwells among us.

As she glanced up again at the lantern, her eye was momentarily dazzled by a sudden beam of light which darted through a piece of openwork in the design as the lamp moved slightly. She jumped to her feet. While he dwells among us! But how much longer might that be, who could know how or why the Starborn came and went? A little upsurge of panic flickered again in Numirantoro. The pack was closing in, she had seen the jackals licking their lips in her own father's house; seen the knowing look in Valestron's eye. Why did she torment herself by imagining endless grim and gloomy years? Whether Caradward went down into the dark or not, she had no future: no future with Arymaldur, and certainly none without him. Now she knew why, in her moments of despair, she wished she had never seen Arymaldur. She saw that in the very instant of their meeting, her chance for peace or contentment was lost: what she had once had, or might have had, would never now be enough: from that day forward, she was fated to yearn for the life of the Starborn alone. So would she falter now, when a lord of the Starborn walked the same streets as she, she who in all her years had looked for the As-Geg'rastigan? A sort of fearful excitement gripped her. Forgard called me steadfast, she thought, but that is more true of him: he is ashamed of his country, isolated among his peers, apprehensive for his wife and son, yet he holds stubbornly to the truth as he sees it. She had been afraid when he voiced his horror of darkness to come, but now in place of fear she was aware of a strange sense of anticipation. It came to her that her days in Caradriggan were drawing to a close, time was somehow running out. She walked swiftly back through the courtyard and into the house with the speed of sudden resolve. The sense of time slipping by returned, stronger than before. She must hasten to Tellgard, look on the gold and silver arrow wrought by Arymaldur, finish her own work, before it was too late.

Work in progress

Finding, to her surprise, that neither Arval nor Arymaldur was in Tellgard that afternoon, and being today without the company of Ancrascaro, Numirantoro seized the chance to work with feverish urgency. Her original idea had flowered under her hand, so that what had been intended as one volume had become three. She was now putting the finishing touches not only to the Salfgard-inspired letter-book, but also to two others in similar style: one was simpler, following the style of the old 'a is for apple' lists, but, she hoped, more interesting and unexpected; and the other was also traditional in form, being a sequence of comparisons, but here too there were twists and surprises to stimulate the imagination. All three were illustrated by Numirantoro to match her choice of words, and would be finished to the highest quality in the book bindery; they would be too fine for everyday use, but Arval would keep them for special occasions, to be brought out and looked at by his young charges as a reward for progress.

Numirantoro smiled to herself, imagining Arval turning the pages and reading from them. "E is for Elderberries, F is for Frost". "As silent as standing stones". She looked at the circle of huge grey stones she had depicted, brooding in a massive solitude amidst a landscape that seemed somehow primeval. Where had such an image come from? She had seen nothing like it during her own lifetime and yet she felt she recognised it or remembered it in some way. Arval might be able to throw light on the mystery. Suddenly it occurred to her that she was taking for granted that Arval would still be in Tellgard, instructing the generations to come. On that autumn day when Arval had comforted her sorrow, he had gently deflected her curiosity about his long life and she had never raised the subject again. A shiver ran over Numirantoro, a chill that swept by like a swift breath of cold wind disturbing the surface of a lake. It was unusual for Arval not to be somewhere in Tellgard and as she packed away her work she wondered where he could be. But the absence of Arymaldur meant that she had no hesitation about entering the precious metal workshops before she returned home.

The master silversmith was an old friend and he greeted her warmly. 'Well, here's a stranger! Come in, sit down, tell me what you've been doing with yourself. Haven't seen you in here for months, thought you must have sworn off silver for good.'

As luck would have it, only two youngsters were in the room, working together at a crucible over a small intense flame, and the silversmith was obviously rather bored with his supervisory task and keen to chat. Numirantoro had spotted in an instant the work she had come to see and sat at the bench where it rested, but with her back casually turned.

'I've been taken up with pen-work, but it's almost finished now. And then as well, I've been doing some teaching; Arval asked me to help with the youngest children, and sometimes I bring little Ancrascaro down for a few hours.'

'Yes, I've seen you together. Nice little lass, very well behaved. But is it too much to hope you've got something planned now in the silverware line?'

To her own surprise, for she had planned no such thing, Numirantoro found herself telling the silversmith that she wanted to take half an hour or so to work on an idea which had come into her mind.

'No problem, here, be my guest,' he said, leaning past her to sweep a clear space on the bench. 'You know where everything is, just help yourself to whatever you need.'

At last she was free to look at what she had come to see, while apparently engrossed in her own work. She saw immediately what Issigitsar had been trying to put into words. The arrow lay supported on a workstand, obviously not yet finished. It was full-size, a clothyard in length although slimmer in section than one intended for use. The shaft was of silver, pure and flawless, and along its length ran veins of gold. They looped around it in finest spirals, as if the arrow had plunged through liquid gold as it flew, and taken the molten metal to itself. In a clamp Numirantoro saw an unfinished golden feather. Others lay in various stages of completion, and one or two had been already attached to the arrow. She saw how the encircling veins of yellow gold were continued to form the structure of the feathers, which were finished in perfect detail with red gold spun gossamer-thin. There was no sign of any point or barb as yet. Numirantoro gazed at this work of Arymaldur's hands, wondering what had prompted its creation. It was like him: austere yet beautiful, enigmatic but with an integrity that was absolute. When it was finished it would fly with the speed of thought, unerring of aim like the piercing light of his eyes. But above all, it made her think of light itself: golden, glorious light, ancient silver starlight, light wreathing into flames of red, life-giving warmth.

That night, Numirantoro dreamed again the old dream of Arymaldur; and as ever, the shadow fell before she could know what followed as their eyes met. She woke with a sigh, oppressed as she always was when this happened by an unaccountable sense of loss. Then as her mind began to shake off sleep, she realised that there had indeed been something different about the dream this time. The darkened room, the wordless calling of her heart, the slow turn of Arymaldur's head, all these were the same; but the strange radiance that grew, that globed the scene and pushed back the dark with an edge of sparkling light, that lit his face in the instant before she met his eyes: now she saw, or rather, now she knew, somehow it came from her. Before the day was old, she was hurrying through the streets on her way to Tellgard. She had said the first thing that came to mind yesterday, any excuse to give the silversmith for her visit to his workshop. But now she was possessed by an idea indeed, an inspiration so bright that she burned to begin, would dare the risk of working where Arymaldur might be present. For once more, as she passed near the tree where the robin sang under the louring clouds of the gloomy dawn, she was assailed by the sense of time running like sand in the glass, of the end of days coming.

Yet the weeks passed, and though Numirantoro half hoped, half dreaded to find Arymaldur at the workbench before her, or to feel the unmistakeable, unearthly energy which charged the room as he entered, she never encountered him. Sometimes she could see that he had been there, for one by one the golden feathers were finished and attached to the arrow; but it seemed that this happened when she was teaching, or talking with Arval; and if she was working, he would be at sword-drill, or out on exercise, or helping in the dispensary. She wondered what he thought of her work, which he must surely have seen, even as she had watched the arrow taking shape. Delicately, with painstaking accuracy and infinite, skilful patience, she was crafting an intricate jewel, an heirloom small but freighted with significance for those who knew how to read its layers of meaning: As y'm Ur, the Star of Earth.

Hidden motives

Strangely, as Numirantoro edged closer to achieving for the first time a work of hand which truly seemed to match the vision of her mind, she attained a serenity, a quiet joy that walked with her so that she seemed happier than before; and since Vorynaas was much enjoying his unaccustomed role of public benefactor, he was animated and cheerful, so that on the surface the tension at home seemed lessened. Both of them would laugh and play with Ghentar, and Vorynaas was more often at home in the evening, spending time in talk with Arythalt. But with regard to the great hall that he was building near the south wall of the city, Numirantoro had mixed feelings. Work had started on it soon after the street skirmishes she had seen from Tellgard, and Vorynaas had announced the project to the council with a flourish. His plan, he said, was for a large building, of a dignity suitable to the grandeur of Caradriggan, in which feast-days could be fittingly celebrated and civic ceremonies performed.

Numirantoro had heard that Forgard asked what the necessity was for a new building, when the ancient hall in Tellgard had been the setting, time out of mind, for honouring the As-Geg'rastigan; to which Thaltor had responded with a sneer that no-one was proposing to change that, for such superstitions would find no home in the new hall once it was finished. At this, Arval had warned the council that they turned from the old ways at their peril, but the majority had been won over when Vorynaas had revealed that he intended the building works to be a source of employment for the needy, who were to be given priority when men were taken on. Such magnanimity did not convince Numirantoro, who knew her husband too well to believe that his reasons for paying for such a huge civic project out of his own pocket were to be taken at face value; but so far his true motives had not revealed themselves.

The domestic harmony was indeed deceptive. There was still no brother for Ghentar, and with Sigitsiro now out of the way Vorynaas turned to his wife more frequently, persistent in his attentions as he hoped for another child. At one time, as he well knew, she would have made it clear to him how unwelcome this was, but now it was as if she scarcely noticed him, as if all her mind was elsewhere. Although he had never admitted it to himself, Vorynaas had always felt inferior to Numirantoro in some way; and now, if she laughed, he began to suspect she laughed at him; if she smiled, he looked for mockery; if she seemed happy, he sought for reasons that were hidden from him. The more she seemed sustained by some inner exaltation, so his own secret insecurity grew: it gnawed at his confidence and self-esteem until he avoided her by day and sought her less often at night. Gradually he became consumed by an obscure feeling of threat, a formless jealousy. Brooding on this one morning as he sat waiting for a progress report from Poenmorcar, casting about for a reason for his doubts, it came to him that what he most resented was the time Numirantoro spent in Tellgard.

But before his dark mind had done more than begin to focus on this idea, the news which Vorynaas had been expecting broke in Caradward. Rumours began to run that the price of grain from Gwent y'm Aryframan had been set at a higher rate than ever before, and when this was confirmed as true, there was consternation in Caradriggan. Stories of panic buying began to do the rounds, with accusations that the richer men would stockpile grain and leave nothing for the poor; and those who had connections with Gwent y'm Aryframan, already feeling insecure enough as the city filled up with refugees from the Ellanwic seeking a livelihood, began to fear worse than intimidation. Some decided to cut their losses and leave, but there was little welcome for them in the Outlands where the Sigitsaran themselves had smarted from haughty dealings at the hands of Caradwardans, so the traffic was mostly towards the border at an ever-increasing rate. Others came to Tellgard and appealed to Arval for help, and none who did so, whatever their origin or circumstances, was ever turned away; but there were limits to how many could be taken in, or how much practical succour he could dispense.

Divisions in council

The mood was black in Tell'Ethronad, and voices were raised as the temper of the meeting worsened. However Vorynaas, with the advantage of his prior knowledge of the news, had laid his plans carefully and his cronies were well primed. At first they stayed silent while man after man spoke in the heat of anger, the younger members of the council in particular being afraid that their families would suffer under this new financial strain.

'Now at least you see what those already disadvantaged by our own actions have had to endure,' said Arval, 'yet you had scant sympathy for them in their need. I ask Lord Arymaldur to give us his counsel in this matter.'

Before Arymaldur could begin, Valafoss intervened. 'Words, words. Who gives us deeds? Lord Vorynaas would not put himself forward, but he at least has taken action. Those who work on his new hall need worry no more; with his money in their pockets, they can put bread in their mouths.'

Arymaldur rose in his place and gradually silence fell in the chamber, for there was not a man but sensed the force of his authority and dignity.

'With regard to the subject of our present debate, I recommend that we send messages to Framstock. Let us exchange words of friendship once more with Val'Arad in the hope that we may negotiate on the corn price. And I would say this also. Lord Arval has advised you more than once that your actions are putting you in peril. He is not called Earth-wise without reason. Gentlemen, I counsel you to listen well to Arval na Tell-Ur.'

Forgard knew he had not endeared himself to his colleagues by his contributions in previous sessions of the council, but he had stuck by his principles so far, and would stay true to them now. 'That was well said, and has my support at least. I vote for Lord Arymaldur's proposal.'

An outburst of derisive laughter caused every head to turn. Thaltor pointed at Forgard, not even bothering to stand as he spoke. 'The white hair sits well on your head! You are old before your time, reactionary, backward-looking, no wonder you run after Arval! As for Arymaldur, he always favours the Gwentarans. Perhaps he should think about going back to Framstock himself.'

For an instant there was complete silence at the shock of Thaltor's discourtesy, and before anyone had a chance to speak, Valestron, still comparatively new to Tell'Ethronad, added with a snigger, 'Taking his sword with him.'

Uproar broke out at this, but it subsided quickly when Arval spoke. He faced them down, his thin features wrathful, his eyes on fire, deep and black though they were.

'For shame, such uncouth behaviour does not belong in this council! We will conduct ourselves in a mannerly fashion as befits members of Tell'Ethronad. I am grateful to Arymaldur and Forgard for their support. If there are any others among you who will listen to me, hear this. I tell you it is fitting that we should be discussing the price of corn, for you are reaping now what you have sown!' He paused to let his words sink in. 'We have heard one proposal from Lord Arymaldur. Has anyone any counter-suggestion to put before us? Lord Morgwentan?'

Several people looked round in surprise, for old Morgwentan, stouter and more ponderous than ever, rarely spoke these days unless his murmurs of support for Vorynaas were counted. Slowly he levered himself from his chair and stood supporting himself with a hand on the table before him.

'Lord Arval, before we reach that point, I would just like to clear up a slight doubt which has arisen in my mind.'

Vorynaas watched him covertly, stroking his beard; now he would know whether Valafoss had planted the right question with his whispers in the old bore's ears. Morgwentan cleared his throat.

'I do not presume to comment on Lord Thaltor's claim that Arymaldur favours the Gwentarans; but I have heard it said that those whose connections lie there are turned away from the site office at the new hall. Can it be that Lord Vorynaas favours only Caradwardans?'

He sat down heavily, and all eyes turned now to Vorynaas.

'Ah, if only more of us took the time to consider things more fully, as Lord Morgwentan, with the wisdom of his years, has clearly done,' said Vorynaas smoothly, standing easily before them seeming relaxed and confident.

Too smooth, too relaxed, thought Forgard. Vorynaas showed no surprise at Morgwentan's words, as surely would have been more natural: he knew what Morgwentan was going to say! They have set all this up beforehand, between them – but what comes next? Vorynaas had produced some papers; he glanced at these briefly and then dropped them back on to the table. Inclining his head towards Morgwentan, and moving his hand in a gesture of self-deprecation, Vorynaas spoke again.

'I fear Lord Morgwentan may be correct, statistically speaking. I will have the site records checked immediately, and if it is the case that Gwentarans are under-represented in my labour force, I will take steps to remedy this situation: one which, I assure you, has not arisen through intent.' A murmur of approval ran among his supporters, but he held up a hand for silence. 'However, my resources are not infinite, and you will appreciate that I am running a business, not a charity. To my mind it seems that the Gwentarans have brought trouble on themselves and as Thaltor has already pointed out, albeit somewhat forcefully, they do have the option of returning to their homeland. I feel it is our first duty to look after our own people. Nevertheless, I am prepared to make the following gesture. I will make it known that any man of Gwentaran origin may seek employment with me, for which the payment will be in kind: lodging and a daily corn allowance, both of which I will provide at my personal expense.'

This time when he paused there was louder comment and many of those present tapped the edge of the council table with their forefingers in sign of approbation. But Vorynaas had not resumed his seat and it seemed he had more to say.

'I hope I have answered Lord Morgwentan's point to his satisfaction. But Arval asked if any of us has an alternative to the proposal put forward by Arymaldur. I have such a suggestion to put before you. I say let there be no question of negotiation over the corn price: such hagglings are for those whose bargaining power is weak. We in Caradward are in a position of strength. We are more than mere farmers and herdsmen. We are innovative, resolute, dynamic. Why satisfy the misplaced pride of Val'Arad by suing for a reduction? Let us pay the new price as if we scarcely notice an increase; if necessary let the more affluent among us follow my lead and buy in bulk so as to assist our poorer citizens. Let us rather apply our energies to developing what we have begun in the Cottan na' Salf, where already significant progress has been made. Determined effort will bring more success. Let our own resourcefulness bring us the rewards it promises, and the present burden on us will be short-lived.'

After this, the result of the vote was easy to predict. In favour of Arymaldur's proposal, scarce a dozen hands were raised, although there were some surprises among them: Sigitsar, he who had been a groomsman to Arythalt long ago but who seldom attended meetings of the council these days, holding himself aloof in disillusionment on his estates in the south; Forgard, a couple more Outlanders and two or three landowners from the Lowanmorad; Arval; and also Issigitsar. Poenmorcar glanced at his colleague with something like envy as he cast his own vote for Vorynaas. He knew well enough that one of the results of Vorynaas' proposals would be that soon he would have to deal with a workforce consisting effectively of slave labour, in bond to the master. But what can I do, he thought. Issigitsar is young, he has support among his own folk in the south. I have a wife and family to think of, if I go against Vorynaas I may lose more than my position as his clerk of works: he may see to it that I never work again.

Forgard sat staring blankly before him, mulling over the discussion. The rumours about panic buying had turned out to be partly true, then, although clearly there was not much panic in Vorynaas' case. By his own admission he had already begun stockpiling grain and Forgard was sure he had manipulated the debate. He strongly suspected that

Vorynaas maintained a network of agents; how else could he be so well-informed, always one step ahead of any opposition? Surely there must be more to his actions than simply ambition, avarice, the self-serving of an unscrupulous man; so what, wondered Forgard with a frown, were his secret motives? He scarcely listened as Arval, his voice dull with disappointment, formally announced the result of the council's vote. Men were gathering up cloaks, putting away notes and papers, breaking up into smaller groups as the meeting ended.

As they waited to pass through the doorway of the chamber, Forgard found himself near Thaltor, Arythalt and Arymaldur. Thaltor swung his shoulder and jostled them roughly.

'Excuse me,' he said, insincerity heavy in his voice. 'Just let me through there, will you, I'm in rather a hurry. Ah, but I see we've the friends of Framstock here, no wonder they're a little slow-moving.' He laughed unpleasantly. 'You're rather free with advice for my taste, Arymaldur, so perhaps I can offer you some of my own. If I were you, I'd be off to Gwent y'm Aryframan as soon as I could, before anyone decides to help you on your way.'

Arymaldur halted before them. Although the tallest, he was much more spare of frame than any of the others, yet somehow not even Thaltor pushed forward again. Arythalt felt once more the slight shiver of unease he had often noted in Arymaldur's presence. For the first time, face to face like this, it occurred to him that there was something strangely ageless about the man; it would be impossible to guess his years. Arymaldur spoke quietly, but his eyes were wide and seemed paler than usual.

'Thaltor, beware of threatening me. Know that I shall return whence I came when the time comes. The place is unknown to you and the time will be of my own choosing, however otherwise it may seem. Arval the Earth-wise has warned you that you are reaping now what you have sown. I warn you once more: sow evil seed again, and the harvest will be bitter indeed.' He turned away and passed through the door.

For an instant the three of them stood unmoving. Thaltor, for all his bluster, had felt his stomach contract in fear before Arymaldur's eyes, but now rage flooded his mind and he leapt in pursuit. Forgard and Arythalt sprang after him, Arythalt calling for Vorynaas as he realised with horrified embarrassment that Thaltor had flouted the tradition of Tell'Ethronad by coming armed to the council. Somehow between them they managed to hustle Thaltor away before he had the chance to draw his hidden dagger, Arythalt and Forgard looking wildly about them in desperate hope that Arymaldur would not witness the scuffle, but he was gone. Forgard leaned against the central pillar of the vaulting in the vestibule, trying to make sense of his thoughts. Arythalt had been aghast at the breach of etiquette, but Forgard's shame went much deeper than that. As he left them, Arymaldur had caught Forgard's eye and the faintest of smiles had barely touched his lips at what he saw there. Now Forgard was left alone, struggling to come to terms with the knowledge that he had looked on a lord of the Starborn, and the fear that the recognition had come too late.

Chapter 15

Rumours

A dozen or so small fires, dotted around the compound, smoked into the late evening air. Beside each one sat or lay groups of men, and in the shadows against the perimeter wall were rows of low huts. There was little conversation, just a quiet rumble of talk here and there. It would die away to a sullen silence each time a guard passed on his round and then pick up once more as the footsteps receded. Two of them were on duty, taking it in turns to sit in the gatehouse or to walk around the outer fence. Valestron got to his feet as his colleague came through the door into the lamplit room, and set out on his circuit. Half an hour each, turn and turn about, all cursed night long. He was so bored! There was no longer even much entertainment to be extracted from seeing these peasants flinch if he loosened his sword in its scabbard, or from hounding and harassing them into their sleeping huts before the official curfew time. They were too exhausted to protest, cowed and hopeless.

He glanced up at the east wing of Vorynaas' partly-built new hall. A light showed at the first-floor window, so the meeting must be still going on. For the hundredth time, he wondered what Valafoss, Thaltor and Vorynaas were discussing, and how long it would be before they invited him to join their inner circle. His cousin was employed in some capacity or other in the office now: officially he was a draughtsman or designer or some such pen-pusher, but Valestron suspected his real duties were rather different. Either he knew an awful lot about what was going on, or he kept his ear pressed to a lot of keyholes.

He was always dropping tantalising little hints, just enough to drive Valestron nearly mad with curiosity and the effort of trying not to show it. Weedy little runt, thought Valestron angrily, see him being good enough for Rigg'ymvala or the border patrols! Ah well, not long now till midsummer, and the public feasting-chamber of the new hall was on schedule to be ready by then: surely he'd be included in the top table group. Valestron's humour began to improve slightly.

In the far corner of the compound, an undercurrent of conversation continued, although the men kept a wary eye on Valestron's progress.

'I'm telling you!' One of them was whispering vehemently. 'I heard it when the mule-train came in with the stone from the quarries down south. One of the lads on it was saying he broke his arm, that time when there was the fight at the horse-market, and they set it for him in Tellgard, and he realised then.'

'Go on,' said another voice, 'how could he know? He's probably just hero-worshipping out of gratitude.'

'He said he could tell, just by the way Arymaldur spoke, the way he dealt with him – and his uncle. He was there too, the boy said his uncle felt it as well. It was only when they talked about it later, the fellow couldn't make out why the lad was so worked up, then when he blurted it out, he realised too.'

'I wish I'd tried to get on the mule-trains,' said a third man after a short silence. 'If I'd have known what it was going to mean, when I stepped up for this "payment in kind" deal, I'd never have done it. Look at us! We might as well be slaves.'

'Easy for you – you could take back your token and break the contract if you wanted to. I've got a wife and two children out there, trying to get by on what she earns washing pots at the *Leopard*. At least I'm not taking my food out of their mouths any longer.' This was the sceptical voice again.

'Don't be a fool!' hissed the man who had started the discussion. 'See there where that cocky young whippersnapper's doing his rounds! What do you think would happen to any of us who went up to Poenmorcar and said we wanted out? But if we stuck together, and if it's right there's one of the Starborn here in the city...'

Another man, who had sat silent while this talk went on, now spoke. 'I spent weeks scrounging at back doors and begging for work on street corners all round Caradriggan, and I heard it said you can't trust a man who drew his sword on an unarmed crowd.'

'He did not!'

'I'd follow him if I could!'

'If I could find the bastard who started that rumour...'

'We should risk it!'

'You're mad, we've no chance...'

'*Watch out!*'

The sudden quarrel and raised voices had brought Valestron swiftly over, lamp held high.

'Cut the noise, here! If you've this much energy to spare for arguing, we'll need to see you work harder tomorrow. Now, all lights and fires out, get into your quarters. We're using up no more fuel and oil tonight on wasters like you.'

The first man in Caradriggan

As the month of midsummer drew on towards the feast-day itself, the undercurrent of tension and unease in Vorynaas' house grew ever stronger. Vorynaas was pleased by the progress which had been made on the new hall, but he was distracted both by his suspicions of Numirantoro and by irritation with his partners. Thaltor and Valafoss had begun agitating to know when he was going to embark on the new project, the still-secret enterprise in the valley of the Lissa'pathor. There were angry words at the meeting the two of them had demanded, which went on late into the evening. Vorynaas came home from it, already seething with exasperation, to find his wife sitting reading with Arythalt. He looked at the pair of them and was strongly tempted to turn on his heel and head straight for the *Sword and Stars*. His marriage-father was wearing a long face that was enough to put him off his supper, and as for Numirantoro, he had something to say to her later to which she had better listen if she knew what was good for her. He ate his grilled vegetables and smoked ewes' milk cheese, then added a little more herb-flavoured oil to the bowl and mopped it out with the last of his bread. A servant came forward with water and a napkin for his hands, and then placed a dish of lemon cakes beside the wine. Vorynaas however had rather a sweet tooth, and going over to the wine-table in the alcove he poured himself a goblet of the heavier mead to go with his dessert. Sitting back now, his hunger satisfied, he expressed regret that his late arrival home had meant that Ghentar was already in bed. He asked a few questions about the boy's day, but after a short while Arythalt excused himself and retired to rest. Vorynaas turned to his wife.

'What's the matter with your father? He seems rather down in the mouth tonight. In fact half the time these days he's so damned miserable he makes you seem almost cheerful.'

Numirantoro looked at him, coolly ignoring the spiteful jibe. 'I expect he's concerned at the way you've cut him out of the running of the business in favour of Thaltor and Valafoss, and put yourself in his place as head of the household: a business, and a house, that both used to be his own. He's too worried about the possible reasons for it to tackle you, and too proud to come to me because he knows I told him long ago, before he married me off to you, that this is exactly what would happen.'

Vorynaas jumped to his feet, his face flushed with anger. He took a step towards Numirantoro and stood over her. 'How dare you say something like that to me!'

She stood in turn and as usual he was infuriated twice over, by her height advantage and by the daunting way she made him feel inferior in spite of all his bluster. Her voice was level and calm, almost as if she spoke from a distance.

'I can see no reason at all why I should be afraid to speak the truth.'

For a second or two they stood confronting each other, then Vorynaas with an exclamation of annoyance turned away. Numirantoro resumed her seat, and he went over to pour himself a second glass of mead and remained standing by the wine-table.

'Things are progressing well at the new hall,' he said. Getting no reply, he forced down his anger and continued, 'I'm having it made public tomorrow that midsummer this year in Caradriggan will be celebrated in the new feasting-chamber, which will be ready for use even though not all the rest of the hall and the other buildings are finished. If the evening is fine, I suggest that we set out from home; but if not, there are facilities on site for dressing and washing. The private rooms off the main chamber are also all now furnished and equipped, as well as the kitchens and public areas.'

Numirantoro marked the place in her reading and placed the book on the shelf with a resigned sigh; clearly her evening was over. She moved towards the door as she spoke.

'I shall not be coming to the new hall at midsummer. I shall be attending the traditional ceremony at Tellgard as I have always done.'

Vorynaas slammed his goblet down on the small wine-table and moved swiftly to intercept his wife before she reached the door.

'Listen to me, woman. You will not be rubbing shoulders with charlatans and peasants in Tellgard. You will sit beside me at the top table in the new hall, as befits the wife of the man who built it and who now holds first place in this city.'

He clenched his hands in his sleeves as she smiled slightly, the smile that seemed to him to hold some mocking secret.

'I will not attend a feast-day where the As-Geg'rastigan are no longer remembered. I will go to Tellgard, where they are honoured still, where I have the friendship of Arval the Earth-wise and my colleagues and they in turn have my respect. You cannot compel me to do otherwise.' That smile appeared again. 'Vorynaas, the first man in Caradriggan? A debatable question, I think.'

She was no more than three or four steps up the stairs before he had her by the elbow.

'There is one thing I can compel you to do though, about which there will be no debate.'

But afterwards, in a strange role-reversal, it was Vorynaas who lay wakeful in the night hours. Numirantoro slept beside him, sweetly, peacefully: her fate was out of her hands now that she had embraced her destiny. Vorynaas' mind ran on restlessly. As sometimes happened when he fought with Numirantoro, he had seen Salfronardo in her, which always provoked his desire. He was accustomed to resistance and revulsion from Numirantoro, and had learnt to use this to feed his excitement at dominating her. But tonight it was as if she was totally indifferent, whatever he did or said; she was somehow beyond his reach and he felt baffled, cheated in some way. He was tired, but could not relax; sated, yet unsatisfied. He tossed and turned, listening to her gentle breathing. What was the secret that Tellgard held? Why, why did she spend so much time there?

A choice made

A few days earlier, Numirantoro had entered the silversmith's workshop and seen immediately that Arymaldur had been there in her absence. The arrowhead had been forged and was held in a clamp beside the shaft, which was now fully feathered. She looked at it, noting its unusual shape. There were no barbs or tangs and in section it was rather long and slim, almost like a bolt for a crossbow. Where it differed was in its lack of facets and in the strange metal of its making. She considered the shape: yes, she saw how it matched the rest of the arrow. It was like a molten droplet, elongated by the speed of its flight, as if the rush of air had honed it to a point of needle-like sharpness. Not that it was sharp yet, because it had still to be ground and burnished. But what metal had it been forged from? The master silversmith came in, and seeing what she was looking at, crossed the room to join her.

'Wondering about the metal, eh?' he said genially. 'Wait till Issigitsar sees this, he'll be walking on swarf till he finds out how Arymaldur did it! Oh, the Outlanders don't know all the secrets about metalworking, much though they'd like to think they do.'

'Come on, that's rather unfair,' smiled Numirantoro. 'I've heard Issigitsar myself talking about this arrow. "The simplicity of genius" were the words he used, I seem to remember.'

'Did he now? Well, I reckon he was right. No, I'm only making fun, you can be sure he'll be fascinated by this. See there now, this is what we call sky-steel. It's the hardest metal there is; and take it from me, very, very few metal-masters are skilled enough to make it. But look here what Arymaldur's done with it, see how it changes colour as you get further away from the point? That's because he's melded it with just the thinnest overlay of white gold, almost an emulsion. When this is polished up, it'll shine too bright to look at. And, by my right hand! If it was fired, it would pierce anything: go through four-inch oak as if it wasn't there.'

'It won't ever be used for shooting, though, will it?' asked Numirantoro with a sudden foreboding. 'Surely it's too beautiful for that?'

'Well you would think so, I agree,' said the silversmith, 'although I can't say I know what prompted Arymaldur to make it. But, oak! Forget that – sky-steel will go through anything. In fact, the only thing that's strong and sharp enough to pierce sky-steel is sky-steel itself.'

She was still thinking all this over as she worked, when the moment she had both dreaded and hoped for arrived. Almost before the workshop door was fully opened, she felt the strange, unearthly quality in the air, as if its very atoms danced with life. All her senses awoke to an almost painful pitch of alertness; her ears seemed actually to catch a faintly audible tingle of energy. She dared not turn her head, but there was no need. Arymaldur crossed the room, speaking quietly to the silversmith and to one or two others at work there, and seated himself at his own place where the arrow awaited his attention, and

Numirantoro could see him in her mind as plainly as if he stood before her. An awareness of some curious altered state of consciousness crept over her. She felt the flagstones beneath her feet, she saw the wall before her, she breathed the familiar smells of metal filings and polish, she heard the small noises as a stool moved or a sleeve brushed against a bench. But what had happened, why did she feel that she herself had crossed into some other, unknown dimension? She looked down at the intricate work taking shape under her hand, and saw her fingers trembling. What was this strange place in which she found herself, alone? Then suddenly she understood, and knew she was not alone: for in her heart the voice she loved beyond all others spoke, offering her a solemn and daunting choice. All her life Numirantoro had yearned towards the fate that opened to her now, even as she yearned for him who laid that destiny before her. Her choice was made even before her heart spoke its answer.

At the Midsummer Feast

The Midsummer Feast was drawing to a close and in the ancient hall of Tellgard the silversmith looked up at Numirantoro. There was something different about her tonight, he thought, without quite knowing what it was. People were right to say she was as beautiful as the Starborn. She was wearing a robe of deepest blue, with wide sleeves that fell from the elbow and a skirt swirling from many pleats at the hip. Her long dark hair was bound up and adorned with silver daisies, the only ornament she bore. The silversmith had heard that this was the work of her uncle away in Gwent y'm Aryframan, and he acknowledged a masterpiece from a fellow craftsman. Looking up again as he sipped his feast-day wine, he wondered why Numirantoro was not also wearing the jewel she had made, the As y'm Ur, as it had become known. Maybe she inherited her skill from her uncle, he thought, remembering the day her work was finished and she had shown him the tiny, intricate, beautiful thing. He had been almost afraid to handle it, apprehensive that his fingers would be too large and clumsy to open the minute hinges in order to see what lay at its heart. She had explained its meaning to him and then said, with such a strange smile, 'I have made it for my son.' He had been surprised, for he too had heard tales of the discord between Numirantoro and her husband; and then he had been pleased to think that maybe warmer feelings were growing in the family now that they had the little lad to bring them closer. But now as he looked at Numirantoro he doubted himself, knowing as he did what a headstrong little ruffian Ghentar was. A regular little brat by all accounts in fact, turning out just like his father.

The man's mind wandered off to thoughts of his own family. Last year, his son had been with him but tonight he had felt obliged to join the company in the new hall on account of being sub-contracted by Issigitsar. It was obvious that he was less than happy about it, but what could he do? Still, at least he would be coming back to Tellgard when the contract was complete. The silversmith brightened. He'd spent years hoping for more sons, then dreading their arrival when the council brought in the new regulations about serving on the border patrols. Now the lad was safe from that, and into the bargain they had the twin girls who had come along to surprise them all only a couple of years ago! Too young yet for public occasions, they were at home with his wife. He looked around him again at his companions. Forgard and his wife never missed a festival, and there too was his sister and her husband, the parents of little Ancrascaro. It struck him suddenly that Forgard, with his silver hair and black eyes, could almost pass for a son of Arval with those who did not know them.

His gaze softened as it paused on Numirantoro once more, and then moved on to Arymaldur. It's a bit much to take, thought the silversmith, mellow in mood on the feast-day wine. Not only does the fellow excel at everything he puts his hand to, but he has to look like that as well! He's so, well, so... The smith groped for the words he wanted to describe Arymaldur, but gave it up. Good-looking didn't hit the mark, reserved only said part of it, even enigmatic wasn't quite what he wanted. Not a bad effort though, thought the smith, rather proud of himself for dredging up such an arcane term from his wine-slowed head. Arymaldur was dressed in dark grey, the collar of his robe faced in a lighter shade of the same colour; it made his eyes seem a paler grey than usual. The sleeves were slashed lengthwise to reveal a lining of palest primrose, the only bright touch in his garments on this night of celebration. Low-waisted and falling to the knee at the front, slightly lower behind, his attire accentuated the height and spareness of his frame with effortless elegance. He trod lightly in boots of glove-like softness but wore no jewel or ornament. The light fell on his face, illuminating the proud cheekbones, the strong jaw, the stern nose, the high forehead from which the dark hair flowed back. For the first time it occurred to the silversmith that he saw a resemblance between Numirantoro and Arymaldur. But how, in what way? Father and daughter, brother and sister? No, not a family likeness. Well then, surely not man and wife? No, not exactly, but... a strange little shiver ran over the smith's skin, leaving him feeling suddenly chilly. Otherworldly, that was it. There's something slightly unearthly about both of them, even Numirantoro, thought the smith; and as he looked back up at them to check his intuition, Arymaldur turned towards him. Those grey eyes, steady and unflinching yet so piercing and bright, met the smith's gaze and locked there for a second or two. The man felt an almost physical shock, dismay at his previous blindness mingling painfully with the elation of his new-found knowledge. No need now to search for the right word: now he knew who he looked on.

Once the time-honoured rites of the evening had been celebrated in the ancient courtyard of Tellgard, folk began to drift away. Numirantoro was scarcely aware of where her feet took her. Her eyes had never left Arymaldur all evening long: his face was imprinted on her mind, her ears heard only his voice. She wandered distractedly, almost afraid of the intensity of the emotion that gripped her. Unseeing, she passed through a door and latched it again behind her, leaning back on it with eyes closed. The old thought came back to her, the only words she had ever found to describe what she felt: I love him more than I am able to. Yes, that was it. She could not free herself to love him as she must, trammelled as she was by her bonds to the Earthborn. But Arymaldur had spoken in her heart; she had heard the words of the As-Geg'rastigan, she had chosen her fate: how long must it be before she could embrace her destiny? She opened her eyes and looked up towards the sky, and a shock of wonder passed through her. Stars burned above her, blue-white summer stars blazing in a midsummer sky of clearest, deepest blue, such as she had not seen since she left Gwent y'm Aryframan! But as she gazed, she realised no stars such as these ever shone above Salfgard. And now she noticed that no trace remained of the wood-smoke that had hung in the air all evening from the many beacon-fires lit for the feast-day, but a faint sweet scent, as of dusk-flowering blossom, filled the night.

Where was she? How was it she had never walked in this garden before, she who all her life had known the ways of Tellgard? For she saw that there were small trees about her, bearing delicate white flowers like lace; they looked up towards the stars above and their perfume filled an enclosed garth, surrounded by a colonnade supported on slender pillars. She looked back at the door through which she had entered. It filled a narrow archway and was secured by a simple latch, worn as if with use; there was no lock. Numirantoro took a step or two into the garden, her feet falling silently on soft grass. Was she under some strange enchantment, or could she herself have somehow have conjured this lovely place into being? Then suddenly she saw a movement in the shadow of the colonnade and felt the very air begin to thrill with life. Though half-hidden from her still by the flowers and the night, she knew Arymaldur was there. She took another step forward and saw him. Tall and silent he stood there, half turned away, looking up at the sky.

All the sorrow and loss, the pain and hopeless longing fell away from Numirantoro as her distress and yearning were replaced by an immense calm: a huge, peaceful serenity that was vaster and deeper than the night itself. Around the little court, at the edges of her vision, it was as if a myriad tiny jewels burned, a hundred fireflies danced, a mazy multitude of glowing sparks spun madly in silence. I have seen this place before, thought Numirantoro. I am within my dream: now I will live it out to the end. This time there will be no waking to loss, for I do not sleep: I am awake, aware, more alive than I have ever been before. As in the dream, she called to Arymaldur in her heart. She heard the silent dream words. 'Arymaldur, my lord. Lord Arymaldur, turn to me. Arymaldur, I love you, turn to me. Hear me, Arymaldur, turn to me.' And as in the dream, Arymaldur turned towards her; the stars burned brighter as they lit his face. In the silence of that starlight, Numirantoro stepped forward in trust and went to meet her fate. She raised her head to Arymaldur. At last, she looked into his eyes.

Arval's errand

Much later that night, a man hurried through the streets of Caradriggan on an urgent errand from Tellgard. Groups of revellers were still making merry in the city, but none took notice of the figure that hastened past them with hood and cloak drawn close. A small light burned above the porch as he climbed the steps and rapped upon the door of Vorynaas' house. After a short pause, the door was opened, not by the house steward who had replaced Arythalt's old retainer, but by Merenald. His eyes widened in surprise.

'Lord Arval! Please come in. It is very late, but may I fetch you some refreshment?'

Arval stepped into the house, folding back his hood as Merenald closed the door behind him. He shook his head, taking Merenald by the arm to emphasise his words.

'Thank you, no. I must see Vorynaas at once. I am sorry if he has already gone to his rest, but please wake him if necessary.'

Merenald looked uncomfortable, as if he was unsure how to reply.

'Lord Vorynaas is not at home,' he said. 'He has not yet returned from the feast in the new hall.'

Arval threw up his hand with exasperation. 'I must speak to either Vorynaas or Lord Arythalt tonight. Is there anyone you can rouse up and send across to the hall to fetch them? I will wait here.'

Merenald's embarrassment seemed to increase. 'Lord Arythalt is here,' he said. 'He returned some hours ago and has retired to sleep. If you will come through, I will wake him and fetch him to you. May I know what your message concerns?'

'You may tell him it is urgent enough to bring me here after midnight,' said Arval rather sharply, noting that no-one in the household seemed much bothered by the fact that Numirantoro too had failed to return home. Merenald hurried off and Arval, after taking a turn or two around the room, sat down, deep in his own thoughts. After a few moments the door opened to admit Arythalt, who had thrown on a house-robe over his night attire and looked both apprehensive and angry. It was many years since Arval had been a welcome guest in his house, and the few hurried words he had had time to exchange with Merenald had been enough to let him know that both his daughter and his marriage-son were still not home. Given the time of night, he could guess at the reasons for Vorynaas' absence, and was shamed by them in front of Arval; but when he saw the look on the old man's face as he rose in greeting, he felt a sudden stab of fear for Numirantoro.

Arval wasted no time in coming to the point; cutting through Arythalt's somewhat tepid greeting he spoke quickly.

'I'm sorry to disturb you at such an hour. I hoped to speak to Vorynaas but I gather he's still out.' Ignoring Arythalt's discomfiture and annoyance, he pressed on. 'Don't be distressed, but I have to tell you that Numirantoro is unwell. You'll know she attended the Midsummer Feast in Tellgard and nothing seemed wrong while we were all in the hall. But later she seems to have fainted; at any rate she was brought to me unconscious and we have been unable to rouse her.'

Arythalt sank on to a chair; he looked suddenly old and vulnerable. He sat with his hands to his face, painful memories of the loss of Salfronardo waking in him, his eyes fixed on Arval.

'Here.' Arval took matters into his own hands, pouring wine for Arythalt and passing it to him. 'Drink this. I appreciate you must be worried, but I assure you I wouldn't have left her if I thought she was in danger. She's breathing normally and her pulse is steady; we have made her comfortable and someone will watch beside her through the night, because clearly we cannot bring her home yet. That's one of the reasons I came immediately to speak to you. The other is that, as we have yet to make a diagnosis, I feel it would be best if we kept her in Tellgard where she can receive the most skilled nursing care available in Caradriggan.'

Arythalt put his cup down on the table, saw that Arval had noticed that his hands were shaking and gripped them in the sleeves of his robe to steady them. He felt cold with shock. 'But if she fails to wake,' he said at last, his voice trembling as he fought down his fears.

Arval felt himself warming to the man a little as he saw his distress. 'She has no injuries and we have been unable to find anything physically wrong – nothing immediately obvious, that is. It's possible that she has suffered some kind of shock, in which case I judge that it would be unwise to try to rouse her too soon. I promise you that I have the skill to sustain the life in her even while she lies withdrawn from us and unheeding; and I can promise you also that all the resources of medicine which we possess in Tellgard will be employed to tend her. Not a man or woman there but is devoted to Numirantoro.'

Feeling slightly reassured, but not much calmer, Arythalt drew a shaky breath. 'Lord Arval, thank you for your care and concern, which I deeply appreciate. I am happy for my daughter to remain in Tellgard. If we may, I and my marriage-son will come to see her for ourselves early in the morning.'

After Arval had left to hurry back to Tellgard, Arythalt sent for Merenald and told him briefly of what had occurred. The younger man looked stricken, but Arythalt took him by the shoulders.

'Merenald, I have trusted you before and you have never let me down. Swear to me that you will never speak to anyone of the errand I am about to ask you to perform.'

'Lord Arythalt, I am your man. You have my word.'

'Well then.' Arythalt swallowed his pride as he forced the words out. 'The evening must surely be long over in the new hall. Go immediately to Thaltor's house in search of Vorynaas. Let us hope you find him there, but if he is not, then I think you must seek him at the *Golden Leopard.*' The bitterness and regret could be heard dragging at Arythalt's voice. 'Tell him I expect to see him at Tellgard as early as may be in the morning.'

Vorynaas in Tellgard

But the two were not to meet there, after all. Arval hastened from Numirantoro's side as a commotion outside the room announced the early arrival of Vorynaas. He swaggered in arrogantly, still richly dressed in his feast-day clothes but looking rather the worse for his night's activities and with a strong smell of stale wine about him. Arval flatly refused to let him see Numirantoro unless he toned down his bluster, warning him sternly that too much noise might rouse her so suddenly that the consequences could be fatal. Agreeing in the end somewhat ungraciously, Vorynaas stepped into the room behind Arval and walked over to where Numirantoro lay. For some time, he stood looking down on her silently while Arval waited, expecting him to ask questions; but neither Vorynaas' thoughts, nor his only question when it came, were what Arval had anticipated.

Vorynaas was tired, having had very little rest, and he had still not completely shaken off the effects of the strong feast-day wine. His mind boiled with resentment and malice. He was furious with Arythalt for sending Merenald to seek him out, and enraged that he had had to deal with the fellow in the less than salubrious surroundings of the *Golden Leopard.* By my right hand, he thought, I'll make sure both of them pay for this. They needn't think they can run round Caradriggan with stories of how they caught me in a compromising situation. And is it any wonder I resort to the *Leopard*? What kind of life do I have at home? Look at her, lying there – my *wife*. Wouldn't even come with me to the new hall: I had to sit alone in the place of honour, everyone wondering why she wasn't with me. She spoiled my big moment by running off to Tellgard, and now look what's happened. She's been nothing but a disappointment to me, nothing of her mother in her at all except the rotten Gwentaran strain. Dull, degenerate, reactionary, backwoods peasants! Now she's stolen the limelight again. No-one will be talking of my success, my plans for the future, the benefits I have brought to the city: it will be Numirantoro this, Numirantoro that, poor Numirantoro, so young, so beautiful, just like one of the Starborn! Vorynaas bared his teeth with disgust, wishing that he had the nerve to spit savagely on the floor.

He turned abruptly to Arval. 'Has the old man been in yet?'

'If you are referring to Lord Arythalt, no,' said Arval coldly. 'It seems you have come here without first going to your home, so perhaps you are unaware of just how early in the day it is. I do not expect Arythalt for another hour or so. May I take it that you are in agreement that Numirantoro should stay here to be tended?'

Vorynaas shrugged indifferently and Arval continued, his dark eyes black with distaste and disapproval. 'If she fails to wake within the next day or so, it would help to bring her son to her. The sound of a young child's voice will often reach a mother's mind when no others can succeed.'

'The nurse can bring him down, if he'll come. I'm glad to say the boy takes after me. We'll see none of these fits of Gwentaran vapours from him,' sneered Vorynaas. 'Well, look, this is all women's affairs, or you can fix something up with the old man when he arrives. I can't stand about all day waiting for him to get himself organised, I've got a business to run. Tell him I've been in; if he's happy for his daughter to stay here, it's all one to me.'

He turned with a swirl of his cloak, heavy with dark green brocade, and strode off. His head was pounding from lack of sleep, bad temper and too much drink. The business can wait, thought Vorynaas. I need camomile tea with honey and probably a dish of eggs, and what's more I'm going to the *Sword and Stars* for it.

A mystery glimpsed

Days passed, and Numirantoro lay unmoving in Tellgard. She never woke, or uttered any sound, although someone watched beside her constantly in case her eyes opened suddenly in fright at her unaccustomed surroundings. The women tended her with every care, but Arval would let none except himself supervise her nourishment. With his own hand he fed her measured sips of the spirit of which he alone knew the secret. If it had sustained him over many generations of men, then surely its strength would preserve the life in Numirantoro. Twice Ghentar was brought in to see his mother, but to no avail. Indeed on the second occasion his behaviour was so disruptive and unruly that Arval had the nurse take him out of the room and told her not to bring the child again until he could be better controlled. Returning to the bedside, Arval tried to comfort the woman who sat there: the old cook from Numirantoro's childhood home who, turned off by Vorynaas, now worked in Tellgard. She was spending every hour of her time, when not required in the kitchens, sitting holding Numirantoro's hand, talking softly to her of happier days in the hope that some word, some memory of her voice, would unlock the trance.

Now she sat, weeping silently as she gazed on Numirantoro's face. She turned to Arval as he stood beside her.

'Why has this happened? As if the poor lass hasn't had enough sorrow in her life. Ah, they say right that those as don't deserve it get all the luck. Lord Arval, what ails her? She was as right as could be at the feast, she spoke to me and I remember thinking she seemed happy at last, so how could she be taken ill so soon afterwards?'

Arval sat beside her and looked at Numirantoro.

'This is not an illness such as we are used to dealing with. I think she is not sick, she is somehow withdrawn from us into some unknown place. There's no mark of pain or disease that I can see, no problem that my skill can find. See how peacefully she lies, how serene her face.'

The old woman dabbed her eyes and managed a watery, reminiscent smile.

'She's lovelier than ever, and that's a wonder in itself. Even as a child she was beautiful. We all used to say she was like one of the Starborn, and so she was. I remember as if it was yesterday how she'd pester me for stories of the As-Geg'rastigan, especially after she'd heard tales from Gwent y'm Aryframan. I've heard it said maybe they still walk there at times, the Starborn, and who knows – perhaps it's true.'

She looked again at Numirantoro's pale, still face, framed by the heavy locks of her loosened hair: dark and lustrous it lay on the white pillow, touched with a hint of Salfronardo's fiery burnish.

'You don't think she could have gone across to *them* somehow and left all this behind, left us here and her friends and the little lad and all?'

Before he could stop himself, Arval had moved his foot sharply as his mind leapt to a sudden connection; the sole of his shoe scraped abruptly on the floor and the old woman glanced at him in curiosity. He schooled his face to show nothing, and spoke to her with quiet emphasis.

'Now there's no need for wild talk of that sort. It will start rumours running that will be no help to Numirantoro, either now or later. You are right to be concerned, but I don't believe we need to fear for her. She deserves love and compassion and I know she has this from you. Stay with her now, and I will return and take over the watch again soon.'

Quickly he sought out Arymaldur, in haste to know the answer to the question that burned in his mind.

'My lord, you told me once that when you leave the life of men, you will take something with you. I have to ask you: is it Numirantoro that you take from us?'

Arymaldur's grey eyes rested upon Arval, and though as ever he gazed into them hungrily to feed upon the power and knowledge that their light held, he felt once more an increased remoteness, as if Arymaldur was half-withdrawn from him into some different dimension of existence. Fleetingly he wondered whether Numirantoro already walked there too, unseen by Earthborn eyes, and when Arymaldur spoke, he was unsure whether or not he drew comfort from the words.

'I brought Numirantoro to you from the garden whose door only you, *as-ur* that you are, and I have ever passed. Her choice had long been willingly made; and so it was that she too could enter there. No, I do not take her from you, she has herself run to meet her fate. Arval the Earth-wise, the long years of your life on earth will not be in vain. You yourself told Numirantoro it was she you had waited for, and did I not say to you that I would leave something of myself with you? Remember these words.'

Deep, quiet, yet resonant with authority, Arymaldur's voice fell upon Arval's ears like balm; but when the old man raised his head, he was alone.

Chapter 16

Surprise and suspicion

Autumn drew on. The wagons set off, escorted by Valestron and his troop, to bring Morgwentan's corn back from Framstock. Work continued at the site of Vorynaas' new hall. The huge undercrofts were completed and fitted out, finished to a high specification for the storage of perishable foodstuffs and especially grain. All the granaries and cellars were secured behind strong walls and locks, and the sweat of those who toiled to build them was bitter indeed when they saw to what end they laboured. Poenmorcar became daily more silent and morose and finally sought out Vorynaas. Citing worries for his wife's health and pointing to the successful completion of the first two phases of the project, brought in on time and on budget, he asked to be released from the rest of his contract as clerk of works. His excuses were transparent, and Vorynaas saw through them without difficulty, for he knew that Poenmorcar had purchased land away south in the Ellanwic: a part of Forgard's estates. He thought fit to withhold his lands from the development of the Cottan na'Salf, yet he sold to this artisan with ideas above his station, thought Vorynaas, staring blackly at Poenmorcar as he left the office. Two of a kind, a pair of old women not worth my attention. But I won't forget, and if a chance comes my way… meanwhile, the senior mason could take charge of the remaining construction. Gratitude for the promotion would buy the man's loyalty, and as an extra insurance, young Haartell could be moved sideways to be his second. He certainly had the required expertise for the job and had been Vorynaas' man through and through ever since the time he filched the mine disaster reports for him from under Arval's nose. Thoughts of Arval made Vorynaas' brows draw down once more. Problems with the building project were the last thing he needed now, when his mind was so preoccupied with doubt: doubt, moreover, that his pride forced him to keep secret.

One morning recently, he had been about to leave the house when a message was delivered from Arval, requesting him to come to Tellgard urgently. Vorynaas had hesitated: Numirantoro was still there, and he suspected that Arval intended to berate him for not visiting her. What was the point, when she lay insensible week after week? In any case, her father spent time at her bedside every few days, and as Vorynaas got used to the situation, he found he was happier with Numirantoro out of the way. Then it struck him that the message was strongly worded and he wondered if his wife had taken a turn for the worse, was maybe even at the point of death. He considered this without emotion. In a way, it would be the best thing. He would be free of her without blame, financially secure, and at last in a position to reveal his new scheme and shunt Arythalt off to oversee it. Yes, the thing to do was to make an appearance at Tellgard. He hurried back to his rooms, changed his clothes for something rather more sombre in style, and adjusting his expression to one of responsible concern presented himself to Arval.

He had been completely taken aback when Arval, drawing him into a small private room, had informed him without much preamble that Numirantoro was more than two months pregnant. Gaping foolishly, he had been momentarily at a loss for words. His first question had made him look stupid in front of the old fool too, he thought now angrily, going over the scene in his memory for the hundredth time.

'How do you know?'

'Vorynaas, how *would* we know? In the usual way and from the usual signs, of course. There is no need for alarm at present; Numirantoro appears perfectly healthy. Whether the pregnancy can be brought to full term if she fails to regain consciousness remains to be seen. I have never myself dealt with such a case, but you may be sure that I and my medical staff will research all the reference material we hold in Tellgard to see whether we can find guidance. At the moment I have every confidence in a successful outcome.'

'Two months... so she would be due when, exactly?'

'At about the time of the Spring Feast,' said Arval. 'She must have conceived around midsummer.'

They went through to stand at Numirantoro's bedside. As Vorynaas looked down at his wife, he was suddenly reminded of her as she lay at his side in sleep the night they had argued about whether she would accompany him to the Midsummer Feast in the new hall: peaceful, untouchable, withdrawn into some inner world beyond his reach. Her face seemed to him to show a trace of the secret exaltation, a hint of the smile that had so disturbed and tormented him. His own face was flushed with an uncomfortable mixture of emotions. He had badly wanted another child, and this might be the second son for which he hoped. He remembered how he had forced his attentions on Numirantoro that night, and on many other occasions around the same time: now, at last, she had conceived again. But for some reason a small voice in his heart spoke up and refused to be silent even though he tried his utmost not to heed it. Midsummer, said the voice. She conceived at midsummer; she defied you at midsummer to come to Tellgard; she suffered this strange collapse at Tellgard; she lies here now. Had he not gnawed at his nails many a time before, wondering what was the secret that Tellgard held, what was the reason she spent so much time there? Tendrils of formless jealousy began to twine around his mind, as the small voice that would not be silenced asked the question that his pride would never allow him to acknowledge in words: Is this child mine?

Henchmen

As the time approached for the Midwinter Feast, Valestron and Thaltor were strolling late one afternoon through the newly-finished living accommodation at the east side of the new hall. This wing comprised a barrack-block for the small garrison Vorynaas had installed as a permanent guard on his strongrooms and granaries, with well-appointed quarters above for the officers in charge. Building work was still in progress on a west wing.

'Pity you missed that council meeting when you were away in Framstock,' Thaltor was saying, 'because you'd have found it most entertaining. Poor old Arval!' He laughed quite heartily. 'He doesn't know where to turn these days, what with losing the upper hand in Tell'Ethronad, and Tellgard bursting at the seams with scroungers up from the country, and now this peculiar business with Numirantoro on top of everything else. I must say though, I'm quite surprised at the way Vorynaas has got his knife stuck into Arymaldur recently. I never thought anyone could dislike that high-and-mighty paragon of virtue more than I do, but Vorynaas really went for him in the council.'

Valestron laughed in return, but offered no opinion of his own. He had more than an idea of what was eating at Vorynaas, but was far too shrewd to drop a hint to Thaltor. Vorynaas had often taunted Thaltor about his lack of imagination and Valestron was not going to voice his suspicions to a man who might blurt something out in a moment of temper or indiscretion. For him, there was too much at stake: he was unwilling to put at risk his new position as security chief at the hall, to hazard his rise in the hierarchy of Vorynaas' expanding empire.

'Well, it's all part of the plan, isn't it?' was all he said now. 'Discredit Arymaldur first, to make it easier to get him out of the way, undermine Arval… Now, just you come and look in here, I want to show you my rooms now they're finished.' He threw open a door with a flourish. 'Not bad, eh?'

It was not until much later, when he was alone and preparing for sleep, that it occurred to Thaltor that Valestron, for whom he felt an increasing dislike, seemed appreciably better informed about Vorynaas' long-term strategy than might have been expected. Maybe that cousin of his, that Haartell, had been talking. He was always appearing silently from around a corner without warning, you wouldn't know what he might have heard. Thaltor turned down the lamp and drew the covers over himself with an exasperated heave. Things were all getting too complicated for him; he felt almost nostalgic for the old days. Sometimes he thought life had been much more enjoyable when he was simply Vorynaas' hard-hitting henchman.

Arval's burden

And so the remaining days of that year of strange events and troubled times went by: dark days in Caradward, as midwinter came nearer, and darker still the shadow that settled on Arval's heart. Caradriggan was a divided city now, the fault-lines even plainer to see than at midsummer. The new hall was known as Seth y'n Carad, and its naming-feast was to be on the day of Midwinter itself; all were bidden to it, and who could blame those who flocked there, thought Arval, who see no further than the warmth and food, who care nothing for their empty lives so that their bellies are full. He watched alone beside Numirantoro in the late afternoon of the day before the feast and gloom lay upon him as his mind wrestled with doubt and misgiving. The followers of Vorynaas delude themselves, he thought. He has flattered the lords among them in the naming of his hall, for in reality it belongs to but one, and that is himself. He has bought their loyalty just as surely as he has that of the common people, who are in his grasp because he has fed them and they have paid with their freedom; the others are tied to him because they lust for power. He has ensnared them through their greed for dominance at the cost of their integrity. But indeed all are deluded alike, Vorynaas included, for his promises are empty and vain of fulfilment. What will happen when all is proved false? Will they turn on him and bring him down, or will he tighten his grip still further in the madness of his pride? Either way, we may all be dragged with them into some unknown abyss.

He shifted in his chair, as unbidden the old phrase came into his unwilling mind. *The bad time.* Were men about to repeat the ancient wrong? Was he doomed to stand powerless as once more something too shaming to name was permitted to happen? Why had he given in to weakness, why had he not asked Arymaldur to reveal his knowledge? His glance fell on Numirantoro, now six months into her term. Maybe in my own way I am as guilty of pride as Vorynaas, thought Arval. Can I really bring both her and the child through this alive? Perhaps he too was deluded, his devotion to Numirantoro misguided, his intuition about the child a mistake, his hope for the future unfounded, his faith in the As-Geg'rastigan useless. He bowed his head, weighed down by his age, by the burden he had carried alone for so long. Then the door opened: he saw a radiance form around the flame of the lamp, the room seemed globed in light. Arymaldur trod softly across to him.

'You were steadfast when hope alone sustained you: Arval, will you falter now, when you know the truth? Tomorrow we celebrate the light returning. I will renew the pledge, I will repeat *Temennis y'm As-Geg'rastigan ach Ur*. Will you stand firm, will you guide the people and guard the child? Be sure you will be neither alone nor comfortless.'

Arval stood up and looked from Arymaldur to Numirantoro, noticing that her face too was now touched with the unearthly, remote beauty that lit his. She is lost to us, he thought, but what of the child? He knelt and pressed his forehead to Arymaldur's hand, and standing once more, he spoke his promise.

'My lord, I swear to you, I will not fail.'

Jealousy

The year turned and the biting cold of deep winter gripped the city, but its bite and its grip were as nothing to the iron hold which jealousy now had upon Vorynaas. He could settle to nothing by day, and get no rest at night; his temper became ever shorter and more uncertain, and as his obsession grew, so his appetite failed and he began to lose weight. He would take Ghentar with him down to Seth y'n Carad and encourage him to strut about in imitation of Valestron and his men: the lad was rising three now, and well-grown for his age, but it would take only a moment for Vorynaas' pride in his son to be replaced by exasperation at some childish misdemeanour. For the first time his hand was raised against the boy, who had known nothing but indulgence until then; now he began to fear his father's changes of mood and to resent his unaccustomed harshness. At home, Arythalt noticed the way Vorynaas pushed the food about on his plate and sent it back to the kitchen barely touched. Mistaking the reason for the haunted look in his eyes and the gauntness of his face and hands, he tried to encourage his marriage-son to eat more, to get some rest, to have confidence in Arval and not to worry about Numirantoro. Vorynaas found this almost intolerable and before long the day came when he could bear it no more. Shouting angrily to be left alone, he swept off to Thaltor's house in a towering rage, leaving Arythalt baffled and offended. After that, the atmosphere of icy politeness which the older man maintained was so unpleasant that Vorynaas spent yet more time with Thaltor, but soon even the girls from the *Golden Leopard* became unwilling to answer Thaltor's call. Word went round of what awaited them when Vorynaas was there, and if he appeared in the *Leopard* itself there would be a scramble to get behind closed doors with a client in order to avoid him.

Once only had Vorynaas called at Tellgard after the day on which Arval had sent for him. By then Numirantoro's pregnancy had been far enough advanced to be visibly obvious. As he looked at her, Vorynaas realised that part of his mind had been almost persuaded that the whole situation was somehow an illusion. This in itself had troubled him badly: was he losing his grip on reality? But maybe all would be well, maybe the baby would turn out to favour him like Ghentar did, so that all would see the child was his. Then the door had opened and for a second he had seen the startled face of Arythalt's old cook, before she retreated hurriedly. This had given him an idea, and next day he had despatched one of his own house servants to Tellgard with instructions to engage the old woman in conversation and discover, if she could, more detail of what had occurred at midsummer. When he heard what she had to tell him, he wished he had left well alone.

He sat now alone in the night, wakeful as usual, trying to quiet his thoughts and induce sleep with wine. Around him the house was silent; all were in their beds and every light was dimmed except the lamp over the street-door and the small glim that burned beside Vorynaas. His left hand curled around the wine-cup and his right played mechanically with a small dress dagger, turning it over and over, point to hilt, point to hilt, as he stared before him. Printed onto the darkness he saw Arymaldur's face. He had detested the fellow ever since he had arrived in Caradriggan, resenting his welcome in Tellgard and his status in the city and the council. He bared his teeth and gripped the little dagger more tightly as he reflected that at least he had been able to do something about the last two annoyances. But if Arymaldur… If Numirantoro… He could not bring himself to form the words, even in his mind. All those hours she used to spend in Tellgard! How often he had wondered why she went, what she did there. She had defied him and gone to Tellgard at Midsummer. She had been there the day of the fight in the horse-market. The trail always led back to Tellgard, and Tellgard led to Arymaldur. And Arymaldur had carried her fainting to the bed where she lay now, according to the old crone he had dismissed from the kitchen.

Over and over he turned the dagger, drinking deeply. Vorynaas could hold his wine, but he had scarcely eaten that day. His head swam as he battled for coherent thought. Suddenly a memory sprang up in his mind, clear and precise: it swept away the effects of drink and left his brain icy cold. Valestron knew! Suspected something, at least. Vorynaas remembered Valestron's snide comments over the dinner table, that time when, yes, they had been discussing the famous arrow and *Numirantoro had spoken up for Arymaldur*! How was it he had never noticed at the time how Valestron had insinuated that he knew the real reason for Numirantoro's visits to Tellgard, whatever she and her father might say to cover the situation; when now as Vorynaas thought about it he could hear the very tones of Valestron's voice dripping poison into his ears? Vorynaas found himself on his feet. The blood pounded in his own temples as he remembered something else: the nervous pulse beating visibly at Numirantoro's throat because *she feared to be found out*! With a snarl of rage, Vorynaas hurled the dagger from him with all his strength; there was a soft thud as it buried the length of its wicked little razor-sharp blade in the door-frame.

He sat down again slowly, thinking more clearly now. If this child is born alive, I will have no choice but to rear it as my own: I will not permit even a suggestion or hint that my wife could betray me with another man. He could scarcely contain himself when he considered Numirantoro and put to one side the thought of what he might do with her in due course. But, by my right hand! I will be revenged upon Arymaldur. Vorynaas stood up again, and lifted the lamp high, tilting his head back to look at it. He spoke aloud, quietly but with deadly intent.

'I will have vengeance upon Arymaldur, whatever the cost: let blindworms of Na Naastald take me, if I do not fulfil this oath. I swear I will take his life as I snuff out this light.'

On the word, he pinched the wick and total darkness fell about him, an enveloping shadow that matched the blackness in his heart. He crossed to the window, but the gloomy dawn was still hours away and rest seemed more impossible than ever. An idea came to him and he left the room, heading for the servants' stairs. He had not found anything to attract him in that girl who took Sigitsiro's place and had paid her no attention. But now that he came to think of it, she gave herself unwarranted airs and was inclined to insolence; maybe it would do her good to know who was the master and to work a little harder for her keep. Something of the old swagger returned to Vorynaas' step.

Birth and sunrise

Numirantoro's time came at the Spring Feast, as Arval had estimated. Fearing for what might befall her, he took charge himself and left the rites in Tellgard's ancient hall to Arymaldur. Nothing in all Arval's experience or lore, no case study in his books of reference, no tale that any of his colleagues had ever heard, came remotely near the strangeness of the hours of her labour. Through the night he and the women watched and tended her, and all went well. But though her body strained and suffered in the pains of birth, it seemed her spirit was absent still: no cry, no word, no sound at all escaped her lips; her eyes stayed closed in a serene face, although sweat lay on her forehead. In his anxiety for Numirantoro, Arval scarcely noticed that the night was disturbed by shouts and scuffling from the streets outside; but as the baby was finally delivered in the hour before dawn, sounds of commotion and violence were heard from much nearer at hand. Surely, some disturbance was taking place within Tellgard? Arval's brows drew down in anger, but he could hardly leave his post now. Finally all was done, and leaving the women to make Numirantoro comfortable once more, he took a lantern and swiftly passed through the courtyard and glanced into the hall. Seeing nothing untoward, he hastened back to Numirantoro, his lamplight failing to reach as far as the colonnade where the body of the silversmith sprawled dead on the steps.

The baby was washed and wrapped in a soft shawl, and the room all tidied and put in order. Someone had brought in a spray of jasmine and its delicate scent filled the air. Arval took his first real look at the child: dark haired, with long, delicate hands and fingers. Thick, dark lashes lay against the cheeks of a face whose features seemed more fully-formed than was usual in one so newly-born. Suddenly a murmur arose from his colleagues, and the note of wonder, of joy mixed with fear, made Arval look up to see a light growing on the wall beside him. Some of the women also were staring at it, while others ran to the window to look out. Sounds of slamming doors, running feet, cries of surprise and delight came from outside. Sunrise! A real sunrise again in Caradward, after how many years? The light filled the room, quenching the lamps, glowing on the flowers. It touched the baby's cheeks and fell on Numirantoro's face, and as Arval looked at her, she opened her eyes at last and smiled at him.

Arval drew a sharp breath in his surprise and at the sound, all heads turned to see what he had seen. With a cry of relief, the old cook fell on her knees at the bedside. Numirantoro took the old woman's hand and looked up at them.

'Forgive my haste,' she said, 'but I must speak alone with Arval without delay.'

They scurried to leave the room, glancing back with delight at Numirantoro as she looked at Arval. As soon as the door was closed, she spoke again.

'Let me see my son.'

Arval did not ask how she knew the child was a boy, but stooped and placed the baby in her arms. The child's eyes opened, and for the first time Arval saw their extraordinary colour: tawny, like amber. Those golden eyes seemed to focus on Numirantoro's face, and to be untroubled by the brightness of the dawn light; small sun-sparks waked in the amber as son and mother gazed at each other.

'Little son, my fate takes me from you,' said Numirantoro, 'but remember always that you have seen me, and I have seen you, and I love you.'

She ran her fingers through the baby's dark hair and gently kissed his forehead, then turned once more to the old man.

'Arval the Earth-wise, you have guarded this city and guided me; will you guard and guide my son? Will you love him for me, and keep him safe?'

Touched by a sense of solemnity far removed from a birth-chamber, Arval knelt beside the bed and took Numirantoro's hand, as if she were a queen granting him an audience.

'You have my promise: may the As-Geg'rastigan be the witnesses of my words.'

Numirantoro smiled slightly at this and then spoke again.

'His true name is Artorynas. Keep this in your heart, and keep for him also the As y'm Ur.'

She glanced aside as the golden sunrise began fading rapidly; already the lamplight was gaining strength again, illuminating the room and leaving shadows in the corners. In the distance they heard an ugly rumour of approaching trouble, swiftly growing as it came nearer. Arval half-rose with an exclamation of dismay, his face drawn with apprehension, but Numirantoro gripped his hand and recalled his attention.

'Let him follow the arrow's path and light will shine again: upon the earth, upon men's hearts, upon the choice that lies before him.'

The disturbance was right outside now: yells, cries of pain, the clash of weapons could be clearly heard. Suddenly there was the crash of a door bursting open within Tellgard, and footsteps ran madly down the corridor towards them; a man's voice could be heard calling desperately for Arval, someone was weeping helplessly. Numirantoro seemed oblivious to all of this.

'Remember me, Arval, and love my son,' she said, as she held the child out towards him.

With that, the door was flung wide: Arval spun round to see a young lad with blood running from a cut over his eye, mingling with the tears coursing down his face as he sobbed hysterically; behind him was a dishevelled group of men, some with swords in their hands, two of them supporting the body of the silversmith; and before all came Forgard, his silver hair dark with sweat, his face frozen into a mask of anguish and despair. Forgard's eyes took in the scene before him, Arval rising from Numirantoro's bedside with the child in his arms, but his heart was too full of panic and pain to think what might be seemly. Without regard for the child, the mother, the strangely remote calm of the room, he cried out breathlessly, the horror of his tale dragging at his voice.

'Arval, they have murdered Lord Arymaldur!'

For a second or two they all stood, motionless with shock. Then Arval took swift charge, passing the baby to one of the women, detailing an assistant to tend to the boy, sending the men to compose the body of the silversmith in a private room but not to leave Tellgard until he had spoken with them. All that skill wasted, he thought bitterly, a worthy man cut down senselessly in his prime, a family bereft of a father: what can I say to his widow, left to raise young twins alone? Well, first I must hear what Forgard has to tell. The two of them headed for Arval's tower room, Forgard stumbling on the stairs.

A festival defiled

It was some time before Arval succeeded in calming Forgard enough for him to tell his tale coherently. But though the events of that terrible night would haunt Forgard to his dying day, Arval saw rather that for himself, it was necessary to muster all his resolve if he was to find the strength for the future which he now foresaw. While Forgard paced the room, his voice now raised in anguish, now drowned in tears as emotion mastered him once more, Arval's black eyes stared darkly before him. Behind the mask of deceptive calm, his mind was racing, looking back over the last few fateful months, realising their wider implications. Unrest in the city streets had become ever more commonplace as the expansion of the Cottan na'Salf was pushed through: and not in Caradriggan alone, for word had reached Arval of disturbances in Staran y'n Forgarad also. Heranwark had stayed quiet, but stability came at a high price there, as recruits swelled the ranks of those enrolled in Rigg'ymvala where all were clothed and well-fed. And always that ugly undercurrent of rumour had swirled and flowed, prompted and directed by Vorynaas and his cronies, so that men looked askance at their neighbours, and families were divided; fingers of blame were pointed and voices of envy and greed were raised. But now it seemed that Vorynaas had aimed for more than the estrangement of Caradward from Gwent y'm Aryframan, had wanted much more than power and wealth for himself: he had sought the destruction of Arymaldur. *Beware of what may follow, if you drive the As-Geg'rastigan away again.* The fool! The deluded, vainglorious, misguided, accursed fool, thought Arval desperately, remembering the words Arymaldur had spoken to him long before and dreading to what end Vorynaas' misdeeds had now doomed them all.

'They are all in it together, Valestron and Thaltor, Valafoss and young Haartell and others besides: he had no shortage of supporters,' Forgard was saying dully now. 'But events played into his hands so neatly that the rest of us had no hope of holding them back. If only Tell'Ethronad had listened to you and Arymaldur and negotiated with Val'Arad on the corn price! If Vorynaas had not carried the day then, he would never have amassed a workforce of slaves, there's no other word for it, that's what they are! And without them to keep down, and his dearly-bought grain to keep safe, there would have been no need for that private army of cut-throats he maintains.' Forgard's voice rose again, ragged with exhaustion and grief. 'Law and order! The man is without shame! They are nothing but hired killers!'

'Steady now my friend, calm yourself.'

Arval knew what Forgard was referring to: the council meeting at which they had debated the food riots which had broken out in early spring when last harvest's stocks of meal were almost gone. Had they but known it, Ardeth's prediction that it was in Caradriggan rather than Framstock where grain supplies would need an armed guard had come true all too soon: in the name of restoring civil order, and suppressing further trouble, Vorynaas had proposed to patrol the streets and secure the granaries with a force under Valestron's command. This, Arval had strenuously opposed, backed by Arymaldur, Forgard and his dwindling band of supporters in Tell'Ethronad; but once more the majority had been swayed by Vorynaas, seduced again by the attraction of someone prepared not only to act for them but to foot the bill as well.

Arval made Forgard sit down and moved his own chair beside him, pouring from the jar strong feast-day wine for them both. Now he spoke again.

'There is no man in this city who could kill a lord of the As-Geg'rastigan. You must tell me as quickly and as plainly as you can what has happened.'

Forgard looked up sharply and his eyes searched Arval's face.

'So I was right! But we have raised our hands against the Starborn... and there were others whose lives have been taken.'

A heavy silence fell, then Forgard began to speak again, the words coming unwillingly as if the taste of them was foul on his tongue.

'When the rites were over in the hall, I walked back to my home in conversation with Issigitsar. The night was warm and pleasant and so we continued our talk, sitting beside the fountain in the gardens across the street from my house; after a while, we were joined there by Arymaldur. We were not the only group to delay our rest: folk sat outside before the *Sword and Stars*, and family parties went from house to house here and there. And of course the revels were still in progress down at Seth y'n Carad, though they were soon to be savagely disrupted.'

He paused and sighed, rubbing his hands over his eyes: Arval noticed that his fingers were blood-stained. After a moment, Forgard resumed.

'It seems now that what happened there must have been some time in the planning. The tied labourers rose in revolt against their servitude. They fell on the guards, killing Valestron's second and a couple of others, and rushed the gates of the compound; they'd armed themselves with a variety of makeshift weapons, sharpened lengths of iron stolen from the site, mostly, and a few improvised slings and clubs. But they took the weapons from the dead guards, and then they spilled out into the streets, calling for Arymaldur.'

'*What!*'

'I know, it was the worst possible thing... but what they seem to have wanted was not so much for him to lead them, but to find him so that they could acknowledge him and have him speak for them. You could hear more about this part of it from the lad with the cut eye, him that was in such a state downstairs there – according to him, they all knew Arymaldur was one of the Starborn, they wanted to pledge their loyalty. He seems to have been sure himself that Arymaldur would sort everything out on the spot; he saw it all, he's completely devastated. Well, in no time others ran to join the throng, and of course the noise and yelling brought everyone rushing out of the new hall in hot pursuit. When Vorynaas and the rest of them arrived up at the gardens, they will always claim now that what they found was Arymaldur at the head of an armed insurrection. Whereas in fact he was speaking quietly to the crowd, who were gazing at him, hanging on his every word, until they were set upon by ruthless, fully-armed professional soldiers.'

Arval groaned in disbelief. 'Were many killed?'

'More than there should have been. We tried to come between them, but Arymaldur was unarmed and Issigitsar was wounded in the first scuffle – no, it's nothing serious, he'll be all right. That young fellow fought like a madman, biting and kicking. You'll have to keep him here in Tellgard, I wouldn't give you much for his chances if he's picked up by anyone from Seth y'n Carad. Arymaldur was calling for everyone to back off, but Valestron's men took no heed. Several late-comers and many of the labourers were cut down, but three of them, shouting out they'd got nothing to lose and no families to mourn them, leapt up on the fountain and refused to surrender, so Thaltor had archers brought up and all three of them were shot dead. They fell into the fountain and with archers covering our every move, no-one made any attempt to pull them out; they floated there in the bloodstained water like dead dogs in a ditch. So then, Vorynaas gave the nod to Thaltor and Valestron, and their men shoved everyone over to one side while he stood there with his jackal-pack behind him, eyeing Arymaldur. He was like a man with a huge weight suddenly lifted off his shoulders: you know how he's been recently, but for years before this he's never missed the chance to belittle Arymaldur in the council; you could see he knew his moment had come at last. Oh, Arval! How did we let this happen? Now I see how Vorynaas has worked for this, maybe he was even behind last night's rioting: what would innocent men's lives lost mean to him?' Once more Forgard's voice cracked and broke as grief washed over him.

After a moment or two, Arval prompted Forgard gently. 'What did Vorynaas say?' he asked.

'He told Valafoss to bind Arymaldur's hands and bring him down to Seth y'n Carad. And Arymaldur looked at him quite steadily, he showed no sign of fear or even anger, but he must have made some sort of impression on Valafoss, because he hesitated and looked around as if for support; but when Vorynaas glared at him he came forward again with the rope. Vorynaas stalked off down the street, Thaltor and the archers kept back those of us who might have made trouble, and the rest of the rabble followed after Vorynaas with Arymaldur captive in their midst. Vorynaas was obviously keen for us all to see everything, though, because after a while a runner came back up from Seth y'n Carad with the word for Thaltor to bring us down under guard. When we got down there…' Forgard stopped suddenly and clenched his hands, fighting for mastery of his emotions. Eventually he spoke again.

'When we got down there, Arymaldur was bound hand and foot and standing against the wall and a large crowd had gathered as word spread of what was happening. Valestron's squad from the hall was very much in evidence, and Thaltor's archers. Vorynaas looked slowly round at everyone. What he had to say was just, well, I don't know what the right word would be. He said Arymaldur had come to us from Gwent y'm Aryframan, that we'd made him welcome, given him honour in the city – he laid all that on really thick, it was disgusting. Then he said we'd been far too trusting for our own good, that we should have seen from the start that Arymaldur was really working for the Gwentarans all along. He reeled off various examples from debates in Tell'Ethronad where he claimed Arymaldur spoke in favour of them – not true, as we well know, but Vorynaas is so skilled at twisting words, and how many would have the wit to realise they were being tricked, who were not there anyway at the time to hear the truth of it? Some of us tried to make our voices heard, but Vorynaas' supporters shouted back, and scuffles broke out; and then, after his own thugs had moved in to restore quiet, he had the effrontery to stand there and claim that disturbances of that kind had been unknown in Caradriggan before Arymaldur's time!

'I think the next thing was the fight at the horse-market – no, I've got that wrong. The next thing he brought up was the developments in the Ellanwic. Did people realise, he asked, that Arymaldur had opposed the expansion of the Cottan na'Salf; had tried, in fact, to block a scheme to feed the countrymen who had made him welcome? And there was something else too, which he had never mentioned before, unwilling as he'd been to add to the tension between the two countries, but events had now forced his hand. Caradwardans should know what Valestron had seen and heard with his own eyes and ears when he travelled to Framstock last autumn: men were threatening to dispossess those from Caradward who held property or business interests there, and the rise in the corn price had been introduced deliberately so as to bring hardship in its wake. Valestron had seen troublemakers who'd been expelled from Staran y'n Forgarad: they were being sheltered by one of the leading families in Framstock, one of whose members had told him to his face that he'd voted for the price rise in the hope that we here would be reduced to eating acorns! Who could be in any doubt now that the Gwentarans were conspiring against us?

'Well, you can imagine how all that went down. Vorynaas had most of them fairly baying for blood by this time, but he held his hand up until they quietened down again, and then he produced the real clincher.

'"Don't worry about the Gwentarans," he said. "We're more than a match for them. But the time has come to let them know we won't tolerate their spies or agents in our midst! Maybe we were too soft the first time Arymaldur showed his true colours, that time our fellow citizens were forced to defend themselves against a mob and he weighed in against them. We should have shown him to the border then, but what did we do? We made it clear to him that he'd outstayed his welcome, yes, but when he brazened it out, we did nothing, and look what's happened now! A man who has got away once with drawing his sword in our streets will try it again, and tonight there has been open revolt in his name, in which blameless men have died! Will we tolerate this?"

'There was uproar then, and I noticed Thaltor and Valafoss grinning at each other. Then Valestron came forward and said something in Vorynaas' ear, pointing at Haartell; Vorynaas smirked and stroked his beard in that way of his, then he nodded and clapped Valestron on the shoulder. He and Haartell went off at the run, taking two or three of the guard with them, and when they came back, about ten minutes later, they'd got hold of the arrow that Arymaldur made.'

Arval recalled hearing ominous sounds inside Tellgard. While he tended Numirantoro, violence had been done within its hallowed halls: he remembered Haartell from his student days and knew immediately what must have happened. Haartell had broken into the casket where the arrow lay, while Valestron and the others were there to cover him and take out anyone who tried to stop them. And the silversmith had stood in their way, who lay now dead in a chamber below having paid dearly for his courage. Another life to Vorynaas' account, although no-one will ever be able to prove it, thought Arval. He nodded for Forgard to continue.

'Vorynaas turned to the crowd and came out with some hypocritical stuff about not presuming to take matters into his own hands: in his opinion, Arymaldur deserved to die, but what were the wishes of the men of Caradward? A huge roar went up, but he asked if there were any who wished to speak for Arymaldur. Plenty of us did shout then, although not nearly enough. But that young fellow, somehow he wriggled through from where they were keeping us back, and he cried out in front of everyone that we were all mad, that Arymaldur was a lord of the Starborn. There was a moment of complete silence: Arymaldur just smiled at him, it was as if the two of them were alone and enjoying a quiet discussion. Extraordinary, you'd need to have seen it to know what I mean. Who is the lad, do you know?'

'He got his arm broken in the fight at the horse-market and Arymaldur set it for him.' I know what you mean, Forgard, thought Arval: how well I know it.

'Ah, I see... Well, Thaltor and the rest came leaping down to grab him, but he jumped out of their reach and yelled, "If we kill him, the bad time will come again!" That made some of them think, but Thaltor swung his fist at the boy; he was wearing a mailed glove, that's how the young fellow got that split over his eye. They heaved him out of the way, and then Vorynaas....'

He paused, searching for the right words. 'Well, it was as though for an instant or two Vorynaas lost control of himself. Up to then I'd had the strong impression that everything had been planned, but now he pointed at Arymaldur and I could see his arm shaking: his face was contorted with rage.

'"Listen to me!" he screamed. "I tell you, get rid of him and the sun will return! I promise it!"

'That was what did it, really. Fists were waving in the air, everyone was yelling, and Vorynaas beckoned Thaltor and half a dozen archers forward. He lined them up about twenty paces from Arymaldur, but as he turned, Arymaldur spoke for the first time.

'"Turn back, Vorynaas," he said, quite calmly. "There is an instant of time still remaining, but turn back now, or it will be too late."

'Vorynaas seemed to have regained his grip on things now, though. He stepped up to Arymaldur.

'"There is *no* time remaining in which you can give me orders," he said, and spat on the ground before him. "For you, it is already too late."

'He took Arymaldur's arrow from Haartell, and made to give it to the first archer in the line, but the fellow backed away and then all of them shied from it as if they feared to touch it. But Thaltor pushed forward and took the bow from the nearest man, and snatched the arrow from Vorynaas; and they all took aim.'

Forgard's voice began to shake again and he trembled visibly as the shock of what he had witnessed began to affect him. He drank some wine and forced himself to continue.

'Arymaldur was standing against the east wall of Seth y'n Carad, and as the squad drew their bows, light suddenly began to glow on the stones. It flooded over us, it was as if, as if a river of gold poured from the sky. It fell on Arymaldur: on a lord of the As-Geg'rastigan, standing before us in bonds, facing death at our word.'

Forgard doubled up in grief, burying his face in his hands. 'I will never, never be able to forget what I have seen today. Of course everyone turned in amazement, the archers lowered their bows, we all gazed in wonder at the sky. The clouds had parted to reveal the sun; I could actually feel the warmth of its rays on my face as it rose in glory. We stood gaping; although it could only have been for a moment or two, it felt like for ever: long enough at any rate for a groundswell of murmurs to begin, for folk to start running from their houses, we heard them calling out to each other, doors slamming behind them. Maybe Vorynaas felt the situation slipping away from him, who knows? At any rate he shouted at Thaltor and his men to take aim once more, and to fire. And then ...'

Forgard fell silent for a moment, and when he spoke again, there was a new note in his voice, almost a trace of hope.

'I saw them draw, I saw the arrows leave the string. I saw the sunlight kindle on Arymaldur's arrow as its sky-steel flew towards his heart. But he ... he stepped forward from his bonds, his face raised towards the light; he put up his hand and caught the arrow in its flight, took it from the air as easily as a man might pluck a flower from the stem. I heard the other arrows hit and fall, and when I looked again, they were scattered on the ground or stuck in the mortar between the stones; but the silver arrow was gone and Arymaldur with it, leaving the ropes that had bound him lying loose on the ground.'

Forgard drew a shaky breath. 'Then the light faded again, and in the turmoil that followed, we took our chance to cut our way out and fight our way back to Tellgard, bringing the lad with us. We found the silversmith sprawled on the steps outside.'

The given name

Arval sat in silence, overwhelmed by the enormity of what had happened. After a while, Forgard spoke hesitantly.

'Arval, what will become of us?'

Arval tried to reassure him. 'Be comforted by words Arymaldur himself once spoke to me: *there is always hope, if men know where to find it.*'

He fought down the sorrow that rose within him at the bitter thought that never again would he hear Arymaldur speak the words of the rites, never again hear the *Temennis* from the very voice of the Starborn. Suddenly he recalled the reason for his own absence from the Spring festival; for the first time his mind went back to the birth-chamber he had attended. The child had been born with the light: man of the sun, born of the star. Through the tower window floated the stormy song of the mistle-thrush and fear rose in Arval. Why had Numirantoro pressed him for his pledge of guidance and support for the child, why had she asked for his promise of remembrance? He stood up quickly, hurrying towards the door.

'I'll be back in just a moment. I left Numirantoro, the baby was but newly-born when you arrived.'

Forgard ran down the stairs behind him, incredulity in his voice. 'The child! Did she wake, then? Is all well with them both?'

'Yes, yes.'

But Arval had already heard the sounds of sorrow from within the chamber. He opened the door. The child slept peacefully in the old cook's arms, though her tears fell on her shawl. Three members of Tellgard's medical staff were at the bedside and they turned at Arval's footfall. One glance showed him that Numirantoro was beyond recall. Arval looked down as she lay there, so young, her eyes now closed once more, closed for ever. The thought came to Arval that Numirantoro's loveliness was not merely fairness of face; it came from the way the outward form matched the life within, a beauty that was strangely unearthly, like that of the Starborn. Like Arymaldur, thought Arval. He remembered that both Arymaldur and Numirantoro had spoken of a choice. He too had made a choice, long ago, and even now in this moment of fear and loss his restless intellect was eager to probe this new enigma, thirsty to tap new wells of knowledge. He dragged his mind back to heed a voice that spoke beside him.

'She slipped away as the light faded,' one of his colleagues was telling him. A movement caught his eye as a robin landed on the outside windowsill in a flutter of wings. For a second Arval looked into its tiny, jewel-like eye and then it was gone again. He caught a whisper from the old woman, scarcely to be heard.

'She left us when she heard Lord Arymaldur was gone.'

An orderly stuck his head round the threshold, warning them in a panicky shout that Vorynaas was on his way, and quickly Arval bundled Forgard off to the treatment room to get himself cleaned up. Within a couple of minutes, the door was opened with a flourish and Vorynaas stalked through it. Ignoring Arval, he spoke brusquely to the old woman.

'Give me the child.'

He put the shawl back until the baby lay naked before him. The loss of warmth and comfort woke the child, but without crying he looked up at Vorynaas with amber, sun-flecked eyes. In the silence, Arval heard now the robin's sweet, wistful little song from the tree outside.

'There is no-one at my house who can feed him,' said Vorynaas. 'You will have to keep him here until a wet-nurse can be found.' He covered the child once more and made to leave.

'Have you not even a name for him?' Arval's eyes were black and his tone icy. Vorynaas was already on his way, but he turned back.

'Yes, we must have a name for him.' He glanced at Numirantoro and then at the child, his expression unreadable, and gave a short, mirthless laugh. 'His name is Maesrhon.'